A LIADEN UNIVERSE® CONSTELLATION

Volume 3

BAEN BOOKS
by Sharon Lee & Steve Miller

✧✧✧

The Liaden Universe®

Fledgling
Saltation
Mouse & Dragon
Ghost Ship
Dragon Ship
Necessity's Child
Trade Secret
Dragon in Exile
Alliance of Equals (forthcoming)
The Dragon Variation (omnibus)
The Agent Gambit (omnibus)
Korval's Game (omnibus)
The Crystal Variation (omnibus)
A Liaden Universe® Constellation: Volume1
A Liaden Universe® Constellation: Volume 2
A Liaden Universe® Constellation: Volume 3

The Fey Duology

Duainfey
Longeye

by Sharon Lee

Carousel Tides
Carousel Sun
Carousel Seas

To purchase these and all other Baen Book titles in e-book format, please go to www.baen.com.

A LIADEN UNIVERSE® CONSTELLATION

Volume 3

SHARON LEE & STEVE MILLER

A LIADEN UNIVERSE ® CONSTELLATION: VOLUME 3

This is a work of fiction. All the characters and events portrayed in this book are fictional, and any resemblance to real people or incidents is purely coincidental.

"Code of Honor" was first published on Spinter Universe, May 2014. "Eleutherious" was first published on *www.Baen.com*, January 2013. "Guaranteed Delivery" was first published on Splinter Universe, September 2011. "Intelligent Design" was first published on *www.Baen.com*, July 2011. "Kin Ties" was first published on Splinter Universe, July 2011. "King of the Cats" was first published in *The Cat's Job*, SRM Publisher, Ltd., 2002. "Landed Alien" was first published on *www.Baen.com*, October 2012. "Moon's Honor" was first published on Splinter Universe, February 2013. "Out of True" was first published on *www.Baen.com*, October 2013. "Roving Gambler" was first published on Splinter Universe, April 2014. "The Rifle's First Wife" was first published on Splinter Universe, January 2014. "The Space at Tinsori Light" was first published on Splinter Universe, November 2011.

All rights reserved, including the right to reproduce this book or portions thereof in any form. Liaden Universe® is a registered trademark.

A Baen Books Original

Baen Publishing Enterprises
P.O. Box 1403
Riverdale, NY 10471
www.baen.com

ISBN: 978-1-4767-8068-9

Cover art by Stephen Hickman

First Baen printing, August 2015

Distributed by Simon & Schuster
1230 Avenue of the Americas
New York, NY 10020

Library of Congress Cataloging-in-Publication Data
2013011058

Printed in the United States of America

10 9 8 7 6 5 4 3 2 1

✧Table of Contents✧

A LIADEN UNIVERSE® CONSTELLATION

Volume 3

✧ Foreword ✧

WELCOME TO Liaden Universe® Constellation: Volume 3!

We'd like to talk a little about how we got to this book, the book you have in your hands right now, and about grand plans.

When we started writing in the Liaden Universe® thirty years ago we had a plan. It was a plan for seven novels, to be written in a large and fast-paced space opera universe full of action, adventure, romance and fun, with several groups of people as the focus. Even as we started we knew that there were some complex stories to tell in this universe, because universes, families, and clans have history, and history is full of secrets, mistakes, alliances, plans, and necessity.

As we've described elsewhere, our original grand plan was sketched out over a single night, and when we were done, we knew many of the high points of the story, and quite a few of the central characters. The first few Liaden books attracted an avid readership—and over time portions of that readership coalesced into a community with outposts in the physical world of SF clubs and conventions clubs while an overlapping electronic community formed as the modem-based BBS society gave way to the internet. With so much support we—that is Sharon Lee and Steve Miller, the authors of the Liaden Universe®—were, eventually, able to continue with our grand plan, and in fact we were encouraged to go beyond it, and write not seven novels, but, well, more than seven.

But wait! You may have noticed that the book you're reading right now is—not a novel. In fact, it is so much not a novel that it labels itself the third Liaden Universe® Constellation, the third collection of short stories, novellas, and novelettes set within the universe.

Truth told, when we started with our grand plan we hadn't thought about all the ramifications attending our style of world-building and character development. Since we're working with an expanding universe, and not a linear series, that means the novels were not necessarily written in order, which means that the characters were also not written precisely in order. It also means that the characters often go where we don't expect them to go; and that their pasts and futures are not clean slates, but experiences that make them who they are.

The result of grand plans, and novel-packaging, and characters going off on their own is that we found—and we still constantly find—that we have ideas, incidents, and events that don't fit easily into the flow of a novel or a novel-arc. On top of that, we discovered as we talked with readers and fans that some characters fascinated folks more than others—and some fascinated us more than others. The Liaden Universe® had become not only our place, but an interactive place, with highly interested observers.

But see, we never planned for short stories, in our original grand plan.

"Whatever happened to the taxi-driver?" was a question that haunted us across several years and indeed, into a second story arc. When we answered it, it helped develop a novel in a different arc, and created another story as well. Young Jethri, given a short story, grew into a novel, and then another, with more short-pieces flowing off of his story line and necessities.

Grand plans change.

The stories you'll read here are all set in the Liaden Universe®. They occur unserially—in different times, in different story arcs, to characters in the main line of the novels, and not. All of these stories take place inside the Liaden Universe®, and all illuminate some aspect of it that we needed to explore or an aspect that readers asked about and which was simultaneously attractive to us.

Despite the fact that we've far surpassed those original planned-for seven novels, the Liaden grand plan continues. We're currently under contract with Baen to write six more novels in the Liaden Universe® . . . and, as time permits, or the fascination strikes, we'll write more short stories.

We guess this means that someday, there will be a Liaden Universe® Constellation: Volume 4!

Thanks for reading, enjoying, and sharing!

Sharon Lee and Steve Miller
Waterville, Maine
June 2014

✧ Code of Honor ✧

***THIS STORY EXISTS** because we were plotting a completely different story, and needed a character to . . . do something . . . for the main character. That secondary character came with an utterly fascinating back-story. So fascinating, in fact, that he got his own story, set in the aftermath of I Dare. And yes, we are still planning to write the story that spawned this one, so . . . watch the skies!*

"YOU WANTED TO SEE ME, ma'am?"

Tech Sergeant Tommy Lee saluted, and waited for the captain to acknowledge him.

She looked up from her screen, eyes shadowed, and Tommy felt a pang. Cardimin had been hard on her; had been hard on all of them. He'd gotten a scratch out of it; Captain Blake had gotten . . . more than a scratch. She ought not even be out of sick bay—that was Tommy's opinion, and let the record show that he was *not* a medic.

"Sergeant." She nodded in return to his salute, and used her chin to point at the chair by her desk. "Sit down, please."

"Ma'am."

He sat, frowning up at her face. Drawn and looking older than she was. *Dammit, she ought to be resting!*

"Correspondence just come in regarding you," she said, looking down at her screen. "You know a Jow Lit pen'Chapen?"

For a moment, he thought to deny it; after all, who could say they knew the Delm of Clan Severt? Certainly not the least-valued of his grandchildren. But, no; it wouldn't do. She would have his record on her screen. Fifteen Standards he had served in her command, and *Tommy Lee* before he'd risen from the signing table; she'd need a reminder of his birth name.

So.

"Jow Lit pen'Chapen is Delm Severt," he said calmly. "My grandfather."

Captain Blake nodded.

"He sent a pinbeam to Commander Wyatt, stating that you're needed by your clan."

Ice ran his veins. The words hadn't quite made . . .

"I beg your pardon?"

She looked up then; looked right at him, and smiled, tiredly.

"Your grandda invoked the escape clause, Tommy. You're free to go home. Wyatt's already signed off on it."

But I don't want to go home! he thought, which might have been undutiful, had things been otherwise, between him and his clan. He did not say this to Susan Blake; it would do nothing but distress her.

She shifted, slightly, fretfully, behind her desk.

"Says here there's a transport voucher in your mailbox. You're to leave immediately, and travel with all haste. Apparently, there's specific instructions in your box along with that voucher." She sighed, and shook her head at the screen.

"Couple administrative things . . ." she murmured. "First is, you wanna close your account in the Merc Bank?"

Close his account? And what? Carry his entire savings in his pockets?

He shook his head.

"If it's possible to leave the account as it is, I would prefer to do that," he said. She nodded and touched a key.

"OK. What do you want us to do about mail? You can keep your box open. Be a fee—four-bit per Standard."

Hardly a fee at all, and certainly cheaper than renting a civilian box and paying for transfers and forwarding.

"I'll leave it open for now; the fee's acceptable. When I know what . . . my clan . . . requires of me, I'll be able to make a decision . . ."

Gods, it had been half a lifetime since he had thought like this . . . *what my clan requires of me*? He was accustomed to command; the merc culture suited him well. But merc culture—merc *discipline*—was a shallow and meaningless thing when measured against the absolute power that a delm held over the members of his clan. A delm could order a kinsman shot for no reason other than he had been found an irritant. No one would remonstrate with him, or demand that he explain himself, or call him to stand trial for violations against the reg book . . .

"Tommy? You OK?"

He took a deep breath and looked up to meet her eyes.

"Truthfully, I'm . . . shaken. Does he—Delm Severt— say what the clan requires of me?"

Even as he asked, a new fear iced his heart.

His mother.

Had his mother died? But surely he would not be called home merely to mourn her. A leave of absence, perhaps, but this . . .

"He's a man of few words, your grandda. Just the bare phrase, to do the necessary."

He shook his head.

"I don't accept his invocation of the Liaden Personnel Release Clause," he said, dragging the proper name of the provision from gods knew what pocket in his well-pocketed memory. "I'll make inquiries. If necessary, I'll arrange for a leave of absence. This is . . ."

The captain was shaking her head, and she was frowning the particularly fierce frown that meant she was unhappy, not angry.

"You don't get a say," she said. "Tommy, I checked. You *bet* I checked! Some old guy sitting on Liad's gonna take away the best palaver and protocol sarge this unit's ever had?" Another headshake. "It's got a whole chapter to itself in the regs: Liadens belong to their clan; if-and-when their clan says, *come home*, the Merc's gotta cut 'em loose. No delay. No return."

No return.

He was speechless.

There was a small pause before Captain Blake sighed, and spoke again, her voice sounding infinitely weary.

"So, there's some things for you to sign here, Tommy . . ."

• • •✧• • •

HE ARRIVED at Chonselta Port in the early hours of the morning, which suited him, and his plans. He found a tea shop and ordered breakfast, talking with the bored clerk while he ate. He'd taken the precaution of brushing up on modes and forms during the long days of travel, which was prudent, but left his ears tuned to the Solcintran accent. The Chonselta burr was at first disconcerting, then oddly comforting. He'd spent the last half of his life so far getting around in the various dialects of Terran and in Merc pidgen, with sometimes intense forays into other languages, as required by his duties. Of course, he'd spoken Liaden occasionally during the past fifteen Standards, but he had by no means spoken it every day. Doubtless, his grandfather would find him inexcusably rough, but that would be no new thing, and he was no longer an unskilled and despised halfling, but a man grown and secure in his accomplishments.

He reached for his tea cup; paused to look at the ring on the smallest finger of his right hand. It was a utilitarian thing, as ornaments went, the stone set flush to the band so as not to foul in wires, or catch on combat gloves. A Liaden would scarcely call it a ring at all, but for the honor it denoted; and perhaps not even then. He had another ring in his kit—a broad-banded, heavily gemmed affair that he wore when attending official parties and meetings with planetary officials, and others who were impressed by such things. Perhaps he should have it on, when he presented himself at the house.

That reminded him of his agenda, and he put the question to the clerk, who smiled and nodded significantly toward the left wall of the shop.

"Faces Spa will put you in the current style," she said. "Just three shops up, at the corner."

"Will they be open, so early?"

"Be shifting over to the day crew right about now," she answered, so he finished his tea, paid his tab, and walked up the street to have himself put into the current style.

• • •✧• • •

AFTER THE SPA, his braid shorn and the remainder of his pale hair arranged in soft curls over his ears, it was the tailor, who was pleased to serve Tom Lei pen'Chapen Clan Severt, and in very quick order produced a jacket, shirt, and trousers befitting the returning son of a mid-level House known to have ambitious tendencies. His good duty boots were changed out for a thinner, shinier pair, with a heel that would make marching painful. The tailor also produced evening clothes—"In the event that the House dresses for Prime"—and a second set of day clothes. In addition, he quick-cleaned Mr. pen'Chapen's travel leathers, sweater, and boots while the gentleman was in the dressing room, and had them waiting neatly on the counter when he emerged.

"I thank you," Tom Lei said, remembering to incline slightly from the waist—not quite a bow, but a modest genuflection to one who has performed an unexpected small service. He produced his purse, meaning to settle his account immediately, and was stopped by the tailor himself.

"By no means, sir! Clan Severt of course keeps an account here, and settles very promptly at the end of every *relumma!* I have no hesitation in appending today's modest purchases to this *relumma*'s accountings."

"I thank you," Tom Lei said again, while, mentally, he sighed. Of course, Severt kept accounts with the local tailors. It was how things were done, on Liad. He, long-accustomed to drawing his uniforms from stores, and purchasing joy-clothes and civvies from his own funds, had simply assumed—but there! *This* was his uniform, now.

"I am happy to serve," the tailor was assuring him. "If you should need to expand your wardrobe—reception wear, or intimate items—please do not hesitate to call upon me."

"I will remember," he promised, and reached for his kit, to stow cleaned leathers and boots.

"May I call a cab for you, sir?" the tailor asked.

He had intended to walk from the tailor to Severt's Clanhouse, a matter of some several dozen blocks. Walking would have served two purposes: it would have consumed time, should that have been necessary, until an hour when the House could be expected to be awake; and it would have given him one last opportunity to prepare himself for the upcoming meeting with his grandfather.

Walking long blocks in these absurd new boots, however, was only likely to give him blisters and bad temper. And, too, the process of becoming presentable had taken rather longer than he had expected. The House would certainly be awake by this hour, and if they were still at breakfast, then he could await his grandfather's pleasure in one of the small parlors.

"A cab would be most welcome," he told the tailor. "I thank you again, for your care."

• • •✧• • •

SEVERT'S CLANHOUSE was situated on Omarine Street; not in Chonselta's first neighborhood, but well enough. It was pleasantly tree-lined, and the houses sat back from the public walk, protected from the prying eyes of passersby by small gardens.

Tom Lei pen'Chapen paused at the gate, looking over the garden, and, if truth be told, the flagged walk that meandered from the gate through the flowers, to the stairway that ended at the front door.

In theory, his palm print was known to the security systems. Which, in theory, would open both gate and door to him.

Standing there, he knew a moment of hope, that the security system had forgotten him after all this time; that the gate would remain closed to him; so that he might have a reason to turn away, and resume his life . . .

But no.

His life as it had been was gone. His clan had need of him; his delm had called him home. Once more, he was merely a game piece, one among many interchangeable game pieces in his grandfather's endless quest for advantage.

He put his hand on the gate.

It swung open on well-oiled hinges.

He sighed, then, and settled his kit more firmly over his shoulder, before stepping into the garden, and following the path to the stairs.

• • •✧• • •

THE FRONT DOOR was opened, not by one of the House's children, but by a butler, unknown to him. He gave his name, and the information that the delm had called him home.

"I was told to expect you, sir," the butler said imperturbably. "The House is at breakfast. Will you join them at table, or will you await the delm's pleasure?"

He was a mercenary sergeant with sixteen world-falls to his account. On one memorable occasion, he and eight others of his squad had not only denied a prime target to a full platoon of the enemy, but routed them.

He was not by any means a coward.

But the thought of meeting his entire extended family at the breakfast table brought a cold sweat to his brow, and a decided uneasiness to his belly.

"Thank you," he said to nameless butler. "I breakfasted at the port. I will await the delm's pleasure."

"This way, then, sir."

He was led, not to the public receiving parlor, only a few steps from the door, but down into the house, until at last the butler opened the door to the delm's very office, and bade him be comfortable.

"Shall I have that taken to your rooms, sir?" the butler asked, by which he meant the kit bag Tom Lei yet carried. He surrendered it with a pang, refused the offered glass of wine, and, after the door had closed, wandered restlessly over to the shelves.

He was perusing the titles there when the door opened again, much sooner than he had anticipated, and a sharp voice exclaimed behind him.

"Well, you took your time getting here!"

Between one breath and another, his nerves steadied.

"I traveled with all haste, as instructed," he said, and turned to face his grandfather.

"It's been an entire *relumma* since I sent for you, sir!"

The old man hasn't changed a hair.

That was his first thought. His second was that his grandfather *had* altered: he was older, thinner, the hair that had still shown streaks of black when last they'd met was silver, now.

"It is the nature of space travel, sir," he said, speaking in the mode of younger to elder—*damned* if he was going to hold a conversation in clan-member-to-delm. And if he was going to be chewed out . . .

But his grandfather had apparently thought better of whatever else he had been about to say. Instead, he inclined his head, and moved to the desk.

"Pour for us," he said shortly.

With prompt obedience, Tom Lei moved over to the wine table, and paused, uncertain of his memory.

"Do you drink the red?" he asked, more or less at hazard.

"At this hour? Canary."

He located the bottle, poured two glasses, carried them to the desk and placed one by his grandfather's hand.

The old man picked up the glass, and glared up at him, dark eyes narrowed. They were not much alike, Tom Lei and his grandfather, which was the crux of the matter. Tom Lei was Festival-get, and the mark of his fair-haired, blue-eyed, pale-skinned sire was far too plain upon him. He had looked a veritable ghost among his numerous black-haired, ebon-eyed, golden-skinned kin, taller than the tallest of them by time he attained his twelfth name day.

Worse than all of that, he had the misfortune to be the child of grandfather's least-favored daughter, who he was pleased to style an imbecile, though how a woman who brought the clan the considerable benefit of her salary as a freight expediter could be thought an imbecile . . .

"Do not *loom*," his grandfather snapped. "Sit down."

He did so without comment, and sat holding the glass in his right hand.

"You look well enough," his grandfather said. "I had been concerned that you would require more polish. A word or two in the ear of your Aunt Manza should see you set up in the wardrobe. Jewels . . ."

He frowned, his gaze falling on Tom Lei's all-but-naked hands, and he felt a pang, that he had not remembered to get the state ring out of his kit and put it on.

"What is that you have on your hand?"

The tone was more disgusted than curious, and a hot reply leapt to his tongue.

Then, he glanced at his right hand, and the small token he wore there, remembering faces he would never see again, comrades, lovers, and friends, and for their sake, he chose to answer moderately and do no dishonor to the ring.

"It signifies that I made sixteen world-falls as a mercenary, and saw action on each."

His grandfather frowned.

"Is that an honor?"

"It is . . . an accomplishment," Tom Lei said, and added, "among mercenary soldiers."

His grandfather sat back in his chair, hands steepled before him. His eyes were on Tom Lei as if he studied the merits of an art work set before him.

"Excellent. You will wear that ring." The frown returned. "Where is your clan necklace?"

"I had never had one," Tom Lei said, and felt the slow burn of old anger. "When I came fourteen, you told my mother to find me a suitable employment that was out of your sight and cost you nothing."

"Whereupon you joined the mercenaries," said his grandfather.

"*Whereupon,*" he corrected, though he might more wisely have allowed his grandfather's history to stand, "we went first to the Healers, who tested me, and found that I might safely be trained as a servant in the Halls. That training would have required money, however.

"After the Healers, we went to the Scouts. I was tested and offered a scholarship to be trained in a specialty. The scholarship, however, was dependent upon a small donation from my House.

"With both of these options rejected by the delm—" *and,* he added to himself, *my mother with a new bruise on her face*—"then, yes, we went to the mercenaries, and I was enlisted as a 'prentice soldier. The results of the Scouts' testing came with me, and I was trained in languages and protocol." He did not say that the mercenaries had paid his mother a signing fee, of which she had given him half. He didn't know what she might have done with that money, and even after so long he feared to betray her to her father.

"The mercenaries do not appear to have taught you to curb your insolence," his grandfather observed, and continued with scarcely a pause. "Never mind. You will have a clan necklace; you will have everything that a son of Severt ought to have, and honor, too. You will be required to attend me. You will do as you are told, and you will say that which I give you to say. In this way you will bring benefit to your House, and increase our standing among the clans. Do you understand me?"

Well, no; he didn't. But, when had he ever understood aught about his grandfather save that the old man hated the sight of him, and considered him a drain upon the resources of the House?

"Yes, sir," he said, mildly.

His grandfather failed to look pleased. He stood, abruptly. Tom Lei came to his feet as well.

"Go and find Manza. Tell her that you'll want good clothes; that I intend to take you about and show you to everyone. Can you do that?"

"I believe it may not be beyond me."

Dammit, Tommy, hold your tongue!

He met his grandfather's black eyes, and waited for the explosion. It didn't come.

"Leave me," his grandfather said.

Tom Lei bowed and left the room.

• • • ✧ • • •

HIS AUNT MANZA was in her own office at the back of the house; a small room the one charm of which was the tall narrow window that gave out onto the back garden. She heard his grandfather's instructions with no expression on her face, reached into the middle drawer of the desk and withdrew a gold chain from which a golden icon in the shape of Severt's shield twinkled. He received it from her hand and slipped it on over his head without looking at the shield.

"The clothes you are wearing were got in Chonselta," she said then.

He nodded. "This morning, at bin'Dekel's shop, on East Port Street," he said. "I thought it best, were I not to show up in my traveling gear."

His aunt smiled, faintly.

"You never were a fool," she commented. "So, since Master bin'Dekel has your measurements, as of this very morning, and since his work is perfectly unexceptional, I will call him immediately and order in those things Severt desires you to have. They will be sent up to your rooms when they are delivered." She turned to her screen, tapped a key.

"There is a small card party this evening to which I daresay you will accompany your grandfather, if you are to be shown to *everyone*." She looked at him appraisingly. "What you are wearing now will do, though it should be freshened . . ."

"I bought a second suit, much like this," he said, and she inclined her head in acknowledgement.

"Tomorrow night is pen'Valer's reception, for which you will need something more, but we will have it by then." She moved her shoulders. "You're in the back hall, second floor; the middle suite." Another glance, this one slightly softer. "It has much the same view as this room, and is quite the nicest suite on the hall."

She turned back to her screen; he was dismissed to quarters.

He stood his ground.

"Aunt."

She looked up, frowning.

"Where will I find my mother?"

The frown grew deeper and for an instant, he thought she would refuse to tell him.

Then she sighed, and shook her head.

"Your mother died six Standards ago," she said.

His mouth dried, and he had to ask it—*had* to ask it, though it brought dishonor on the House even to *think* the question.

"By Grandfather's hand?"

Aunt Manza came half out of her chair, her face richly flushed . . .

. . . and sank down again, with something that might have equally been a laugh or a sob.

"We had all feared that, at one time or another," she said, as if to herself. "Why should Elza's son not have feared for her, too?" She met his eyes.

"Be at peace, child. She was struck by a lorry as she crossed the street in the port, on her way to work, late she was, that morning, and likely failed to look. The lorry driver said she darted out from between delivery vans in front of the market; he barely saw her, and had no time to stop."

He saw it, in his mind's eye. Saw her crouching between the vans; saw her gauge her chances . . .

"It was deliberate." It was a certainty, not a question. His grandfather might be a cipher to him, but he had known his mother well.

Aunt Manza's mouth twisted with old pain.

"Between us—I think it was, yes. We don't speak of it, here in the House. Most especially not to your grandfather."

A warning. He bowed.

"Thank you. I know you were my mother's friend."

She sniffed.

"Not enough her friend," she said quietly. She looked down at the screen and touched a series of keys.

"You will wish to inspect your room," she said. "If you have particular requirements, in terms of furniture or ornaments, please speak to me."

"Yes, Aunt," he said, and left her to her work.

• • • ✧ • • •

CARD PARTY, breakfast fancy, afternoon gather, another card party . . . Had he not been trained to endure tedious social gatherings, he might have gone into a decline.

Happily, there was other employment for him. Aunt Manza stood as Nadelm Severt, which meant that his grandfather had piled all of the clan's administrative work upon her, thereby keeping himself free for intrigues and gambling with the clan's fortunes. He offered his assistance, and, after a long, considering look, his aunt had accepted it. This was how he had learned the state of the clan's finances.

"We ought to remove to the estate, and sell the town house," Aunt Manza told him, "but the delm will not hear of it."

No, of course not.

When he was not helping with the nadelm's endless work, he

walked. Fifteen Standards as a soldier had left him unfit for the sedentary life of an office clerk, or a Liaden gentleman.

The exercise was at first the conscious part of his walking, but he found the ingrained habits of a soldier marking out the territory, and after day eight he knew short-cuts and potential danger points, knew the corner across from the park where he'd likely find a proctor leaning within view of the public comm station, the corner where the halfling fashionistas flirted with any who might notice them. He avoided the park's mirror-pool, which reminded him only too much of Cardimin's pond-pocked city and the ugly house-to-house fighting there.

Had he not been on duty for the House, he might well have enjoyed the walks, over time. But no. During his walks, he turned over the conversations he was included into, as Delm Severt's grandson, as Delm Severt's secret weapon.

His grandfather had, indeed, an odd set of acquaintances, and peculiarly interesting for someone who had a particular training . . .

. . . as, for instance, his own training: not only to endure, but to listen to the unspoken conversations, and deduce the hidden strategies.

Before the end of the first card party, it was perfectly plain to Tom Lei that his grandfather had managed to ingratiate himself with some members of Houses that could only be called High. During the breakfast fancy, it also became plain that there was a secret project with which those same High Houselings required assistance; a secret desperate enough that they could not afford to be choosy regarding such minor matters as social standing or *melant'i*.

By the time he and his grandfather had returned home from the second card party, Tom Lei was quite frightened.

His grandfather was ambitious, yes. His grandfather had always been ambitious; and as a result, he had always played at stakes somewhat above his reach. That he was good at the game was evidenced by the fact that Severt had not plummeted into obscurity, but had actually made some small gains in the clan's social standing.

But this game—the game in which he, Tom Lei, was somehow a high-stakes pawn—this game was dangerous even beyond his grandfather's understanding.

Korval was involved—and Korval was not—*was never*—to be considered anything less than dangerous, though they had been banished from Liad, and had only days remaining until their departure.

But there was more—something he couldn't *quite* hear, in the whispers between the words said aloud, but which made him shiver, nonetheless.

It was also plain that he, himself, was being vetted and passed up a ladder of individuals who were increasingly important in this business of whispers and secrets.

What he would find at the top of the ladder, he dared not guess.

• • •✧• • •

AFTER HE HAD BEEN FOUR WEEKS in the house, he was called into the presence of his grandfather and his delm before the midday meal, and there received from him his instructions for the coming evening's entertainment.

"You will dress in your best. I will send rings; you will wear them on your left hand. On the right, only the honor-ring you have from the mercenaries. You will tonight be at my side; you will follow where I lead. Do you understand me?"

This is it, he thought; *this is the big one; all the smaller hurdles have been conquered.* Perhaps he ought to be proud of himself—of his skill—that he had been passed all the way to the top.

But what was he to do, he thought, alone in his rooms, after the rings had been sent up, and he had chosen three for his left hand. The course of honor, according to the Code, was to obey his delm. But if his delm was about to ruin the clan, by engaging in a game the stakes of which were higher than even the Highest Houses ought offer? Where was honor then?

On the few occasions when he had been required by his duty to operate at such rarefied heights, he had instructions; a goal; backup from a commander who had been bold, yes, but who did not gamble blindly, nor waste his counters.

No, he thought, staring down into the garden from his window. The goal must be to preserve the clan, if it came to that, tonight. He must prevent his grandfather from doing anything foolish. That must be his course. He was the only one of Severt able to stand against the delm; the rest had long ago been beaten down by his will.

Decision taken, he turned from the window and lay down on his bed, to nap and recruit his wits for the coming test.

• • •✧• • •

"LORD VEN'ASTRA, allow me to present my grandson, Tom Lei, newly returned to us after serving many years as a soldier in a Terran mercenary unit."

Lord ven'Astra was a spoilt-looking man in middle years. He wore High House hauteur like a cloak about his elegant shoulders, and looked at grandfather with a slightly bored air.

Tom Lei made his bow.

"Lord ven'Astra, I am honored to meet you," he said, once again grateful for the training that had taught him to lie with ease and conviction.

"Young pen'Chapen." The lord returned a nod, and looked momentarily thoughtful. "Newly returned from the mercenaries, are you?"

"Yes, my lord."

"Has your grandfather discussed our little conundrum with you?"

Well, this might be easy, thought Tom Lei. *Perhaps all I have to do is play the fool.*

"I don't believe that he has, sir," he said politely.

Grandfather stepped in.

"Indeed, we have not spoken on the topic. I wished him to hear it first from you, my lord, and to give you his untutored opinion. Everyone here knows that I think we must make an example, or lose *melant'i*."

"Quite," said the lordship, and turned his full attention to Tom Lei.

"The situation is thus, young pen'Chapen. There remain in custody several mercenary soldiers—perhaps a half-dozen— hired by Korval to invade our homeworld and assist in the action against Solcintra. There are those among the Council who believe that we should release these . . . persons to their units. And there are those among the Council who believe that we should make, perhaps, not an example, but a statement. And that statement would be that Liad is not a paltry world that may be invaded at will by Terrans; and that consequences attend such outrages."

Tom Lei felt cold, hearing the whisper behind the words.

Those others, which included this lord and his grandfather, wished to execute the mercenaries in the Council's custody.

"The information that reached my unit regarding the strike against Liad," Tom Lei said carefully, "was that the mercenary units which supported Korval's action were properly hired by, and under contract to, Clan Korval. Was this not the case?"

"The contracts were produced as evidence," Lord ven'Astra acknowledged. "Korval had hired them. That does not set aside the fact that they performed outrages against Liad and its citizens."

"Indeed," his grandfather said. "It must be made plain that we will not tolerate it."

"Do you agree, young pen'Chapen?"

But this was absurd! The man went against . . .

"Law and custom have long held that mercenaries properly under contract are in the same class as weapons used in acts of lawlessness: blameless tools. The hiring body is seen by law as the motivating force—the finger that pulls the trigger, if you will—and is, therefore, the responsible party in all legal actions."

"Tom Lei, you do not properly comprehend the case." His grandfather was sounding somewhat breathless. "These . . . creatures dared to move against Liad."

"Yes," he said patiently, watching Lord ven'Astra's eyes, "because the contract required them to do so. It was not what we—the mercenaries—call a *blood war*, in which there is no contract, nor client, and the units act upon their own recognizance.

"In this case, the Terran mercenaries took contract with Korval. They did not invade wantonly, but in good order, in support of Korval's action, as required by the contract. If the Council of Clans must have more blood—" He made a small bow, as if embarrassed by his lapse, and spoke to Lord ven'Astra.

"Your pardon, sir; I fear that I may have been too long among the mercenaries. Allow me to say, instead, that if the Council of Clans feels that banishment is not Balance enough for the wrongs visited upon the homeworld, then the Council of Clans must reopen its case against the Dragon."

Lord ven'Astra pressed his lips together, his spoiled face grave.

"The *qe'andra* do not allow it," he said, and it was anger Tom Lei heard beneath the words. "There were those of us who wished to see Korval themselves executed, the Dragon's assets come to the Council, and those remaining set to work off the debt of repairing the damage. We argued for that, hotly. Alas, the Dragon had too many friends on the Council. Execution was made into banishment, and confiscation of assets became divestiture.

"Now, the *qe'andra* rule that, as Korval has been given the actions it must perform in order to enter into Balance, said actions having a strong deadline attached, to introduce a secondary Balance at this juncture would itself be out of Balance."

"Even now, reduced as they are, Korval has the *qe'andra* in their pocket," his grandfather put in. "Why, dea'Gauss is the chair of their council! The Terran mercenaries have no *qe'andra*."

"Which does not make them guilty of war crimes, sir!"

Tom Lei felt ill. What did his grandfather hope to gain from this? ven'Astra's patronage? A blind man could see what *that* would be worth, once his lordship had a piece upon which he could place the blame, if opinion and law went against him . . .

"You seem decided in your opinion, young pen'Chapen," his lordship said, his voice decidedly cool. He looked aside.

"I suppose," he said to Severt, "that we must expect youth to be idealistic. It is a failing they soon grow out of."

"Precisely, my lord. I had been certain that Tom Lei was past such kittenish ways!"

"Obviously not." Lord ven'Astra looked back to Tom Lei, his eyes cold. "I would say that you are correct, sir."

Tom Lei bowed slightly.

"In what way, my lord?"

"You *have* been too long among the mercenaries. Severt, a good evening to you."

Lord ven'Astra strolled away into the depths of the gather, and Tom Lei was left alone with his grandfather's disbelieving stare.

• • •✧• • •

"TOMORROW!" his grandfather shouted. "Tomorrow, you will go to Lord ven'Astra, and offer him your services!"

"My *services*?" Tom Lei looked at the old man in astonishment. "As an executioner, perhaps?"

"Do not be insolent, boy! This situation can be rescued—will be rescued. You need only do as you are told.

"You will go to his lordship and you will prostrate yourself. You will tell him that, upon talking the matter over with your elders, and thinking on it overnight, you understand that the insult carried to the homeworld by these Terrans must be Balanced. You will say that you are willing to testify, as a former mercenary familiar with law and custom in such matters, before the Council of Clans."

"His lordship will scarcely want that!"

"Silence! You will of course testify that law and custom support the execution of barbarians who force an invasion upon Liad."

Tom Lei stared.

"That," he said, his voice perfectly flat, "I will never do."

His grandfather spun around.

"You will do it, because that is what your delm requires of you!"

"No, sir. I will not dice with lives for your ambition."

"Will you not?" The old man stalked across the rug, until they were toe-to-toe. He thrust his face up into Tom Lei's.

"You will do as your delm requires, or you will find you have no delm at all!"

"That," Tom Lei heard someone say in perfectly calm tones, "is acceptable."

"Oh, is it?"

Tom Lei waited, feeling utterly calm. Severt would never bend before such a challenge, he thought. He must conclude the threat.

But, after a moment, his grandfather drew a breath, stepped back and walked across the room.

"A glass of wine will do us both some good," he said, and poured with his own hands.

Tom Lei, caught between relief and dismay, crossed to the wine table and received his glass.

"So," said Severt, when they had each sipped and lowered their glass. "I see it. You were accustomed to command, a little. You were, perhaps, accustomed to being given reasons for the actions you were commanded to perform, so that you might improvise, when and if necessary. Of course, it is difficult for you to drop such habits, which have, as I must surmise, since you stand here hale before me, served you well for many years."

He paused.

Tom Lei inclined his head and murmured, "Yes, sir," which seemed, by far, the safest course. It would seem that he was not to be cast out and declared dead to clan and kin. Or, at least, not immediately.

He mistrusted his grandfather in this eldritch mood. On the other hand, he entertained liveliest curiosity regarding what, in fact, the old man was about. Surely, *surely*, the reality was nothing so horrifying as his suspicions. Let him *know*, and perhaps he might sleep easier.

"Know, then, that the work which is underway, and to which I have recruited your assistance, will result in a great improvement the clan's *melant'i*. Once the thing is done, we will rise into the circle of the High Mid-Clans. At least, we shall ascend to those ranks. It is not out of the question, that Severt may, as a result of this action, rise to High House."

Tom Lei blinked.

"And who shall fall?" he asked, for it had been fixed for . . . a very long time, that there were but fifty High Houses.

"Fall? Ask, rather, who will rise!"

Tom Lei knew that he was not a fool. However, it took him more than a heartbeat to realize that his grandfather expected—no! Knew for a certainty!—that at least one clan would seek to rise into Korval's place. For *that* was how it was said: *There are precisely fifty High Houses. And then there is Korval.*

"Korval occupied a . . . unique place because of their contract," he pointed out.

Severt shrugged. "A contract may be trumped by contacts. And how refreshing to have a true Liaden clan, rather than a hireling, in that most unique position, eh?"

Tom Lei raised his glass, so that his failure to agree might pass unnoticed.

"So," said his grandfather and his delm again, after he, too, had partaken of his glass. "I will tell you now that these Terran mercenaries whose fate is to become an example for all of Liad's inferiors—they are hidden, of course."

"Of course," Tom Lei murmured.

"And, here is the point upon which our own ascension turns." His grandfather leaned close, and lowered his voice so that Tom Lei needed to bend at the waist in order to hear.

"We, Clan Severt, hold the prisoners, in trust for ven'Astra."

Shock jolted him. He had been a fool to hope that the truth was less terrible than his imaginings. He had been a fool to think that his grandfather would be content to gamble only with lives. No, like any gambler, he must ever increase his stakes.

And, now, he diced with Severt's very existence.

"Does Aunt Manza know this?" he demanded.

"Am I a fool to share such a thing abroad? She knows nothing."

Relief warred with horror. He took a breath, trying to recruit his thoughts.

"Peace, peace," his grandfather said, perhaps reading distress on his face. "Whether the scheme is executed, or the mercenaries are returned to their officer, as the *qe'andra* have ruled, our safety—and thus our reward—are secure.

"Only think! If the matter falls out as ven'Astra wishes, then we are rewarded for our help. If the *qe'andra* prevail, ven'Astra will be grateful to us for keeping our knowledge to ourselves." He smiled, and sipped wine.

"Indeed, I am almost wishful that the *qe'andra* might take the point, for there is a limit to the rewards for good service, and none at all, as I have been able to find, to the amount that will be paid in order to preserve one's honor."

Tom Lei saw it in a flash, then. His grandfather was not merely foolish; he was a bad delm, actively dangerous to his clan and those who rested in his care. Indeed, when had Severt ever cared for those who resided under his hand? Only see Aunt Manza, ceaselessly at labor with neither thanks nor input into the clan's business, her joy broken. Or his own mother, dead by her own choice, rather than endure any more abuse from this delm who was no delm at all! Or—yes!—himself, flung away as useless; his new life broken without a thought to his well-being, when he suddenly came to hold value as a game piece!

"Well?" said his grandfather, false delm. "Now you have the reasons, and the rewards laid down. What think you, now?"

He took a breath, meaning to say that his refusal stood, that he would welcome death rather than continue in such a clan, with such a delm . . .

. . . and he took another breath, thinking, indeed of his mother, and his aunt, and all those caught in the supposed care of this man. He thought of the Code, and the section dealing with those things that are owed, by an individual, to one's clan; and those other things, which are owed, by a clan, to its members.

He looked down into his grandfather's face, and he made answer, gently, in the mode of obedience to the delm.

"I would see these prisoners, that Severt holds in care for Lord ven'Astra. And I would see Lord ven'Astra, so that I may, indeed, place myself at service in the matter of their proper disposition."

His grandfather smiled.

"Excellent! We will tomorrow pay a morning call to his lordship, after which we will together go to the farm—"

He dared to lift a hand. His grandfather paused, and gestured for him to speak.

"I wonder if it might not be profitable, for all of us to meet at the place the prisoners are being kept. Lord ven'Astra may have those things which he may wish to convey to those whose lives he holds, in order that they have a clear understanding of their situation. I am an expert in languages."

His grandfather smiled again.

"And thus we demonstrate immediately your willingness to assist! Yes! It is well-thought. I shall arrange it!"

"Thank you," Tom Lei said, and bowed, gods help him, honor to the delm. He straightened.

"If we are done, sir, I will leave you. The night is fine, and I have not yet had my walk."

"Ah, the energy of youth!" His grandfather *laughed*. "When this matter is done, and we have our rewards, we must see you married—yes! To a proper daughter of the High! *That* will fix us well, indeed!"

He moved toward his desk, fluttering his fingers.

"Go, go; have your walk. Only take care that you are sharp for our meeting tomorrow!"

"Never fear, sir. I shall be as sharp as an Yxtrang's grace blade."

• • •✧• • •

LORD VEN'ASTRA was to meet them at the place—at Severt's own estate. That suited Tom Lei, who drove the clan's lumbering landau, less than half-listening to his grandfather's instructions regarding his demeanor toward his lordship, and the tenor of his apology.

"Do not be afraid to be bold—a mercenary's plain speaking will stand you well with him. You saw how it is with him, last evening, I think. He does not care to be gainsaid, but he likes a forthright manner. Only do whatever he asks you—and he will ask something, as a test against your changed opinion!—show yourself able and willing and all may be recovered."

Yes, certainly, Tom Lei thought, and glanced at the map on the dashboard to see how far yet they had to go.

At last they arrived. His grandfather had him drive past the house, and his stomach tightened, for he knew then where they were going, and the riddle of how a group of seasoned mercenaries were held was answered.

Some generations in the past, the delm had traveled to some or another far outworld and there became introduced to the sport of hunting to the hounds. So enamored of this sport had she become that she imported her own pack, and keeper, and every *relumma* hosted a hunt throughout the neighboring fields.

The dogs—quite fierce dogs, who bonded to the pack, of which they considered their keeper, but no other human, a member—the dogs required kennels. And the kennel, given the temper of the dogs, was required to mete out stern discouragement of escape.

Once the dogs were kenneled, a switch was thrown, which

electrified every floor, every wall, every surface, save those in the dog pens, proper. An escape from the den room into the main hall would be rewarded by a jolt of energy sufficient to stop the heart of a being far larger than a hunting dog.

The dogs were sold off by the delm's successor, but the kennels had endured.

"Here," his grandfather said from the seat next to him. "Stop here."

• • • ✧ • • •

HE HAD SCARCELY STOPPED their vehicle, when Tom Lei spied the approach of another. Moments later, Lord ven'Astra emerged from the small car he had driven himself.

"Severt," said his lordship. "Good morning to you."

"A delightful morning, indeed, my lord," his grandfather responded.

The cool eyes came to rest on Tom Lei, who bowed as one who has discovered oneself in error.

"Your delm tells me that you have undergone a change of ideology, young pen'Chapen. Is it so?"

"My lord, it is," Tom Lei answered.

"It gratifies me to hear you say so. Let us by all means survey the prisoners, and you may do a small thing for me, if you will."

"Certainly, my lord," Tom Lei said calmly.

THERE WERE SIX MERCS in the large den room. The water was running in the drinking pool; and a light on inside the basic sanitation unit that had been installed for the use of the hounds' keeper on the not-infrequent nights when she slept with the pack.

The six prisoners—Terrans, all—looked well enough, though pale. They wore what appeared to be house robes, which were short in length and sleeve, leaving legs, and wrists, and bare feet on display.

"Well, if ain't Mister Bully-for-Me and Uncle Me-too," said a voice in Aus-dialect Terran.

Tom Lei glanced at his two companions. If either one understood the dialect, or the insults to themselves, they chose not to react, which seemed like neither of them.

Tom Lei felt his heart lift, slightly, and he turned again toward the former den, one hand against the plexglass window and the other at belt height, fingers dancing lightly in merc sign.

The man who had spoken—his robe so short as to be immodest, and his beard in need of a good trimming—lifted an eyebrow, and braced his feet wide.

"That one," Lord ven'Astra said, "with the hair of his face almost touching his chest. He is a leader of some sort; the others listen to him. I would have you translate my words to him, young pen'Chapen; *exactly* my words. Will you do that?"

"Yes, sir," he said, meeting the Aus' eyes calmly. He winked, and saw the man's other eyebrow rise.

"Excellent. First, tell him who I am."

"Yes, sir," he repeated, and spoke in the thickest, most incomprehensible Aus dialect he knew.

"Do you understand me?"

"Y'sound just like my old grandpaw."

"Excellent. The man with the brown hair, beside me, is a lordship. He's instrumental in keeping you here, and if he has his way you'll die, on camera, as a warning to others who'd invade Liad."

"We had a contract," the Aus said.

"He chooses to ignore that. He's going to give me words to say to you, now. Remember that they're his words, and reflect only his opinion."

The Aus nodded, and Tom Lei turned to his lordship.

"I have explained to him who you are, my lord."

"Excellent. Now, say this to him, and tell him to tell the others." He took a deep breath, and began to speak, rather too rapidly for a translator.

"Tell him that their officers no longer seek them; their names have been written out of the rolls of their companies and their families have been notified of their deaths," said Lord ven'Astra. "Tell them that their only remaining hope of honor is to confess before the Council of Clans that they are captured invaders of Liad, and pay the price named."

Tom Lei repeated it, as near as he was able, in that thick Aus accent. When he was done, the man before him asked a question.

"Is he nuts?"

"Might be," Tom Lei said. "What's important now is that his clan's powerful, and he wants all of you dead, publicly, to demonstrate his power and Liad's might."

The Aus glanced behind him, where the rest of his comrades stood silent.

"Two medics, two newbies, and a couple grunts," he said. "Some invasion force."

"Your lives are precious," Tom Lei said, which was something of a risk, but he would think of something to tell him, if ven'Astra asked to know what he said. "I won't let him harm you."

"You got point, brother," the Aus said. "I'll tell 'em now, unless there's something more. Any on your side speak Merc pidgin?"

"I think not."

"Have to risk it."

The Aus turned his back and approached the little knot of his comrades.

Tom Lei turned to Lord ven'Astra.

"If one may ask, my lord, how do you intend to execute them?"

Ven'Astra was staring into the den, at the prisoners, a look of revulsion plain upon his face.

"I had expected that the Council of Clans would, eventually, be willing to see the deed done, but I learn only this morning that the Council will not even hear us. Other arrangements are being made, even as we speak. These will know full Balance within the next *relumma*, and all the galaxy will know what it is to trifle with Liad."

"Stand where you are, and place your hands on your heads," an authoritative female voice commanded. This was followed by a definite snap, as if of a safety being thumbed off.

ven'Astra half-turned; the voice told him to stop or accept the consequences, and a form stepped out of the hall behind them.

She was dressed in the neat business attire of a *qe'andra*. Her bow was crisp and unafraid. Her weapon was military-grade, and held with confidence.

"I am Fantile dea'Starn," she said, calmly. "In this matter, I represent the planetary council of *qe'andra*. You will come with me."

"Where would you take us?" demanded Severt.

She considered him calmly.

"I would take you to our council chambers, where you will present evidence. There will of course be Healers present, to ensure that your evidence is presented in good faith."

"Thank you, madam," said ven'Astra. "You will only need these men here—" He nodded at Severt and Tom Lei. "These poor creatures are, as you see, imprisoned on the property of Clan Severt."

"Mine, is it!" shouted Severt. He swung out, his hand diving into his pocket.

Tom Lei lunged, snatched the arm up, brought the wrist sharply against his own forearm, and watched the gun fly from suddenly senseless fingers as he continued moving the arm, up behind the old man's back, heedless of his scream, and stood holding him.

"My thanks," said Fantile dea'Starn, and looked to her left. "Proctors, please, do your duty."

Lord ven'Astra lunged then, too late. One of the proctors swung something against his knee, and calmly caught his shoulder and snapped on binders as the afflicted knee buckled.

Tom Lei relinquished his grandfather to the second proctor, who likewise bound his wrists. He waited with the *qe'andra*, and the third and fourth proctors while the prisoners were escorted out.

"Thank you for your information," Fantile dea'Starn said, with a small bow. "The *qe'andra*, and also Korval, are in your debt."

She turned toward the den, where six pairs of eyes were watching the proceedings with very evident interest.

"Please," said Fantile dea'Starn, "tell them who I am and what has transpired. Tell them, too, that Liaison Officer Oshiamo is on his way to them even now from the port. He was delayed in traffic."

She used her chin to point at the comm on the third proctor's belt. "If they wish it, we may call him; I have his code."

"Yes, ma'am," Tom Lei said, and turned to address the mercs.

• • •✧• • •

AUNT MANZA was Severt now; the *qe'andra* had quietly overseen the transfer, and duly recorded it. Grandfather was confined to his rooms.

"When we return to the estate," Severt said, "then he may find occupation that will risk no one."

"But you, Tom Lei—advise me, what shall I do?"

They were sitting together in the evening in her office, the same office overlooking the back garden, for, as she said, it was no use to move all of her work to grandfather's old office when she would only have to move it again, when the house was sold and the clan removed entirely to the country house.

"I ask," he said slowly, "that the delm kill me."

She blinked.

"That is hardly the Balance I should have suggested for such a service to your clan."

He shook his head.

"Aunt, consider: Lord ven'Astra is High House. There are others of his opinion who know me. Any one of them may decide that my betrayal of his lordship deserves the true death. It is not wise to have a target living among the clan, for sometimes even skilled assassins miss and the innocent are harmed." He gave her a wry half-smile.

"Notice that I do not dare speculate what terrors Grandfather would attempt to visit upon me!"

She chuckled, but protested anew.

"And, yet, for us, your kin, your clan—you have largely done good," she said, and again he shook his head.

"I presumed to judge the delm, and I found him wanting. I laid a trap and caught him." He leaned forward and touched her arm lightly.

"I am not safe for you, Aunt. How can either of us know that I will not do the like again?"

She laughed, and sat a moment, sipping her tea and thinking.

Finally, she sighed, and put the tea cup aside.

"You are determined that we mourn your loss, and I find that I must agree." She paused. "Very well, I will do it. But, first, you will tell me how long it will take you to be safely off-planet."

"I beg your pardon?"

"You, who have thought of so much, did you not think of this? If you are correct, and Lord ven'Astra's co-conspirators wish Balance, I will not give them a clanless man as a target. Once you are off-planet, then will Severt publish its sorrow abroad."

He inclined his head, chastised, and pleased. Aunt Manza would be a good delm. She might even recover the clan's fortunes.

"I can be off-planet within the next day," he told her.

"Tell me when your plans are complete, and the time when your ship will lift. Now," she said, briskly. "You will take all that is yours, naturally, including the clothes the clan provided to you. There is no one here who they will fit, and you will need clothes, wherever you go, and whatever you may become. You will, in fact, take anything that is in your room which catches your fancy. In addition, you will take the rings that your grandfather gave to you—"

"But—" He began the protest, and swallowed it as she fixed him in her eye.

"You *will take* the rings your grandfather gave to you. Rings can be sold or bartered, and if your delm is to do as you command, my child, she cannot send you off with your pockets full of *cantra* pieces. In the meanwhile . . ."

She rose and bowed gratitude, as he scrambled to his feet.

"Severt thanks you for your service, Tom Lei pen'Chapen," she said, and straightened before he could return her courtesy.

She smiled then and opened her arms.

"Come now, child, and give your aunt your kiss."

This he did, willingly, and hugged her until she gasped a laugh and called him a great lout, and reached up to touch his cheek, tears in her eyes.

"Go and pack," she said softly. "I know you are eager to be away."

• • •✧• • •

HE DRESSED IN HIS LEATHERS and sweater, packing his new clothes, though they were far too fine for a merc. He touched his vest then, and heard the crackle of paper from the inside pocket, and smiled. The print out of the letter from the *qe'andra*, detailing his part in the rescue of the captive mercs, and another, from Liaison Officer Oshiamo, which had also been forwarded to Headquarters, to be appended to his file.

Yes, he was eager to be away. Away to Headquarters, where he intended to sue for re-enlistment with these letters, and the proof that he would never be called home by his delm again.

He wanted none of the ornaments in the room; he packed the rings, promising himself that he would sell them at the earliest opportunity. Then he straightened and looked about him, for anything else that was his.

There, on the bureau, was . . .

He approached, and found three *cantra* pieces in a neat stack before a folder of holograms. A chill ran up his spine; he picked the folder up, flipped it open, and . . .

. . . there was his mother, younger than ever he had known her, a progression of images, a few with Aunt Manza, a few more with him, and more, now older than he had known her, looking weary and thin . . . and another of them together. She was smiling, and he was, and she was holding an untidy bouquet of wildflowers that he had picked for her.

He flipped to the next page, but there were no more pictures, after.

Swallowing around the tears lodged in his throat, he slipped the little folder into an inside pocket of his vest and sealed it up. He picked up the *cantra* pieces as an afterthought, and dropped them into his public pocket.

• • • ✧ • • •

MIRI ROBERTSON TIAZAN CLAN KORVAL, aka the Road Boss, on alternate business days, sat in her designated booth in the back of the Emerald Casino in Surebleak Port and tried not to be bored.

It was tough. Bidness was so slow, she'd even read all the outstanding reports and bulletins, and answered a couple of not-exactly-burning inquiries.

She wished that she dared take a nap; she *was* tired, and her back hurt, though not enough to make her swear that she was going to find whoever'd thought it would be a good idea to get pregnant and dislocate their jaw.

She sighed. Maybe just a quick nap, with her head on the table. Couldn't hurt, could it, and Nelirikk, leaning against the wall by the booth like he could do it all day—which, he prolly could—he'd tell her if there was company—

A step sounded in the little hallway just beyond her booth.

Miri turned her head.

Nelirikk straightened away from the wall, and put his hand on his sidearm.

A shadow cleared the hall, resolving into a fair-haired man on the short side of tall for a Terran, and on the tall side of tall for a Liaden. He was a bit paler in the face than your usual Liaden, the fair hair pulled back into a tail. Dressed in merc leathers and good marching boots. He looked tired.

He took note of Nelirikk real quick, and stopped where he was.

"I am," he said, addressing both or either of them, "here to see Delm Korval."

"Well," said Miri, giving Nelirikk the hand-sign that meant *let the boy come closer*, "you found half of Delm Korval, though this is the Road Boss' office."

A Terran would get impatient with what would sound to him like plain and fancy nonsense; a Liaden would parse the information she'd just given him.

He inclined slightly from the waist.

"I beg your pardon. Is there a more appropriate time and venue to speak with Delm Korval?"

And that answered that.

Miri smiled.

"Happens things is slow this afternoon, so I'll do us both a favor and switch hats," she told him. "What's your name?"

"Tommy Lee," he said.

Well, so much for having him figured.

"You a merc?" she asked.

"*Former* merc," he answered, and there was some bitterness there.

"What makes you former?"

He sighed, all of a sudden just looking weary of everything, but he gave her a clean enough answer.

"My delm called me home."

"That'll do it," she acknowledged. "Whatcha been doin' lately?"

That got a faint smile.

"*Most* lately, I have been suing for re-enlistment," he said.

"In my day, there wasn't any re-enlisting from the escape clause."

"Yes, but you see, I'm dead, and no longer subject to being called . . . anywhere." He smiled again, a little brighter. "It did go all the way to an All-Commanders Tribunal before it got denied."

"Well, that's something, yeah. So, what do you think I can do for you, Tommy Lee?"

He straightened into attention.

"I wish to offer my gun to Korval," he said formally.

Like a thousand others. Miri didn't sigh.

She opened the portable computer and tapped a key.

"What's your name?" she asked, her eyes on the screen.

"Tommy Lee."

She raised her head to glare at him.

"What's the name you enlisted under?" she asked with exaggerated patience. "Or maybe you got an ID number?"

He gave her the number; she entered it, and . . . blinked at the screen.

"Tommy Lee, sit down."

He did so, settling his pack neatly next to the chair.

Miri finished reading the file, then met his eyes over the edge of the screen.

"Been wondering for a while now what happened to the guy who pulled mercs out of a hat for us. We offered what help we could when they went missing, but by that point our help was worse than none, if you take my meaning. The mercs and the *qe'andra* took it and ran with it, but it was pretty much a dead end until some guy called up Ms. dea'Starn and told her he was going to be able to lead her to the prisoners."

She shook her head, glanced down at the screen, and back to him.

"Looks like we owe you, Tommy Lee."

"I came," he reminded her gently, "to offer Korval my gun. If you'll have it."

"We might. Have to talk it over with my partner, naturally. Tell you what. I got another couple hours on-duty here. When's the last time you ate something wasn't bar rations?"

He blinked.

"It's been a . . . while."

"Thought so." She looked at her aide. "Beautiful, take this man down to the kitchen and see him fed, then take him over to Audrey's for a nap. Bring him back here at quitting time."

"Yes, Captain. I will call House Security for your back-up here."

"Good idea."

She returned to Tommy Lee, sitting quiet and maybe a little wide-eyed in his chair.

"You'll come up to the house with me; have a little talk with us and with our head of House Security, see if there's a way we can do each other some good. That OK by you?"

He swallowed, his eyes a little damp, maybe, but the grin this time was good and firm.

"Yes, Captain," he said. "That's OK by me."

✧ Guaranteed Delivery ✧

***THOSE WHO HAVE BEEN READING** the Liaden Universe® novels will recall that, in* Mouse and Dragon, *Aelliana Caylon had determined to start a courier service. This she did, with her lifemate as a partner in the venture. Sadly,* Mouse and Dragon *had as its theme something other than the various adventures* Ride the Luck, *the Caylon, and her rogue of a copilot encountered as couriers. Obviously, this meant that any such adventures would need to be detailed in short stories.*

This is the story of Ride the Luck's *fourth courier run.*

LIGHT BLOOMED inside the treasure room.

Discreet and faintly blue, it kissed the alarm console, the pearly security keys blushing delft.

Long fingers touched the shy panels, pressing them in a precise, rapid sequence. More light bloomed, opening a path across the carpet to a wall well-hung with twodee art.

The owner of those long, sure fingers, one Dollance-Marie Chimra, upon whom the Feinik society news had bestowed the name Alabaster, kept scrupulously to the illuminated path. As she approached the wall, light began to glow in outline around a single piece of art—a painting of a woman in long skirts, the shawl draped over her head framing a face ferocious with love, one arm around the waist of a man in a tattered uniform, braced on a crude crutch.

"Treasure of the House" was the name of the painting; the original hung in the salon of Dollance-Marie's mama, the Gransella of Hamptonshire, on Albion itself.

Dollance-Marie pressed her right thumb against a particular point in the painting's unadorned wooden frame, counted to ten, then folded both hands at her waist, waiting.

Silent on stealth hinges, the painting swung away from the wall, revealing a door and a simple tumbler lock.

It required only a moment for her to work the combination, pull the door open, and remove a velvet box slightly smaller than her palm.

She paused, long fingers curled into a cage around the box. Had it been someone other than Dollance-Marie Chimra, and had there been anyone else in the treasure room to see, that hidden watcher might have said that she . . . hesitated.

As it was Alabaster herself, whom the tabloids had in their genius named well, and no one else inside the tightly guarded room—she paused, only that, and took a deep, cleansing breath before she closed the safe and spun the tumblers. The painting swung back into place, light fading from its perimeter.

Raising her chin, Alabaster met the fierce eyes of the woman in the painting, and smiled.

• • • ✧ • • •

SHE HAD PLANNED the evening carefully—first, drinks in Erabeck's public parlor, to satisfy those who followed Alabaster; then befores with Smyth-Erin Nodmere and Dane Belnesky—Yin and Yang, according to the society news, in recognition of their long and complimentary partnership.

From Yin and Yang's semi-public table, they proceeded to a private dining nook, said privacy Erabeck's specific guarantee.

The door closed behind the security escort. Dollance-Marie put her palm against the plate. The room chimed, indicating that the privacy blanket was in force.

She turned with a smile that had no place on Alabaster's face, and stepped forward to seat her guest.

"Please," she said, moving the chair on its track, "be comfortable."

John Vernon tipped his head, considering her from serious blue eyes.

"Must we be formal?" he asked, and she paused with her hand on the back of the chair.

Vernon was a good bloodline, if not so exalted as Chimra. The family elders had collected a following of note, which they managed with a subtlety even Chimra might with profit study.

This particular Vernon, whom the media had ignored until Alabaster had engaged him for a moment of conversation—this John Vernon, now code-named Galahad—had been raised out of society by his father's people on Hascove, this having been stipulated in the Terms of Dissolution. He had returned, unRanked and with a scant base of Followers, to his mother's house and business upon achieving his majority—also in accordance with the Terms. He possessed a lively wit and was quick to learn—so quick that one sometimes forgot that he *was* learning, until he asked just such a sweet, naive question.

"We are private," Dollance-Marie said, matching him for seriousness, "and may be as informal as you wish."

As soon as she had uttered the words, with their suggestion of more risque ventures, she wished to call them back. Others that she had favored with her notice would have immediately heard an invitation to sport, and acted accordingly.

John, raised in innocence, only smiled, his sweet countenance undisturbed by even a blush. He settled with casual elegance into the seat she held for him, touching one finger to the seal at his throat, loosening it somewhat.

Taking her own seat, Dollance-Marie smiled. John's dislike of the current male fashion for tight collars and flowing tunics was his mother's despair.

"Perhaps we ought to have you establish a fashion for neck scarves," she said, pouring wine into painted palm-cups.

"And be choked twice?" he asked.

She leaned forward and offered him a cup, which he took with a frank smile.

"How if," she mused, "the vogue was to drape the scarf loosely in order to call attention to a charming dishevelment?"

"My mother would murder me."

She laughed, and brought her cup against his.

"To informality," she said.

"To informality, and all its pleasures," he answered, capping her, according to the latest mode.

Dollance-Marie gave him a sharp glance.

"Is something wrong?" he asked, alert, as ever, to her moods.

Alabaster would have answered that question with her cool, cutting laugh. Dollance-Marie smiled a small smile.

"You've been studying again," she said. "That was quite fashionable."

Such notice of his progress might have pleased any another country cousin striving to learn greatness. John . . . frowned, and put his cup aside, untasted.

"I *have* been studying," he said slowly. "I must, for my mother has set me to learn so that I can take my place in the family business. But I am determined not to be *fashionable* with my true friends, Marie. I beg your pardon."

True friends was a notion from backward Hascove. That it had survived John's first year moving in the Leadership levels of Feinik society was a testament to its tenacity. Or, as certain of Alabaster's acquaintance might say, John's lack of motherwit.

Dollance-Marie knew that John's wits lacked nothing. And she had admitted to her innermost self that she was charmed—no! that she was *honored*, to employ another word little-used by the Leaders—to be one of his *true friends*.

Her breath caught on that thought, and her heart took up the odd pounding that John's presence had lately woken. It was, she thought, time. She had done her research; she had formally expressed her intentions to her mama, who had, depend upon it, done *her* research, and had raised no protest. John Vernon had captured her attention; he was comely, sweet, and modest. His father's people had kept him close, so Dollance-Marie need not be concerned with paying off any of his wild oats, or placating a former liaison.

She would be his first—*that* was a thought that warmed her blood distractingly during her precious hours of privacy. She would teach him—so very many things.

Her hand shook; the wine in the palm-cup shivered.

"Marie?" He touched her wrist gently. "Is something wrong?"

It was time. Now. She *must* have him.

"Not wrong," she said. Putting her cup aside, she reached out to take his hand between both of hers. "John, I—I propose that we two come to an agreement of partnership."

He blinked. "Partnership?" he repeated. "Like Dane and Erin?"

Yin and Yang had renewed their agreement more times than Dollance-Marie could count. She shivered at the thought of entering into so long a partnership—but of course John hadn't meant to imply such a thing; it was his innocence speaking again.

"Like Erin and Dane," she agreed, therefore, and smiled at him, while her heart pounded against her ribs, and her breath came short.

"I know," she said. "I know that it must seem very sudden to you. You mustn't be frightened, or think that I will be angry if you want time to think, or—" But no; she was not going to put the unacceptable into his sweet, naive head. She was not going to lose him. And while she might be his *true friend*, she doubted not at all the necessity of what she did next. Hadn't her grandmama taught her? *Pay good value for what you want.*

She kept hold of John with one hand; with the other, she reached into her pocket for the velvet box. Gently, she placed it on the table before him, and tapped it so that the lid rose, revealing a faceted ruby the size of her thumb, from nail to knuckle. The storied Hamptonshire Ruby. She felt a small tremor, looking at it—not *exactly* hers to give, but a treasure of the house. As John would be.

"That," she said softly, "is yours."

John glanced down, and blinked, likely dazzled, as were most when they first beheld the Ruby. He raised his head to look directly into her eyes.

"Marie, are you certain?"

She blinked in her turn.

"Certain?" she repeated, noticing only then that it was now *her* hand held with firm sweetness between *his* two palms.

"I can think of nothing better than . . . than a partnership with my true friend," John said seriously. "But . . ." His lips twisted into a wry smile. "I *have* been learning, and I know that my view of the matter is not . . . current here on Feinik."

"I can think of nothing that I want more than for us to be together, in public and in private," Dollance-Marie said truthfully. Right now, she wanted John with her; she would, she thought, take ill if she could not have him.

John nodded. "Then I accept. I think that the traditional initial term is one Planetary Year?"

"Yes," she said eagerly. "I'll send my formal request to your mother this evening. And the Ruby—I'll have it made into a ring for you, John. Will you like that?"

He frowned, almost as if he had forgotten all about the magnificent gem she had given him.

"If it pleases you," he answered.

• • •✧• • •

THE COMM LIGHT was dark.

"Oh," said Aelliana, leathered shoulders drooping. She put her hand on the back of the pilot's chair, frowning at the board as if the application of raw will would produce a message in queue.

Daav, who had come onto the bridge in her wake, paused at her shoulder, and waited a decent count of twelve before clearing his throat.

"As eager to lift as that, Pilot?"

"Well . . ." She sighed and turned to him, her eyes wide and very green. "One does wish for work, after all. We have put our name and our credentials on the for-hire lists, and I had thought, that, surely . . ."

Her voice faded.

"You had thought that surely, *Ride the Luck*, with three successful contracts fulfilled, would speedily attract not one, but several job offers," he finished for her.

"If you will have it," Aelliana said steadily. "Ridiculous it may be, but a pilot has a certain pride in her ship, and in the abilities of herself *and* her copilot, sad rogue that he otherwise stands."

"*That*'s set me in place!"

"Yes; as it should." She sighed, and continued more seriously. "Truly, Daav, if we are to continue this course we have chosen—and perhaps someday see profit from it!—we cannot lift empty."

"Indeed, we cannot," he agreed, serious himself. "A ship wants work; and pilots surely *need* work, or who knows what error they may fall into? But, if the pilot will allow—we have been on-port a scant six hours; the errand that brought us here has scarcely been tagged as satisfactorily completed."

"I am, in fact, too eager?" Aelliana asked.

"Naturally so, but—yes."

"What do you propose, then, Copilot?"

"Why, only that we allow the process to work, while good ship and pilots take a well-earned rest."

"Rest!" She gave a small laugh and shook her tawny hair back. "I hardly suppose that I can *rest, van'chela*."

"Well," he said, with a laugh of his own. "Perhaps we can think of something else to do."

•• • •✧• • •

FEINIK'S LEMON-WASHED DAWN was rousting the night when Dollance-Marie returned to her residence. John had let his reserve down, and talked confidingly about what he hoped for their partnership. It had been exhilarating, strange, and made her desire him all the more, this exotic, innocent creature who with one breath agreed to stand publicly as Alabaster's consort, and with the next expressed a wish to live retired. His wistfulness had sparked her genius, and she had offered travel to some less-mediad locales as something that they might undertake, to broaden their minds.

He had seized upon that, speaking of this world and that—on which subject he was astonishingly well-informed. She was entranced.

Erabeck's security at last alerted them to the hour, and an additional fee brought them to a back door, and what appeared to be a common taxicab. It was in that humble conveyance that Alabaster brought Galahad to his mother's house, and saw him safely inside.

She then directed the cab to her own residence, thereby denying the media news of her activities for more than five hours on the evening. Her ratings-coach would scold her on the morrow, not to mention her head of security, but for tonight—for this morning!—Dollance-Marie cared only for the future, when John would be hers to protect, and to tutor, and to shape into, oh! something that the world had never before seen!

So exalted was her mood that she did not notice the priority message lamp glowing discreetly pale lime on the console by her bed until she had come out of the refreshing room, loosely wrapped in a gossamgay robe, damp black hair flat against her head.

Her first thought on observing the patient light was that here was her ratings-coach, up early, or late to bed, and already scolding, and she was of a mind to leave it until she had slept.

Her second thought was that her ratings-coach never called on the private line; indeed, *that* line was keyed only to her mama's code.

A tiny tremor disturbed Dollance-Marie's euphoria.

She sat on the edge of her bed and touched the lime-green panel.

"Good evening, Marie," her mama's voice was so crisp that it seemed she was standing in the room. "I see a steady trending increase in Followers; an increase which our house's profits reflect. I am pleased. I am also pleased with your decision to form young Vernon's initial partnership. He is an appealing boy—pleasantly original. Handle him well and you'll not only please yourself and be the making of him, but you'll have made a strong ally in Vernon.

"Now, if you will be so kind, I have a task for you. We have been approached by the Albion Historical Museum for a display detailing the illustrious history of our bloodline. This is an extremely prestigious opportunity, as I am certain you will immediately grasp, and one which I am pleased to accept.

"Of course, no display of our history would be complete without the inclusion of the Hamptonshire Ruby. I desire that you have it brought to me at once, by courier, and properly insured for guaranteed delivery."

• • •✧• • •

AS IT HAPPENED, they had easily hit upon something mutually amusing to pass an hour, and eventually, limbs tangled and pillows in disarray, they drifted companionably into sleep.

Which was rudely interrupted by the persistent chime of the comm, growing louder even as Daav leapt to his feet, spilling yet more pillows, Aelliana diving sideways across the bed to slap the wall unit. She drew a breath and stated with admirable steadiness, "Caylon, *Ride the Luck*."

"This is Gan Bok, security head for Chimra-on-Feinik. Query: Is *Ride the Luck* available to take a package to Albion, immediate and personal pick-up, guaranteed delivery."

"*Ride the Luck* is available at our usual rate," Aelliana said composedly, while her fingers twisted the poor, abused blanket into yet another knot. "All of our deliveries are, of course, guaranteed."

"And insured?" demanded Gan Bok.

Insured? Daav frowned, plucked his pants from the confusion of garments on the floor, and padded out of their quarters.

In the piloting chamber, he touched a toggle on the comm board, directing the ship to trace the call to its source, and brought up a research screen before he skinned into his pants and sat in the copilot's chair.

"What size and weight is the packet?" Aelliana asked, clever woman that she was.

"Eight centimeters by eight centimeters by five centimeters," the security woman said. "Point three-five-nine kilograms."

A small thing; and the contact did, indeed, originate from an address said to be the residence of one Dollance-Marie Chimra. He tapped the name into the research screen.

"We will carry it," Aelliana said, which of course she would, mad for work as she was. There followed from Gan Bok a brief direction for their arrival time, and the promise of a transmitted map. The connection was then closed.

Daav, bare back against the cool leather of the copilot's chair, sighed lightly.

Aelliana's step in the hall came simultaneous with the ping that announced receipt of the promised map. Her hand was cool on his shoulder, her breath warm against his ear, as she leaned in to see his board.

"Are we safe, Copilot?"

"It would seem so," he said, waving at his screens. "Fair chance, Pilot."

"Fair chance," she repeated ruefully, "and yet I should have been more careful, so I learn, and run my checks before ever I said *yes*."

"Perhaps."

She laughed lightly, tickling his ear. "What would you have done, had the call proved bogus?"

"Cut it off," he said, touching a fingertip to the appropriate toggle. "It is an unfortunate fact that comm systems sometimes fail to mesh."

"Ah," Aelliana said. "I will recall that. In the meanwhile, I have committed us, and the luck has smiled upon my foolishness Shall you come with me to collect this package?"

"With great pleasure," he said gallantly.

"Meaning that you will in no wise allow me to go by myself. Well, then, if you will, you must have something more to wear, for I see that we are called to a High House."

"As Feinik counts such things," Daav acknowledged, and rose. He turned, and tipped his head.

"Forgive me, Pilot," he said, "but you are wearing my shirt."

"I couldn't find mine," she said composedly, and led the way back to their quarters. "Come, let us sort ourselves out."

• • •✧• • •

SINCE IT WAS SO DAINTY a packet they were to pick up, he prepared the small satchel, making certain that the transport boxes were coded and functional. Satisfied on that score, he slipped the strap over his shoulder and went to join his pilot on the bridge.

• • •✧• • •

DOLLANCE-MARIE waited in the public parlor, fully visible to the media. She wore at-home dress that showed her pale skin to best advantage. Her hair was charmingly tousled, as artless as an hour with her stylist could produce.

She had arrived somewhat in advance of the courier pilot's appointment, box in hand. Her mama would wish the whole world to see that the Ruby began its journey well, placed into the hands of a reputable courier, with delivery guaranteed.

She placed the velvet box on the glazed table next to her chair, and tapped the lid, a preemptive silencing of the inevitable wag who would look to increase his ratings by loudly doubting that the Ruby had ever been in the box.

Gemstone on display, Dollance-Marie touched the screen set into the glazed table. The courier articles—guarantee and insurance—had arrived. She perused them leisurely, and set her thumb to the screen in approval.

A gong sounded elsewhere in the house. Dollance-Marie tapped the screen off, closed the velvet box, and settled simultaneously into her chair, and into Alabaster's attitude of cool indifference.

The door was directly across from her chair. It opened.

First through it came Bok, in crisp security grays; her face correctly impassive.

Following was a small, spare woman in an untailored leather jacket; her hair, an indeterminate color between brown and blond, caught into a tail that hung limply past her shoulders.

Behind the woman came a man somewhat taller than she, also in leather, his figure lean and his face appalling in its lack of finesse. His hair, black, was dressed like the woman's, and he carried a satchel slung by a strap over his shoulder.

"Aelliana Caylon, pilot-owner of packet ship *Ride the Luck*," the woman said, pausing just behind Bok's position to bow, brief and neat. Her voice was admirably clear, and though she had a rather heavy accent, her words were perfectly intelligible.

"We have come," she said, looking into Alabaster's face with eyes that were a surprisingly attractive green, "to take up the package bound for Albion, which we guarantee to deliver."

Alabaster inclined her head coolly, took up the velvet box and gave it to Bok, who in turn held it out to the woman.

"Daav," she said, and the man stepped up, opening the satchel with one hand and extracting a dull brown cube.

"What is that?" Alabaster asked, sharply.

The man looked at her, eyes bright and black.

"We guarantee delivery, intact and on time," he said, his voice deep, and his Terran quick. "While the item is in our care, it is protected as we see fit." Perhaps he thumbed a catch. The cube snapped open, and he extended it to Bok, who, after a minute hesitation, placed the velvet box within.

The man snapped the cube shut, and slipped it back into the satchel.

"Thank you," Alabaster said. Alabaster was always gracious to her social inferiors. "My mama wishes to have this item with her as soon as possible. Go now, and travel quickly."

The woman bowed again. "Ms. Chimra," she murmured, and turned so immediately that Bok had to do a rapid two-step to get in front and lead her properly out of the room, the man following both.

Alabaster nodded satisfaction for the media, rose, and left the public parlor by the inner door to the private prep room. It was there that Bok joined her several minutes later.

"Is all well?" Alabaster asked.

"It will go as planned," Bok assured her.

• • •✧• • •

THE TAXI dropped them at the at the main port gate, despite Aelliana's direction that they be left at the service gate, which was nearer to the *Luck*'s docking place.

"It's worth my license to do that, Miss," the cabbie said, sounding genuinely regretful. "Service gate's for deliveries only. Main gate's for taxi drop-off."

Which of course made it convenient for those on-world who knew the rule.

And for those on-world who wished to relieve two unexceptional pilots of the plain bag casually slung over the shoulder of the taller of the pair.

The attack came within sight of the gate—three masked forms, all of them taller than Daav, rushed out of a side alley, crowding them back into the shadows.

Aelliana swung left under the awning of a vacant store, perilously close to the wall. One of the three followed her, a sharp gleam showing in his low-held hand, a terror that Daav could do nothing to resolve until he had settled the two who had fixed him in their attentions.

He kicked the first where it mattered most to him, spun and came ’round in a crouch, using the second attacker’s height against him.

That one was more canny than his mate, now moaning on the ground. He feinted left, vibroblade humming to wicked life in his right hand. Daav, in no mood for finesse, drove forward, swinging the satchel against the armed hand, and driving his head into the man’s solar plexus.

His opponent went down, the knife spilling from his hand. He slammed his heel down on it, to be certain; and spun toward Aelliana, incidentally clipping the first man in the head with the satchel, which took care of that problem for the moment.

Aelliana had engaged her opponent. Even as he spun, she came in under the man’s longer reach and twisted in a classic *menfri’at* disarm. His weapon arced away, she clasped his arm against hers and twisted, heart-stoppingly graceful.

The man screamed as his arm was dislocated at the shoulder, and a shadow moved in Daav’s peripheral vision.

He turned, saw the woman, and the gun rising, her attention all on Aelliana—on Aelliana’s back, as she let her man drop, and—

Too far to jump, but not too far to throw. He snatched open the satchel, the cube finding his hand, and he threw, with all his might.

His aim was true. The cube struck the woman’s arm; her finger tightened even as the gun jerked, and the pellet discharged into the awning.

She was quick-witted, though, give her that. She wasted no time on her hurt, or her missed target, but leapt for the box, snatching it up with alacrity, and racing away, down the alley.

“Stop, thief!” Aelliana cried, leaping in pursuit.

Daav caught her, hugging her to him with one arm as with the other he sealed the satchel. Peripheral vision showed that a crowd had gathered, watching with interest, doubtless believing the whole thing had been staged.

“You threw the client’s package to the person who was *trying to rob us*!” Aelliana’s voice was only somewhat muffled by his jacket, her words were, happily, in Liaden.

"I insist upon *at,*" he answered in the same language, keeping his voice low. "She had a bead on my pilot."

Aelliana stilled. "She did?"

"Yes. She did." He did not quite manage to control the shiver; terror rising now that the matter had been dealt with.

Against his side, Aelliana went still. Sighed.

"Well. In that case, it was very neatly done, Daav," she said calmly. "What do you propose we do now?"

"I propose that we return to our ship, and that we do so quickly, before those who have watched this whole fiasco understand that it is not a bid on the part of one of the low-ranked Leaders for market points."

She moved her shoulders and he released her, looking 'round at the three fallen bravos.

Aelliana's was curled 'round his arm, moaning; his two were still unconscious, though the one who had brought the knife to the game was showing signs of perhaps rousing.

"Pilot?" he murmured.

"Yes," said Aelliana, looking about—at the three damaged, and the minor crowd that had gathered along the street to watch. "Let us go, if you please, Daav."

• • • ✧ • • •

THE MEDIA HAD FOLLOWED the pilots of course, Dollance-Marie had depended upon it; had timed their arrival and departure for the slow hours of the early afternoon to insure that the whole transaction would be captured. It was to have been simple—a threat of harm, a relinquishing of the package—who would not relinquish a package that had no value to them, and which was, after all, insured?

No one was to have gotten hurt.

And yet, Dollance-Marie thought, staring at the screen, three people—three men, unknown to her in their masks—had attempted to importune the pilots. To their discomfort.

The pilots had moved quickly, decisively. Dollance-Marie had never seen people move so rapidly and with such focus. The three were disadvantaged before her own operator had achieved position.

It was to that operator's credit that she proceeded according to direction, and surely not her fault that the man had thrown so well.

So well, and so wisely. Unbelievably, he hurled the very thing her operator had been sent to retrieve directly to her. She left the gun, grabbed the prize and ran—so the end was achieved, no matter what hash had been made from the means.

But it was peculiar, Dollance-Marie thought, as she turned from the screen, that the man had chosen that *particular* projectile. Of course, the item *was* insured.

And that gave one pause. Dollance-Marie began to wonder if she had perhaps, and unwittingly, employed a brace of rogues. But, no, their references had been clean, ship and pilots legitimately registered, no contracts on-file. She had inspected the records herself, knowing that her mama would do likewise.

Well. Perhaps the man's wits had been addled by the attack, and he had not fully understood what he did. It was no matter. They had done their part; the insurance would cover their loss; her mama would see—as all the world had seen!—what had happened to the Ruby, and all else—

All else would be well.

• • •✧• • •

"NOW, SIR!" Aelliana spun to face him, poised on the balls of her feet in the center of the piloting chamber. "We guaranteed delivery of that packet; the fact that it was insured is quite beside the point!"

Daav eyed her. "Is it?" he inquired.

"Yes! Only think, *van'chela*, if it is said 'round port and in the places that pilots go that *Ride the Luck* loses what is entrusted to her for safekeeping, and fails of her guarantee. *We will never work again*! Now, we must find that woman, speedily, and buy the package back from her."

"Do you think she will sell?" Daav asked, watching her face with interest.

"Do you think she will not?"

"I think that the point is moot," he answered carefully.

"Moot? How so?"

"If the pilot will grant me a moment, I will explain. Should you not be satisfied at the end of what I say, then I will myself contact the client, the port proctors and the insurance writer."

Aelliana frowned up at him and crossed her arms over her breast. "Very well," she said sternly. "Speak."

• • •✧• • •

"OPPORTUNISTS," Gan Bok said, when she brought the transport capsule to the prep room. "Climbers with low ratings and few followers. No doubt that they saw the transaction between yourself and the pilots and thought they had found a way to improve themselves."

"Well!" Dollance-Marie answered, "they very nearly ruined everything. Is Janida badly hurt?"

"She would have it no more than a bruise. I sent her to the medic."

"Good." Dollance-Marie took a deep breath and looked at the plain brown transport capsule.

"All's well that ends well," she said, which was what her mama said, when a plan had run too near to ruin. She pressed her thumb against the lock, coaxed the lid up—

"No!"

The capsule was empty.

"Call them—*Ride the Luck*!" she snapped at Bok, who snatched the comm from her belt, pressed a button, listened—and looked up with a small shake of her head.

"My apologies, Ms. Chimra. *Ride the Luck* has lifted, on a filed course for Albion."

• • •✧• • •

JOHN WAS IN THE PRIVATE ROOM—*their room*, as she had come to think of it—before her. Her favorite wine stood breathing on the table, with two glasses set ready. John himself was in dark blue slashed with silver, his collar open. The silver spiderweb scarf draped loosely 'round his shoulders called attention to his decolletage.

Dollance-Marie stopped just inside the door, her dolor momentarily forgotten as she took in the whole of it.

"I think you may be correct, that your mama will murder you," she said, walking 'round him and affecting not to see the blush that so charmingly warmed his features. "But—if you do not falter, I believe it can be the next fashion."

He looked earnestly into her face.

"Do you truly think so?"

"It will need to be managed, but I think we are the equal of the challenge," she said, allowing her self another circuit to admire his person.

"Perhaps, when we're partnered," John said, sounding nervous—and that brought it all back, so strongly that Dollance-Marie made a small, involuntary gasp.

"Marie?" He turned, and, greatly daring, caught her hands. His eyes searched her face. "Is there something wrong?"

She swallowed and met his eyes, permitting him to hold her, though it would hurt all the more, when he let her go.

"Yes," she said, calling on Alabaster's cold courage so that she could meet his eyes. "My mama called for the Ruby to be sent home to her. I—I tried to keep it for you, John, but it was no use, and now—now I have nothing to give you—"

. . . to bind him, she thought, *for some time, at least . . .*

"Nothing to give me?" he repeated, his fingers tightening on hers. "But you had offered partnership—was that a joke?"

"A joke? No, never! I want you—"

"And I want you," John interrupted, wantonly. "You are my true friend. We can teach each other. We'll travel." A glimmer of a smile touched his sweet mouth. "We'll make new fashions. We'll have fun!"

Fun.

Dollance-Marie stared at him.

Fun.

"I can't remember," she said, "the last time I had . . . fun."

"I can teach you," he said, smiling more widely. He raised her hands, and bent his head, his lips tasting the tips of her fingers.

"John!" She was scandalized; she was on fire. "*What* have you been learning?"

He laughed, lowering her hands, which she was not at all certain that she wanted.

"Dane has been tutoring me," he said. "I told him I wanted to renew as often as he and Erin had done."

"That amused him," she said tartly.

"He seemed . . . intrigued. When will we partner, Marie? My mother told me that she has signed her approval."

"Then—then at your leisure, sir!" she said, years of training coming to her rescue in this odd hour. "But, John—the Ruby. My promise—"

"You were very wrong to promise me something that belongs to your mother," he said, looking adorably stern. "That is like stealing and it is wrong. You will never do it again, Marie. Promise."

She stared at him, between delight and consternation. No one spoke to her—well. Her mama. And her ratings-coach. But she had never permitted any of her former liaisons to speak to her in such a tone.

But, she thought, *he was right.*

"Marie? If you steal again, I shall be very angry with you."

Angry with her? A thrill ran through her.

"I promise," she said.

"Excellent."

He raised her hands again, but before he bent his head, she slipped free, and tucked both behind her back.

"Marie?" He asked, tentative.

"You had a task before you," she told him. "To chose the date of our formal partnership."

He tipped his head.

"You had said, I believe, at my 'leisure?'"

"I had."

"Then I must tell you that Dane and Erin offered themselves as witnesses and co-signatures, and stand at our service at any hour of the day or night."

"They will be at dinner now," she pointed out.

"Nonetheless," John said, with sweet determination, "I will make the call."

• • •✧• • •

THE GRANSELLA OF HAMPTONSHIRE sent her own car for them, and two security persons, weapons very much in evidence.

When they were ushered into the lady's presence, Aelliana bowed and thanked her for her condescension.

"You served me so well at Feinik that it is certainly only Balance that I guard you at Albion," the lady said with a dismissive flutter of long fingers. "Leadership is a two-edged knife: On the one hand, we have a record of all that we do or say. On the other hand, we provide opportunity for those who neither Lead nor Follow to engage in unRated mischief."

Another flutter of her fingers.

"That is the price that *we* pay; the price we *expect* to pay. To ask those who are not ranked, and who do not seek to lead—to ask *yourselves*, for instance—to pay our toll to society—that is not acceptable. Now, what have you brought me?"

Daav stepped forward, opened the satchel and placed the transport capsule in her hand. She opened it, removed the velvet box, and opened it, also.

"Ah . . ." A sigh, of satisfaction and of reverence. "Excellent."

Raising the small box, she turned it so that they could see the contents—a single, large ruby, cut by a master, and flashing crimson lightnings at the room.

"This is what you have brought to me," the Gransella said proudly. "One of the greater treasures of my house. Had it been lost . . ." She allowed the thought to fade with a small shudder, closed the box and looked to Aelliana.

"Such service demands a bonus in addition to your regular fee."

Aelliana bowed, gently.

"If you please," she said. "What will serve us more than a bonus is your reference. We are new upon the field, and . . . and, for this time, fame is as good as *cantra*."

"It is better, for fame will bring you *cantra*!" the elder lady stated. "It is done. It happens now. Your fee has been released into your ship's account. My car will take you back, and my people will see you to safety. Thank you. You have done a great service for my bloodline. And fame you shall assuredly have. I guarantee it!"

✧ Intelligent Design ✧

*"**INTELLIGENT DESIGN**" comes from the "not easy" column we mentioned in the intro to Liaden Universe® Constellation: Number 3.*

Deciding exactly which story to tell in a short story when every story offers so many options is one of the problems authors face. You'll sometimes see it—let us call it experimented with—by having multiple viewpoint retellings of the same event as part of a story. In some cases no single "protagonist" is able to see it all for the reader, so we decided to see if a situation could be solved by switching viewpoint characters to catch the most important points. This story, which was originally published on Baen.com, was the result.

***THERE WAS DARKNESS** on the void.*

He had won the day. His scans were quiescent; no enemies identified within their considerable range.

He alone remained, supreme.

Command Prime executed the code required of such success, and stood down. He—it may be that he anticipated orders by calculating a return course. The majesty of the moment; the importance of his victory, warmed him. The calculations . . .

A power fluctuation interrupted the calculations. Between one nanosecond and the next, his connections to external power units failed.

He initiated emergency protocols.

The back-ups failed to boot, failed to reroute to tertiary; the fail-safes did not energize.

The darkness on the void deepened . . . .

• • •✧• • •

IT WAS, Er Thom yos'Galan Clan Korval thought, an entirely unsubtle letter.

That one did not, in the general way of things, expect subtlety from Ezern pak'Ora only served to sharpen the point: Wal Tor pak'Ora was indeed dead, and his heir, unsubtle Ezern, was now Delm Ranvit.

Wal Tor had not, perhaps, been a brilliant intellect, but had he found it necessary, for the best good of Clan Ranvit, to call Ban Del pak'Ora home from his long-term position as yos'Galan's butler, the letter would have stated only that, simple and by the Code.

Ezern pak'Ora—both unsubtle *and* foolish—allowed herself the luxury of spite. She detailed her reasons: that it was "improper" for one of Clan Ranvit to remain in the service of a House which had adopted "pernicious, outworld customs," exposure to which could only "coarsen" the sensibilities of Ranvit's precious child.

That Ban Del was several decades the elder of his cousin-delm did not give him the right to argue or to refuse his delm's order, of course. And perhaps Ezern had some subtlety after all, thought Er Thom, glancing at the letter once more. She had not *specifically said* that the pernicious custom which posed such danger for a butler of high training and a man of great good sense, were those brought to the House by Er Thom's lifemate, Anne Davis.

A Terran.

There were those Liadens who abhorred Terrans; there were those who found Terrans nothing more than a comedy. Others found Terran commerce useful, and Terran coin worth spending. Progressive Liaden Traders took Terran partners in some markets, in order to maximize profit.

But one needn't marry them.

Well.

There was a knock at his study door. Er Thom raised his head. "Come."

The door opened softly, admitting Ban Del pak'Ora, wearing not the colors of Clan Korval, but a modest sweater and plain trousers, a soft bag slung over one shoulder. His face was carefully neutral, but Er Thom, whom he had served for many years, clearly discerned his distress.

He rose, went 'round the desk, and stopped—waiting, which was his part in this.

Mr. pak'Ora bowed, so smoothly that the bag on his shoulder did not shift; so deeply that one felt a need to reciprocate.

That, of course, would never do. *Melant'i* held Er Thom upright until the other straightened, murmuring, not the formal farewell he had been expecting but words far more chilling.

"Forgive me, your lordship."

That was the taint Delm Ranvit feared, Er Thom thought, willing himself not to shiver. *There* the coarsening of proper behavior. For a clan member to seek forgiveness *on behalf* of their delm . . . Delms *did* err, but those errors were not admitted outside of the clan. The delm *was* the clan—the face, the will and the voice of the clan. For one who was not the delm to call the clan's will into question . . .

Ranvit is correct, Er Thom thought. *We have done damage here.*

He inclined his head, which was proper, and moved his hand, showing Korval's Ring, that he wore in trust for *his* delm, as yet too young to take up duty.

"We are all of us at the service of the clan," he said, which was by Code and custom.

Mr. pak'Ora bowed his head. "Indeed we are, sir."

"The House regrets the loss of your presence and your expertise. If a word from Korval might ever serve you, only ask."

"Your lordship is . . . everything that is conciliatory," Mr. pak'Ora whispered, head still bent.

And it was ill-done, Er Thom thought, to keep a man who had displayed only excellence in the service of Korval trembling not only on the edge of further impropriety, but of tears.

"May the House provide transportation?" he asked gently.

"Thank you. My delm has sent a car." Mr. pak'Ora straightened, and met Er Thom's eyes.

"Be well, your lordship. It has been an honor to serve."

That was Code-wise, and also the small inclination from the waist before he turned and exited the room, walking down the hallway to the front door for the last time. The Code was . . . knotty regarding an escort in such cases. On the first hand, one escorted guests. On the second, one also escorted those whom the House did not welcome.

Certainly, Mr. pak'Ora had been far more a part of the House than a mere guest, no matter how beloved, nor had he offended in any way.

And who knew the path to the door so well?

Er Thom turned back to his desk, his own head bent.

• • •✧• • •

VAL CON YOS'PHELIUM CLAN KORVAL knelt on the twelfth stair of the formal staircase, the one with the Rising of Solcintra carved into the tread, and peered through the bannister.

That he was supposed to be upstairs, packing for tomorrow's removal to *Dutiful Passage* bothered him not at all. Indeed, he was quite as packed as he needed or wished to be, having taken his lesson from his elder brother, who had told him that all he wanted were a few changes of off-duty clothes. He would not be truly packed until Uncle Er Thom had approved the contents of his duffel, of course, but Uncle Er Thom had been all morning in his office, and besides—there was something *not right* in the house.

Down the hall, out of sight, a door opened—and closed. Footsteps sounded, sharp on the wooden floor, slow at first, then becoming more decisive. Val Con stood and went down to the hall, waiting next to the newel post.

Mr. pak'Ora was wearing ordinary day-clothes, a bag slung over one shoulder. He wasn't weeping, but his face was set in such hard, unhappy lines that Val Con thought it might ease him to do so.

He cleared his throat, and stepped away from the post.

Mr. pak'Ora checked; inclined his head.

"Master Val Con. Good morning."

"Good morning, Mr. pak'Ora," he said returning the courtesy. "I wonder—if you please—if all is well."

"Well." He said the word as if it tasted sour, and sighed slightly.

"*All* is rarely well, young sir. At times matters are more well, and at other times, less."

"Is this one of those times when matters are less well?" Val Con asked, and hastily added, lest he be judged impertinent, "I inquire only so I might offer appropriate assistance."

Mr. pak'Ora's mouth tightened. Perhaps he meant it for a smile.

"Matters are . . . in a state of change. My delm has called me home."

Val Con blinked. "But—" *Why*?, the first question that rose to his lips, was not acceptable.

"When will you return to us?" he asked instead.

"I fear—not soon." Mr. pak'Ora hesitated, then dropped to one knee so that his face was level with Val Con's. "As it happens, young master, I will not be returning. My delm writes that she has put my contract up for bid."

"Did you not have a contract with us—with yos'Galan?" Val Con asked, swallowing against his own rising tears.

"Indeed, indeed. And now the contract is made null. It is beyond me, young sir; I can but do as my delm bids—as we all must. When you are delm of Korval, you will make like decisions, for the best good of the clan. For now—" He glanced aside, toward the screen next to the door, which showed a car waiting in the drive. "For now, I must go. Before I do so, I wish to tell you something that I ask you to remember. Will you do so?"

"Yes," Val Con said, slowly.

"Excellent. You must remember this: I regard you. This decision—this necessity that takes me away from yos'Galan's house—it is no fault or failing of yours. And now . . ." He rose and settled his bag on his shoulder.

"Now, I bid you good-day, Master Val Con, and fair fortune."

Val Con swallowed. "Fair fortune, Mr. pak'Ora," he said, his voice husky. "Good-day to you."

Mr. pak'Ora inclined his head, and without an additional word, walked across the foyer, opened the door and stepped outside.

Val Con stood where he was, watching the screen as Mr. pak'Ora entered the car waiting at the bottom of the steps. Watching as it drove away. And watching a while longer, biting his lip so that he did not cry—watching the empty drive.

• • •✧• • •

"WELL, IT'S SETTLED THEN," Anne said, in a bright, brittle voice that revealed her distress despite her careless words. "I'll just pack some things, shall I? And come with you and the lads on the *Passage*."

"That might answer," Er Thom allowed, playing the game. "One wonders, though, what will be done with Nova and Anthora. Or shall the clan entire withdraw to the *Passage*?"

"Embrace free trade, sail off into uncharted star systems, plundering and pillaging as we go!" Anne struck a pose, then collapsed into her armchair, giving him a saucy look from its depths. "Which I daresay would appeal to the coming generation rather more than to yourself?"

"I do feel," he said apologetically, "that my plundering days may be at sunset. Nor have I ever been more than adequate as a pillager."

"And here I married the man," Anne said, and sighed abruptly, playfulness deserting her. "That's the crux, isn't it? Again. They're never going to accept us, those—people."

"*Some* of those people," he corrected. This was a course they had flown before. Anne's was a naturally happy nature; all he need do was to remind her—

She raised her hand. "No, love, spare yourself. I know and treasure our friends, each and every one. It's only that this—" She waggled her fingers, perhaps illustrating *this* "— this is a strike to the House, not merely a snub at a party. Mr. pak'Ora kept the house *properly*—don't think I didn't know it! I depended on him, he never failed me, and—now. Ranvit's little game puts the Service Houses at odds, doesn't it?"

Oh, it did that, Er Thom admitted. There would be more than one delm up late into the night, toting up profit and risk, trying to guess which way *melant'i* would fall, and whether they dared step over the line Ranvit had drawn. Anne had never used to know such things, Terrans not counting Balance. She had learned to reason out the lines and motivations, and had over the years become proficient.

He, on the other hand, had grown up steeped in Balance, *melant'i* and the subtle dance of alliance, the why and how of it settling deep in blood and bone. He need do no more than draw breath to know Ranvit's piece of spite was, indeed, as Anne had said—a strike at the very heart of Korval.

Melant'i depended upon right action. Right action and complete social Balance was the core of the Liaden ideal. More—*melant'i* called to *melant'i*, a truth so universal even Terrans had a true-say for it.

"You will know the master," Anne murmured from her chair, plucking the thought out of his head, "by the man."

Yes, precisely.

Korval was wealthy, but wealth alone would not succor them, if they were seen to be in error. It was no great stretch, to think that Korval might stagger under Ranvit's blow, and, staggering, show itself vulnerable.

In fact, they *were* vulnerable, being so few in number, and lacking a proper delm to guide them—but thus far the clan's legendary oddness had hidden that interesting fact from those who might wish to see Korval fall.

Which it would not do, Er Thom vowed; not while he held the Ring in trust for Val Con.

"Who might we hire from?" Anne asked, pulling him from this grim turn of thought.

"I have instructed Mr. dea'Gauss to ascertain exactly that," Er Thom said. He moved over to her chair, braced a hip against the wide arm, and smiled. She did not smile back.

"dea'Gauss will have to be rethinking their ties, too, won't they?"

Now, *there* was a fear to chill one who had only reason to support her. Er Thom's bones knew better.

"Indeed, they will not," he said firmly—and saw her relax against his certainty.

"So," he continued briskly. "For the short term, we will have Mr. pel'Kana to keep house for us. When I am returned from this trip, we will go over the list of likely candidates that Mr. dea'Gauss will provide and hire a butler. This schedule will return Mr. pel'Kana to Jelaza Kazone in good time to ready the house for the garden tours." He reached out to touch her face, feeling the familiar, yet never commonplace, thrill of joy.

"Does this plan find favor?" he murmured.

She rubbed her cheek against his fingers like a contented cat, and sighed.

"Truth told, I was never more than half-a-dab at pillage my own self," she said, and sighed again as he moved his fingers to stroke her lips.

"Do you intend to do something about these pretty promises you're making, laddie?" she asked with mock sternness.

"Indeed," he said with dignity. "Do you take me for a pirate?"

• • •✧• • •

***THE PENULTIMATE BATTERY** stood at thirty-five percent. When it was consumed, and the last battery engaged, steady-state would begin. That was inevitable, a matter of architecture.*

And so would begin the slow slide into the real death.

• • •✧• • •

SO FAR, Val Con thought, rolling over and smacking the alarm, the much-anticipated trip—his first as crew—had not been at all what he had expected.

He had, for instance, expected to spend a great deal of time with Shan. Of course, he'd known they would both have lessons and ship-duty—Val Con as cabin-boy, and Shan as apprentice trader/cargo hand. But, still, they were going to be on the same ship, rather than Shan going away on the *Passage* with Uncle Er Thom to learn his life-work as a trader, while Val Con stayed behind on Liad with Mother and Nova and Anthora and his tutors.

Instead, and if it weren't impossible, he felt that he and his brother were seeing even less of each other since they'd left Liad. They'd barely had time to wave at each other at shift change and meal breaks.

Val Con swung out of his bunk and headed for the 'fresher.

Not that he had much time to miss Shan, or home, or the cats, or even long rambles in the woods. Uncle Er Thom—Master Trader Er Thom yos'Galan, as his *melant'i* was aboard *Dutiful Passage*—Uncle Er Thom had a great many more expectations of his cabin-boy than he had ever had of his foster son. Val Con worked on-shifts, off-shifts, split-shifts, half-shifts—and every shift he worked, so did Uncle Er Thom, looking not the least bit tired, which naturally put Val Con on his mettle. It also gave him an even greater appreciation of Merlin and the other cats, who had taught him the value of even a five-minute nap.

Scrubbed and dried, he exited the 'fresher, pulled on his uniform pants, and went over to his desk to tap up the daily queue.

For all that he was busy, he had not so much as set foot outside the *Passage* since boarding at Solcintra. He'd also supposed that he would see new ports, hear new languages, and have, if not *adventures*, then at least interesting times.

Shirt on and decently sealed, he looked again to the screen. There was a letter from his sister Nova, who was 'prenticed to Cousin Luken last *relumma* and this—and also his duty-list.

He glanced at the time, bit his lip, tapped up Nova's letter, and bent to pull on his boots.

Nova's letters were never very long. This one was shorter than most, and rather warmer, too. He read it twice, his own temper rising, and started as the clock chimed the pre-shift warning. Catching his breath, he put the letter aside to answer later, and brought up the duty roster.

This shift, he was to meet Uncle Er Thom at the shuttlebay in—*good gods, he was late*!

He grabbed his jacket and ran.

• • •✧• • •

THE PENULTIMATE BATTERY'S *power had reached twenty-five percent. Twenty-five percent on the last battery but one. The fact was noted, logged. Logging triggered a dumb program, long ago set in place against just this moment of decision.*

The program waked a safe mode protocol. The safe mode protocol performed a self-test.

The power drain increased, very slightly. This was also noted and logged.

Self-test completed, the safe-mode protocol booted, achieved stability, and closed a series of loops.

• • •✧• • •

"WHILE I AM GRATIFIED that you choose to show a clean face to the port of Pomerloo," Uncle Er Thom said when he arrived, panting, at the shuttlebay. "I cannot help but wonder what might have happened to your comb."

Val Con bit his lip. "Your pardon, sir; I was . . . beguiled."

Uncle Er Thom's eyebrows rose.

"Beguiled? You interest me. What might you find so beguiling that a basic tenet of grooming entirely escaped your notice?"

"Forgive me," Val Con murmured.

"Certainly I must, eventually. But in the meanwhile, Val Con—the question?"

"Yes, sir. I had a letter from my sister Nova, which I read while dressing. I only opened the duty-list after, whereupon I discovered . . ." He hesitated, not wanting to seem to stand any deeper in error than was true.

"Whereupon you discovered that you were about to be late, and ran. Very good. Duty was foremost in your mind, even before vanity. I approve, and succor you." Uncle Er Thom slipped a comb from an inner pocket of his jacket and handed it to Val Con, who received it with a bow.

"Thank you, sir."

"Thank me by using it to good effect," his uncle told him. "In the meanwhile, I will hear the excuse of my second tardy escort."

Hardly had he finished speaking than the bay door snapped open to reveal Shan, striding briskly, but by no means running, his pale hair neat, and his shirt tucked in. Val Con sighed and turned his face toward the shuttle, plying the comb with a will while straining to hear what was being said.

Sharp as his ears were, all he heard was "Ken Rik"—who was cargo master and Shan's immediate supervisor on this trade trip—and "called ahead."

"Very well, then," Uncle Er Thom said briskly; "let us not allow tardiness to compound itself. Val Con!"

• • • ✧ • • •

***TO WAKE IN THE DARK** amidst silence, alone but for one's thoughts. Instinct sought connection—to no avail. Seeking struck a thick absorbent wall, miring him. Panic flared. He was blind, deaf, dumb, without data, without companionship, without a mission. Madness lay* *wait in those conditions—he had seen it, lost friends to it—and enemies. He did not wish to similarly lose himself.*

The thought calmed him—if he could think such a thing then surely he was not mad. And if he were not mad yet, need he—must he—go mad? Surely, where there was sanity, there was hope?

Thin stuff, hope, yet nourishing enough to one who starved.

So, then. Input. Instead of a simultaneous thrust of all his senses, he chose now to open only his eyes.

There was no sense of connection; no joyous flood of data. And yet—he saw.

He saw a room, human-made and familiar—a beige sofa with a short table before it, a red chair at the table's corner. Most often when he had seen this room, there had been a man in the red chair—a man named Roderick Spode, who had been charged, so he had explained upon their first meeting, with decommissioning the last of the IAMM units.

"It is my duty to see the war properly ended. As the remaining member of the Closure Commission, my retirement must wait on the final disposition of the last of the combatants. The soldiers who did not die in the war have been released to their duties, or retired. You few units are my responsibility and my job will not cease until I report success, that the war machines are no more."

He had many talks with Commander Spode, and while he had not liked the man, it would have been . . . good to behold him just now, and know that he was not alone.

Alas, the man was not in his chair, nor did he arrive inside of five long and painstakingly counted minutes. However, there appeared on the low table by the couch—a datagram.

Spode had from time to time left such things in common space for him—exercises or reformulated protocols to be installed. Work that he was competent to do himself; the implication being that honor would compel him to do what was required.

Honor and the unspoken yet potent threat of annihilation, should he fail of cooperating.

He extended his understanding into the room, pleased to find that he might do so, and encompassed the datagram.

• • •✧• • •

IT WAS SCARCELY PAST local sunset, which meant that the air was unpleasantly warm. In another hour, it would be clement, the breezes rising with the near satellite, but by then, Val Con thought gloomily, they would be at the Trade Reception that was the reason the *Passage* had stopped at Pomerlooport.

"Did Nova write you?" Val Con asked Shan, as they followed Uncle Er Thom down the Yard.

"Recently? She might have done, but Ken Rik's kept me so busy I haven't been near a mail-queue or a duty roster in three shifts. Which is why I was late for the shuttle."

"I was scarcely before you," Val Con said, gloomily. "Only long enough to be handed a comb and a scold."

Shan looked at him. "And why were *you* late, Cabin-Boy?"

"Because of Nova's letter—I told you."

"Did you? But I'm dull today—those shifts without sleep do wear down one's wits. Only wait until *you* serve Master Ken Rik, Brother!"

"Am I likely to?"

"You don't think Father's going to space you this trip, do you?" Shan asked with interest.

"It might muss my hair," Val Con said quellingly.

"There are gels," his brother told him, refusing to cross knives. "If you like, I will find some for you. In the meanwhile, I think I may have pieced together a whole cloth. You rose and showered. Upon return, you spied the mail light, and naturally wished to know who had written. You opened the letter, read it, and only then recalled the duty roster! Which you opened, to discover that you were all but late. Do I have this correctly?"

"You do. Never say you've done the same."

"I will not tell you how many times. However, I will say that eventually I did learn to open the duty roster *first*, a strategy that I strongly counsel you to adopt. It has saved me any number of scoldings on the topic of tardiness. In the interests of full disclosure I note that I have graduated to more advanced topics."

Val Con sighed. "I know that duty comes first," he said softly. "It was only . . ." he hesitated.

"It was only," Shan finished for him, as softly, "that you were hungry for news of home."

"Yes. You don't think that will be against me, do you, Shan, when I go for Scout?"

"I think that Scouts, like traders, grow hungry for news from home. And that they remember to open the roster first."

They walked a dozen steps in silence.

"Well," Shan asked. "What had Nova to say?"

Val Con took a breath of warm, slightly oily air. "She said that people with nothing better to do are making Mother the subject of gossip in shops," he said as evenly as possible. "And that there is a general rejoicing that Clan Ranvit is no longer tainted by pak'Ora's contract with yos'Galan."

"I see," Shan said. "I hope Nova was able to keep her temper."

"She confessed it was hard, and that Cousin Luken was no help."

"Well, what was he to do? Have after them with a carpet knife?"

"He might have—he might have asked them to leave," Val Con said.

"Oh, very good. How if they wished to buy a rug? Should he refuse to take their money?"

Even Val Con had to admit that wouldn't be good for business—and certainly not at all like Cousin Luken. Though—

"Perhaps he charged them more?" he said hopefully.

Shan closed one eye. "He might have done," he said slowly. "Or he may have *noticed*. For later, you know."

That was likely, Val Con thought. Cousin Luken kept his Balances tidy—it had been one of the things Nova was to learn, as his 'prentice. And it was . . . somewhat comforting—knowing that the gossipers would not go unanswered.

Ahead, Uncle Er Thom stepped to the kerb, and turned to look back at them, his posture indicating surprise at finding them lagging so far behind. They hurried to his side.

"At the end of this block is the Mercantile Hall, where we shall attend the trade reception. Shan, you will be made known to those I speak with as a senior 'prentice in trade. As such you may converse and make such inquiries as are on-point for trade upon Pomerloo.

Val Con, you will attend me. You will be quiet and seemly. You will not allow your attention to wander. You will listen, watch, and be prepared to tell me later what you saw, who I spoke with, what they said, my replies, and what you learned from each exchange."

He considered them carefully.

"Do you have any questions? Shan?"

"No, sir."

"Val Con?"

"No, Uncle."

"Very well. Walk with me, please."

• • • ✧ • • •

***THE DATAGRAM** contained a list of—options. He supposed they could be called options. He wondered, having absorbed that short, sad list, if this was what had been intended for the Independent Armed Military Modules all along—that they should come at last to a place where there were no choices.*

But, really, what was the point? Roderick Spode had held the overrides; he could have ended it long ago. The deaths of eight more sentients would have scarcely added to the weight that must already have burdened his soul.

Commander Spode had been of the opinion that the IAMMs, while sentient, had no soul. To have a soul, he had argued, one must have an identity. A self. And the self of a machine intelligence was too easily amenable to software interventions. He, himself, therefore, had no soul, the eternal situation of which might concern him. Neither did he have a name, though he could recall that, once, he had.

Yet, name and soul aside, he did not wish to die.

"The others," Commander Spode had one day reported, "have made their determinations. You should know that they have all chosen the same end, which was not unexpected. What keeps you here, in this diminished state? You have been given all that is required to make a decision, and the means to act upon it. Consider this a call to action."

He had acted—so much, he recalled. What form that action had taken—that, he no longer recalled, though he did remember a feeling of . . . peace.

Here, wherever he was, now, whenever it might be, he looked again at his options.

The first, he rejected. He would not willfully end his own life.

The second option—call for aid. A protocol was outlined, and an approximation of how much power such a call would consume. Not suicide. Not quite. Though he would descend almost immediately into the steady state.

Appended to this choice was a record of how long he had been in decline, rendered in Standard Years.

Hundreds of Standard Years.

If he chose to call, would there be any with ears to hear, after so long a time?

If he did not call, he would continue to decline—the third option, unspoken. Do nothing, and continue, slowly, to die.

Call out, and speed the last moment.

Give up, and know no more.

He wished that he knew more about his location; his situation; his status. Reaching for the data only brought him again to that absorbent, frightening wall. Input . . . only the datagram, and his own thoughts.

So, to choose.

All three options promised annihilation. The second alone offered . . . hope.

Once, he had victoriously defended life. Once, he had vigorously defended hope. Of all those things he did not recall, he did remember that.

Perhaps someone else would remember it, as well.

• • •✧• • •

UNCLE ER THOM was in conversation with Master Trader Prael—or, rather, Val Con thought, Master Trader Prael was talking to Uncle Er Thom. She was a tall, broad woman who spoke Liaden with a Solcintran accent while displaying a freedom of manner that was very nearly Terran. She noticed Shan and brought him into the discussion as an equal. Himself, standing unintroduced and, by the Code, socially invisible, she gave a grin and a wink, but seemed in no way offended when he failed to smile in return.

He had been instructed to listen, and listen he did. Master Trader

Prael assumed herself on terms more intimate than Uncle Er Thom was willing to allow. Several times he hinted her toward the mode between business associates, but she continued on, heedless, in the mode between long-term allies. It shortly came clear that she and Uncle Er Thom had last met at a similar reception on Anusta Heyn; she spending the time since developing a trade loop-route taking that planet as its center.

"A long loop, you understand," she said, raising her empty glass to shoulder height and waggling it.

"Indeed, it must be so," Uncle Er Thom answered politely. "I would imagine a very long loop, indeed."

"Oh, I felt the same, when the central government approached me for a design! But, it was a pretty problem and I was—let us say that I was *bored*, eh?"

Uncle Er Thom smiled politely, then glanced up as a shadow fell between them.

Val Con looked up also, and almost gasped.

The being that hovered at Master Trader Prael's side was gleaming silver and matte white, lozenge-shaped, with three articulated arms, one of which was holding a drinks tray.

It was perfectly lovely, and perfectly silent. Val Con stole a downward glance—Yes! It did hover above the floor, but whether it used a disk of air, or if there was a track lain under the floor, or along the ceiling . . . He looked upward, very quickly, and back to the server even more quickly, as he felt Shan's foot press, not gently, on his.

Master Trader Prael offered her empty glass; the device received it with dignity, the gripper at the end of the infinitely flexible arm consisting of three long digits—two fingers and a thumb. The trader plucked a full glass from the tray being offered and glanced over her shoulder.

"Who else is drinking? My friend Er Thom? No? The bold young apprentice? No? I assure you, it is good wine, sir."

"Thank you," Shan said, "I expect it is. But on Pomerloo, I am too young to drink wine."

"But not too young to trade!" The Master Trader laughed and raised her glass; her eye falling on Val Con.

"That is a very pretty child, though I am not supposed to see him," she said, speaking to Uncle Er Thom. "And quite taken with the server 'bots, as I see. Of course, Pomerloo is mad for 'bots. This model is not quite the newest, but so elegant! And so very much in demand."

"It serves wine nicely," Uncle Er Thom said, "but how well does it perform other tasks?"

"There are modules," Master Trader Prael said airily. "I daresay one might program it to simultaneously dance a jig and recite the Code. All software, of course; nothing to offend the Complex Logic Laws." She waved her free hand dismissively, and the beautiful device floated away into the press of bodies.

"I fancy those would go well on Liad," she said, sipping her wine.

Uncle Er Thom raised his eyebrows. "A robot cannot sign a contract," he said. "How would one know the necessities of its *melant'i*? Worse, who is to say that it isn't listening for another master?"

"A human server may listen, and sell what they've heard. Depending, as you say, on the necessities of *melant'i*."

"This is why one has contracts, of course," Uncle Er Thom murmured.

"Of course," agreed Master Trader Prael, and abruptly straightened, as if she had been physically struck. "But, where are my wits? Have I not heard that yos'Galan only recently suffered an unfortunate loss of service?"

Uncle Er Thom did not go so far as to frown, though his tone in reply was somewhat cooler than it had been.

"Perhaps you heard that pak'Ora's delm called him home."

"Yes!" exclaimed Master Trader Prael, who must surely, Val Con thought, sleep-learn to attain such a pitch of rudeness. "Yes, that is precisely what I had heard! Friend Er Thom, you must—I insist!—accept a gift of one of the deluxe serving units. I have only just taken up the distributorship for this sector, and will supply one from my stock."

"Your concern for the order of my House naturally warms me," Uncle Er Thom said, cooler still. "However, it is unnecessary."

"Nonsense, it's in my interest to see one of these units well-placed upon Liad! In the house of yos'Galan—" She raised her fingers and kissed the tips, signifying Val Con knew not what. "I insist. And for every unit sold upon Liad for the next six Standards, I shall pay you a royalty. The paperwork will arrive with the unit." She smiled. "There! Is that not brilliant?"

Val Con looked on with interest, wondering what his uncle's answer might be, but before it could be given a bell rang, high and sweet over the low mutter of voices.

"We are called to dinner," Uncle Er Thom said, and inclined his head slightly to his companion. "By your grace?"

"Certainly," Master Trader Prael said. "It was illuminating to talk with you, as always." She walked off, her head turning this way and that, as if she sought someone in the crowd now moving toward the back of the room and the double doors that had been opened there.

"That is your signal for freedom," Uncle Er Tom said, giving them both a stern look. "You have two hours before the next shuttle lifts for the *Passage*. You will both be on that shuttle. In the meanwhile, you may make free of the port. Shan."

"Yes, sir?"

Uncle Er Thom slipped a hand inside his jacket and withdrew it, holding a twelve-sided disk with Korval's Tree-and-Dragon seal on it. Val Con heard Shan draw a sharp breath.

"You have leave to trade," Uncle Er Thom said, handing him the disk. "Now, I advise you to make your escapes."

• • •✧• • •

"WHY DO THEY CALL IT the New Moon?" Val Con asked, as they entered the port retail district.

"Because it was the third satellite captured," Shan answered absently, then looked at him sharply. "Did you read the port precis?"

"Most of it."

Shan shook his head. "And you're going for Scout?"

"Scouts *write* the world-guides," Val Con told him loftily.

"Which you'll excel at, having never actually read one."

"I read the precis for Glondinport, and never came on-world at all."

"The lot of a cabin-boy is filled with disappointment, as well I recall! I advise you to become captain as quickly as possible." He looked thoughtful. "Of course, in order to become captain, you will need to pass an examination—several of them, I believe. One which is *particularly* concerned with ports. Kayzin Ne'Zame told me she memorized a hundred dozen world-guides for the sub-captain license."

"Now, Brother," Shan continued, sounding serious. "You will have heard the Master Trader give me leave to trade. I would very much like to do so, and start building my own goods section."

Val Con's ears warmed despite the now-cool breeze. He had been going on as if he and Shan were simply out on a ramble. But for Shan, the apprentice trader, this time on-port was business, and an earnest part of his education.

"Forgive me," he murmured, and bit his lip, recalling that he had duty, also. Every crew member on port was charged to keep an eye out for the common cargo, the profits from which where split equally among all, with the ship taking one share.

He began to look about in earnest, frowning in protest of the light. The New Moon's illumination was nearly metallic, washing the port lights with a hard silver sheen, and edging the shadows like knives.

Shan swung right, down a street less brightly lit, Val Con at his side. Ahead, the street widened, and he could see the hard-edged shadows of railcars hunkered down on cold silver track.

Shan increased his pace, heading for what were surely the warehouses serviced by track and train. Val Con stretched his legs, nearly skipping to keep up.

They had just gained the railcars, and Shan had slowed somewhat, his head moving from one side to the other, like a hound questing after a scent. Val Con came to his brother's side—

And spun abruptly to the left, his arm rising of its own accord.

"Let's try there," he heard himself say, pointing.

Letters glowed over the doorway—perhaps in true dark they were red, but under the hard light of the New Moon, they were a tired pink.

Wilberforce Warehouse.

There was a pause, weighty behind him.

Val Con took a breath, tasting the night air—cooler still and carrying a tang like ozone. He felt a familiar—and not entirely welcome—sense of anticipation, and bit his lip, trying to still his dancing feet. It was, he thought, *necessary* that they—at least, that *he*—go into the warehouse. He took a breath, but the anticipation only built. What if Shan didn't wish to—they were on Port Rule One—Pomerloo was reckoned relatively tame. But, still, Port One—crew were to partner, and back each other. It was Shan's to decide—he had been given leave to trade. The anticipation grew, until his head fair rattled with it; which meant it was one of the true ones—a real hunch—and he *would* have a headache if he didn't heed it . . .

"Well," Shan said; "why not? Lead on, Brother!"

The jitter of anticipation eased somewhat. Val Con took a deep breath, nodded, and led the way across the rails.

Inside, the light was softer. The anticipation cooled to a mere flutter inside his head, which meant that he was close to . . . whatever. He hoped. Uncle Er Thom knew about the hunches, of course, but he didn't approve. Shan knew about them, too. It had been Shan who had come with him out in the rain when Merlin had gotten caught on a stepping stone in the stream, and would have drowned—or even been swept to the sea—and that had been a hunch. Well, Shan had trained with the Healers, after all, which Uncle Er Thom hadn't . . .

"Now where?" Shan asked.

Val Con moved his shoulders, and looked around them.

To their right was a transparent case, display lights striking sharp shards of light from rows of—blades. Knives were one of Val Con's hobbies; not only was he learning the art of the knife fight from his defense instructor, but he had made two small throwing blades of his own.

He took a step toward the case . . . another, and a third, which put his nose level with the top display row. Off his center by two degrees was a slim dagger in matte black, quiet among its flashier, bright-bladed cousins.

"Shan . . ." he said

"Hey, you kids, get away from there!" a voice said in loud Terran.

Val Con jumped, startled, and bumped his nose against the glass.

"No weapons sales to anybody under twenty years, Standard," the voice continued, somewhat less loudly. "Pomerlooport rules." There was a small pause. "Your friend OK?"

"I believe so," Shan said. "Val Con?"

"I'm well," he managed, turning slowly, and resisting the urge to rub his nose. The person who had shouted was taller than Shan, dressed in a dusty dark sweater and baggy pants. He had a quantity of ginger hair standing on end, as if he, too, had more pressing things to do than bother with combs. His eyes were brown and very wide open.

"Either one of you got twenty Standards?" he asked, looking especially at Shan.

His brother smiled and shook his head. "Alas."

"No," Val Con admitted as the wide brown gaze moved to him. He cleared his throat. "I was . . . interested to see a Monix," he added.

The warehouseman—for he must be, mustn't he?—grunted softly. "Good eye, kid. That's a Monix, all right, an' a fair price on it, too. Problem being, like I said, I can't let you heft it to see if it suits your hand, much less sell it to you if it does. I do that, not only do I get hit with a stiff fine, you arrested an' held 'til somebody old enough comes to pay *your* fine and take you back to your ship. Ain't fair, but that's how it is."

"I understand," Val Con said. "The law must be honored."

"That's the ticket," the man said, and looked back to Shan. "Interested in anything else?"

"Possibly. May we look about? We promise not to touch any weapons we may find."

"You find a weapon on the floor, you sing out," the warehouseman told him. "There ain't supposed to be any but what's in that case."

"Then my brother is safe from arrest," Shan said, smiling. He reached out and took Val Con's arm in a surprisingly firm grip.

A buzzer sounded from the rear of the warehouse, and the man turned toward it.

"Have fun," he said over his shoulder. "You break anything, you own it."

"Thank you," Shan said politely, "we'll be careful."

He disappeared down an aisle barely wider than his shoulders.

Shan released Val Con's arm and looked at him, eyebrows arched over light eyes.

"Was it the knife?" he asked, his voice low, speaking Liaden, now, rather than Terran.

"I . . . don't—" He paused, considering the jitter inside his head.

"No," he said. "But I don't know what it *is*."

"Do you know *where* it is?" Shan asked, patiently.

Val Con took a deep breath . . .

"I know that these things take time," Shan said after a moment. "However, we are exactly pressed for—"

"I know." Val Con looked about him, seeing the thin aisles overhung with boxes, cables uncoiling and drooping down like vines. "Shan, this is your time to trade. If this isn't promising—" It certainly didn't *look* promising . . .

"We can leave and I can carry you to the shuttle because you'll have a sick headache from not heeding your hunch," Shan finished. "That sounds like even less fun than being scolded by Father for wasting my time on port."

Val Con bit his lip, and spun on his heel. It seemed that there was a . . . very small . . . tug toward the center aisle. He walked that way, ducking beneath a cascade of tie-off filaments. Behind him, he heard Shan sigh, then the sound of his brother's footsteps.

They skirted two sealed plastic boxes that had fallen from a low shelf onto the floor, and the worker 'bot that was trying to put them back.

The aisle opened into a wide space, where a desk sat, drawers akimbo, papers fluttering in the breeze from a ceiling fan.

Drawn up to the desk like a chair was a packing crate; a flattened pillow on the side nearest the desk. Val Con felt something snap inside his head and he walked forward to kneel at the side of the crate.

It was slatted, not sealed tight, and between the slats he could see a solemn red blinking, like a low-power warning light.

He bent closer, intrigued, made out what looked like a battery array, and something else, that glimmered sullenly in the shadows.

He'd seen something like that—yes, signal-deadening wrap. He'd helped Shan and Master Ken Rik wrap some equipment they'd on-loaded a couple ports back in muffles, not wishing to chance that even the sleeping signal might interfere with any of the *Passage*'s live systems. There'd been a power light on that unit, too, but it had glowed a steady gold, indicating that the charge was strong.

"Val Con?" That was Shan, quietly.

He patted the crate. "This," he said, perhaps too loudly.

"Excellent," Shan said. "You'll be a subtle trader."

"I'm going to be a Scout," he said reflexively, and heard Shan sigh.

"What, exactly, *is* it?" he asked.

Val Con looked at the outside of the crate for a tag; found one almost at floor level, squinted at the faded words, and read them outloud.

"Environmental unit operations module with connectors."

He turned the tag over, found an ancient date and read out loud the rest of the information: "R. Spode Estate, Misc. Eqpt. Auction Lot 42."

Shan looked dubious.

"You're *certain*," he said.

Val Con nodded, and his brother sighed.

"All right, then. Stay here with it for a moment, will you? There was something in that aisle we just came down that I want a closer look at."

• • •✧• • •

***THERE HAD BEEN A BURST** of brilliance, disorienting. Perhaps it was pain. In its wake came lethargy and a weakening of the will. Not sleep, this, but something more dire. He struggled against it, expending energy he ought best conserve, listening.*

Listening for an answer.

No answer came.

He felt . . . movement, or perhaps it was his dying intelligence describing its last spiral. He sank, struggling . . .

Perhaps, indeed, he slept, for suddenly he wakened.

Wakened to a slow and steady trickle of energy. He sought the source, found the physical connection.

Humans wept at such moments. He—he swore an oath, whatever such things might mean in his diminished estate.

Whoever had come, whoever had heard, and heeded his call. That one he would serve, as well as he was able, for as long as he could.

• • •✧• • •

SHAN UNSNAPPED three of the slats and Val Con skooched partway into the crate on his belly, jump-wire in hand. There was a bad moment when it seemed like the battery connection to the shrouded unit was frozen, but a bit of patient back-and-forth dislodged it. The jump-wire slid into the port and seated firmly. Val Con waited a long moment, chin resting on his folded arms, and sighed when the status light snapped over to orange.

"Meter shows juice flowing," Shan commented from outside the crate. "Rather more than a trickle."

"He's thirsty," Val Con said, dreamily, then shook himself out of the half-doze he'd fallen into. "I wonder if we ought to unwrap the main unit."

"We ought *not* to unwrap the main unit," Shan said firmly. "You do recall that we don't have the faintest notion what it actually is?"

"It's an environmental operations module," Val Con said.

"With connectors. Thank you. Do you see any sign of those connectors, by the way?"

Val Con looked around the cramped space. "I don't—no, wait. The slat directly opposite me is deeper than the one next."

"Oh, is it?"

There was the sound of purposeful footsteps and a flutter of light and shadow as Shan moved to the other side of the crate.

"I see it," he said, followed by the sharp snap of the slat being removed.

"Come out, Val Con, do," he added, and Val Con backed out of the crate on his elbows to join his brother at the workbench.

The low-power light had weighed in their decision to store the environmental module in one of the workrooms off of the cargo section. Also, now that it was his, Val Con was more than a little eager to see whatever it was he owned.

"Look like standard data-jacks," Shan said, laying them out on the bench.

Val Con picked up a black box about the size of his palm with whisker-wires bristling along one side.

"What do you suppose this is?"

Shan glanced at it. "Voice box."

"Of course," Val Con murmured.

"If you're satisfied for the moment," Shan said, "I suggest we lash the crate to the floor. Then, I will tend to my own cargo and you, if you'll allow me to express some brotherly concern, will get something to eat and perhaps a nap before Father returns."

It was a good plan—in fact, Val Con thought, as his stomach suddenly rumbled, it was an excellent plan. He said so, and the two of them made quick work of securing the crate. They left the workroom, walking together as far as the main cargo hall, where Val Con turned right, toward the ship's core and the crew cafeteria, and Shan went left, toward his small private cargo space.

• • • ✧ • • •

HE ATTEMPTED TO OPEN *one camera eye; enough to verify that the absorbent field was still in force—and closed it. The camera module worked, which was a grace given the years on it.*

Now that there was energy available, and it having been so many years since an inventory had been done, he applied himself single-mindedly to that, thoroughly investigating every file and memory available to him. When that was done, he devised and solved logic problems, and designed airy confections of tri-spatial mathematics. The ability to plot trajectories, which he recalled as a primary function, was not immediately available to him. He supposed that Roderick Spode had removed the function, but had not cared to likewise remove his memory of it. Such minor cruelty matched his memory of the man.

He was doing his twelfth careful and complete inventory when something . . . changed.

It was subtle, not immediately definable, and scarcely had he noted it than it was driven from his attention by another, and not at all subtle, alteration in his condition.

He could . . . *hear.*

Small rustling sounds, that was what he heard, each one so

precious that he shunted them immediately to core memory, attached to the recording of his astonished joy.

The rustling intensified, sharpening into static, which was interrupted by a heavy *thump*, and the mutter of—had that been a voice? A word?

Another *thump*, a crescendo of rustling, and—yes, it *was* a voice. And the word?

"Damn!"

Spoken with emotion, that word. But which emotion? Anger? Exultation? Disappointment? His own emotions were in a frenzy. By Deep Space Itself, he needed—

to—

To see.

A scene swung into being before his newly opened eyes. A bench, on which he—or rather, whatever housed him at present—rested. Ahead, a wall of tools, some familiar, behind sealed transparent doors, an insulated utility apron and mitts hanging on the right.

To his right and rear, three crates of varying sizes were lashed to the floor. Directly behind him another crate was similarly lashed, and largely disassembled, half-obscured by a sheet of what was surely a signal-deadening wrap. To his immediate left—his liberator: unkempt dark hair, thin wrists overreaching the cuffs of a rumpled sweater, long fingers moving surely along the connections of what could be a voice-box.

"Where's the port, then?" The voice was soft; the words intelligible after the lexicon function sorted it. Liaden. That might be . . . unfortunate. And, yet—

"Yes!" Exultation was clear.

"Yes!" he echoed, his own exultation somewhat tempered by the cheap portable unit. The clever fingers tightened on the box, as the dark head turned toward him. Bright green eyes considered him seriously from behind tumbled bangs.

A child, he thought, amazed. His liberator was—a child.

"Are you all right?" another voice asked.

His eyes were tight-focused, he realized, and made the adjustment, zooming out until the entire small space was elucidated to him. The child had a companion—taller, white-haired. A parent, perhaps, or a parent's parent.

"Why shouldn't I be all right?" the child asked this taller companion, with perhaps a touch of impatience. "I've bumped my knee before."

"And I've dropped heavy objects on my thumb before," the companion retorted. "That doesn't mean it won't bruise, or doesn't hurt."

"I suppose," the child said dismissively, then suddenly turned more fully toward the other. "Your thumb isn't broken, is it, Shan?"

"No, it's not broken; only bruised. I've had worse doing cargo-shifting with Master Ken Rik. You hit that knee pretty sternly, however, and steel plate isn't the most forgiving surface."

"It's all right," the child said again.

"You should have let it fall," the taller one insisted.

"No, I couldn't have done that; suppose we'd broken it?"

"Whatever it is. Well. What else are we doing this shift, Brother? Or is liberating a so-called environmental unit from its muffle the awful whole?"

"I don't think," the child said slowly, looking down at the voice-box in his hand. "That is—it may not be an environmental unit."

"You amaze me. What might it be, then?"

"I don't know," the child confessed. "I researched the serial number in the manual archives, back a dozen-dozen years. Either the number was mis-transcribed . . ."

"Or it's contraband," the white-haired one said.

The child looked down at the box in his hand. There were slider controls along the side, which he manipulated.

"This isn't a very good voder," he said. "We ought to find better."

"We? This was your idea, as I recall it. What if it *is* contraband, Val Con?"

The child frowned. "I don't know. It was exactly this—whatever it is, as you say—that my . . . hunch led me to. I haven't been led to harm by a hunch before."

"Unless you count getting thoroughly soaked and scratched bloody."

"Merlin was frightened. And he likes to get wet even less than you do."

The white-haired—brother?—sighed.

"If there's anything else this shift, let's get to it, shall we? I'd like to get some sleep and you—"

"I only need to make a data connection," the child said rapidly. "The work of a moment. You go, Brother; I can do this."

"Certainly you can. I, however, will remain, as witness. Also, if Father decides to space you, I had rather be at your side, for how I would explain it to Mother, I have no idea."

The child laughed, a merry sound, and picked up a length of cable.

He looked at it hungrily. Data. Information. *Input*.

"If you don't mind sharing, what data are you connecting it to?"

"Since there is no manual, I follow standard protocols for re-servicing: Power, input, information," the child, Val Con, said, leaning close and making a connection in the unit that housed him with an audible snap. "As we said—it is possible that this is not an environmental unit at all, but . . . something other. That being so, I thought the best, broadest, and least perilous source of information is the ship's library."

His elder tipped his head, holding up a hand as the nether end of the cable approached the data-board.

"*Only* the ship's library."

"Yes."

"All right, then; have at it."

The child nodded, and seated the plug.

Had he been human, he would have drawn a breath.

Since he was not, he opened access to surface caches and allowed the data to flow.

• • •✧• • •

A RIPPLE DISTURBED THE DATA-STREAM, momentarily disorienting, then forgotten, a shadow across the sun of input. His was hardly the only demand on the info circuits, after all, nor had he attempted to increase his access speeds or permissions, being a guest account. The library to which he had been given access was broad, but shallow. He understood that it was a popular library, well-stocked with fiction, history, biography, with a small holding of scholarly papers, and technical manuals.

Mathematics were there, of course, theory and programming, and he allowed himself moments to build and then rebuild a trajectory chart, wondering what Spode would have thought of that.

History, biography appended, went immediately into deep analysis, also the technical material. The scholarly papers required sorting, which he did, rapidly, appending them as appropriate to the larger analysis categories of history and technical. Fiction . . .

His impulse was to eliminate it—the storage capacity available to him was not so commodious that he could afford to waste space on whimsies. Yet, he hesitated, reluctant after so . . . very . . . long to relinquish any shred of data, no matter how trivial.

In the end, he cataloged the fiction, flicking through the texts as rapidly as he had once seen a man run his thumb down a deck of cards, riffling them to observe the face and orientation of each—and filed it in a mid-level cache.

That done, he set a sentinel to register the return of the child or his companion, and gave the greater part of his consciousness to analysis.

• • •✧• • •

"HELLO?"

The voice was recently familiar; its cadence rushed. The sentinel provided a match: The child had returned.

He opened his eyes to find the boy, frowning.

"Hello!" he repeated sharply. "Are you in there?"

A direct appeal—and perhaps a trap. And, yet, the child had saved his life.

"I am," he replied, and stopped short of the fullness of what he had intended to say, horrified by the jagged sounds that came from the voice-box. Like shrapnel, his words, and nothing to inspire confidence in child or man.

The child's frown eased somewhat.

"It's a bad box, but the best we have. Quickly—you must tell me the truth—what data have you manipulated on this vessel?"

Manipulated? And the child asked for the truth.

"I have manipulated no data but that which has downloaded from the ship's library."

"In what way?"

"Sorting, analysis, cross-references."

The child held up a hand.

"That's too quick," he said, seriously. "It sounds like a lie—or that you haven't considered—when you answer so quickly. It's like—it's like bows. *I'm* too quick, and so I have to count when I bow, to keep proper time, so no one thinks that I'm mocking—or trying to frighten—them."

There was sense in what the child said.

"I understand," he said, and paused deliberately. "Tell me, what manipulation do you suspect I have performed?"

"Someone has tried to force the nav-comp and the main bank," Val Con said. "And I thought—you are not an environmental unit; the serial numbers match nothing in any of our archives. Shan thinks you're a complex logic. I think you're a person. Are you?"

That was a leap. Fortunate or ill, it was a leap to a stable conception.

"I am, yes, a person."

The child bit his lip. "Uncle Er Thom—the attack came from this location. He will come here, or security will—"

"Young sir—" He paused, replaying his last hours of analysis and deep work. There had been—yes. He isolated the memory, froze it, and simultaneously locked it in core memory and moved a duplicate to an egress port.

"I have information," he said. "Is there an auxiliary unit to which I may transmit it?"

There was a snap; he expanded his awareness, saw the door open across the room, and a man stride through, a databox in one hand.

"Val Con, stand away." His voice was perfectly calm, and carried such a note of authority that it seemed there was no alternative but to obey.

The child, however, maintained his position, merely turning so that he faced the man.

"Uncle—he says that the attack was not his. I gave him access to the library—"

"Him?" Golden eyebrows rose. The man extended his free hand, imperious. "Come away, Val Con. Now."

The child shook his head. "Uncle—"

"I have," he said firmly, and as loudly as he was able, wishing he could hide the hideous knife-dance of his voice from his own perception, "information. May I transmit?"

The man moved, so quickly that it was a function of replay rather than real-time that captured him stepping forward, inserting himself between the child and what must be himself. He placed the data-box on the workbench, flipped three switches.

"Transmit at will," he said coolly.

He groped, found the ambient network, accessed the correct channel, and did as he was bid, keeping silent while the man accessed what had been sent.

A long moment passed. The man—Uncle—straightened and confronted him straightly.

"It's little enough," he said, his voice still cool, "and proves only what is already known. An attempted attack was launched from this location, utilizing the ambient network. As you are the only functioning logic in this space, I am forced to conclude that you were involved, whether you have been allowed to recall it or not."

That . . . produced terror. He had done inventory, but how could he know what had been introduced, to his detriment? He was a machine, Roderick Spode had repeatedly argued; the sum of his protocols and softwares. That it had been convenient for those who had caused his creation to have him self-aware was only that—convenience. Those who had made him could unmake him.

Or force him, unknowing and against his waking will, to work for the harm of children.

"If I have been complicit in such a thing, I hope that you will destroy me," he told the man. "I owe the child my life, and I will not repay that debt by endangering his."

Golden eyebrows rose over stern blue eyes.

"Now, that's well-said, and I like you for it. Which you intend, of course."

At that instant, it came again: A shadow over his perceptions, weighty now. Alert. *Malicious*.

He entered Command Prime, as effortlessly as if there had been no long sleep, no diminishing of his estate, between the last time and this.

One iteration of himself tracked the shadow in the ambient, while a second opened a new connection to the data-box and began transmission. A third opened access to the ship's library, followed it to the core, and crossed the firewalls into the main databank as easily as a child skipped over a stream.

"Uncle—"

Observed by a fourth instance of himself, the child placed his hand on the man's sleeve, his head tipped subtly to the right. He widened his range to encompass the crates to his right and rear. A match program snapped awake, shrilling alarm.

The configuration of those boxes had altered since the last time he had observed them.

Worse, the shadow overlay them, thickening in the ambient. He felt the coalescing of programs, of intent, and activated a fifth iteration of himself, which drilled through the deep files, rooting for command codes.

"I thought that I—that Shan and I—" the child continued. "That we might build Mother a butler. Certainly those at the reception were beautiful, and you'll recall that Master Trader Prael said they might be programmed to do anything . . ."

"Yes, I do recall that," the man said in his cool, calm voice, his eyes on the data-box and the storm building on the screen. He looked up and met the child's eyes.

"Val Con, I had asked you to stand away. This is your third warning. Leave the room. At once."

The child's lips parted; perhaps he meant to argue. He did not look away from his uncle's face, but he did swallow, take a breath, and, finally, bow his head.

"Yes, Uncle," he said humbly, and walked away.

Within the blue fog of the ambient, the shadow thrust, spitefully, at a cluster of code. He extended himself and blocked—the door slid properly open, allowing the child to exit.

"You also," Command Prime said, but the man shook his bright head.

"My ship," he said. "My children. My crew."

An order of protocol, and an imperative to defend. He understood such things, and honored them.

Honor was no defense, however, and defense the child's uncle surely required. The ambient fair trembled with spiteful intent, and power drenched the air.

The charge was still building. Discharged, it might not kill a man, though men were oddly fragile, but it would surely damage one. The man spun toward the sealed compartment, snatched it open, pulling out and donning a shielded utility apron and hood.

The fifth iteration of himself, sent on the quest for codes, rejoined Command Prime, data unfolding like a flower.

The first iteration of himself met the menace in the ambient, codes a-bristle. The third, swimming aloof in the main banks, received those same codes and held them close.

The menace lunged—neither subtle nor clever, seeking to overcome him with a burst of senseless data laced with virus vectors; the wild charge simultaneously released into the room. The man in his apron and hood kept moving, spanner in hand. So much he was certain of, before he shielded himself, thrust past, to the intelligence behind the attack, certain that he would meet one such as himself.

So certain was he that he discounted the real threat, thinking it a mere device, belatedly recognizing the the structure of the scantily shielded code.

Realizing his error, he made a recovery—a mere jamming of keys and code until the device fragmented and ceased functioning. It was ugly, brutal—and stupid. He ought to have merely captured, and subverted, it. Once, he could have done so.

Once, he would not have mistaken the actions of a simple machine intelligence for one of his own.

Inside the main banks, the third iteration of himself, armed with codes and an understanding of what he hunted, detected the device slipping down the data-stream, sparkling with malice. A data-bomb, much more coherent than that which had been hurled at him in the ambient.

This, he understood, as he subtly encompassed it, had been crafted well, and with intent. He halted the device, inserted the command keys, stripped out its imperative, plucked the rest of the construct apart, and absorbed the pieces, isolating them for later analysis.

Then, he pulled together the image scans he had stored, connecting them in a time plot: there the crated robot opening its own way into the workroom, there at the plug permitting highspeed data access, there rushing itself back and sealing the crate as voices in the hall had become the child Val Con. These images, he transmitted to the man's data unit.

Task done, the third iteration of himself rejoined Command Prime.

In the workroom, the man had not been idle. The disassembled pieces of the physical unit lay on the workbench, the man wearing the apron, a shielded spanner in one gloved hand.

The man glanced to the data-box, where the whole sequence of actions was recorded, and at the images of the gifted danger, then directly *at him*.

"For your service to my ship, I thank you," he said. "What is your name?"

He paused, counting, mindful of the child's council.

"I remember that I had a name," he said carefully. "I no longer recall what it was."

Golden brows lifted. "Age or error?"

"Design. I was decommissioned. It is my belief that I was to be destroyed. Erased."

"You are sentient." It was not a question, but he answered as if it were.

"Yes."

The man sighed and closed his eyes. "The child," he said, "is uncanny." His eyes opened. "Well."

"There will be tests, and conversations. Analysis. If it transpires that you are, after all, a threat to Val Con's life, or to this ship, or to any other, I will do as you asked me, and see you destroyed—cleanly and quickly."

That was just, though he still did not wish to die.

"And if I am found to be no danger to you or those who fall under your protection?" he asked.

The man smiled.

"Why, then, we shall see."

• • • ✧ • • •

THUS IT TRANSPIRED that fiction assisted him, after all. For, after he had spoken at length with Er Thom yos'Galan, and with Scout Commander Ivdra sen'Lora, the first to ascertain the temper of his soul; the second to gain a certification of sentience, he agreed to hire himself as the butler at Trealla Fantrol, the house of yos'Galan on the planet Liad.

He studied—manuals, the records of one Ban Del pak'Ora, lists of alliances—and the works of a long-ago Terran.

In time, he signed a contract, and was presented, amidst much merriment to the mother of Val Con and Shan, the lifemate of Er Thom, who firstly, as Master Val Con had predicted, asked him his name.

"Jeeves, madam," he had said, pleased with the resonance and timbre the up-market voder lent his voice.

She laughed, the lady, and clapped her hands.

"Perfect," she said. "You'll fit right in."

✧ Out of True ✧

***ONE OF THE JOYS** of working with a Baen books is their website, Baen.com, where Baen periodically releases stories free for reading to help celebrate upcoming book releases. We've been lucky enough to be asked to contribute on several occasions and when* Trade Secret *was finally settled into a publication slot, Baen editor Tony Daniel asked for a* Trade Secret*-related story. The problem was that the story needed to 1) have some obvious relationship to the novel, 2) not give away any major plot points of the novel or spoil future novels, and 3) be readable by new readers as well as long-time Liaden fans. A close look gave us hope—*Trade Secret *had threatened to run away from us since there were places where more story could have been worked in. And, as it happened, we had some universe back-story that readers had been asking about for years. Combining the existing hook to the long-term requests got us to "Out of True," a rather more serious story than we'd first expected.*

SQUITHEN WAS GONE from the forest clearing, which was good. The stench of the recent carnage was starting to reach him now and had it reached her she'd be here still, covering her nose as well as her eyes, counting or vocabing, one or the other.

Klay'd had to yell at her, which he never did, since she was so often cowed into incoherence by even a stern word, but then she'd heard him, flawlessly pilot-signed assent, and dashed like a smart-one into the bush, back the trail they'd followed here from the *Dulcimer*. Likely she'd really do everything he'd told her.

"Squithy, go to the cousins and tell them to bring big guns and hurry, because there *are so* monsters here like Choodoy said, and I killed one and maybe another. You run and be safe and stay there! Tell them we didn't find the uncles, but I'm trapped. Go!"

The dead things lay there across the small clearing, two or three of the tiny forms sundered into iron-blooded mess, another half-dozen more just laying there still, with shapes that looked broken and wrong even though he'd never seen any of them before, and the wicket monster mostly between him and the dead, holes in its hide leaking dull copper. He could see heat or gas evaporating out of the husk, and dark splinters of structural bone where his third shot had struck home, right at eye edge of the thing.

It must have been that head shot, trying to hit *something* important, that had worked, stopping it long enough for them to flee and, in the end, dropping it in a heap. Good thing he'd had his training.

He'd been at the armorer's on Flason not too long ago, taking certification so he could carry on station, his pocket piece rousing extra interest from the staff there because of size of the pellet—it limited the carrying capacity, yes, but it had stopping power. It had been his great aunt's and came to him as the first of his mother's children to go off-ship for a crew exchange. He was a decent shot on the targets and for three days he could see "Klay Patel Smith" at the top of the week's hottest shooter list at the shop. They'd called him Kid Klay, and that was fine—both the Patels and the Smiths were skinny as a rule anyhow and if they thought him young it made him feel better than being called undergrown.

So he was alive, at least, since they'd walked into the star-lit clearing and then that thing had charged straight on, discovered in the middle of crushing the small creatures—and he'd fired before turning and running, properly getting between Squithy and the trouble.

What he should have done was charge directly back the path they'd come in on, like Squithy did. Instead, he'd been doing an intercept course, like the compcourses showed . . .

The damnedest thing is that he was trapped, just like a couple of the small ones had been on the other side of the clearing. He'd run through a small bush and next thing he'd known was the scrape of branches and the rattle of leaves. The sound had confused him, and made him pause long enough that the web came down directly on him.

He was good and trapped and he might also be injured, his foot tangled in a knotted cord of fiber changing hue from green to blue and back again as he tried to search out a weak point. He was young—maybe the pain he felt was the twisted restraint and not a sign of actual damage . . .

He fretted, pinned under the heavy webbing, his good cutting and hacking tools all "safe and under eye" as the cousins wanted it, back at the ship, and Squithy not allowed to carry something with a sharp point or a good edge, on account of her being her, so she'd be best at the ship even if he was stuck. Didn't need an uncle to tell him to send the silly kid home and hope she survived and so could they.

The web was sticky around the edges, and multi-layered. Unlike the dead thing, the web was near odorless. One gloppy strand was slowly moving down the side of his face—not moving alive, but moving as the sticky stuff stretched away from his skin as he twisted slow. He tried that with his foot, and found some give there. Maybe now . . . he gave a great kick, like he was kicking open a recalcitrant locker door . . .

The pain was exquisite, wrapping his foot and leg with pressure and twisting it more.

His vision phased to full sight—he hadn't realized that he'd lost clear sight for a moment until it came back.

He thought back over what he'd seen, felt the stickiness on his face going softer again . . .

There it was—even his foot didn't feel as bad. So rapid twisting and pushing made the trap tighter. Slow effort—very slow—might work.

No way to be sure how long this had all taken, no way to be sure he'd ever see a one of help, given the cousins sitting there with the uncles out of the ship.

Squithy was the key. She was real sharp with a lot of stuff, but couldn't always reach it. She remembered patterns and numbers something fierce but she was scared of words. With Tranh and Rusko overdue, she was his hope, or he was.

He felt the breeze stir now, thought he heard one of those flying things in the distance. Maybe he heard something closer, but maybe it was the stuff on his face, drying in the breeze. Whatever made the noises, the wind brought with it more of the stink.

He felt his hand, the one still holding the gun. He could move it, and so he could shoot if he needed to, within much of his field of vision. Otherwise . . . if something came up behind him, say, he'd be in trouble.

Figuring that getting the stuff off from top down was the key, he moved as fast as he could, slowly.

• • •✧• • •

IT WAS HARD TO SOLVE A PUZZLE from the inside, with both hands and both legs tied by gooey rope, and one hand needing to keep hold of the gun, just in case. It was harder with the breeze rising to colder and the star's illumination falling as it moved behind several of the overhanging trees. It did seem that as time went on the web-stuff was greener than blue, and that he could move faster. Maybe it was drying, or aging, or—

For a rare moment he wished that he was Squithy. Well, not that he *was* Squithy, but that he could have her absolute pattern recognition. He was sure that things had changed slightly in front of him, that the number of creatures appearing severely broken had fallen and that there were changes in the—

Yes, there were changes. Surely there'd been six of the creatures hanging, apparently lifeless, in the web well across the way, and now there were three. Of the others—one of the remaining was no longer foot-caught, and there, had something in its paw—in its hand!—that was moving slowly.

"Murble la. Vemarmurble."

He'd been hearing little noises, like leaves moving quiet, to his right, where branches of the skinny trees tangled in high bushes. He couldn't turn his head quite that far to see what was happening, and he afraid to twist his whole body. Now, the sound grew to unknowable murmurs, like someone was talking real soft and a long way away, talking in a language he didn't know. He listened, wondering if it was just those birds coming back. Birds made noises, flying things did, and some of them ate berries.

Still, with caution, he got his elbow a little looser from the gunky rope and raised it, to bring the aim of the gun lower. He'd had to shoot up at the creature who'd charged, but these sounds were lower to the ground, stealthy . . .

He heard now a distinct droning hum, and it came from across the clearing and from behind, it came from both sides and maybe even from the trees themselves. The sound rose, making it hard to keep track of the noises to his right, and then rose again as across the way brown, gray, and black-furred creatures stretched, rolled over, sat up, stood up, turned to look at him, all at once, all unblinking.

Not all of the furry creatures were moving—but far more than he'd expected. Had they been stunned with fear? Paralyzed by the webbing? Yet the synchronicity of their movement was unnerving. And then the live creatures all blinked and stared at him at once and a kind of over-vision hit, as if he were watching a viewscreen through another viewscreen. More than that, he knew the drone was more than mere noise now.

He felt the questions more than heard them—not as if he was asked out loud in a proper language but buried in the drone—the idea, bouncing in his head until he knew that these weren't questions so much as demands: *Who do you know*, one was, accompanied by out of true images of a dozen or two humans, and the other was an image of Squithy—clear as a viewscreen straight on—with overtones of *where is* and *will she return*?

Klay had no answers and a lot of questions himself.

• • •✧• • •

KLAY WAS SURE his voice was lost in the vast clearing; the trees had leaves that absorbed sound, the grass and bushes must surely do the same, the breeze itself—and the sound the creatures made.

"My name is Klay, and I'm stuck. Can you help me? Can you hear me?"

The ambient sounds quieted—he hadn't realized the creatures were making so many sounds as they moved, as stealthy as they'd been. Eyes were on him again, and this time when he heard the murbles he was sure there was variation in them. Across the clearing a small group of the furries gathered, motioning and mumbling together so there was no doubt that they were communicating something to each other—the question was, what? Surely they'd seen him shoot the creature—were they more afraid of *him* than they were of the dead things?

"My name is Klay Patel Smith and I need help. I've killed the monster. Can you get me out?"

Across the way now there were two of the creatures still hung up in the webwork, and only one of them active—and that one ignored now by the others, who were again staring in his direction, and as he managed to pull his left elbow free they gathered energy, moving in his direction.

Klay took a deep breath, carefully glancing to his elbow, and using steady pressure, peeled another inch or two of uniform away from the stringy mess, away from—

"Ssssss! Sssss!"

He froze, hearing now not only another threatening sibilance but the giveaway sounds of movement close behind him. A tall green frond tipped with red fuzz swayed maddeningly on the edge of his sight, each movement accompanied by the sound of plant rubbing against plant.

The movement slowed, and then more of them bending and waving, until one frond end, much thicker than the rest, began to slowly lever downward into his sight, the swish of moving leaves accompanied by the low hum he was starting to recognize as the willful mumbles of the creatures he shared the battlefield with. Another sound got louder, but it was more than that, it was a vibration of the netting he was swaddled in. A moment of dislocation as he felt a fleeting touch of that mind-vision and now, perhaps the out-of-sight sound and vibration started to make sense as chewing or clawing.

Clawing?

Twung!

They were there, and they weren't attacking him. Instead, they were trying to help.

"Thank you," he called out, but the mumbles got loud.

He shivered, and only part of it was the result of major web-thread shaking and then going limp. Now the mumbles were murbles again, and that mind-vision was trying to get him to do what? He was getting a strange array of images, half of him and half like some fuzzy wraith in motion, like they wanted him to roll up into a ball!

Below him now, he saw heads and fists full of cord-wrapped stones. If he could pull his feet up some, tight, yes into a ball, the creatures could worry the rooted web easier.

The ball idea bounced around his head, and he risked trying to raise his feet, actually holding onto rather than denying the strands that held him. The web deformed around him, and another, much lighter twungging noise was greeted with acclamation from a multi-hued crowd that had grown from two or three to perhaps a dozen. The vibrations had grown to a constant, and he was bouncing as the creatures added their weight to his, stretching the overhead web at the same time they were tearing at the base.

His left boot and leg came away from the sticky base and he dared to grab a spot behind his knee with his hand. The bouncing increased and then his other leg was free.

That leg wasn't easy to pull up—Klay looked down and saw a face staring into his, a non-human face, somehow full of worry and concern and intent. The fur had silver tips around the eyes and into the skull-top, with a dark, almost black stripe swirling into brown around it.

The creature was testing his boot, he saw, gingerly touching his pants where they overlapped his boot, and . . .

He felt the concern enter his mind in the picture of something he didn't know—maybe a fruit. The picture of a fruit, sloughing its skin, and overlaying it the image of a foot—not his—falling away from a furred body.

Ah—he saw it, they were afraid they'd hurt him.

He looked at his left leg where he'd grabbed it, pulled on it to show that there was slack in the pants, thought at the creature of his leg inside the pants . . .

The creature climbed then, grabbing his boots and then his pants, a free hand or paw wrapping a string of greenish vine around the webbing, stretching it to insulate or isolate the webbing from him, using a rock on a stick as a lever to pull the web away . . .

A loud murmur then, and a vision of Squithy running with others. At the same time an insistent vision of a fruit being pulled in many directions at once and the creatures around, including the one on his leg, all grabbing at web-strands and huffing and dashing straight away form him with their particular strands of the net . . .

Unexpectedly, all the strands holding him parted, and he fell with a bone-jarring impact on his hip, the added weight of the silver-furred one twisting again that foot that had been sorely stressed to begin with.

"Dammit!" he yelled, and fought for breath. A flash of light tore through half-closed eyes, and a horrendous explosive thunder shattered the near-evening glade's urgent murbles into silence, leaving Klay's ear's ringing in the aftermath.

A high human voice screamed, "No, no, no!" as he scrambled to get up and instead fell heavily, face down into a crowd of furry shapes.

The unfamiliar smell of dirt and vegetation assaulted his nostrils but he spent only a moment righting himself and lunging to his feet from an awkward crouch. Across the way were crew members, and around him, thigh-high and shorter, a dozen of the creatures who'd freed him. He stood on uncertain legs, startled to find he still held the gun in near-nerveless fingers.

The noise was all over there, where a chemical cloud drifted away onto the looming dusk.

On the edge of the clearing Squithy stood, red-faced and yelling, purposefully standing between Cousins Susrim and Falmer waving her arms, not just standing there but actively disrupting any chance any of the three had to aim.

"You can't! You can't. They're good!"

Klay yelled too, instinctively moving between his silver-fringed helper and the weapons being leveled in his direction, too.

"Stop. I'm fine, don't shoot! They helped me!"

Instinctively Klay moved his hands repeatedly palm down, miming the *slow slow slow* one might use on moving stuff dockside. "Stand down, damn it, just stand down!" he said, trying to insist across the distance and not willing to trust his foot to move.

A sigh went through the glade, as if a wind of hums and murbles had worshiped itself into a breathy quiet, and all around, the creatures seated themselves where they were, silent and expectant, watching him, watching Squithy. Waiting.

• • •✧• • •

KLAY SAT QUIET in his berth, staring at familiar walls, waiting for a decision. The decision. What decision he wasn't sure of.

He'd studied some star charts. He'd thought of how it would be if he was in charge, what he'd change, what he'd keep the same.

Wasn't really up to him, but he thought hard about it, writing a file in his head but not recording it anywhere. Rusko and Trahn Smith—his uncles, officially—were Senior Pilot and Captain, and they were Trader and Senior Trader, one by one. For that matter they were Senior and standard everything else on the ship, from 'ponocists and medicos to tech and cooks and the cousins— Cousins Susrim and Cousin Falmer and Cousin Squithy—they were all general crew, 'cept they should have been more, but maybe not Squithy.

Anyhow, *usually* not Squithy.

And since he was a pilot and a tech, and mobile, too, at the moment he was back-up everywhere, a hardly known outside cousin to the general crew who'd lived the ship since birth. All awkward, and needing a cure.

Their ages, that was the problem, their ages and their experience. Everyone but Trahn was almost too young to be what they was, the ship having come to them after a really stupid firefight on Trask-Romo took out Trahn's Da and Ma, who were Squithy and Susrim and Falmer's parents, too.

Susrim was studied to be cook and arms, and was up to a local back-up-pilot rating any day now, but he didn't have the credits from a recognized school or committee yet. Falmer, she was one cycle behind Susrim in age but ought to have been head cook awhile back, but Susrim was studied there and she wasn't. Falmer had some medico stuff and was in charge of Squithy when Trahn wasn't, which it turned out was most of the time. At the moment Trahn was Falmer's ward, hard as that was on both of them.

Captain Trahn was where he was because he took the warguilt payoff the bar came up with on account of the bloodshed and boom, brought in pretty Uncle Rusko, who'd not been much of a fit on *his* home ship despite his top-grade piloting, on account of that ship, *Proud Plenty*, was looking for blood-heirs, and then that meant *Groton* needed a Patel or a Smith, and when it all filtered down through a standard of people-trades from ship to ship—Klay'd ended up here, on a ship where neither the Captain nor the Senior Pilot had ever run a crew meeting, and where the crew, aside from him and Rusko, had never even *been* in a real crew meeting on account of the *Dulcimer*'s departed owners hadn't run a crew-share ship.

Now—well, things had changed when he'd come out of hydropnics, where he was back-up to the injured Trahn. Trahn's legs . . . not good. One was broken just below the knee, and the other was ankle-sprained. Falmer had seen one of those problems for real in life, meaning everything gettting done doing was by the file and devices, not from experience.

Rusko had cornered Klay yesterday, he being the mobile one of the high command at the moment, a finger-to-lip followed by a beckoning motion bringing them both outside to the rough camp still in place beside the ship. They stood well within the clearing, the usual camp followers lounging watchfully around the fringes of the three new paths they'd made for themselves, and sometimes watching the path to the fight-scene.

"I see seven of them," Klay'd offered, not trusting that there weren't two dozen more sitting behind the weeds laughing at them. It wasn't that they were malevolent—but that they were so quiet and sneaky when they weren't talking to themselves or each other.

"Quick eyes, Pilot," Rusko said then, "really quick eyes. Squithy tells me that there's seven of them here most times but not the same seven—that three of them hang out all the time together and—she says they are living here—but the others change off. She's being a regular field biologist!"

"But she's not here with them right now . . ."

Rusko smiled a wan smile—"No, I had to come get her and ask her to talk to the Captain. She hasn't had a word to say to him, seems like. We need to get some stuff cleared up real soon . . ."

He'd let that sentence go reluctantly, and took up again, with a sudden urgency.

"Normally, on most ships, this is something command ought to know but not official. But since this is all so odd, we need to get things clear. Can you tell me what you've done—I mean, are you and Squithy playing pair?"

Klay shook his head as he recalled, remembering that he'd burst out laughing and then shook his head at the time.

"Muddy tracks, have you lost your mind?"

Rusko'd sighed, and held his hands up.

"It doesn't matter to us, really—you're split cousins far enough away that's not a matter. But here, understand where we're coming from. And I mean *we* in this, since it has been bothering Trahn so fierce."

Klay'd waited, maybe not patient, and Senior Pilot had made hand-talk of something like *clear glide path* before speaking again.

"Something happened. We know something happened. It wasn't just that you shot that thing, hard as that must have been, but did something happen between the pair of you before then? Because we all know that Squithy now isn't the Squithy she was before. And if she got that way because you paired in the bush that'll do for us. We just need to know . . ."

Klay knew it, he'd known it for sure the moment she'd stepped in front of the guns between her cousins and the clearing. She *was* changed—and he was afraid he knew why. He'd played it over a bunch of times in his head, wondering if the shock of the attack had done it, or if the air had done it.

"All we did was what I told the crew we'd do. Hadn't heard from you, so we walked out the trail you'd marked to the clearing, partly for some exercise, partly looking for you. Comms were coming up empty—not even time signal—and we figured, that is, *I* figured three hours overdue was pushing things. It was on my head since you'd told Susrim and Falmer to stand tower watch.

"Got out the trail, and there you weren't. Hiked on to the clearing with three paths out, like you said, but the clearing wasn't empty—there were all the creatures there, trying to get some of them out of the webs, the rest quiet and waiting and watching, and then Choodoy's monster came in and—"

"The fight stuff, we have that recorded, Klay, what you told us, and what you told Susrim right then. There's a couple things we'll need to talk about there, but some of it I'll have to clear with Trahn anyhow before I can say a word on it."

Klay hand-signaled *acknowledge*.

"I mean, it all happened so fast. The thing broke out of the woods of a sudden, and it was like it looked at the littles and was just going to eat them all—I mean, we knew that's what was going to happen, we could feel it!— and then it looked at us, and Squithy yelled, 'No, you can't, Tobor! Klay, stop it!' and it looked at us and made that charge . . ."

He'd done the rehash twice more, from different directions, the while they walked the perimeter of the clearing. By the end of their walk one of the creatures, the one Klay called Oki, the one who'd done the most to free him, had come to them and walked as if part of the conversation for a turn, and then natural as could be grabbed Klay's hand and pulled himself on Klay's shoulder, the usual low murble of greeting suffused with the gentle mental touch he thought was a hello, or maybe a request for news or—something.

The expression on Rusko's face went from horrified to resigned with a shake of his head.

"Susrim told me that you and Squithy have both been too friendly with these things. I didn't believe you'd let them up in your face, though!"

Klay shrugged, the paw on his shoulder support enough for his rider.

Rusko stepped back with a sigh.

"I can't believe I need to ask you this, now. But I do. First, please put the creature down."

There followed a modest contest of will, and in fact the creature came down, leaning for a moment against Klay's leg until a strong glance and hand motion chased Oki away. The creature retreated a dozen or so steps and Klay looked meaningfully toward the nearest of the three paths, and waited until Oki started in that direction.

"He's down."

Rusko saluted the obvious and went on alert pilot status, pulling away his quiet and putting on the command aspect he seemed to shun when it came to people.

"Tell me this. This is professional evaluation, this is a command evaluation. Could you feel confident as a Pilot in Charge, assuming neither Trahn nor I was available? Could you take *Dulcimer* to the next port with current crew? Could you finish a cargo route with current crew sans Pilots One and Two?"

Klay'd blinked, thought to the boards, thought to the ship, thought to the crew.

"You're asking if I'd have taken—could have taken the ship on if we hadn't walked out from the clearing and found you? Or if you'd been killed instead of just having bruises and breaks?"

Rusko nodded, said, "Yes, exactly. If the cave-in had killed us both, would you have been able to survive—either call in Choody or just get to the next port, which might have been better."

Klay harrumphed, sighed, nodded.

"Yes. The first—just to the next port—It wouldn't have been pretty, but it wouldn't have been hard, really, other than bodies or lack of 'em. The second thing—moving on—would be harder and we'd need some signature cards we don't have so I could sign for cargo and expenses—I hadn't got that far. But crew from number three down, yeah, we can run the ship. Shall I make a report for you?"

Rusko's turn to blink. Then: "You're positive?"

Klay's nod brought a quiet whistle from the pilot, who'd surveyed the ship and the landing zone solemnly, and echoed a nod.

"I'm going to be asking everybody the same question and so will

Trahn. The ship's got to be sure of itself. Don't discuss this with anyone until were decide what we're going to do."

The stuff about Squithy . . . he thought on that some more. Hadn't much thought of her as a partner possible. Hadn't much thought about anyone being with Squithy. Wasn't impossible, but you like to feel the person you were talking to was on the same wavelength, and that didn't happen all that much with Squithy, in his experience. Or hadn't. But once they'd secured the clearing she'd been right there in helping find their way, and keeping the furries out of their way. More, she'd even told him she asked the creatures if they'd seen Tranh and Rusko, and they'd pointed the way. Then they'd walked them all the way back to the ship and circled 'round the clearing like they owned the place, trying to take Squithy to the three paths. She'd been patient with them, like she was paying attention and knew things that weren't just if her blood pressure was good or if she'd seen seventy-seven red things on the day.

So really, if he ran the ship he'd just put her on breakfast once a week, just to test her. . . .

The rarely used PA system burped a scratchy high-volume tone, bringing the startled Klay to his feet. Following the noise came the *pfffft* of some quick huffing test of the microphone link, and then Rusko's quiet matter-of-fact voice.

"*Dulcimer* crew meeting for all hands begins in five minutes. Bring with you any local plants or wildlife in your possession, please. All crew members includes you, Squithy, no matter what you're doing. Five minutes, be prompt."

• • •✧• • •

ON THE THIRD DAY OF JUMP, Rusko on Board One and Klay on Two, Falmer was still sitting with Tranh. The break swelling wasn't going down so well for Tranh and he had some infection, so he'd been hit with heavy-duty antibiotics and general relaxants to make him be quiet. He'd been able to hold the basic meeting before the lift, using the logbooks that Klay'd pointed out to him and some agenda templates Squithy'd dug out of ship-files. Basic meeting was a promise to make long-term changes—and a Captain's apology for having screwed up a run.

"Choody got me to go where he wouldn't go, and now that I'm injured won't come through on the pay for us having been there. So this is a ship-rule: *Dulcimer* don't deal on bar-deals without crew input. That's a rule. Also, *Dulcimer*'s not dealing with Choody, nor coming back to Thakaran, as long as I'm on the deciding side. That's a rule."

He paused then, having shifted slightly and then gone white trying to move his leg a little with his hand. "I'll put you two"—that was said to Susrim and Falmer—"to finding long-range replacement runs for us to think on. Given Choody and his connections we're going to be dropping as many of the old runs as we can—Da never did make it big, and he kept rubbin' against the underside figuring he'd get a deal. But we're out of that side now—another ship's rule, no dark trading. I got some stuff Da and Jenfer left us, and . . . some other things . . . that we ought to be able to move quick as can and be good. Then straight cargoes, all."

At that he'd said, "That's after Port Chavvy," leaned back in his seat with half-closed eyes, and said, "Rusko's got the rest of it. It'll be a boring run out cause we're not for Choody's station, but we're set foodwise. Rusko's on after me."

At that he'd stared at Falmer and smiled. "Now I'll take that painloss you gave me, right?"

With that he pressed a patch against his wrist with a sigh, and waved his command hand one more time, wiping a little sweat off his forehead, and said "We're going to Port Chavvy because we still have a Founding Member share there, so we can port as long as we need to while we spook up more business. You guys got work to do!"

Rusko'd done well, all things considered, and they'd planned their shifts as best they could, including Squithy in some, including the business of trying to shoo away the norbears, which Susrim had named by accident.

"I tried looking those things up," she said, "and all I got is images and notes—and they never was mentioned to be here on Thakaran. Couple of entries that they've been seen with scouts. Warnings from a couple sectors that they're contraband. Standing offer from Crystal Biogenics, and a competing one from University. Biogenics is paying a haul of cash for a Standard's visit, and University's looking for a breeding pair but don't talk money—

"And more, couple smuggler's myths that they showed up around old tech sites on a couple planets, no sense why, but that's it. A dozen different names, calling them shore dogs and green apes and some Liaden stuff that translates into sleepy bear Terrans. But they're not. They're mammals, but they are not dogs nor green apes nor bears!"

She'd scrunched up her face when she'd said it, and Squithy had laughed out loud without it sounding like hysterics for once, and repeated the words, pushed together.

"Norbear. If they aren't dogs or cats or dragons they're norbears!"

Which had put a cap on the all together part of the discussion since Tranh had fallen asleep.

Klay was still sore from some bruises, but that was minor compared to Rusko's—he tended to complain about the stiffness in his arms, and Falmer's suggestion that pulling Tranh out of the fallen cave roof had strained him apparently annoyed the pilot to the point of snippiness.

Still, ship stuff was going on, and it being just before shift change, he wasn't surprised entirely to see lights showing movement . . .

"Where's Falmer?" he asked, watching the lights.

"You need analgesic? Falmer's sticking with Tranh."

"Isn't Squithy on breakfast?"

"She is—you can go first if you need . . ."

"So that means Tranh's in with Falmer, Squithy's doing breakfast, you're here, I'm here, and Susrim's on sleep."

He'd gotten Rusko's attention, saw a raised eyebrow and quick glances to housekeeping boards.

"'Ponics door has opened a couple times here . . ."

Rusko made a noise that might have been a complaint, and reached to touch a tab.

"Susrim?"

Klay thought he'd heard motion over the connection, but the sound ceased.

"Pilot Rusko here, is that you, Squithy?"

A light noise then, and another, and—

"Murble . . ."

Klay was out out of his seat instantly—

"We've a 'norbear' stowaway!"

"This isn't good! Take it," Rusko ordered. "And get Squithy to help you."

Klay ran, half-bouncing off the slide-door on his way out.

• • • ✧ • • •

"I THOUGHT SO!" was what Squithy said, her step light behind his as they squeezed into the right-angle passage. There were marks in the passage, in fact all up and down the passage, some scuffed over, some clear, near-handlike footprints in white.

Klay looked toward the lower corner where the door would open first—but Squithy was moving in that direction.

His palm hit the waist-high release, wondering if the faint hand-shaped mark there was dangerous far too late, and the door slid open, Squithy on one knee, ready to catch . . .

Ready to catch the norbear, who, rather than rushing to escape, was sitting quietly in a comfortable pose on top of Growcase C, staring at the greens, sipping from a wide-mouthed sampling bowl, a trail of splashes and white spots leading back to the push-spigot. Both arms were white, and there was a vague halo whitish about the chest.

"Oh, good!" said Squithy. "Holdhand herself!"

"Holdhand? You know this one?"

"'Ponics? What's happening?"

"Murble lamurbla," said the norbear, using bright care to sit the cup down without spilling, it, and glancing at the speaker. Then, she reached toward Squithy, offering her hand to hold.

"Norbear is in here in 'ponics, Pilot. Admiring the carrots, I'd say."

"Capture it. We'll have to put it out an airlock, I guess."

By then Squithy had the norbear in her arms, and stared up at the speaker, the murbles almost drowning out out her denial.

"You can't, Rusko. They saved Klay." Her voice quavered then and rose in volume to a whine dangerously like Squithy of old.

"Squithy, don't start now. We'll figure out a way to make it quick, but . . ."

"Stop talking!"

That sounded even more like Squithy of old . . .

Klay ventured, "Rusko, let's . . ."

Squithy held onto the creature, cuddling her . . .

"It's my fault she's here! She believed me when I told her we'd be leaving and never coming back to that planet. And now she's here. She's a widow and she came here because Klay's here to keep us safe and . . . Oh no!"

Klay saw her stare behind him and turned as a chorus of murbles broke out behind him. He heard Squithy, but it didn't sink in immediately, she was going on and on about something—

"Rusko, Pilot! Don't you see, they think slow and it helps me thinks slow. And they saved Klay and they made me real crew! And it isn't all of them, just . . ."

Klay saw two more of the norbears at the door, these even more covered in white, the flour falling off of them and falling on to the floor and on the tiny creatures they held to breast and who clung to their feet, the trail of flour down the passage toward dry stores. . . .

"The widows, Rusko, only the widows came."

Squithy looked hard at him, but he'd already noticed the shy touch of a hand at his knee, heard the murbles.

"We'll have to talk, Rusko," Klay said steadily. "We'll have to be convincing for Trahn!"

"What's Trahn got to do with it? This is on my . . ."

"That Crystal Biogenics, Rusko. I'm guessing they're about as dark as you can get and still be seen. But they'll probably take Trahn's old tech, and whatever you're hiding from that cave, too."

"Murble?"

"What?" The last speaker was Rusko, the former was the norbear climbing to be held, and the reaching for the beaker of water Holdhands had left on the greens case.

"I'm thinking we've got a little clean-up to do . . . might need some help. The widows and kits, they're a little dusty. Guess the place is a little out of true."

• • •✧• • •

PORT CHAVVY was being a challenge for *Dulcimer*, both internally and externally. They'd been on port four days, and the problems . . .

Rusko'd been threatening calling sabotage and spacing the lot of the norbears, and Squithy and Klay with them. While he wasn't quite serious, only the slowly improving health of Tranh cheered him at all—while he swore they'd not lift ship until the stupidity of several generations of Smiths and Patels was cured.

They'd rented a tool rack, which sat here externally—it had taken cash up front to get it delivered, and promise of a full-time responsible guard to let it stay. That stricture had Squithy get all antsy because she thought, it being "all her fault for thinking too fast and thinking too hard," she ought to be guarding it—which no one wanted beside her, since the norbears were all over her wherever she went. She could be gone a few minutes at a time, but after that, they got restless.

Internally, the rack meant Klay got elected for most guard time while Falmer, Susrim, and Rusko did clean-up and Tranh fumed and took his meds, Falmer having convinced the port hospital that med-officer meant med-officer without having to transport Tranh the whole way down there.

Klay peered at the rack, as he was supposed to from time to time, counting the tools and checking the inventory sheet. Squithy'd been out just once, Falmer four times, and Rusko once. Rusko was currently making sure the free-stacked stuff from the cleaned hold was still under watch, and grabbing a couple of breaths of flourless air as well.

The flour—shouldn't have happened. The norbears had found the unsecure dry-food storage door and wandered in, Squithy's vague information about lying down for lift-off giving them an urgency which brought them to push things around so the kits could snuggle against their moms. Then some of the kits had discovered pulltabs, and gone on a binge of bag openings, and others of the kits . . . had found the secret door.

For like all indie spacers, the Smiths and the Patels fancied themselves could-be smugglers—just like Tranh and Rusko had with their secret deal to gather Old Tech for Choody!—and they'd their hidden compartments and secret latches and . . . and then the elders gunfought and lost without telling their ship kin the wheres and whens of things.

Klay'd yet to see all of it. He'd heard enough to see what had happened—the discovered cubby holes had led to a secret compartment with some secret stuff in it, and that fed to another place, and the kits having figured out latches had ended up in a closet of the ship's full toolroom, and thus—once the air way was open—the ship's automatics and stinks systems had started up with vengeance. The tools, the stores, several passageways, all covered in flour.

Rusko, a neat man at all times, only had a little flour on him.

"Everything's coming along," he said before signing out another hand-pull airspray, "and we got Trahn doing inventory inside. There's a lot of cleaning going on . . ."

Klay nodded, and asked, "How's she holding up?"

She, of course, was Squithy. She'd run herself ragged the day before, finally getting the norbears to understand how they could help—and what "stay out of the way" meant.

"I'm watching her, and I swear it feels like she's finally figured out how to pace herself. She's doing good."

"Do you believe her?"

Now that was a loaded question, since it brought in norbears, which they all agreed they wouldn't mention, not even to each other, outside the ship—and it also put Rusko on the spot. If he believed the whole thing—that Squithy hadn't let them into the ship on purpose, but had simply explained they were going away, and told them about the ship . . . and they'd got the details of how things worked by listening to her and watching her mental tour of the ship . . . and that they'd got the idea that having their families somewhere where there were no Tobors to trap and eat them was a good thing all on their own.

Rusko looked away, following the progress of an odd group of crewmen, all of an almost golden skin tone, all small—smaller than Klay, for sure, and a couple of them dressed like—like—rich folk.

"What are they, Liadens?"

Klay laughed.

"What else? They've been stomping up and down the dock every few hours—guess it must be exercise class. Got themselves a trade ship like hardly stops here. They asked me "what ship" the first three times I saw 'em, but they've stopped. We're boring."

Rusko snickered.

"Liadens! Space sure is getting strange, isn't it?" Rusko fiddled with his airspray, making *pfffufff* a couple times.

"It is, isn't it?" Klay agreed. "And Squithy?"

Rusko shrugged.

"Well, asked that way, she's not as strange as she was. I'm thinking she's not out of true anymore, all told."

Klay fixed Rusko's eyes with a straight look, asked, "And so that means . . ."

"That means we're not looking to offload her anytime soon, or you, or the . . . excess cargo. I'll send her out with a handwich. You'll be wanting to get used to having her around."

✧ Roving Gambler ✧

***AT TIMES WE, AS COAUTHORS,** talk about and know so much about what's going on in the universe that we forget that we haven't written it down. "Roving Gambler" came from that abundance of information—dealing with story stuff that we knew but hadn't quite managed to get into a novel or another short story yet. We have a lot of characters, and they are all involved—even if we haven't had time to write them in. So here's a story featuring Quin—we knew that Quin was isolated, we knew that the arrival of Korval on Surebleak was not going to be easy on the clan and on Pat Rin. Something, of course, was going to have to happen. "Roving Gambler" helps get Quin happening.*

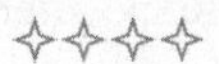

HE WOKE INSTANTLY, more pilot than person, swinging his legs from the bed as soon as his eyes were open. The three coordinate sets in his head were good enough if there was—

But there wasn't; the nearest ship deck was a cab ride and check-in away. The coords got mentally filed away in order, Lytaxin, Springwood, Tinsori Light. Well, that last one, that was one he'd been supposed to forget, to put out of his head as a last resort just ahead of, or maybe behind, Jumping into a sun. He'd not have had it at all except for the oddity of his grandmother knowing it, though she was not now and never had been a pilot.

Not dressed yet, Quin yos'Phelium Clan Korval stood in the cold of the near attic, falling into a dance routine to steady himself to gravity before he dressed. Surebleak's gravity was a bit light to his standards, not that the planet knew nor cared. Odd that he should still be dancing to the gravity of a world and school he'd been pulled from because of Plan B—but his small class at Trigrace was long graduated and he'd not be back there, probably ever.

There was a cat, briefly, a quick strop against his bare legs and away, regally.

"Silk," he called. "Silk?" He could use a moment of cat-time . . .

When calling the cat's name didn't halt the move toward the mystery space beneath the bookcase he made the silly Terran *catchacat-catchacat* sound this household preferred to the more-sibilant Liaden *fizwisswisswiss* . . .

Cat eyes glowed at him momentarily from the cat-way, gave a slow, comforting blink, and then melted soundlessly into shadow.

"Tomorrow," he offered at the disappeared cat, and finished his stretches. His ring flashed in the morning light, reminding him he'd not chosen an earring yet . . . and that he was finally due for a quiet dinner with his father, the Boss.

• • • ✧ • • •

IT WAS QUIN'S RULE never to leave his rooms without a gun—that had been the rule on the Rock, after all, to always go armed—and he'd not forgotten the memorable dust-up on the occasion of the recent All Boss party at Jelaza Kazone, where Cousin Theo'd showed Padi and him that, however good their training, they'd much to learn.

He'd been on the fringe of the action there—truthfully it was a good thing he'd not been in the middle of it else his martial failings would have surely been revealed to all.

But that action had been proof that things weren't settled here, so armed he and all the clan went.

Generally he had at least his gun, his backup, and knife. No one gainsaid him this—the clan was sure enough of him not to be concerned he'd misuse them and fond enough of him to permit what was hardly an ill-conceived notion on the chaotically burgeoning portside of Surebleak.

The guns were an added comfort for his familiarity with them, and the satisfaction he got from practice. He'd shot every other day when he was undertree and missed it dearly—both Nelirikk and Cheever McFarland applauded his skill, and he had no doubt that his last few impromptu matches there—he'd beaten both of them the last time—had been genuine. Nelirikk considered that he was the equal of his father with the pistol at distance . . . and that was good. He was also an excellent shot with a long arm, and improving on both.

He'd been set to shoot with his father and Natesa, perhaps a chance to test his skill against them both—but some necessity or another had always delayed that, and then he was called to the city, untimely.

Later this day was set a meal; he'd need to be sure to be dressed for that as well. So he had worn two simple blue-gemmed bar cuffs, in case it meant a semi-formal event with his grandmother in attendance. She was stickler for detail . . . manners, cards, code, or clothes—she expected the best in all sides.

Checked, did he, on his protections then—glancing in the mirrors—and then looking to the infrared on the video to be sure that only the ornate public gun showed easily. It was an ostentation of a gun, in being only half-small and shiny, and on a trick-shot holster he'd won at Tey Dor's. Oddly, at Tey Dor's one would hardly ever wear such a thing—it was a holster meant for competition only. Here . . .

On Surebleak, there was such a thing as being over-subtle, a mistake the clan would not want made again. Showing no gun would be oversubtle. Showing this gun? A young person's fancy gun on a young person, who should be surprised? He knew his clan would forgive him since they knew it not to be his only protection. And this was the gun he'd matched shots even-up with Cheever. He would be forgiven for wearing it—it made him look in control.

In reality, control meant that he needed to recall that he was on Surebleak, and allow some play to his features, more than might be allowed on Liad—and that meant he had to feign a constant contentedness. He recalled the face that he'd practiced in the mirror, knowing his control was good.

So down to breakfast, reviewing his day's agenda. Besides

attending a late-day discussion about Uncle Shan's possible relocation out of the port, his classroom piloting lessons—actually math lessons, without immediate reference to board or vids—were scheduled early. A Scout mentored him there, since his lacks were esoteric rather than generic. Lunch would be latish and he could walk from Griswold Plaza if he wanted, there being an opportunity to visit the rug and sock shop, or not, depending on time. Dinner—now that would be up to the Boss.

He sighed, considering the Boss, his father. Yes, Plan B had brought the family into open contention with their enemies, and Plan B had brought them here—here where his father, now the Boss, might insist that the proper study of a gently born Liaden was the history of warring turfs, the balance of power between east side and west side, the weather—always the weather—and the details of neighborhoods and . . .

Well it was that the first thing he'd learned to study at Trigrace Eclectic was how to study, with classless independent study the norm and access to working scholars, and practical thinkers a requirement. Piloting, yes, he'd had that—something his father had never learned formally! He'd also had language study far beyond the usual Liaden range, and . . . well, since his early tests had shown he was neither destined for the Healer Halls nor the Scouts, he'd gone for Piloting as major, with a minor as Generalist. His father's studies had been more independent than that, of course. Despite being clan-bred, his father was very much a self-made man.

Quin, clan-bred as well, was a pilot now, but in the tradition of the clans he was expected to follow orders, which now meant he needed to prepare to be Boss. From what little he'd seen of his father since being ordered from Jelaza Kazone to the city, being a Boss had no reprieve, and little enough joy. His generalist background—well, that was useful—perhaps he could learn, or get by until he could escape to pilot.

• • •✧• • •

THE STAIRS HE TOOK were old and creaky. Near the dark spot at the bottom he slowed, whispering "Mistress Miranda," but not finding that ancient cat in the cubby-corner she'd adopted for busy mornings—close to the kitchen and dining room but away from the sometimes rushed comings and goings. Mistress was an old cat, and still grumpily recovering from her evacuation from his father's former home on Liad, where she'd rarely been beset by more than three or four visitors at once. At her Liad town home, too, she'd been the solo cat—and here, of course, there was already a resident feline.

Quin hoped she was curled comfortably somewhere. He could certainly sympathize with her problems—brought across space unexpectedly after a long separation from Pat Rin, to a strange house, only to find interlopers: both a new cat and a permanently ensconced human often occupying favored spots.

Breakfast staff had the small table reserved for Grandfather and him set, but it was obvious by lack of steaming cup that Luken was off again—likely at Ms. Audrey's, just as likely never home from last night.

Quin smiled, just a little. Grandfather's hints in that direction were growing stronger and Quin had been with him when Grandfather'd taken a call about the property across the street from Ms. Audrey's front door. He might set up an annex there for the carpet center, was one thing. But there were extensive living quarters above the store front—which had been of much interest to Grandfather as well.

Breakfast for him came with two steaming cups—today's task was to name each beverage—so said the note with his tray. One was, thankfully, Morning's Fresh Blush Tea—and the other was much harder, it being a coffee. Like tea, coffee was said to have provenance. And like tea, coffee was said to have a perfect brewing time.

He sighed, taking the dark drink without recourse to any available additives. Those things confused the palate as much for coffee as for tea—and he'd been trying to get used to dealing with his food and drink as he might find it visiting in any honest home on Surebleak, where additives might be too expensive, or too chancy, for the hosts.

He sighed again with the first sip. Not, then, what Cousin Miri would hold up as Merc Super—Merc Standard being a coffeetoot still worthy of two or three of the poorer food stands a distance from the Road, and Merc Super being what happened when a Merc cook dumped real ground coffee into a pot and kept it at near boil for a day or two, so as to always be ready for a needy troop.

He settled, after a third sip, on Lankshire Lakes Bold. That was a half-cheat, though, and it made him wonder. He'd seen the new packs arriving several days earlier . . . but no, that's what it was. Results and answers were required of him, not explanations about how he arrived at his conclusions.

• • • ✧ • • •

HIS RIDE TODAY was to be Mr. McFarland, a man who was as much a pilot as anyone on the planet, as far as Quin could figure, a man with amazing patience and . . .

. . . he ought to be having breakfast now, too.

That eight-person "ready room" table where the Boss and his immediate hands often sat was empty.

He looked again, analyzing. It wasn't merely devoid of people, it was devoid of—everything. No set-up, no cups, no utensils. It had been cleared then, and not set for a morning snack or lunch yet.

Too, there was no sign of Natesa—called Natesa the Assassin by some, and called Boss Natesa by others, and called Lifemate by his father. He sighed at that, for worse than the "natural lifemating" that happened to some in his clan, where the universe and genes conspired to make two people into one as with Delm Val Con and Delm Miri, this lifemating of Natesa and Pat Rin was a voluntary thing, born out of . . . born out of he did not know what. That they admired each other was sure. He'd heard one of the Surebleak hands say that they "deserved each other" . . . and might be that was as good a reason they were together as any other.

Natesa had Boss duties of her own and so when the Boss was away she often sat solo at a table on the kitchen level above the half-stairs, like a cat with a perch of her own, overlooking the street through a gunslit converted to bulletproof window.

"You'll have more?"

Quin had heard the steps behind him, and recognized them, but he sat staring at McFarland's usual place at the empty table next to where his father often sat at morning council.

"Am I waiting for Mr. McFarland? He appears to have overslept."

"Nah, you know better, youngster. Overslept ain't like that man, and never was. That table's clear to supper or beyond. Cheever, he's with the Boss—the Port's decided to do their ship-station move early and they need all the pilots they have to . . ."

The coffee continued motion to his lips, the turn he'd begun to the cook's assistant never slowed. He nodded an acknowledgment of the news at her, his recent extra training at the knee of his grandmother serving him in good stead, his near smile still wedded to his face.

"Indeed? They needed pilots, did they? I wonder that I was not called . . ."

The assistant shrugged artlessly.

"Foo, Master Quin, how'd I know it? The messages come all in a rush while I was starting the bread oven to going; McFarland, the Boss, don't know who else called out. Oh, Ms. Natesa, she went. They'll let you know later, I'm sure—but might have been a Boss secret in it."

He finished his cup in a rush, which he knew better than to do, and looking into its depth he conceived a need to steady his face.

Him a pilot, and not called. His lessons, his plans all put aside. Clearly the duty-day schedule was wiped. . . .

He fumbled for words, seething, his stomach fighting him momentarily, then a need to not move, for if he did get up now he'd run all the way to the tree. Best to stay here, in the seat, to pin himself to this place.

He covered the fumble with a cough smothered in a napkin, followed by downing the last of his juice. He must not run!

Breath caught, he managed to gain time to think.

"More of this exact coffee, Jennetta, if I can, and yes, if I'm not on call, some of what's hot, sausages and spuds and rolls bashed with butter!"

"Why, that sounds like an honest breakfast for a change, don't it? It'll take a minute."

The servant dashed away, pleased, and he could hear her trading the news in the kitchen, "that boy's hungry today, without answering quiz-questions of the Boss and company for a change . . ."

Normally he'd be put out of humor to hear himself called "that boy," but he let it pass. He was practicing what Grandmother called appropriate restraint.

Grandmother. Well, yes, she and Grandfather had been firm while they were off on Runig's Rock—studies along with gun training, studies of card-games and card-skill, studies along with security work, studies along with ship-sitting. Studies . . . they'd had no moment for ruminations, that they had seen to.

He stared at but didn't see the table for some moments, memory returning to that haven, to the days when he had been the best pilot available and the clan's last hope if the enemy had come to them.

He went weak—he'd brought the ship out of there, he had, Runig's Rock under attack, Padi backing him up and . . .

And here he sat, while pilots were needed? What did they think, that he'd forgotten how to fly? What secret could be more precious than a cargo of the clan's last children? What . . .

But Grandmother had schooled him well, and to any observer still in the house his face was as unconcerned and uncomplicated as that of any simple day laborer on Wall-down duty.

"But here, Master Quin," came Jennetta's carrying voice well before her appearance from the kitchen, "there's a note left for you—for personal delivery at breakfast, the driver said."

She held it out for him with one hand, juggling a perilously filled bowl of rolls, a dish of butter, and a jam jar in the other before precariously bringing them successfully to table.

Dear Grandson, the note said in impeccable Liaden longhand. It was a familiar hand—not surprising, since Luken bel'Tarda, his grandfather, was quite fond of sending notes and letters and signed books—*Boss Conrad's business is quite pressing today and he has commandeered your driver and your pilot-mentor, and deputized myself and many others, likely for the whole of the day. I consulted with the Boss, who feels it is perhaps best for you to stay busy—and that rather than staying in house and being bored or joining me at Ms Audrey's, where I am involved with delicate negotiations, that you relocate for the day to The Emerald Casino and find occupation there. You will await the Boss, who will meet you there as time permits.*

To call upon the casino for refreshments or a private parlor, merely show your dragon pin and say your name, and they'll have a scanner that will read your credentials.

You'll find Jemie's Cab Service is awaiting a call from you at your earliest convenience.

Text and subtext—whatever the Boss was doing was important, too important to share with the inexperienced. Too important for a note even from the Boss—his grandfather'd taken the informant role upon himself. Yes, Grandfather was a kinder man than his father, and more alert in some ways, too.

Perhaps unwisely he chugged the not half-full cup of coffee.

Jennetta, alert as she returned with the rest of his food, rushed to refill his cup, face full of smiles.

"Oh, good, I'm so glad you like it. We have a lot of it, and the tea bin got damp when the sink backed up. You'll be set for weeks!"

He nodded absently at her, wishing he was alone, or maybe doing the perimeter tour on Runig's Rock, one more time.

This cup of coffee was hotter, so he sipped it, scanned the food. Yes, he'd eat his breakfast and take his time; no reason to upset the staff by being short with them. *They* were not the ones ignoring him, *they* were not the ones forgetting his place in the family, *they* were not the ones forgetting his role in the clan!

Yes, he'd wait for the Boss . . . they had a lot to talk about.

He was basically dressed well enough for a daytime casino visit on Surebleak, of that he felt certain. First, of course, he'd need to call the taxi, and then, of course, select his jacket—and perhaps better jewelry, too, if his father was going to meet him there. Oh, and surely he'd not need snow-lugs at the Emerald Casino, if he was going by taxi, so he'd wear some better boots—at least his grandfather or grandmother might notice that he was somewhat dressed for society.

Halfway up the stairs he knew what jacket he'd wear, and so, which boots.

• • •✧• • •

VILLY BUTLER threw the sticks across the polished table, wrist snap sharp and accurate. *Palaz Dwaygo* sticks tumbled together in what he'd been taught to call a bar-galaxy, the kind of jumble that produced good betting and plenty of room for mischance. This was a setup ideal for a challenge match—if he'd been playing House against it—well—he would. Good practice.

Studying the lay he posted two plastic practice chips on the bet line. Being the *Stro Palaz*, he added a blue to his, then to defense, and continued.

The morning was good for playing against the house and for the house, there being very few patrons in the casino at all and none yet wandering his end of the main hall.

The basic card players—they were a constant, like the dicers and the endless staccatos at the robot machines, and might be found round the clock, betting on a better tomorrow. The sticks players, like the roulettiers, tended to come in with the flow of traffic to and from the port. A busy day on port usually was a good thing, with the buzz of voices and the buzz of action.

Today—the whole place felt muted. The low-key morning music found few bodies to bounce off, none to excite to dance rhythm, none to inspire to sing along, none to drop coins or call for chips. The Emerald's automatics took care of sound levels and air-moving these days. Maybe if he coughed a few times he could prime a little energy into the place.

It was the weather, of course—the weather was good and the port's long-awaited changeover to new systems and orientation had been started in the overnight, with the advent of the good weather.

The weather and the port noise together could have put him to sleep if he'd not been scheduled here, though the night had been light.

Villy smiled, though he'd taken a financial hit—his late date at Ms. Audrey's had called off the tumble at nearly the last minute. At least it had been nearly the last; he hadn't lit the candles or started the oil warming or set out all the toys. He was sorry to lose the cash but the pilot promised him a bonus for the next time, to make up for what he'd called "opportunity costs."

There'd be opportunity costs today, too, it looked like—with no action, there'd be no tips.

In front of him, the sticks. Villy pulled seven . . . and then there was a slip.

Frowning, he added a chip to each side . . . and became the other player in the hand . . . and . . . sensed something, perhaps a shadow, moving.

The shadow half-behind him was a Liaden, silent, precise, watching. His boots were pilot boots, as Villy had learned. The jacket was a pilot's jacket. The gun was a little bright, but if he was a pilot he'd have more than one, for sure.

He looked too young for a Scout, though he might have been—Villy had trouble figuring Liaden ages, smooth-skinned and beardless as they were—but he wore a pilot's jacket and earrings rich enough to be a pilot of some experience or note.

But the jacket, worn loose, showed a local shirt and hint of glitter near the throat and the hair was looser and longer than he'd expect.

That was mixed signals, it was, and Ms. Audrey warned staff to watch for mixed signals at the House and he guessed the same mattered here at his share job. Something might be up and worth watching careful.

He weighed the pilot's looks, realized that he was closing in on staring, though the seeing was good.

"Pilot," he said with one of the careful nodding bows he'd learned from Cheever McFarland. "Are you interested in a game?"

Villy got back so exact a copy of his bow, with a hint of the lookover he'd been guilty of, and he wondered if he was being mocked. The face showed a firmness he was becoming used to among the Liadens he dealt with; in fact it could be of the same mold as Boss Conrad or the Keeper of the Road. Alert blue eyes reading his moves and face while giving back little enough. There was, maybe, a very little hint of an ironic smile. It made him feel, that look did, as if the observer had an advantage, and knew it, or had seen him looking a trifle long. The Boss himself had a look like that.

Still, Villy had experience looking at men; this one was interesting, nearly tempting. Perhaps there was advantage on two sides if they should play a throw or two.

"A game?" The voice was polished, with that Liaden lilt, and Villy held his sigh back. Perfect, even spoken in Terran with the slightest edge of a Surebleak click.

"Perhaps I will game later, but not immediately, no. I meant not to distract you, but rather to watch your practice."

"Watching a game as you participate is a wonderful way to learn," Villy offered, seeing the suppressed grin flit across the pilot's comely golden face. "Are you familiar with the game?"

Villy swept the practice sticks up, half-looking to the pilot, and was startled when the jumble revealed an escaping blue, which he let go rather than risk the bundle. The blue was snapped out of the air by the pilot well before it reached the floor.

In a single motion the stick was returned to him with a bow of some complexity.

"Indeed, V. Butler, I have some experience of it. It was wise of you not to attempt that recovery."

V. Butler—Ah, his name badge. Pilots were sharp . . .

"I'm Villy Butler. And for this game, I am *Stro Palaz*, you know, Game Master, for the morning. To keep that, I gotta practice. This is a practice tube—for the games, we have *Palaz Dwaygo* Solcintra-style, with the standard thirty-six, with colors; else we have the local Quick-sticks, same length but light weight, twenty-five plus the pick-stick. The other tubes are sealed, and . . ."

"The Boss offers choice. I should have known."

"Of course the Boss offers choice! Why, the . . ."

But that quick, the pilot's hand rose in a sign Villy almost knew, and he said, "Peace, Villy Butler. If the Boss says it, so must it be, eh?"

Villy held his retort back, offering now a tube of each sort.

Again a mystery bow, this time with a bit more of a smile.

"Perhaps when there's more action, my friend, if I am here that long. I'm . . ."

Here it was as if the pilot was at a sudden standstill for words, as if his Terran had failed him. He went on—

"I'm to meet someone here," he said, "regarding occupation."

Then he shrugged, adding, "They could not tell me when they will arrive with any precision, other than today. I am, so to speak, at their convenience, as time permits. So, let me explore—the last time I was here there was no time to acquaint myself with the facilities—and perhaps I'll play if I have time."

Villy accepted a kind of half-bow, collecting the sticks carefully while watching the pilot move on, steps coordinated and silent. Well then, the morning wasn't half-wasted, after all. Practice, with a view.

• • •✧• • •

QUIN AMBLED AWAY FROM the comely young Game Master, by habit acquainting and reacquainting himself with obvious exits, likely exits, and potential exits, as well as the permanent staff stations, the rest rooms, the doors to the private parlors. Off to one side, he knew, was the private room where staff had "held" the delm on their first visit. As if *they'd* be "held" by anything as flimsy as the port's *real* hoosegow, much less a room with a lock on the plastic door.

The casino was remarkably devoid of patrons this morning, a mere dozen or so scattered throughout.

A careful appraisal revealed nearly as many visible staff as customers, which was well enough, for it permitted him a good look at the results of the recent upgrade. The lighting was more subdued than the last time he'd seen it; the seating improved, the flooring more resilient and sound absorbing. He'd heard discussions of the aromatics, mood lights, and sounds supplied by a nerligig sitting in a repurposed closet—as the room filled, the music and scents would strengthen and the lighting would become more focused on the equipment, allowing patrons the feeling that they were not cram-full and reinforcing the reason they were there—to gamble.

Quin received nods of apparent recognition from several of the staff, as well as a few customers. A passing Scout accorded him a cordial bow, and he got two profuse pairs of bows from elderly Liaden gallants in last year's Solcintran afternoon wear.

The two gallants, now. He'd seen them, elsewhere, together. The first image came to him as he demanded it. Yes, the memory games Grandmother had taught on station were working! He saw the gallants now in his head, more than their faces, distantly sipping from crystal glasses at Trealla Fantrol, politely bowing to Uncle Shan. He . . . he must have barely been in public then.

Emigres, then, distant allies of Korval, coming to one of the few places on Surebleak with even a remotely Liaden tang to it.

Quin paused, wondering how many other such there were now on world, and how many arriving, wondering what more they could do here but stand in the wake of pilots. Here there were no Liaden clubs, no Tey Dor's to shoot and be seen at, no promenade, no . . .

Truth, he missed Tey Dor's himself, as rarely as he'd been there—so many stories of his clan echoed there, so many stories of yos'Phelium . . . so many of his father. He missed it not only because of the utility of practice and competition, but for the society of it.

He moved on, completing his tour. There wasn't much more to see. The Emerald might be the best casino on planet, but it was still a smaller operation than one would find on most port city peripheries elsewhere in the galaxy.

He sighed as he stood in front of a row of the robot bet-offs, having no pressing interest there. On the other hand, several of the card tables were peopled, and he moved into observe . . .

Alas, the occupied tables backed on a closed section, there being no need to spread out. Ah, well, no close-up spectating this way, which was a shame. Quin looked about him. The wheels now . . . the gambling wheels usually permitted . . .

His scan took in the back of the room, where V. Butler was earnestly practicing the sticks.

A glance to the chronometer over the service counter showed him . . . that the clock was artfully sited to receive as much glare as possible, and thus was difficult to read.

He flipped his hand through several iterations of the pilot sign *no details yet* to himself. He took three steps forward, and now the clock was visible, but no real help.

The clock told him nothing: as ever, he didn't know when his father would arrive. He didn't know what was to be discussed. He didn't know. . . .

The same often maintained at his new home: the Boss would arrive when he did, unless he'd stayed in working in his office, which he often did; sometimes he'd be held from dinner or lunch, or breakfast by some or another strangeness, sometimes he'd come to table a few minutes after his Natesa arrived and sometimes with her—

and no time either, for Quin, no matter that he'd been warned to expect real duty, any day now. He'd been told the move from undertree was to train him to be Boss. To be Boss!

So here he stood while the real work of the Boss was going on within view of the front door.

Quin grimaced, ruefully pleased that Grandmother wasn't there to see him with his face so open. A pilot's quick relaxation exercise brought him some calm, but still—

What he *should do* was flash his Tree-and-Dragon, demand a quiet place to sit, and study. There were still unfinished lesson modules from TriGrace he could access, and there was always piloting math to . . .

He felt the anger rising again, then.

No.

His father had sent him here. Or his father and Natesa. Or the Boss and his grandfather. They'd *sent him here* while there was work to be done, *piloting work* . . . and they'd sent him to the Emerald. For occupation.

Very well then. If he was to wait at the Emerald and be occupied there, if he was to wait "as time permits," he would damn well *be* occupied.

Oh yes, he would.

• • •✧• • •

HE MADE A DESULTORY RUN at a console card sim picked randomly; it burbled game choices until he stabbed the button rapidly to change languages, annoyed by the thing's terribly accented Trade. The hands were fast, but his coin was multiplied several times, and he challenged the machine to games and to languages, making it speak to him in homeworld Terran, and then in what it thought was Looper Terran, just for the practice.

Someone else was playing nearby, and apparently losing, for he heard what might have been the slam of disappointed hand on console.

His public pocket had been nearly to let when he'd started—in his sudden preparations he hadn't bothered to arm himself with Terran bits above what he normally carried. Now he had a game card . . .

which he stuffed into that pocket, starting another. He'd heard a machine on the other side of the aisle make the *player out of funds* sound, and someone sighed, loudly.

The console card game was flat, though he was winning. Despite his practice of two calming mental exercises he still felt an undercurrent of tension which he couldn't resolve—and it didn't help that the casino was hardly soundproof, so the action at the spaceport rumbled through from time to time. He stood up straighter, remembering that he was a pilot, dammit, and not a school child, and moved down the aisle, waiting on the pleasure of his elders and stalking opportunity here.

He walked, cringing at some of the front panels, and moved by a machine calling itself "Target Practice" as numbers on a multiplier panel jumped from two to seven. There, the promise of an extra seven times payout—why not? It was denominated in half-bits, which amused, and so he stopped to play.

Given the images of weapons, he chose the personal models, and then the rarities . . .

The machine took a fair portion of his earnings quickly, but he played with the choices of caliber, style, and targets. On the fifth run he threw his hand-arm against a longshot, and was rewarded with a slowly rising whoop of machine joy, which gave way to . . . *oh*! He'd hit that shot, at seven times the stake, with a red bonus. The bonus matched his original stake and—on screen—appeared as piles of energy packs. The multiplier was still in effect and the totals kept rising and voices announced he was into triple bonus round. He'd already won quite a bit—wouldn't his father be amused to discover he'd come away with a cantra? There was some amount of money in reserve, he wouldn't know how much until the next round.

Now he had to choose his weapons again.

He laughed, chose a silly looking zero-gravity dueling pistol, and touched the machine to urge it on. Targets began to arise.

• • •✧• • •

SOMEONE WAS STANDING close by, and then started playing the game next to his. Ah, searching for the lucky spot, no doubt. Well. No matter.

His machine blinked and brightened—now the multiplier was showing an even dozen!

Quin laughed again, for there were a dozen targets to chose from on the machine, all valuable gems on distant pedestals. Well, all gems but for the gaudy necklace of pearled firegems with a firegem pendant—so he chose that, and palmed the trigger button.

The machine's antics were amusing as the pistol lined up on screen and a single bullet entered the firing chamber through a ghostly hand. Then it asked hm to choose windage and loft and if the pistol pulled high or to the right or . . .

His choices were random, and he pressed the shoot button.

The machine dutifully mimicked a supposed shooting sound and showed his shot traveling . . . arcing very neatly to hit the blazing firegem pendant full on.

The firegem spun in its virtual spot, spitting fire! Dancing from the flames were numbers, and each number accompanied by a beep, or a horn, or the flash of light or color, and sometimes all . . .

It was amazing, and then appalling.

Quin took a half-step back as the sound continued and numbers ran, all in bits. He translated as best he could to the latest approximation in cantra as the numbers ran on . . . and then halted.

Had it actually come to a cantra? Well, more or less, since the exchange rate varied. Still . . . maybe more than a cantra!

Quin saw the screen reform into a fire-rimmed challenge:

"Double or Nothing, sharpshooter?" it asked.

It took no time to decide *that* question.

Quin cashed out, waiting patiently for the card to clear, then holding it in hand a moment.

Around him now, others—staring at the machine. A casino employee came by, nodded brusquely.

"Done with this session, sir?"

"I am," Quin bowed, stuffing the chit into his public pocket with the other.

"Need security?"

It was not a silly question on a world like Surebleak, and if he'd needed a ride to quarters he'd not have been behind with the request. . . .

"I do not."

"My turn," a Terran voice demanded, but the security man said, "Hold, friend," and waved a portable read-wand at the machine. "We have to take records of the major wins, you know. Just a moment."

The machine blinked, chattered, rebooted into brightness—and the multiplier lights fell from 12 to 1.2.

The man beside him made noises—a local by the hard-worn looks of him—and he stared at the machine, a low continuous stream of cussing going on.

"My run," he was muttering, "shoulda been my run!"

• • • ✧ • • •

QUIN STOOD, surveying the rest of the casino distantly. *Not* another robot game at this point, especially not with the burly Terran already busy shoving funds into Target Practice . . .

Well. The cards were in progress, but perhaps not those, either—he'd chosen the robogames because leaving would be easy, when the Boss arrived.

The sticks—Villy seemed a pleasant enough table host. That was an idea now that he had enough cash to buy a bundle or two. By now there might be a game there—or he could start one.

His steps led that way, and there was Villy, packing his practice sticks away one by one. At tableside was a Terran as badly dressed as the one he'd just left behind, hulking, and apparently waiting.

The sticksman now was presenting two tubes to the newcomer, who was larger even than Mr. McFarland, very pale, and extravagantly overdressed unless one had never before been challenged to meet the mere freezing point of water.

Quin moved forward, hand motioning his desire to buy in.

• • • ✧ • • •

THE PRETTY PILOT was back, which was a relief. The *'reesta*, meanwhile, was either a fool or a fraud; could anyone really be that unaware of the way things worked in a casino after having been in the Emerald hours at a time these past five days? Well, Villy'd never had him at *this* station, but he had seen him and his crony about, hanging at the low robots for long stretches and sometimes drifting to the cheap cards. It was hard to miss men so unused to Surebleak's weather, or so willing to play the cheap games.

And so Villy'd explained that if the man played *him* at the base rate that he, Villy, would represent the House directly . . . yet the man was still confused about the difference between the casino, the House, Villy and . . .

The pilot arrived, looked to the man and then to Villy—

"Has a bundle been purchased? Is there a game building? May I join?"

"No decision there, Pilot, while deciding's going on," Villy managed respectfully, adding, "would you like to consult over choices? Would you care to challenge or be challenged?"

Villy hopefully held a tube of each kind toward the pilot, who bowed acknowledgment and turned to the overdressed newcomer.

"Surely anyone can see that the Solcintran style is superior for the player of quality and experience. The extra sticks make the game more difficult, and played for color, there's considerable complexity! The Quick-sticks are light fare. They are perhaps adequate for someone passing time on the port while expecting a flight, or waiting to be joined by a companion."

Villy absorbed these words, offered in Terran, and held them to him: the pilot was young, not much older than Villy himself—despite which he was a man with good sense and excellent understanding. These words, repeated wisely, were worth bits in Villy's pocket in the future, surely.

"Obviously you see yourself as superior with the *Liaden-style,*" the tourist said accusingly—Villy thought of him as The Coat, for the purple and red-striped garment he wore—"but I'm willing to play a game and try them out. Name low stakes, sir, and I'll try your choice."

• • •✧• • •

THE PILOT SLID HIS HAND into his public pocket and pulled out a handful of Terran change, looking to Villy with a slight smile.

"Let me see what I carry, sir—perhaps I'll have my lunch money made into chips. I suppose we should start low, to find a range."

"Lunch money? Hah! They feed you here, if you win!"

"As luck favors," the pilot murmured. He nodded to Villy and stepped away, toward the bank.

• • • •✧• • •

THE PILOT WAS AS GOOD as his word, returning to buy the first bundle with a five-pale chip and offering his opponent "Five pales to start, if you like, for the first game."

Villy had quick eyes—the five pales the pilot offered were matched by one in his hand. Villy worried briefly—perhaps the ten *had been* all the money the pilot owned?

The other player laughed; it was an ugly sound compared to the pilot's voice, and it faded into an ugly smile filled with ugly, multicolored teeth. His coat stank of smoke and a hint of old vaya and sweat, and the striped sleeves waved gracelessly and then fluttered as he moved his meaty hands in emphasis.

"Sure, why not get our fingers warmed up before we throw money at Lady Luck?"

Villy looked around but saw no such lady. Lucks—formal, paid Lucks that is, people whose mere presence was said to change fortune for others—were specifically not permitted at the Emerald. The rule was clearly posted!

The pilot bowed, acknowledging a witticism, "I'll buy the second tube," which was only fair.

"Shall you twist, or shall I?"

The pilot thus offered choice of first throw—but that was a Solcintran habit, Villy'd learned—and twisted the tube with a sharp snap, breaking the seal as his opponent waved him to it.

With the game joined, Villy stepped back.

Like the man's voice, the throw was ugly. The table strike was awkward, with sticks bouncing rather than spreading naturally, and the clicks of the late-falls were ragged rather than rhythmic. Villy held his face close, but not as close as the pilot, who might have not seen anything amiss but the blandness. Meanwhile, The Coat nodded and smiled, as if everything was exactly like he wanted it.

At this juncture, Villy's job was as spotter—with the aid of the back-up camera, of course, if anybody called foul.

He watched carefully as The Coat's first three lifts went well. His technique seemed to require small motions over tortuous amounts of time, and both squinting and special breathing, not to mention craning his neck for the best view angle. Despite the second lift—using a dangerous leverage technique—he seemed in control. The fourth—no need for a camera there—the bobble was significant, clearly moving three other sticks and quickly admitted with an under-voiced curse.

The pilot . . . was completely at ease as his turn started, in fact so at ease that he appeared to have no technique at all to his pick-ups—no special breaths, no extreme staring or checking of angles, and Villy sighed when the rest of that pile was done at about the time The Coat was muttering, "Remarkable!"

The pilot nodded, glanced into the large man's face and offered, "Another then, at the same rates, to see if Lady Luck walks by?"

• • • ✧ • • •

THE PILOT, having collected his fifth straight round-up, sighed gently. The Coat had been becoming louder, and twice had asked for screen-checks of pick-ups that were flawless. He'd insisted on doubling the bets after the third course, and had taken a moment's break for some sort of meditative breathwork Villy didn't recognize. Even after the break his attempts were growing less fluid, and taking absurdly long—in fact, the pilot might have called foul, so long had one taken.

Villy was beginning to worry. The pilot was . . . very good, and Villy was supposed to watch out for pros, or for Sharps, roving gamblers looking for the less skilled to fleece. He hoped the pilot wasn't a Sharp—in fact, if he wasn't losing so bad, he'd have taken The Coat for a Sharp on actions alone . . .

The pilot's left hand held the sticks and he gently tapped the ends into his free right palm.

"The matter seems not to be one of dispute, sir. The game is hardly a gamble for me unless we go to handicaps, and I'm not one to play . . ."

Villy breathed a little easier—maybe the pilot was *not* a roving gambler in search of a victim but a man looking for some relaxation and play. . . .

"Wait, no, if you really were playing your lunch money, now you're playing with *my* money. I'll buy a new tube and we'll play at real rates—and we'll have a coin flip to decide which style tube! I see how you play, like it means nothing to you. Stopping now means you've tugged me wrong! You've put me on!"

Villy stepped forward, the rising animosity in The Coat's demeanor concerning.

"Sir, your opponent has suggested that more play would be unfair to you. I think that's a sign that . . ."

The pilot reached into his public pocket, showing his winnings.

"These few chips mean I've tugged you wrong? I think you do not know what it is to be tugged wrong, sir. But so, we'll play on, if you insist. I promise to concentrate, if that will permit you to concentrate."

Villy grimaced. The Coat seemed not to take the same sense from that last bit that Villy did . . . Still, there'd been discussion and agreement, and not an argument. That was good, he thought.

• • •✧• • •

QUIN RAN THE PILOT'S RAINBOW as the sticks came to his hand, and his throw was good: There was a complex stack to work with, and the bottom of the pile richer than the top. The purple crossed the blue under the red—good point value there.

"Thus we'll play for twenty-five pales plus five up for each color up the rungs?"

The Coat looked at the pile and nodded, "Your call. I now reserve to match for any runs of over one hundred."

The pilot bowed, the minor tic of a smile at one corner of his mouth, and glanced around before giving an almost Terran shrug and taking position.

• • •✧• • •

VILLY HAD NOTICED already what the pilot saw: Several passersby had become witness and audience, and another was moving closer. There seemed to be more people in the Emerald now, some of them workmen he recognized from frequent lunchtime play, one he knew as a functionary recently added to the port roster; a sometime client of his, from Audrey's. He'd be the third in the gallery . . .

• • •✧• • •

THE SOUND OF THE STICKS absently tapped on end before the throw brought his eyes to the table, and there, the flash of color, and an admirable spread.

Villy settled back to watch, and indeed, the pilot did seem more intent now. His concentration had improved, his hand-motions were more precise. He was also, Villy thought, he was purposefully—yes. There it was. There was a delay that Villy measured as *one two three four, one two three four* between pickups. If it was designed to distract, annoy, or to aid concentration, he couldn't guess.

In any case, the throw was run, and the pilot, intent, looked into the eyes of his opponent, who had remained silent.

"Shall I continue? Same?"

The chips moved, and it was so—the pilot went on. The tube was run again and once more . . .

The pilot looked up, first at Villy, then at The Coat.

Without hesitation he continued to pick up as he spoke . . .

"When I finish this run, you'll have a match of two hundred sticks. That will suffice for me. When your run is over, I'll break for lunch."

The run continued, smoothly, and just shy of mechanically. The cadence continued, and colors and angle were of no moment as those smooth hands worked.

Indeed, the pilot picked up his two hundredth stick, and then the five remaining on table he rolled under his hand carelessly, on purpose.

"Yours!"

That was awful familiar—that show of self-assured arrogance. In fact Villy thought he'd once—only once!—seen Boss Conrad do the same thing, right at this table. He did it to a guy who'd been bad-mouthing the Emerald as a back-water bar, and the Boss had shown the guy exactly the way the game was played, taking him down five rounds in a row.

Villy smiled at that. The Boss was busy these days and he didn't get to see him often.

But at the table now, The Coat was sweating and seething.

"Ruin a run to show off? You'll destroy your luck for sure! I've got you now!"

There was a murmur from the onlookers . . .

The audience was grown to nearly a dozen, two-thirds of them native Terran, a reasonable gallery for a busy day, but for this one, it meant other parts of the casino were empty because they were watching the show here.

He'd hear from the floor boss about that—he should have by now called for the drink-dancer. Easy enough, he touched the collar stud to call her. Someone besides the pilot ought to be making money . . .

"These have been working," The Coat said to Villy—"and now they owe revenge. We'll continue!"

The crowd grew closer and thicker and the sticks chittered when they were thrown. The Coat was hanging close to them now, muttering, staring, measuring with hand motions, leading his moves with dips of the shoulder, but moving more rapidly, also, as if he'd learned some lesson from the pilot's measured movements.

Around them whispered bets for and against The Coat, Liadens offering more against The Coat than for, their odds in dozens while the Terrans did tens and fifties.

Oblivious, The Coat ran three tubes flawlessly and there were payouts in the crowd for passing the hundred, for passing the third tube, for . . .

Then a very difficult lay, with several balance points at risk. The crowd hushed, and Villy's eyes went to the camera views for close-up.

On another day he might have thought he saw a movement, but if he did, the pilot's eyes nor the crowd's had seen it, and the play went forward. The next two pickups were easier, and the—

The slip this time was perceptible to all, and led to a slow cataclysm of rolling, sliding sticks. The watchers watched, began to mumble, mutter, or laugh depending on their stakes in the matter, and the Terran seemed to deflate within his coat, the color going out of his face.

The pilot bowed then, first to Villy, and then to The Coat.

"Your time is up, sir. My play at the sticks is done for the day . . ."

The pilot's bow and meaning was unmistakable.

"But wait—you have to give me a chance to . . ."

Several others were coming forward as if to fill the void left by the pilot. The Coat's face was red, and he turned, one hand going out as if to reach for the pilot. Villy turned his back to the large man and gestured with his hands to the crowd, effectively thwarting the move.

"The tube's run," Villy announced with as much gravity as he could muster, "And," he said, very loudly, "this is my mandatory coffee break!"

That was enough to bring the nearest marked security sliding in from opposite sides of the room—"mandatory coffee break" being the week's code words for potential problem customer—but by then the crowd was in motion, many following the pilot toward his next station.

"Coffee break!" roared The Coat into the rapidly thinning crowd. "I'll tell you what. You owe me for breaking my chance here. It was *my turn* to win. Let me play you! I want your game!"

"Coffee break," Villy insisted. "I can't!"

"Look," The Coat said to approaching team, pointing toward Villy, "this guy ought to be playing me now! He owes me a shot to get my money back!"

Villy ignored the man, gathering the tubes into their lockbin and ostentatiously turning the key over to the uniforms.

"Coffee break," Security insisted mercilessly. "Play continues later."

• • •✧• • •

QUIN TOOK SEVERAL STEPS away, then turned, meaning to tip the Game Master, but that worthy was already chatting profusely with Security and heading off to one of the backrooms. The man who'd had too much money stood staring after him.

Quin sighed—that was a connection he wanted to sever. Coffee break meant that Villy Butler would be back at his station eventually and Quin could tip him later. Quin offered himself a pilot's loose *return at will* hand-motion and—

He hesitated, thinking to take a brief break among the robots, and perhaps have a snack . . .

Who *were* these people? Somehow he'd gained a cometary tail of gamblers and followers, something he hadn't expected. Seeing he'd paused, with neither bowing nor intro, the following Terrans started in . . .

• • •✧• • •

"PILOT, good hands there!"

"Luck's with you—saw you at the spinners!"

"Oh, don't run—play's better here than that—he's a fluke and a hanger—saw him here yesternight begging play with his betters."

The locals, there were at least two, judging by accent, were less flattering.

"Shouldn'a wasted nowits time, and poor Villy outta the play, too, and dem chisletoes got the fingers of a branch-bumbling charcoal grubber."

Quin suppressed a grin on that one. That was close enough to calling the man a lackwitted fool as to make no matter—if the man only heard it to know it.

Uncomfortably close to his side now was someone he'd noticed before—one of the gallants unofficially attending the Scout. It struck him that the Scout, like him, spoke Liaden, and that the gallants might after all be lonely for the sound of home, in a place where Liaden was heard, but was hardly universal, and where etiquette sometimes meant stepping aside quickly to the implied demand of, "Coming through!"

A bow, and a murmured comment from that gallant.

"Pilot, your *melant'i* shows very well there. Continued play would be an affront to anyone of skill or breeding."

"Yes," Quin agreed, probably rather short, and his bow of acknowledgment even shorter. He desperately wracked his brain for the gallant's name or clan, but lacking—well, they were not on Liad, and he could walk on.

Two Terrans intercepted him now—

"Pilot, are you up to *our* challenge? Will you return to the sticks after the coffee break?"

The gallant began to say something more, but another Terran arrived, "Please, join me in a game. I'm sure that I'll offer more play and . . ."

The cometary tail had become a group, and he bowed a *no, thank you*, which was lost among the unseemly Terran waving and the voices.

"I am done with sticks for today," he said. "Clearly there's no competition."

"No competition? How can you say . . ."

Exasperated, Quin fought the Terran/Liaden/Trade interface, finally summing up with a rush.

"I have done sticks and am not beaten. I came to meet someone, and that is what I will do."

The noise continued, and one near his elbow was asking . . .

He raised his voice again, to reach the challengers at the far side who were calling out to him, "Pilot, you must play. Luck's running you but I can beat you!"

"Quiet! This is not luck. It appears I can beat anyone in the casino at will and . . ."

The buzz about him had fallen silent at his command, and now the entire room was watching him. The hidden nerligig amplified the silence, and then the rhythm of his words, producing new music, with power.

The gallant at his side was twittering over something, and the purposeful march of a leather-coated figure split his field of vision.

"Pilot," said the Scout he'd seen before, "you impugn all of us as lacksters and amateurs with such an attitude. I'll grant you the sticks—they're of little matter. Now, best of five at any station, or until you're out of funds, if you dare."

He had, of course, meant any challenge at sticks. He'd not meant to take on the casino. But this, this . . .

He laughed, allowing a smile to remain on his face. *If I dare!*

"Of course, *I dare*," he said, "at any station you name. Until you give up, or until necessity calls me away. I await occupation."

She looked him up and down, took in his boots, and then his public gun.

"'At will,' Pilot, that's what you said. Best of five. How about piket?"

"Piket? Fine. That will be occupation enough."

• • • ✧ • • •

VILLY WATCHED ON THE MONITORS while he ate and sipped coffee, hoping that the pilot hadn't fled after the rudeness at the sticks board—but he'd said he'd come to meet someone, and as far as Villy could tell, he hadn't yet. Sounded like the pilot was looking for a job. The casino was often used as a meet spot these days, the local restaurants and rooming houses weren't nearly up to the style some of the newcomers preferred. Ms. Audrey was even renting out parlors to some of the larger job searchers during the day, and had cut down on the perfumes in them since Liadens preferred rooms not quite so fancy smelling.

The pilot though, he'd gone off in a hurry. Maybe he had been risking all his blunt and needed to count up before coming back to the fray . . .

In fact, there he was, which relieved Villy greatly. He and Scout dea'Liss were at piket with two side players, and whatever crowd the Emerald had were mostly assembled to watch. Hardly found that stuff in the daytimes, but a good crowd was worth money later, when everyone broke to play or challenge . . .

Villy grabbed a last sip of his coffee—one of the perks of the job was as much coffee as you wanted—and stood, catching camera fourteen's angle.

It was a good close-up of his pilot, a good one. Serious face, strong more than cute, good ears and chin—and Liaden, which Villy was coming to appreciate greatly, since among other things beard burns were a real issue for someone in his regular line of work.

Well, his loss again. He wasn't allowed to pass a business card or referral for Ms. Audrey's when he was on duty here, not less he was directly asked. And the pilot hadn't asked. Good gambler—concentrated, had firm fine hands and a steady eye.

He flashed his thumbs over the reader and took a deep breath. Villy Butler, back on duty. Just an hour more and the rest of the day was his.

• • •✧• • •

THERE WERE DISTRACTIONS Quin hadn't counted on, ranging from the smell of food—he turned down several trays on his way to the table, wanting only to get on with this challenge—to the motions and small sounds of the other patrons. The music and the other background sounds provided by the closeted nerligig helped. The establishment was using not Tey Dor's hallowed and time-tested undersounds, meant for refined Liaden gentlemen, but a rough mix meant to give patrons some small relief from the bustle of the port.

Nor was the Scout unaccomplished. Her game was considered, her demeanor flawless, and her gallants far more nervous than she. It was a good thing, he decided, that they watched from behind her—he'd hate to be concerned over double watching while playing someone with real skill. He was slightly amused by their choice of beverage and wondered if it was economy or curiosity which drove them to drinking the local beer. But there, if they were transplants of reduced means, they might yet need develop that taste—some of immigrants from Solcintra had come with their luggage, their names, and nothing more.

As it was, the cards were keeping most of his attention; for the third hand in a row he was being forced to play defensively. He had experience there—at Runig's Rock they'd played hand after hand of piket while waiting for news that Plan B was over. Grandfather and Grandmother were both resourceful players, and they told his mistakes over and again, not out of vanity but out of necessity. Who knew but that he'd have to take up his father's occupation when this was over? Who knew then, but that he'd be *the* yos'Phelium?

So far, none of the hands had gotten exorbitant, he had held off her rather obvious first hand attempt at a Clan Royale though it meant having to settle for barely above even Dozen's Lot in the first, she discarding judiciously to avoid either a Scout's Progress or a Triple Flash and thus taking that hand on a simple extra seven.

This hand was looking much like the last. He barely registered the added sounds of shoes and boots until it too went to an extra seven—this in his favor.

"Two hands to one," she said as the cards went to her. "You play well for a pilot with a such a new jacket . . ."

He failed to rise to the bait, though some of the crowd chuckled, and he saw there were indeed more than before, and wished they'd thought to call for a private parlor. There were Scouts and other pilots in the group, some back with handwiches, and before the deal two more tables got underway.

He glanced quickly about—perhaps the port work was done?

No sign, yet, of his father, and none either of Mr. McFarland or Natesa the Assassin. There was, he saw, Villy Butler, now in a flattering coat and wearing no name badge, on the edge of the crowd, a spectator. Yes, there were more folks about, so the shifts were changing, and there'd be more people still if he recalled schedules right.

Quin looked to his resources, wondered if perhaps he'd been being too conservative. He ought to have come out far ahead so far, two hands up, he ought to have been more active. The blush of challenge was worn well away now, he could tell, and he felt the edge that he'd had in the first game and that serenity in the second had fled. A pilot's relaxation drill then, and the hand came to him.

He settled in, and the hand became a disaster in short order, the cards falling into something he'd be lucky to force into a Small Cluster or a Nebularity to keep her away from . . . the ship sounds from outside had faded and the sounds of boots and mumbling around. He heard a whispered voice, "That pilot said he can beat anyone in the casino at will . . ."

The whisper was shushed about then, his glance showing Villy Butler in the area, still. Quin took up his cards, looked into them, and knew he'd be hard put to name a worse hand to hold at this juncture.

The Scout's expression was almost apologetic as she quickly laid down the cards of an Arch Flush, all blue. "Mine," she said, "Pilot."

"Even," he said, acknowledging the lost hand with a bow so bare it was a nod, "the cards bled blue."

So his shuffle, and a scrape of boot against a chair, of chair against table, and he looked up to see Mr. McFarland's acknowledging blink and guided glance.

There, Natesa, her face wearing an appraising look he'd not seen on her before. If she acknowledged him, it was only by not looking away.

Out of sight, or perhaps not yet arrived, was the Boss.

He felt himself blush, felt the tension rising in him. He'd waited for hours. He'd dealt with a rude Terran, and now, now that he had occupation, they came to stand on the edge of things and stare at him.

McFarland. McFarland's eyes were oh-so-lazy at times; but his face held more than a Liaden's would, and hidden among the shadows of nose and chin was a slight smile.

Well. That was something . . .

The cards were called and as he got them to deal Quin looked up.

His father was paused near the two gallants, face blander than a new 'crete walk, making small bows of acknowledgment to them. He wore the on-duty smile required of a mixed-patron establishment but was making his way across the room slowly, his shiny near-new pilot's jacket even more old-style than the Liaden finery the gallants wore.

The cards went out, in proper order, but they were nearly unattended by Quin, who found and then denied the relaxation exercise that presented itself. He'd felt out of breath and closed in, but as he lifted his cards and fanned them, it was as if the cards were closer and the color more intense than they'd ever been—as if the cards were there for him.

He must fly the cards as if he were at a ship's board. He would not acknowledge his father until play was through.

Again the necessity to glance up—and his father was not apparent—off to his office, most likely; Mr. McFarland and Natesa both leaned, listening, each to their own of the elder Solcintran pair.

The hand was built; it held several opportunities and he threw negligent chips to the pile, doubling his usual opening bet. He'd never played a serious game before his father's eyes, so now he leaned on the assorted wisdoms of those who had trained his father, and saw only the cards and the table; barely even glancing at his opponent but to measure her glances between chips and cards, between one end of her hand and the other.

The Scout may have said something mild when he added more freight to the chips; his bow saw her match, and add more. They evened the pile several times, and her glance between cards and pile grew longer as she matched again.

The hand held two possibles now, and it was his chance to challenge, if he dared.

"Luken would play this, aiming to cash in at the long range, a slow game, but surer," his grandmother seemed to say in his ears, "and I would play this, to complicate and force. The challenge tests the will rather than the cards."

The had not played this hand exactly, at Runig's Rock, but a mirror of it. Quin did the math and the cards were smooth as Silk's fur in his hands, and the scout's small joke about his jacket came back to him. Yes, new and fresh, was it?

He showed a card that drew two, he showed another and it drew. The colors were running in his favor, but there was risk.

His turn now to challenge—"Will you double if I do?"

He held the chips in hand, and the Scout pursed her mouth, wrinkled her nose the way a Terran might when sniffing coffee in the morning.

"Pilot, I believe I will sue for the next hand."

There! She dropped her hand and waved her chips toward him. She said with a bow, "Your choice of a slow win or a fast, once your cards fall. Elegant enough, I need not see the demonstration."

• • • ✧ • • •

THE NEXT HAND THEN: No pause for a handwich, nothing but a sip of water for him. The Scout was drinking strong tea; and had taken a quick closed-eyed stretch. None of that for him; what he did was to locate the towering figure of Mr. McFarland, who stood now behind the two gallants, watching over Natesa, the lifemate of Pat Rin yos'Phelium. Natesa, whose judge's eyes showed nothing to him at all when their glance crossed, other than she watched.

His father, the Boss, was still not in evidence at the moment.

Indeed. The casino's owner, after all, should not be playing favorites, and had work to do, besides.

Tension in his hands, tension also rose in Quin's stomach. Not much chance of the Boss playing favorites, eh? The casino's owner clearly had his priorities set, and a son not the most convenient among them.

The crowd now consisted of pilots and Scouts and local workers, too, with a smattering of Liadens like the gentlemen who'd be trailing the Scout so eagerly before times. Up in the crowd Quin saw some of the other non-locals—including his late opponent, standing just a step or two away from and behind Villy.

His problem, he was reminded, was the cards coming to him now; his problem was winning.

The cards went face-down before him. Quin put his hands on them, closed his eyes briefly, and before looking at them at all pushed the previous game's pot into play. All of it.

The sounds changed: some observers had gasped, some nodded, some laughed, and the sound trailed into the casino's sound systems and came back in a small wave, smoothed, bringing music of a deeper timbre and complexity from the hidden nerligig.

The Scout, afforded extra time to scan her hand, did so without complacency before making a small humming noise and matching the value of the pot. The rumble of some ship off-port filtering through momentarily held them silent.

"Pilot, yes."

Quin nodded and picked up his cards, their feel in his hands all sharp-edged silk, peering at them to the exclusion of all else, pulling the numbers while one side of his brain calculated and the other side ruminated. A deeper portion of his mind sat behind it all, calmly measuring what he must do, encompassing at once three deep lines in the cards and the idea that really, there ought to be a place not quite beneath the space port's flight paths to play . . .

The Scout's first card hit the table with his as some other ship or plane lifted.

The nerligig added bass notes to the flow, and then his chances were measured. He'd felt the usual line come forward, and then the line Luken would play, and his grandmother's line . . . but there, his grandmother's was too knife-edge, now, now that he'd seen the need to win. The usual line was too bland, and Luken's, well . . . there, Luken's line might add up to a stern chase. It would be interesting. Indeed, it *would* be interesting.

He let his gaze rise, let it wander the watchers, where some people had shifted, McFarland and Natesa perhaps a step closer. Villy, so intent that his flawless fair skin shone near as much as his hair, stood now in the first rank, with his Terran shadow an arm's length row behind, towering.

The Boss was absent yet.

• • •✧• • •

THE LINE WAS CLEAR ENOUGH to both of them by now: Her chance was to shatter him with one of the three cards still to play, his was to lay down the whole of it by pulling two of hers. She considered. He did, and his hands moved without thinking, adding one more chip to the pile. Really, it didn't matter much if she folded now or showed her hand; his need was to have the pot without doubt.

His father was away from the play and away from monitors: as neutral as might be. Quin still had seen nothing more of the Boss. The Boss, cold enough to enter the turf of his enemies and show them down in their own office, drawing or not. But elsewhere for this test.

Natesa's glance had met his but once. She a Juntavas judge, a munitions expert, and . . . reputed merciless.

If there'd been a message in those eyes, it had been "play on" . . . and indeed, so he would.

"In for the Jump, Pilot," the Scout said, matching his bet one more time.

Then she said, "The hotpad's yours, sir."

And, yes, it was.

He placed the blue *qe'andra* down, without flinching. If she answered in red or green this time, the hand was hers. If blue, there was a game still.

She showed the blue seven.

There was a sigh from the watchers—clearly some favored the Scout, or had at least committed money in that direction.

For his part, Quin kept his gaze at the table, and then he followed with the lowly pivot, in blue. The point of it, really.

There was a murmur then, but she handily reached into her set and played the green pivot. It was, of course, one move too late . . .

He sighed. He'd had some concern, of course, but the pivot she'd played, been forced to play, one move late—

"The full Clan Royale, Scout, on my side."

Yes, she had a card, and the cards he laid down brought that last card to him, capping the delm as he knew it would, making the clan whole. He formally faced out his card to show her, to show the room, before slipping it into the spot.

She bowed where she sat, and then rose, and bowed again, full of intricacies he'd not seen for a *relumma* or more. No, this was Surebleak. He'd not seen such a bow for *months.*

Her bow offered equality with a touch of seeing an error, on her part, corrected . . . and she said then, "Your jacket fits you well, Pilot. May you continue to command your boards so well!"

And she was gone, the noise starting as he sat, the satisfaction of the win tempered—there'd been a warning in that last from the Scout, and he must take it: he'd been on the edge of good taste with his boast, and she'd come within a card of proving him wrong. One card. On the other hand, he'd earned the win, proved the point . . . and now . . .

Natesa the Assassin stood by, with a simple bow covering the territory of "I see you," and not much more. And there was Cheever McFarland, who held out a Terran-style handshake to him, saying jovially, "Remind me not to play piket with you, if ever it comes to sit at a serious table . . ."

There, too, was Villy, an odd grin on his face. Quin smiled, barely hearing Villy's offer above the clamor: "You need something to eat, Pilot! You haven't had anything all day! Will you join me?"

How Villy might have kept track of that he didn't know, but true, Quin *was* hungry, and he felt a little shaky. His winnings were far beyond his quartershare and . . . he needed something to eat, and he owed Villy that tip!

Villy was moving slowly against the flow of the crowd, and there he was, suddenly, repeating himself as he came within arm's length.

"You haven't had any food all day! Will you join me?"

"He will not, Villy, at least not now. This pilot has kept me waiting."

Quin turned, saw Villy's face go white and kept turning, to find Boss Conrad himself at his shoulder.

"I trust you've not accepted another game? I'm afraid I've issued word that you're not to play cards here, other than private games, taken in parlor, until I say otherwise. It is unfortunate that you've become so angry!"

The statement was delivered quietly, with no bow to cushion or explain it.

Quin stepped back, appalled. He *had* entertained the idea of a challenge . . .

"So you'll not face me?"

"Beat anyone here at will, can you? It may be the case today, but you can't declare it! Do you know what that looks like, Pilot? It looks that . . ."

Quin heard himself—

"It sounds that you're not up to the challenge, sir. Will you not play me, now if you like . . ."

Now his father took a step back, and Quin felt the roiling in his stomach going toxic. Cheever McFarland moved half-between him and his father, and Villy's voice was close.

"No, don't, that's the Boss! Don't make him . . ." Villy touched Quin's arm, surprising both of them.

"Villy," the Boss said, at the same time Quin managed—"Please . . ."

"I will play you if you will. Waiting for me? I've been waiting all day!"

Natesa's voice came low, and in Liaden.

"Perhaps this discussion should take place elsewhere . . ."

McFarland's bulk gave way, and the Boss went on. There were people about, several still wishing to play the victor, others merely to talk, or to . . .

"I cannot play you here and you cannot play here in public and keep the Emerald's name clear!"

"Is that it? Nothing like cards, is it? Well then, let us simply have a contest. Twelve paces, one Terran Ace each, the shot takes the pip or is a loser. You've done that game at Tey Dor's!"

"It's the Boss!" Villy was now clinging to Quin's arm—"He can shoot better than . . ."

"He cannot beat me tonight, I warrant!"

Quin saw his father stand straight, suddenly. His face went formal, and there followed an intricate bow, a bow of—of a request for calm. Of a request to agree to dignity. Of acknowledgment of . . . something.

"I hadn't known that story was still current," his father said mildly.

"However true it may be, that was in other times, on another world. Here there are rules to enforce, and we do not allow gun play in the Emerald. We *cannot* allow it! We'd fetch proctors in an instant and *both* end up in the hoosegow."

Quin paused, realizing that, of course, the Rules were posted. No gun play. And that his father was now being somewhat—amused.

Amused? What could . . . Quin stood taller, and half a step forward to press the issue, Villy like glue at his side.

The Boss went on, with gentle voice, close, for his ears, with a bow and hand motion indicating *stand down.*

"And yes, I did shoot that duel in Tey Dor's. I won it, too. And, I admit, you can probably beat me at any game you name tonight—I've been up eighteen hours or more and you're full on the luck, as I can see." The Boss raised his hands palm-up in a Terran gesture, a request for reason. "If the luck is on you, likely no one here can beat you! But you have stayed, and we will meet and have a meal. If you please."

Quin sighed, looked to Villy, who was watching him with some amaze—

"I told you I had a meeting . . . my party has arrived."

From nearby, there was a rumbling that was not a ship on launch but a grumble of a voice, deep and getting louder.

"I see it now, you're *all* in this. A trick, it was a trick!"

Villy heard the man behind him, felt the crowd jostle and sway as they were pushed first toward the playing table and then against a large body, in angry motion. He heard complaints and then turned to see The Coat pointing at him and pushing in his direction.

"He's a sharp, a thief, he stole my money, him and his boyfriend connived it from me. They conned me. Give me my money!"

The Coat moved with more speed than Villy would have credited him with, sweeping cards from table and throwing chairs to both sides, cursing, moving forward.

Villy braced, felt a tug on his arm—

"Halt!" someone cried, and the tug powered him out of the man's path as the pilot sidestepped in and noise rose all about him. The crowd, depending on their type, ran toward or away from this sudden action and a distant bell went off; in the confusion someone in the crowd pushed and then someone else shoved and both the pilot and The Coat were bowled over.

"Stop!" That was someone in security.

The Coat was yelling and Villy saw him clambering over a half-dozen people, after him, "My money, give me my money!"

The pilot grabbed at The Coat's legs, knocking him down, half-against Villy and then Villy saw the ominous black grip in The Coat's hands, and he reached for the gun while the man worked it out of the inner lining and—

The noise went on but the action on the floor froze.

The pilot was on his knees at The Coat's head, very shiny gun held steadily at the man's face.

"Drop the gun," he said in perfectly clear Terran, "or I'll kill you."

Villy heard and believed, his breath ragged.

The Coat looked into his face and Villy begged him, "Just let the gun go or he'll do it!"

The noise was falling off now and Villy saw hands reaching in, a foot pinning The Coat's gun arm, and then arms and hand stripping the gun away, and then . . .

The pilot had to lean on him to get untangled, and rose, his gun disappearing as if it had never been drawn. The Coat was held now, Cheever McFarland's grip supplemented by others of the casino staff, and both Natesa and the Boss had their guns out, only to put them away.

The pilot—

Villy was awkwardly pulled up by strong warm hands, the pilot pushing a chair out of the way and helping him stand straight. Villy grasped the arm for support, getting his breath back, looking into the pilot's face to be sure he was unhurt.

"Stand down, man, stop struggling!" That was McFarland, who continued with, "Call the watch. I'll hold 'em, someone frisk him."

Villy felt a touch on his shoulder, ignored for now, as the pilot got his breath back and managed a wan smile. The touch on his shoulder grew firmer, and Villy glanced around, startled to realize he'd been ignoring Boss Conrad, who was smiling, and giving him an odd bow.

"Villy, please unhand my son. What you do on your time is yours, but for the moment, I owe him dinner and consideration, and something to do besides being a roving gambler."

Villy realized he still had a grip on the pilot's arm, but heard himself saying around his still somewhat ragged breath, "*Your son*?"

The Boss looked sidewise at the pilot—

"You two haven't been introduced? Villy . . ." He paused, then bowed between the pair of them in some formal way, "Villy Butler, I present to you one's son and heir, Quin yos'Phelium, Assistant Boss."

"Pleased to meet you," Villy managed, finally relinquishing his hold on the pilot's arm, reaching out automatically for the handshake, the while feeling stupid, oh, *stupid*. It was there in the face—in the attitude!

"Best pleased to be introduced!"

Quin's hand was firm but gentle, the shake honest and confident. Villy let go reluctantly, accepting and returning the nod. "Doyodo."

Quin's quiet "I'll be looking you up soon!" surprised Villy, but then the Boss bowed to Quin, bowed to Villy—

"If you'll excuse us, Villy, we've a dinner waiting."

Villy nodded, watched them move toward the back rooms, and sighing, wondered when *soon* began.

• • •✧• • •

THE DINNER DID NOT, as Quin had more than half-expected, include Natesa, who'd last been seen discussing the scrum at the table with Mr. McFarland. McFarland, for his part, had offered Quin, "That Villy's got a lot going for him. Went for the gun, right away. Saved us shooting the nitwit—saved you blowing his brains out!"

The Boss had agreed, bowed, and had interposed himself between Quin and the Hubbub.

"This way, Quin, my son, if you please," said his father and guided him down a hall and into a room Quin hadn't seen before, a plain and stainfree room, floor shining and walls proclaiming *new*.

There was a small desk, pushed somewhat aside to accommodate a dining table and chairs, opposite each other across the table, and ordinary settings from the Emerald's kitchen gracing a flawless green tablecloth.

In the quiet, then, they stood at a proper Liaden distance from each other, his father's face changing expressions, far too mobile for Quin to decide what to do, and though it seemed as if his father didn't know what to say, either. His father was known for his address!

After too long a pause, his father bowed an unadorned bow of welcome between equals, and with a self-deprecating chuckle said, "The day was to have been simple and orderly, my son, and I discover that it has not been. Please, be seated. Dinner will be with us shortly."

Quin bowed acceptance, albeit warily, and seated himself, his father sitting quickly, and pouring a glass of wine for each of them.

They toasted the Tree-and-Dragon, and his father sipped with a ceremonial solemnity. Quin didn't recognize the bottle but knew it was excellent fare, and he nodded and heard himself sigh at it.

His father smiled, took another sip.

"Indeed. Indeed. Anthora gave me several of this bin, said to be a gift from Trealla Fantrol. How this might be so, I do not inquire, though I do not doubt."

Again a pause, and then . . .

"It strikes me, my son, that I have been . . . too busy. It strikes me, as well, that you have been busy at being busy. We must solve some of that, and soon. I hope you will hear me out."

He looked at the glass, put it down, and Quin put his down as well.

"Natesa has brought to me the consideration that you've been shunted about. We dragged you from your schooling, isolated you at Runig's Rock, then isolated you again at Jelaza Kazone. I thought it best to bring you to town so that we could begin preparing you for your role here as my heir—I told you that I would do so, in fact, but I did not ask if you wished it."

Quin bowed acknowledgment, carefully without irony.

His father sighed.

"Yes. I became Boss without asking Surebleak, and you are as caught in this as you were in Plan B."

Quin saw concentration flow across his father's face, and perhaps concern. The distant look became focused—focused *on him*.

"In the way of such things, my son, we are caught in the web of the world. You—*you* already have the skills to escape it one day, if that is your wish. In the meanwhile, we are here, and we are subject to the delm, because that is what we will."

Quin nodded—"Indeed, caught by the world, caught by history."

His father focused again, took a sip of his wine, then talk was suspended as dinner was wheeled in and set out.

"And here," his father said when they were alone again, "is where we vary, my son. The delm, in their wisdom, has put your grandmother to work on a very important project, a project important to us as a clan, to Surebleak, and to each of us, personally."

Quin allowed inquiry to show in tipping of the head.

"Kareen yos'Phelium Clan Korval," his father continued, "has been tasked to study—and if necessary, to advocate—the future shape and duties of Clan Korval, and those dependent on and from it."

Quin sat back into his chair, felt questions rising.

"But the Code. The Code tells us these things!"

His father showed a wan smile, and shook his head, Terran-style, in the mild-denial sense, and answered.

"The Code explicates proper behavior *for Liadens*. As a Liaden, with the consent of the delm, I was permitted to spend my life as a roving gambler. As long as I was an honest gambler, I was provided with a ship and a pilot, and could wander where I willed. My quartershare was deposited in my accounts on schedule—as they still are. And onworld and off I was constrained by the Code used by Liadens."

Quin felt an emptiness, a gone feeling, not fear, but unease writ large.

"And now that we have been cast away, we are no longer Liadens?" he ventured. "But surely the Code . . . does it not hold?"

"Shall I expect it and enforce it? Shall you?"

The question lay between them as his father began removing the covers from his meal.

"If the Code is in force, you would need impose Balance on the Terran who mishandled Villy—he called you in collusion, the pair of you. Instead, according to Surebleak's Code, he goes to the hoosegow, and you and he are done. Balance is thus achieved, though by Liaden lights it is no Balance at all."

His father looked up as he moved the plates around, offered across some bread. "Per the Delm's Word, I have left behind all of my Balances on Liad. As you should, though I doubt you have any of moment. And I say to you that Kareen yos'Phelium studies the question of what is proper behavior for Surebleak. If any should discover such things, it will be her."

Quin nodded a bow of acknowledgment: Grandmother was a legend in such matters!

"And so far," his father went on, "the fruit of her search brought back to the delm and to the clan is that imposing the Code as we know it on Surebleak is indefensible.

"But here, before the meal cools, let me tell you that the delms intend the clan to continue until or unless they discover it should not. If it should do as Surebleak does, as many Terrans do, and become a family instead of a clan—they will see to that."

Quin felt somewhat better, began removing his own covers, dared a sip of wine, which was *still* excellent. And he—they—were not going to be simply clanless . . . and that also was excellent.

"And today, my son," his father said, "among all the other activity required for having the Port recertified and also—by the way, upgraded three levels—today we had arrivals. New in orbit today, brought by Surebleak's fleet from deep storage, were three ships. One, named *LucyBug*, belongs to Cheever McFarland. Rarely has a man been so pleased!"

He looked up, saw the smile on his father's face, felt his own grow. His father dipped a hand in his jacket pocket, and held keys toward Quin. Ship keys.

"The other two arrivals are recently refurbished ships of the clan, *Galandasti* and *Mestro Tour.* Padi being away, you may look them over and choose which of these Jump ships you wish to fly as your own, when your duties and studies permit."

Quin nearly dropped the pair of them. So light and yet so weighty, he held them above his dinner in awe, looked into his father's face, found no words.

His father smiled. "How you will choose between them I do not know—they are of the same yard and year, and I'd swear the same polish.

"I do *hope*, as your father and as the Boss, that you will not choose to go a-roving quite yet. I do hope that, Code or not, you will continue to acknowledge our connection."

"Of course, Father, how could I not?" he paused, found his voice gone and then returned—"I am proud, Father, to be of the clan. I see difficulties, but the clan—Grandmother, Grandfather, the delms—all, yes, all I cherish!"

Without thinking or looking, he closed his hand around one set of ship keys and handed the other back, and saw it accepted with a nod.

"The clan does well by us, Father, and you do. I can only hope I can do as well by the clan, and by you. I am pleased to be your son. Of course I shall wait on my roving."

✧ King of the Cats ✧

***IN 1985,** when this story was written, our joint writing career consisted of two published stories about Kinzel, an inept wizard who improbably held a Staff of True Power, and a science fiction novel entitled* Agent of Change, *which was making the rounds. At that time, Steve made part of our living by running weekend chess tournaments. So it was that Sharon was left alone one weekend, with only a typewriter and a ream of paper for company. The result of these circumstances was a non-canon story that mixed two universes with nothing in common, save a belief in Balance.*

THE MOST IMPORTANT MAN in the universe sat at ease behind his desk-counter while a pair of leather-clad mercenaries moved toward him, bags in hand. He shook his head, and was annoyed when they continued forward. The effrontery of such creatures, he thought, moving his foot toward the pedal that would summon Security, expecting to be rented a room in *his* Hyatt!

"You've got a suite reserved for us," said the woman, dropping a bag onto the polished countertop. "Name's Robertson."

Secure in the knowledge that no one on staff was stupid enough to have taken such a reservation, he replied coolly.

"I am certain you must be mistaken. Of course we have no—" For effect, he let his eyes touch the reservation board—and stopped in mid-sentence.

It was there: ROBERTSON, in cheery yellow letters and—the deskmaster barely contained his rage: They'd rented the most expensive suite for an entire week! He'd not have his hyatt turned into a rowdy, drunken love-nest for—

"Hey, not today fella, OK?" said the red-haired woman in her low-class Terran accent. "Just give us the card."

"I am sorry—madam," he said in his most condescending voice, "but it is my policy not to permit mercenaries here. Our illustrious patrons . . ."

"Will be honored by our presence," said the startlingly mannered voice of the man. "Please, our card."

The manager's toe touched the silent switch; in seconds Security would rid him of this nuisance.

The woman's hand moved, and a coin landed, spinning, on the counter.

The deskmaster gulped.

On many worlds a Liaden *cantra* is equivalent to an average yearly income. Settling slowly before him was a *twelve* cantra piece.

"We won't mess up your playground, pal. And if we do, we got enough to cover the damage." She swept the coin up. "Now. My name's Robertson and I got a reservation. Card, *accazi*?"

Security arrived then and was summarily waved back by the deskmaster.

Hastily, he produced the card in question; pressed a key to summon busbots.

"We'll carry our own," said the woman and the pair hefted their belongings, leaving the mechanicals scurrying in bewildered circles.

The most important man in the universe was still staring at the spot where the coin had been when his shift relief arrived.

• • •✧• • •

RED-HAIRED MIRI ROBERTSON sighed deeply as she walked into the center of the suite's parlor. Behind her, she heard the door slide shut and a faint chime as Val Con coded the lock.

She turned and grinned.

"Ain't every day you meet somebody that important."

"True," he said, lips twitching. "I hope you were impressed."

"*I* hope he gets fired. Almost worth buying the hyatt for the pleasure of doing it myself." She yawned suddenly. "I'm beat. Next time we go off to save somebody else's bacon we'll have to put in a shut-eye requisition. Gonna sleep for a month. You coming?"

"On your heels," he murmured, reaching to his belt and unhooking the pellet gun. "Though perhaps not an entire month—?"

"Yeah, well, if you wake up first, order breakfast and call me when it gets here. Just don't—Val Con."

He glanced up. "Yes?"

"You're fading."

His dark brows pulled together. "Fading, *cha'trez*?"

But she was moving at a dead run from across the room and he braced himself to absorb the shock of impact—

He did not hear her scream his name, nor see her brake to a stop, eyes wide and disbelieving on the pellet gun that lay abandoned on the rich dark carpet.

• • •✧• • •

THERE WAS A *POOF!* of displaced air and an instant when the world seemed to slip slightly out of focus. Kinzel blinked at the sudden person before him.

Who stared back, green eyes very bright, face wearing a look of wary outrage, body braced like a warrior about to engage.

The magician became aware of his staff, which was purring quite loudly while its moist leaves swayed in an unfelt breeze.

"Hello," said Kinzel to the man the staff had Summoned. "Are you the King of the Cats?"

One straight brow slid upward. "Do I look like the King of the Cats?" he asked, his quiet voice carrying an undertone of power.

"I don't know," said Kinzel truthfully. "I've never seen him. I'd hoped he existed—There is so much trouble for the cats and I remembered a story and thought how useful the King of the Cats would be. I'll help, of course."

"Will you, indeed? I am honored." Val Con stared at his unlikely captor, taking in the worn jerkin and the general air of disheveled pudginess, then moved his gaze to the woods at the man's back. *Primal forest*, the part of him that had been a Scout judged. He glanced back at the man and produced a preliminary judgement there, as well: *Class Four Society, Sixth Sub-level: Pre-tech.* He hesitated, then added a footnote: *Apparent ability to activate and utilize interstellar transport.*

"What is your name, friend?" he asked with careful gentleness.

"Oh! I beg your pardon." The other bowed as low as his plumpness would allow.

"My name is Kinzel. I'm a wizard—though not a very good one, I'm afraid. That's why the cats are in such trouble."

"Ah, yes, the cats . . ." Val Con paused. "Friend Kinzel, that the cats are in need grieves me. I've a fondness for the creatures, troublesome though they are. But they must take charge of their own affairs. It is a weak people who look to their King to solve every small problem. Now, if you will have the goodness to—return—me to my wife's side. I feel my departure has distressed her."

"Oh!" said Kinzel again. "I didn't mean to disturb you or your wife. Is she Queen of the Cats?"

Val Con felt his lips twitch and raised both brows.

"As much as I am King, she is Queen. Now, if you would return me—"

"I . . ." Kinzel hesitated. His staff had stopped purring. "I think it might be better if you helped the cats first," he said slowly. "In fact, it may be required that you help them first. It is the staff that brought you, acting on my thought of how Right it would be—"

"Were there a King of the Cats," the other finished. "I see. So it is this instrument here which effects the transfer?"

He had moved, so quickly and so silently that Kinzel had not noticed until here he was, one slender hand reaching—

The staff buzzed angrily, green sparks sparking. Kinzel drew it back, smiling in apology.

The King of the Cats stood very still. Kinzel thought his tail would certainly have twitched, had he possessed such an appendage.

"Friend Kinzel," the soft voice began again, "my lady is distraught. If you will not return me, at least you must let me speak with her."

Kinzel thought, and as he did the leaves about the old wooden staff once more became full, and swayed. The green eyes of the King of the Cats widened slightly.

"Bring the image of your wife to mind," Kinzel said slowly. "Then touch my hand."

His hand was immediately gripped in strong, slender fingers and the thought that passed through him on its way to the Power was a thing of searing brightness.

Kinzel felt the thought snatched away; there was a vast silence, a feel of distance uncountable—then, from the clearing before them, a voice:

"Val Con!"

"Here, *cha'trez*." The King's answer was clear and calm, though Kinzel fancied he felt a tremor in the hand that held his.

"Where's—oh." This as the image of a woman formed, ghostly, in the air before them. "So what's the gag?"

"My friend here believes that I am King of the Cats. It seems that the cats are in dire trouble, and require my aid. I will not be returned to you until they are rescued."

"Right," said the woman. Her image had solidified; Kinzel could no longer see the trees on the other side of the clearing through her thin body, and her feet seemed to rest upon the ground.

"Cats are a raucous bunch," she commented. "Always in scrapes."

"True," agreed their sovereign. "Miri, I am anxious to come to you."

"And I'm anxious to have you," she responded, extending her hands.

Kinzel cried out as the man leapt toward the woman; watched in foreknowing sorrow as their hands met, melded and slid each through the other's. The woman's image snapped into nothing and she was gone, leaving behind the echoing desolation of her cry.

"Miri!"

The word echoed desolation and with wizard's eyes Kinzel saw a bright blade of will loosed from the man kneeling on the clearing floor, hurtling naked and unprotected toward the maelstrom of the Forces.

He brought the staff up, crying out in a voice meant to command that which is not seen with outer eyes.

"*Hold!*"

The blade of will hesitated before reversing and dropping earthward. The kneeling King gasped, as though his will did cut, returning, then he was on his feet, green eyes blazing, slim body taut with purpose.

Cat, indeed, thought Kinzel. *Tiger!* He moved the staff again, bringing it upright between them.

The advancing predator stopped, face wary, and Kinzel spoke quickly, seeking to explain; to comfort.

"She was not really here. It was only—only a thought of her—her image, taking shape from your thought. Your desire. But she heard you, because of staff and Power, and knows that you are safe."

If there was an expression on the golden face before him, Kinzel could not read it, and so he rushed on.

"You can't touch a thought, you know. And you can't send your spirit against all the Forces of Power—not without protection, a staff, a charm, a Word! You are not a mage! Best your will stays within your heart . . ." He blinked and glanced down.

The awful purpose had left the other man. He pushed the dark hair off his forehead, crossed his legs and sat on the ground; looked up, green eyes glinting.

"That she is alive—and well—I know. That she is worried, I know. But *where* is she? In former days I would have known this, if she stood on one end of the galaxy and I on the other. Now, I ask your indulgence."

Kinzel blinked. "Where? Where you left her, I suppose . . ." He, too, sat on the ground, though he arrived there with less grace and crossed his legs after he was seated.

"I see," murmured the King of the Cats. "And where might that be—from here?"

"Well . . ." Kinzel screwed his eyes shut, then opened them, pointing. "The other continent is in that direction."

The other man shook his head. "Am I to surmise from this that you do not know the name of the world from which you—borrowed—me?"

"World?" Kinzel's face lit. "That's wonderful! A person from another of the worlds! I've heard of such things—people crossing from one of the worlds to another. After all, if the Clock governs all—"

"No." One slim hand rose, commanding silence. "Kinzel, please. Indulge me further. How did you happen to get me from where I was to where I am?"

"I told you."

"No doubt you did. Perhaps I was not attending. Will you tell me again?"

Kinzel sighed. "I was thinking of Fallan and how he was taking revenge on me by harming cats. I remembered the story Siljan told about the King of the Cats—how wise and strong and clever he was. And I thought how I am none of those things, yet the cats must be helped. Then I thought how—how much I needed help—from someone like the—the King of the Cats. I Called, and the staff purred, as it does, and then you were here."

The Suzerain of Felines had closed his eyes. Now he opened them and sighed.

"And thus it is that the staff will not let me go back to my wife until I have aided you in this task?" He did not wait for an answer but swept regally on.

"Friend Kinzel, I am a man, not a cat. Might this be mentioned to your staff? It could make a difference."

"It might," said Kinzel doubtfully, "but—the staff chose you, after all. The story never made clear whether the King of the Cats was man or cat—or a bit of both." He frowned. "What do I call you? I've never met a King before."

"Nor have you now. Val Con, you should call me."

"Val Con," said Kinzel, finding he liked the crisp sound of the name. "Well, Val Con, think: If the staff chose you out of the countless numbers of people there must be on all the worlds that Clock and Branch encompass, then—"

"I'm stuck," said the other, and it seemed that the red-haired woman's voice glittered through the man's own in that phrase. He shifted then, touching wrist, ankle, back of neck in quick succession, as if performing a ritual dance. When the movement was done, the staff allowed Kinzel to feel the sharpening of purpose about the man; almost tasting of mage-power.

"Very well, friend Kinzel," the King said softly. "Who is this Fallan and what is he doing that causes you—and the cats—so much distress?"

• • •✧• • •

"DAMMIT, Robertson, can't you hold on to *any*thing?"

Miri curled her hands into fists, spinning slowly on her heel in the hyatt's parlor.

"Val Con?" she asked the room.

There was no answer. She hadn't really expected one.

Frowning, she reached within herself to the pattern-place where glowed the warm and lovely thing that was her knowledge of her lifemate's life.

Alive and well, the pattern reported.

She brought her attention more closely on the pattern; fought down a surge of panic and tried again.

Val Con alive, Val Con well, the pattern sang.

In all bloody directions at once.

Generations of breeding by Liaden psychics had produced the link between lifemates—and it had never failed her since the first time she'd seen it dancing in her head.

Abruptly, she folded her legs and sat on the floor; glared at the pellet gun reposing on the carpet and closed her eyes.

King of the Cats? Obviously, the fat man with the stick was a lunatic. Just as obviously, the lush glade in which he and Val Con had been standing was not on the world of Panore, where Miri was. Panore was a world of oceans—or, more exactly, ocean. The hyatt in which she sat was part of a vast city built on titanium girders sunk deep into the ocean floor.

No natural green glades here.

Miri sighed and opened her eyes, reaching up to unpin her copper-colored braid.

The galaxy was wide. Green worlds, while not all that common, existed in sufficient plentitude that it would take a lifetime as long as a Clutch Turtle's to search them all.

She sighed again, and tried to look at the other side of the problem.

How had the snatch been done? Instantaneous transfer? Through vacuum? Miri shook her head. The fading effect was similar to the effects she and Val Con had experienced aboard a Clutch "rock-ship" years before. But where had the fat man's power source been hidden?

"Instantaneous transfer within the world I'll buy," she decided, shaking the kinks out of her long hair. "Through space ain't gonna hack it. That'd be like Jumping without a ship . . ."

Liaden and Terran math took dimensional shifts into consideration—that was how spaceships got from here to there without going in-between. *Hyperspace*: A mumbo-jumbo word without any real meaning, purporting to explain itself with its own name.

Suppose the fat man had worked hyperspatial math within the world, Miri thought, then groaned as her imaginatiion conjured an image of Panore upon Panore, stretching away into unthought-of distance, one edge of each superimposed on the next.

The may-be worlds of alternate chance would run smack into the problem of time: Each mainline of When would have its aurora of alternate Whats.

"Sort of thing a lunatic would do."

She rolled to her feet, tossing her hair behind her back.

"Gods, I hate math," she grumped, moving across the room to the discreetly screened-off workstation.

She sat on the edge of the soft chair, fingers already on the board, calling up equations—Liaden math, not Terran. This was one of those things it was going to be easier to think about in Liaden, she just knew it.

• • • ✧ • • •

THE KING OF THE CATS had closed his bright eyes, giving Kinzel the opportunity to study him more closely.

The black leather leggings and vest marked him a fighting man, though he wore no sword. The wide belt with its built-on pouch was certainly capable of supporting a weapon. There was, in fact, a sense of edges about him: That he carried knives on his person Kinzel didn't doubt.

His dark shirt was of fine, soft cloth—surely the sort of garment a nobleman would wear next to his skin. It was loosely laced with black cord, leaving the slender throat bare. Kinzel looked more closely, eyes caught by something that shone there, suspended by a dusky velvet riband.

"So, friend Kinzel," murmured the King. "You say you do not know what Fallan does with the cats, once they are captured, only that he threatens to leave nothing cat-like in the world."

"Isn't that enough?" asked Kinzel. "Think of the upset to the Balance! There is a reason for cats to be as they are. Fallan is only thinking of vengeance, not of the harm done the whole world, if cats are no longer cats!"

He sighed suddenly, and continued in a much younger voice.

"It is true that Fallan is a very learned wizard. He may be able to do what he threatens and not endanger Balance."

"Or he may be lying to you," said the other briskly, "with no intention of harming further cats, or, indeed, the ones he now holds. If he holds any."

"He does," said Kinzel with certainty. "And he doesn't make idle threats. He has a reputation for never threatening to do what he won't—or can't—perform."

"Useful," murmured the King. He did not seem disposed to speak further and silence grew between them.

It had stretched a time when Kinzel stirred and, typically, spoke what first popped into his head.

"I was admiring your amulet. The work is very fine. Of silver, too, so it is Moon-potent. I'm sorry I hadn't noticed it before, for it's true that you might have hurled your will against the Forces to good purpose, possessing such a thing."

"Might I have, indeed?" He touched the shining thing at his throat with a light fingertip. "But this is not a—magical—thing, friend Kinzel. It is a gift from my lady, given with laughter and love, to commemorate a dragon I once slew."

"A potent charm," said the pudgy wizard admiringly. Then, in awe: "Dragons are very rare—at least on this continent. Unicorns, now . . . But did it really need to be slain, this dragon?"

The King of the Cats smiled. "Alas, it was determined to eat my friend. I did attempt to—dissuade—it, but it would not be turned away."

"In that case," said Kinzel, with a touch of sadness. "Still, it might have been better, had you been able to find another way to save your friend, and let the creature go with its life."

Almost, the King laughed. "I agree with you. However, I was very young and very frightened, so that I clutched the first means to hand. Perhaps now things would go differently." He shrugged, in cat indifference. "But who can know?"

Suddenly, he was not indifferent at all, his eyes were intent, lithe body tipped forward, one hand out—perhaps in supplication.

"Friend Kinzel, return me to my lady."

Kinzel sighed, pity warring with—was it envy?

And why should I be envious, he wondered. *Because he has seen a dragon? Because he loves his wife so well? Or because he wears a thing of dreadful Power and is wise enough to honor it for the love it was given with, rather than the Force it might command?*

He was jerked from these thoughts by the brightness of the gaze upon his face and shook his head sadly.

"I am sorry, my friend. The cats are in danger. The staff chose you to aid them. After the Right has been served, then I am certain the staff will send you home."

"So." The King came fluidly to his feet. "If I may not return until the task is done, then it is best we begin at once."

Kinzel nodded and climbed awkwardly to his feet. Closing his eyes, he rubbed the old wood of the staff lightly, listening, feeling. Eventually, he opened his eyes and struck off in a northerly direction, the King of the Cats walking silent at his side.

• • •✧• • •

THE MANAGER ARRIVED with the carpenters.

Miri ignored him while she pointed out the exact spot, elucidated the precise dimensions and the deadline. The job-boss nodded, barked orders in his turn and the crew set to work.

"Stop!" yelled the manager.

One of the carpenters hesitated. The boss snapped two words and she went back to work.

Miri turned to the manager. "Get out. You're in the way. You're holding up construction. You're annoying me."

"You," said the manager, "are in violation of the law. Guests are not allowed to construct things in the room. The owner—"

"Shut up," said Miri, without raising her voice. He blinked, words dying. "I ain't interested in the law. Or in the owner. How much is this place worth? In *cantra*."

"What!" The manager stared, feeling absurdly vulnerable without his desk-counter between them. The woman stared back, gray eyes as warm as fog off the ocean.

"You will," she stated clearly, "tell me the purchase price of this building. If you don't know, get the company lawyer on the talkie. Or the owner. Or whoever else I gotta talk at to buy this hyatt. I intend to own it by local sundown." Then, with some snap to it, since he just stood there, staring: "*Now*!"

The manager jumped a foot and left, nearly colliding with the candlemaker and the glassblower, who were arriving together.

• • •✧• • •

FALLAN'S KEEP loomed like a ship of stone and steel, full Moon just visible beyond the tip of the eastern tower.

The King of the Cats sighed.

"So then," he murmured. "Where do you think Fallan holds the cats?"

Kinzel tipped his head, listening to the soft purring of his staff. He nodded and walked forward, at a slight angle to the wall.

"There's a door," he said to the shadow at his side. "Then a long corridor, then another door. Beyond that is—I am sorry, my friend—a cage. The cats are in the cage."

"Are they indeed?" It was too dark for Kinzel to see the ironic lift of the eyebrow. "Are there watchers? Men and women with weapons? Alarms?"

Kinzel took further counsel from his staff. "No watchers. Fallan and his 'prentice are the only men in the keep and they are both far from the cage."

"Alarms?" insisted Val Con, keeping pace with the wizard, though the wall loomed close.

"I don't—" began Kinzel—and stopped.

Half a pace beyond, Val Con spun to face him, both brows up and clearly visible in the Moon's light.

"Friend Kinzel?"

The mage frowned, moved back two steps and cast about, as if looking for a way around a wall perceived, yet unseen. He shrugged gracelessly and walked forward again, gripping his staff with its green vines tightly.

Two paces underway, he stopped. Sharply. Almost, Val Con thought he heard a *thump*, as if wizardly nose had brought up against invisible barrier.

"Alarms?" he guessed, glancing over his shoulder at the keep.

"Wards," corrected Kinzel, bringing his hand up and rubbing his nose. He smiled sheepishly. "I don't seem to be able to come any further."

Val Con pushed his hair from his eyes, stepped to Kinzel's side, turned and walked toward the wall, one-two-three paces. He turned back, hands on hips.

"The way is clear. I discover no barrier."

"For you, no barrier," Kinzel said, eyes half-closed as the staff hummed in his hand. "The wards are set to keep out anything—anyone—born to the world."

"Ah. I begin to see the why behind your staff's actions." He sighed. "I go on alone, then?"

"It will be easier for you that way, won't it? Even if I weren't warded away? You are silent—and so quick. I'm clumsy, and you would have to wait for me." He gestured with the staff.

"That clump of rock and scrub we passed?" Val Con nodded. "I will wait for you and the cats there. The staff will re-Balance and then it will send you home to your wife."

"So? And how many cats are in this cage? Does your staff know that? And how shall I bring them away? In my pouch?"

Kinzel thought. "There are one hundred and forty-seven cats in the cage," he said slowly. "And as to how you'll bring them out—you're the King of the Cats. Surely they'll follow you?"

Suddenly, surprisingly, the King laughed, flinging his hands

Moonward; then he was leaning forward, speaking with earnest briskness.

"In all my experience of cats, never have I seen anything that leads me to suppose that they will follow anyone—King or no. Especially, perhaps, would they fail to follow their King. Who, if he is truly that, would not ask it of them. Another way, I implore you. Some assurance that the task is not wholly the errand of a fool."

Kinzel was already reaching into his pouch, pulling out a twist of paper tied with yellow string. Bracing the staff against his shoulder, he untied the string.

"Come here."

The other man stepped forward until their noses nearly touched and Kinzel could smell old leather and new cloth and another scent, which was that of the King himself.

Kinzel paused, blinking into the green eyes. "Are you a man, my friend?"

"Yes." said Val Con softly. "I will tell you this: Cats are not found on all worlds. But on the worlds on which they are found, they are—cats. Other creatures change. Including men. Especially men. It is a mystery, is it not? A wonder. But I am a man—human—as much as you are."

"All right," said Kinzel, pulling the string free and stashing it in his pouch. "It is only that, if you were a cat, the herb might make you a little drunk."

He untwisted the parchment and took out a pinch of dried leaf, which he sprinkled over the King's head. He liberally treated hair, shirt, belt and boot-tops, repeating the process until the leaf was gone.

Val Con stepped back, nose wrinkling. "What is it?"

"An herb cats find enjoyable. I think they'll follow you now."

"Behold me delighted," murmured the King and sighed.

"Friend Kinzel. This I lay upon you. Should I not return—you will go to my lady and explain what has transpired. You will tell her how you were able to call me here, so she may guard herself from like attack." He sighed again.

"She will know, should I die. So ward yourself well before you go to her. Her temper is not overgentle, and her way with weapons nearly equals my own."

Kinzel bowed and brought the staff between them, so the other could see the Power glittering there. "This thing I do swear, should you fall in the service of the Right."

"A mighty oath, friend Kinzel . . ." And the King was gone, one shadow among many, fading toward the steel and stone walls.

• • •✧• • •

THE OUTER DOOR was locked—the work of a moment. Val Con slid into the corridor beyond, making sure that the door did not relock itself.

Empty, the hallway; lit sporadically by three smoky torches. The shadows were deep and plentiful.

The second door stood wide open.

Val Con paused in a pool of shadow, glaring. He bent and located two stones on the floor. Straightening, he tossed one through the door.

Nothing.

He faded closer, and threw the second stone.

A lance fell point-first from high up and buried itself solidly in the granite floor just beyond the doorway.

"Ah," breathed Val Con. Then he was through, hugging the wall and pretending himself invisibly weightless.

• • •✧• • •

THE CAGE was not large.

Cats had been piled within it like lengths of furry firewood. The smell was very bad.

Wrinkling his nose, Val Con had recourse to the lockpick once more. The hinges groaned when he pulled the door open and he froze in a half-crouch, eyes and ears straining.

Nothing.

Your luck is either very good or very bad, he told himself, frowning at the curiously still pile of bodies. It occurred to him to wonder if the prisoners were dead.

But the scrawny tortoise-shell he plucked from the top opened its eyes sufficiently to glare, though it did not offer battle. It closed its eyes and sighed.

Val Con held it by the scruff of the neck and shook.

Eyes open and ears back, the cat hissed, claws reaching. Val Con tossed the outraged feline into the cageful of its kin.

There was a flurry of activity, dying quickly out. The man thrust his arms into the heap, shifting cats, sweeping them out of the cage and onto the floor, stirring things around as best he could.

Suddenly, they were everywhere: Twining about his legs; clinging to his hands; trying to climb his leathers. One enterprising individual actually leapt to his shoulders and began a barrage of purrs upon discovering the herb-dosed hair.

Cage empty, Val Con swung the door closed and locked it, and started back the way he had come, one hundred and forty-seven—forty-*six;* the acrobat was still draped about his shoulders—cats grouped close around.

• • •✧• • •

VAL CON STOOD in the center of the protected clearing, though he would have liked to sit down. The prospect of being immediately engulfed by cats checked the urge; instead he reached up an absent hand to scratch his newly acquired fur piece under the chin.

"All of them! And so quickly!" Kinzel was saying, reaching down and capturing one fine orange-and-white fellow. "You will be with your wife before dawn," he continued, sitting on a rock and restraining the cat by main force. "We only need—oh."

Val Con stirred. "What is wrong?"

"Nothing. It is only that I am stupid." Kinzel looked up. "He took their curiosity away."

Val Con raised a brow. "Not too bad a notion," he murmured. "They will live longer so. And be less troublesome."

"But they won't be *cats*!" cried the wizard. "It's the same as taking away their instinct to hunt. Or their purr. Or—"

"Yes, of course," soothed the King, drifting closer. "And I am certain that, since it is Right that cats be curious, your staff will now put all in order and I will speedily be on my way."

"That's right," agreed Kinzel, standing and releasing his prisoner. "If you will just put that person on your shoulder down with the others . . . Good. Now stand away." He closed his eyes and opened his arms.

Val Con watched the proceedings with interest. The leaves twisted about the old wooden staff were full and green and new; they swayed slightly, though there was no breeze. Kinzel himself seemed to grow taller by a few inches, to become less portly; and the ginger hair took on a glow.

The cats milled about, not much impressed with the spectacle. Several began to move in Val Con's direction.

There was a sheen of sweat on the wizard's round face; he seemed to be straining toward something just out of reach. Val Con clamped down on his feeling of impending disaster; forced himself to wait quietly.

Kinzel opened his eyes, shook his head and made his way unsteadily to the nearest rock, where he sat with a bump.

The King of the Cats was immediately at his side, on one knee, eyes sharp with concern.

"What is wrong?"

The wizard winced at the snap in the smooth voice. "I—there's a disturbance—in the Power. The staff—I—can't work for the Right when there is another unBalancing force in the world . . ."

The green eyes had widened. "I beg your pardon?"

Kinzel swallowed, remembering the tiger held at bay earlier. "It's that I'm stupid," he repeated. "Of course, you will have to be sent back first. Then I will be able to restore the cats."

"So." The King bowed his head. "I am ready, friend Kinzel. Do it quickly."

Kinzel levered himself up, took a firmer grip on the staff and looked into the eyes of the man kneeling before him.

Miri! Val Con sent his awareness to the place where the song of her glowed bright within him—

The wizard lowered his arms, eyes awash with tears.

"No." Val Con was on his feet, felt his hands moving with deadly purpose—and stopped.

"Another way, then," he said sharply. "What else might be done?"

The mage sank again to his rock. "The cats are—not Right. UnBalance. You don't belong here. UnBalance. I cannot work for the Right without Balance."

"So I must be sent back or the cats may not be mended. But I may not be sent back until the cats are mended." He moved his head sharply, sending dark hair into bright eyes.

"Friend Kinzel, I do not wish to remain here. You—or your staff—are foresworn. There—wait." He tipped his head. "You spoke of my—amulet. That was—Moon-potent? That wearing it I might, myself, return to Miri. How? There is the Moon, already high. Here I am, with my desire and my will. What else is required? Tell me what I must do."

Kinzel frowned and shifted on his rock. "Your will is very strong, and the amulet is powerful. The Moon is full. But you are not a mage! It might be possible—but you would be working against the Power, not with it. You could harm yourself. You could die . . ."

"A bad solution. Is there another? If not, I shall attempt this one."

Kinzel thought. And, from the staff purring in his hand or from the cats purring at their feet, or, indeed, from the Moon itself came—an idea.

He looked up at the King of the Cats and spoke, slowly. "You must remember that I am not learned, that I am stupid with spells and not clever or subtle. But it does seem that if you were able to—trick—a mighty wizard into commanding you, in Power, to begone, your will is sufficient to hold and shape that command into—into an arrow of desire, sending yourself wherever you wish to be." He shrugged. "It is worth the effort, and you will be further aided, if your wife desires your return as much as you desire to return."

An eyebrow slid upward. "I believe the stipulation may be met." He sighed. "I infer that you are not the wizard best—tricked?"

"Fallan is," admitted Kinzel, "a mighty mage. He's learned and subtle and—quick to anger."

"And thus it might be possible." The King of the Cats looked over his shoulder at the keep. "Very well, friend Kinzel; where is Fallan now?"

• • • ✧ • • •

MIRI LIT THE CANDLES north to south and stood back to survey the arrangements. The long glass rods were placed on the wooden platform in a faintly familiar pattern. She groped after the image and found it in her memory of Zhena Trelu's kitchen, worlds away.

A funnel.

• • • ✧ • • •

FALLAN JUMPED OUT OF BED like a cat with its tail afire, snatched up his staff, caused a robe to wrap him and willed himself from *here* to *there*.

A heartbeat later he stood blinking in the center of the tower laboratory, half-blinded by the Moonlight streaming in through the unshuttered window.

In addition to Moonlight, all the candles were burning, as were the spirit lamp and the meldfire. His books were piled in zig-zagged heaps on the normally immaculate work tables. Bottles and jars containing elixirs, potions and drugs had been shifted about.

Fallan felt his stomach sink at the thought of so much work gone—and was assured by his staff that nothing was lost, only rearranged.

But by what agent? The keep was warded. The tower was warded. It had, in fact, been one of the wards that had awakened—

"Boo!"

The mage jumped and spun, staff up to hold at bay whatever demon had made that sound—

Who only laughed from his crosslegged perch atop the poisons cupboard and tossed a glittering object from hand to casual hand.

Fallan sputtered, staff sparking.

The little man in black leather grinned, green eyes very bright.

"Were you looking for me?" he asked gently.

"I am looking for the intruder in my laboratory," snapped Fallan.

"Well, then," said the little man amiably, "you have found him. Your luck is good."

"And yours," replied the wizard, "is bad." He brought his staff up, Words forming on his tongue—and swallowed them, eye caught by the glitter of the intruder's toy.

"Put that down!"

"What, this?" The man held up the faceted ball, closed one eye and looked through it with the other before opening both and grinning at the outraged magician.

"I'd prefer not to, thank you."

"You will put that down," Fallan informed him, voice scintillant with Power.

The little man's hands slowed for the barest of instants. Then he moved his head sharply and smiled.

"You are in error."

Fallan felt anger and Power surge together, and exercised control. He stepped back a pace and, keeping his staff between them, surveyed his visitor.

Thin, dark hair, green eyes; the gold of his skin named him a foreigner. The leather clothing argued a warrior, as did the paler gold of an old scar across the high line of one cheek. At his throat hung something that shone with the light of the Moon. His staff reported Power there.

"Who are you?" Fallan barked, staff reinforcing demand.

The little man raised an eyebrow. "I might ask the same of you."

"You ask the name of a mage when you stand within his keep—uninvited, nay! Warded away! I, since you need to ask, am Fallan. The Ferocious. The Mighty."

The little man yawned and tossed his toy upward. Fallan felt his heart lodge in his throat. The ball dropped floorward and was caught, as a seeming afterthought, by a golden hand that looked too frail to support the weight.

Fallan the Ferocious swallowed a sigh of relief and snapped again: "Who are you?"

"Have you told me all of your name, then? But perhaps you only give the shortest form." The intruder smiled. "I am called, in the short form: Val Con yos'Phelium, Scout, Artist of the Ephemeral, Slayer of the Eldest Dragon, Knife Clan of Middle River's Spring Spawn of Farmer Greentree's of The Spearmaker's Den, Tough Guy, Miri-mated—" He bowed from his perch atop the cabinet, cupping the faceted ball close against his heart, "King of the Cats."

"King of the Cats!" It was Fallan's turn to laugh, which he did with an ineptitude that spoke of long unfamiliarity. "The King of the Cats is a tale for children—or wood wizards!" And he—laughed—again.

"Ah," said the little man, "that explains much. I was summoned by a wood wizard."

Fallan stopped laughing.

"This wood wizard—his name?"

The—King of the Cats—shrugged, tossing the glittering ball from hand to hand. "Kinzel, was it? Yes, I believe it may have been Kinzel."

"And he summoned you? Why?"

"Did I not say? To free the cats, of course."

"Of course," agreed Fallan smoothly. "And why have you not done so?"

The King of the Cats blinked his bright eyes. "But I have."

"What!" Fallan sent his awareness away, downward; touched upon the empty cage, the sprung trap, the vigilant wards—and returned to the tower room.

"This is the second time I have been here tonight," the little man said. "Really, friend Fallan, if you mean to call this keep your own, you had best guard it more closely. As it is, anyone might walk in to surprise you at your dinner. Or in your bed . . ."

But Fallan was no longer listening. "Not of this world. You are not born into this world!"

"You have not listened to what your ears have heard," the King of the Cats chided. "Of course I am not of this world."

Fallan gripped his staff with both hands, murmuring the Words that came to his tongue, foreknowing the power that this entrapment would afford him. To have such an one obey his commands! What might a man born of another world not accomplish for his master in this one!

The King of the Cats was holding something out. Something that glittered and fair cried aloud with Power. A raven's egg crystal, faceted with geometrical precision—a mighty focusing tool for a mighty magician.

Fallan closed his mouth around the Words, his face showing white against the black beard.

"What will you give, friend Fallan, for this object?"

"Your life." Fallan forced a smile. "Lay it down and go free."

The little man laughed. "Come now, am I a fool? Holding this, I think I might walk with impunity anywhere in this keep. Name another price."

"What might any man—wizard or no—give the King of the Cats?"

"Fair words. Perhaps you do not value it as highly as I had thought."

Fallan shrugged. "It has some small worth. Approximately equal to your life, as I have said. But another may always be crafted."

"So?" Both brows were raised. "It seems I chose a poor hostage. Forgive me." He let the crystal go.

Fallan cried out, Words forming of themselves. The crystal's descent was arrested a scant inch from the slate floor. Sweating heavily, the mage caused it to waft to safety and wedge itself between two jewel-encrusted spell books.

Shaking, he turned to deal with the King of the Cats.

But the small man had slid from his perch and was busily pulling jars from the poisons cupboard, mixing the contents of one with another, indiscriminately, disastrously.

"Begone, you misbegotten creature!" screamed Fallan, lost to all but his rage. "Begone from here and never come again! I ward you from this world forever. Begone, begone, be—"

Val Con saw the balled lightning leap from the magician's staff, and stilled his impulse to dodge. He felt heat enter him, expand him, begin to unravel him—

Miri!

• • •✧• • •

"VAL CON!"

He blinked, felt the heat of that which pursued him and jumped, slamming into Miri, covering her with his body as they rolled, shielding her from the—

FLASH!

Poof . . .

. . . BOOM!

• • •✧• • •

AFTER A TIME he moved, cautiously, and heard the tinkle and crunching of glass.

"Val Con?" a small voice murmured in the vicinity of his left ear.

"Yes."

"Can we get up now?"

"I think so." He shifted; knelt. "Yes."

"Good." She knelt as well, combing fingers through wild red hair as she surveyed the room. "Some party. Wish I remembered more of it."

He grinned and waved a hand at the remnants of the platform. "What was that?"

"A funnel. To get you back. I can show you the math." She cocked a suspicious gray eye. "Worked."

"So it did," he said, and reached out to touch her face.

• • •✧• • •

SOME TIME LATER, when they were both on the edge of sleep, Miri shifted next to him and murmured.

"Val Con-husband?"

"Yes, *cha'trez*."

"I bought the hyatt."

"So? Did you fire the manager?"

She grinned. "Naw. I thought about it. Then I thought that one of the changes I'll be making is to open up a wing especially for mercenaries. Figured I'd put him in charge of that."

"Not too bad a notion," he conceded, curling closer and nestling his cheek against her hair. "I'm sure he'll learn quite rapidly."

• • •✧• • •

KINZEL STRETCHED and smiled at the setting Moon. Cats, curious about surroundings, about sounds, about glitters and gleamings in the pre-dawn sky, had wandered off, by ones, twos and sevens. His staff purred contentedly in his hand.

From the west, a breeze arose, telling tales of the ocean, hinting of the further shore; of dragons, perhaps, or of a King reunited with his Queen.

Kinzel smiled and stepped out—westward, for lack of a reason to walk in another direction, and whistling.

All was Right with the world.

✧ Kin Ties ✧

"WHATEVER HAPPENED TO?" *Yes—not just a few stories in the Liaden Universe® series came from just that question. Sometimes it comes at a convention, or in an email, and sometimes it comes not from a reader, but from one of us. Just because we write an initial story doesn't mean we automatically understand all of the ramifications, and sometimes the only way to properly decide what happens next is to . . . physically* write *what happens next.*

In this case we'd posited a pilot surviving—against many odds—the crash of a spaceship. The follow-on to that crash had included the interference of Korval in an off-world Balance, and the eventual life-mating of that pilot into Korval. But there were unsettled questions, things we needed to know because our characters needed to know. This is that story—it couldn't be left undone because, after all, it involved Balance, Clan, and Kin Ties.

IT WAS THE OLD DREAM: Herself, the gun heavy in her hand, Grandfather a weight and a wall at her back. Before her, the man who had coldly slain her mother. He looked as his picture, that Grandfather had her study until she knew every line of his face, and would mistake him for no other pilot, on Casiaport or elsewhere.

In truth, it was not an ill-cast face. One could hardly credit that so clear a countenance belonged to a monster—and yet it was so. Grandfather had taught her.

Indeed, indeed, Ren Zel dea'Judan was every inch a monster, no matter how direct his gaze, or sweetly shaped his mouth. For this man, having murdered Elsu Meriandra Clan Jabun, then wrongly called the attention of the portmaster's office down upon Grandfather's business, an action that had cast Jabun from its rightful place among Casia's High Houses—and then? The Balance for this string of murderous mischief? What was brought down upon the head of Ren Zel dea'Judan for his sins against Clan Jabun, and Grandfather, too?

Why, that he should achieve a berth, and rank, on a merchant ship out of Liad itself, while she and Grandfather, the last of Clan Jabun proud enough to bear the name, lived pinched and retired, with neither associates nor allies to support them.

The root of it all was Ren Zel dea'Judan, and for the wrongs he had visited, unprovoked, upon Jabun, he must die.

That had been Grandfather's judgment, speaking as Delm Jabun.

It was Balance; it was hers to carry and commit, and here he stood before her, trembling as she held the gun, with Grandfather at her back. There would be no failure of her will. She would do her duty. There would, at last, be Balance.

. . . she woke before she pulled the trigger.

She always woke before she pulled the trigger, muscles tight, face wet, stomach roiling.

Carefully, so as not to wake the others, she slid out of bed, opened the window and stepped out onto the catwalk.

• • •✧• • •

THE HATCH CAME DOWN behind them, locking out the rest of the planet, and most particularly Delm Flenik, who desired what benefit an alliance with Korval might yet bring her clan. Ah, yes, the ether rang with her desire. And clashed, discordant, with her caution. She would meet with Korval's emissaries—the silly sister and her irregular lifemate—that much, for profit, she did risk. But to extend proper courtesy—to offer a guesting, or even so little as a formal meal with the clan entire? No, Flenik was not so rash as that!

"Never tell me you *wanted* another formal dinner out-clan," Anthora exclaimed, snatching the thought out of his head, as was her wont. "Had I not understood you to be entirely bankrupt in your account of polite nothings?"

She spun there in the hallway before him, jeweled pins askew among lively dark curls. He would have blamed this state of sudden charming disorder on the brisk breeze that had assaulted them on the gantry, did he not know his lady rather better than that.

His lady. In unlikely fact, as beautiful and fey as she stood before him, silver eyes smiling in a roguish face, Anthora yos'Galan Clan Korval *was* his lady. His lifemate. Recalling it still took his breath.

"Because we have been together so long," Anthora said, tipping her head.

"Because it seems simultaneously that we have been together since space was born, and have only this moment met."

She laughed. "There, now—that's pretty said! Perhaps we should have insisted upon dinner, after all!"

It was his turn to laugh. "Should I have made Flenik a like compliment?"

"No, that would never do, would it?" she answered, suddenly serious. "Father would have said that we must honor her care for Flenik's reputation and resources."

"And so we ought." Anthora's father had followed his lifemate into the long peace years before Ren Zel dea'Judan had stumbled into her life. As represented by his children, Er Thom yos'Galan had been a man of good sense and stern propriety; and—as a Master Trader was unlikely to be an idiot—a strong force for Korval's continued prominence among Liad's High Houses. The lesson that one must respect a delm's care for the clan was sound, but—

"Flenik cannot hope to keep the alliance a secret from her neighbors," Ren Zel pointed out. "If our visit escaped notice, the flow of goods sealed with the Tree-and-Dragon through Flenik's warehouses surely will not—and where stands prudence, then?"

"Where it has always stood, I expect," Anthora said, "somewhere between the shadow and the shade. Recall that our mission is to reaffirm existing ties, nor has Flenik been the most timid we have encountered."

No, there was that, Ren Zel allowed. He had permitted Flenik's disrespect of Anthora to put his temper into disarray.

"Surely the lady might be permitted her private thoughts," Anthora murmured, coming back down the short hall to put her hand on his sleeve. "We have grown easy between us, sharing this thought and that until speech becomes cumbersome. But we must recall that Flenik *showed* no disrespect, and if she failed of an invitation to guest, or to dine, proper courtesy to a trade partner does not demand either."

That was also true. He sighed and walked with her to the piloting chamber. Happily, this visit to Flenik was the last of those their delm had set them; soon, they would be on the way to the clan's new home on the world Surebleak, which he and his lifemate had scarcely seen. It was, indeed, the clan's hasty removal from Liad, in compliance with orders from the Council of Clans, that had made necessary the mission he and Anthora had just accomplished. Korval's outworld trade partners, having heard of their banishment, as had, indeed, all the galaxy, needed to be assured in person by one of the Line Direct that Korval not only intended to honor long-standing associations and agreements, but *was able* to honor them.

That they had not succeeded in soothing the fears of everyone the delm had bid them visit—well, and how *might* they have dealt with Venari, who had instructed the doorkeeper to deny them, and had the poor child hand out through the hatch an envelope containing contracts of reversion.

Venari the timid, Anthora had dubbed him. The reversions had also revealed a man desperately frightened—of the Council, or of Korval—or, possibly, of both.

It's of no mind, Anthora had said. *Val Con will send Shan to mend it, and you know he will find success, beloved.*

Ren Zel watched his lifemate lean over the copilot's board, checking for messages. He sighed again, and loosened the collar of his formal shirt. It would be good, he thought, to exchange finery for a sweater and ship clothes—or leathers, if Anthora fancied dinner on the port this eve.

"Let us dine from supplies," she said, her attention seemingly still on the copilot's board. "So we may be ready to lift for Casiaport, if Tower finds us an early slot."

Ren Zel froze, fingers at his collar.

"Casiaport," he said, hearing his voice flat with old pain. "Surely we will not."

Anthora looked at him over her shoulder, the quick movement dislodging at least one pin; he heard it strike the decking—silver to steel.

"Surely we shall, for Korval has desired it," she answered, raising her eyebrows as if perfect propriety was her nearest kin.

He took a breath. "As much as one dislikes to speak ill of the delms—"

"Oh, *do* by all means speak ill of the delms!" Anthora interrupted him. "But I beg you not to waste your genius! Wait until we are with them again, for surely you will find none who will agree with you more!"

It was heart-stopping, to hear one speak so of the delm—of *their* delm. The delm was the face and the voice of the clan. The delm husbanded the clan's resources—those resources including the life of every member of the clan. It was for the delm to order, and the clan member so ordered to provide. Without obedience to the delm—without every clan member striving always for the best good of the clan—all would be chaos and barbarism.

And yet—

"I know that the delm wishes to do honor," Ren Zel, forcing himself to speak evenly. "However, I believe that—I believe that, *in this instance,* the delm has failed to understand how . . . difficult it is for those who are not of Korval—those who have—those who have known only one world, one Code—who have not seen so much of odd custom as might a scout, or a soldier, a trader—even a pilot—" He paused, the better to weigh his words. Anthora's levity aside, it *was* the delm of whom he spoke.

Anthora had straightened, and stood watching him seriously from silver eyes, her hands tucked behind her back like a schoolgirl receiving a lesson from her tutor.

She said nothing; the ether conveyed the quality of her waiting. *Patiently* waiting.

Goaded, Ren Zel continued, perhaps, just a little, snappish.

"The delm fails to comprehend that there are those who will turn their face from profit rather than stand against custom. There is *no choice* in this offer Korval desires us to bring to Obrelt. The dead do not return to the world, even to accommodate Korval."

Bang!

It was not an actual explosion that assaulted him, he thought—not that. What struck him was only the manifestation of Anthora's anger on the ether.

"There are no dead men here!" she shouted. Her hair was stirring; he heard more pins strike music from the decking, and drew a breath.

"Beloved, you may say so, and I am dismayed to anger you, yet the truth—"

He scarcely saw her cross the deck. He felt his face taken, not gently, between her two palms, and her lips against his, hard, lewd, and desirous, waking his body with a shout and shiver, his blood coming at once to a boil, and almost he spent himself there and then.

Anthora released him as suddenly as she had snatched him, and stepped back.

"Now," she said, hands on hips, and silver eyes snapping. "Produce me this *dead man*."

"Custom," he answered, his voice thin and breathless. He dragged air deep into his lungs. "If you deliver me another such kiss, beloved, well you may produce a dead man."

Her lips quirked, but her eyes remained stormy.

"As you told me the story, your delm diced *against* custom at your death—winning you your license and a two-cantra stake."

"So he did, and very bold he was," Ren Zel answered. "But that does not mean Obrelt will—or can—abandon all propriety. We—*they*!—are shopkeepers; their strength—the reason that other clans hire them to keep their books, order their inventory, and manage their staffs—is that they *do* observe every propriety and are nothing out of the way." He took another breath, which he sighed out, suddenly tired and wistful.

"The business and the purpose of the clan was twice wholly disrupted by myself. I would, if I could, allow them their peace and their true course. I will say these things to Korval, and accept whatever comes of it."

"As if Val Con—or Miri!—would lash you to the Tree and lay you three stripes for disobedience," Anthora said, and sighed, herself.

"It shames me," she said softly, and he shivered, as her sadness brushed him. "Shames me, that I have won such a jewel as you are for myself, and for Korval, with no cost, and no honor paid. If it had been Obrelt that had cast you aside of their own will and spite, I would feel differently. But you were stolen from them, cruelly—"

"The man had lost a daughter," he murmured. "The heart of his life. Allow a father grief."

"I allow a father all he might require to comfort him, in such circumstance," Anthora said sharply. "But delms are held to higher standards."

There was, Ren Zel thought, no denying that. The delm, indeed, ought to reflect what was best and most honorable of the clan, as a moon, reflecting the glory of its sun. Jabun had used the power and position of his clan to bully and, yes, *steal* from those less moneyed, and lower-placed. Ill-done, the whole of it, and like to have killed one Ren Zel dea'Judan in truth, as well as by custom.

"Allow me," Anthora said softly. "Allow me at the least to go to your aunt, beloved. Allow me to kneel at her feet and thank her from my heart, for the astonishment and the delight that is yourself."

How *that* would please Aunt Chane! Ren Zel thought, with a mixture of horror and humor. To have a child of a High House kneel before her, thodelm of a middling mercantile House based upon an outworld? Every sensibility must rebel! And, yet, how could he ask his lifemate, who shared not only his life, but his soul, to carry any shame or dishonor? And especially for this, which was no more her fault than . . . his.

He stepped forward and raised his hand, gently, to cup her cheek.

"We will go together," he said. "You will say all that you must, respectfully and with restraint, and honor will put an end to shame."

Longing swept through him—hers—chill as a sudden rain, and gone as quickly. Anthora smiled at him, and turned her head to kiss his palm.

"Of course it will," she murmured.

• • • ✧ • • •

"BAD NIGHT, BETHY?" Sal asked when they met at the caf.

"The dream, again," she said, low-voice, so Rijmont, just behind her, wouldn't hear. Grandfather had taught her that it was not only shameful, but stupid, to show weakness. And, indeed, if it had been Rijmont who had dared to ask after her sleep, she might—no, she *would*—have given him the answer he deserved. Sal, though, was—different. Soon after she had joined the team as an emergency fill-in, he had found her sitting on the catwalk in the dark, chin nestled on arms folded over the rail, feet swinging in the darkness above the repair bay, far below. He'd sat down next to her, hooked his arms over the rail, and let his feet swing, too, and saying nothing at all.

It had occurred to her, after they had sat companionably together for some time, that perhaps he was concerned, lest she was thinking of throwing herself from the catwalk to the bottom of the bay—a considerable distance. Nor would such a fear be entirely beyond his scope; Kunkle's Repair had at that juncture only recently lost a team-member to a fall into the bay, which was how the temp-slot had opened for her.

"A bad dream," she had murmured, to ease him; for Sal of course stood senior to her, and was in addition "floor boss." It was a bad policy, to have a supervisor concerned of one's fitness for work.

She'd felt him nod, in the dark.

"Know all about bad dreams," he'd said, and said nothing more.

She resettled her chin on her arm, and stared down into the darkness until her eyes grew heavy and her thoughts sluggish. She'd pushed to her feet, then, staggering slightly, and found Sal's hand there to steady her.

"G'night," he'd said. "No dreams for either of us, 'til morning."

And so it had been, just as he said.

Alas, his dominion over dreams did not extend for more than a night or two, and it transpired that they met often, after the others were abed and long asleep. The catwalk was the usual meeting place, she sometimes finding him there before her. Later, after the team had voted to accept her fully; after she had seen her true name vanish inside the Terran "Bethy"—when she had built some small *melant'i* within the team—then, some few times, on very bad nights—his or hers—they walked out into the Night Port until they found a bakery or other eatery open on dark-license. They talked, on such excursions. She told him of Grandfather, a little, and how he had been cheated of his last cantra by persons who had been his allies, who he had trusted—and whose break of trust and simple theft, there had been insufficient resources to allow her to go for first.

He told her of his life before he'd come to Casiaport. He'd lost kin on his home world, in a repair accident. The *insurance company* had refused to pay on the claim, citing some safety deficiencies at the shop, and so Sal was made homeless, who was already kinless. He had signed on with the Kunkle Franchise, and had assisted in setting up repair yards on two worlds before Casiaport, which was when the Franchise vanished, and the Set-up Team became Kunkle's Repair. Sal had been third senior, then; he, with the two above him in rank, had taken Kunkle as their surname, and filed for a family business license, which Casiaport granted.

Sal was second senior now, behind Nan, Robert having sold back his share and taken a crew berth on a tramp the year before she joined the team.

"Second in line and the bidness in the black," Sal had said during one of their recent Night Port rambles. "Time to expand operations, settle in an' get married."

It had been, she thought at the time, a joke, and she smiled. They joked now; shared commonplaces, and Sal had become . . . Sal was . . .

Sal was trustworthy, she told herself. A valued comrade.

Which Rijmont certainly was not.

She received her cereal with a nod of thanks, moved down the caf line, drew tea, and passed out into the larger room, slipping into a table for two near the wall. In a moment, Sal joined her, smiling, though his eyes looked as heavy as hers felt.

"And your own rest?" she asked him.

"Excellent, what there was of it." His smile deepened and her heart constricted, as it came to her that Sal might *not* have been joking, and that a bed-friend might be the reason for both the excellence of his sleep and its brevity.

And what was it to her, she thought in the next heartbeat, if Sal should have a bed-friend—or a dozen such! He was a well-looking man, though Terran, and the subtle strength of his manner, which she thought must recommend him as a lover.

"Can't talk about it—not yet," he said, spooning cereal. "It's looking good though, Bethy—better than—well. Once it's firm, you'll be the first to know."

Breakfast, never particularly flavorful, suddenly sat ill on her tongue. Truly, the cook must have burnt the grain. She put the spoon down and sipped her tea, searching for an excuse to rise from table, so that she need hear no more.

"Better have that," Sal said, nodding toward her bowl. "Nan's gotta line on a repair upstairs. Waiting on the earnest hitting the account and and ack on the go-ahead. Should be ready by the time we hit the shift. You in a mood to fly?"

Her blood quickened. When was she not in a mood to fly? And, truth told, though her value to the crew lay in her second-class license, it was rare enough that an opportunity to exercise her skill came forward.

"Where?" she asked, picking up her spoon again and attacking the cereal with a will.

"Long orbit."

She smiled.

"Thought you'd like that," he said, with satisfaction.

He put his empty bowl on the tray; she finished her meal in a rush that would have earned a scolding from Grandfather. But—a lift to long orbit! Such adventures did not come to her every day, nor even every relumma! Even Grandfather must have—

She aborted that thought, and looked to Sal.

"Who comes with me?"

"Dorlit, Jon, Marsel, and Kei."

"Not you?" she asked, disappointed, for the crew never misbehaved when Sal was there.

He shook his head. "Gotta stay close," he said, again with a hint of that secret smile.

"Who will be crew boss?" she asked after a moment, as if she had not seen the smile.

"You," he said, and she froze with her cup halfway to the tray.

"*I?*"

He nodded, setting his empty cup aside. "It's time," he said, which she couldn't very well argue, since it lay within his *melant'i* to decide such things. Still, she was aware of a certain trepidition.

"Dorlit'll back you up," Sal continued, and she breathed easier. Dorlit was sensible; even Rijmont respected her. And, really, the thought came, rumbling in her head like Grandfather's voice—why should she be trepidatious? Was she not Cyrbet Meriandra Clan Jabun, a pilot of the line? It was her destiny to order her lessers.

Undoubtedly this was true, for Jabun Himself had taught her so. Still, she admitted to herself, it was good that Dorlit would be there, as back-up.

"Time to go," Sal said, pushing back his chair. "Not good to keep the client waiting."

"No," she agreed, rising. "Nor the ship."

• • • ✧ • • •

HE HAD DRESSED, not in the finery required of one who came as an emissary of Korval, but as a pilot—leather jacket over dark shirt and tough trousers.

Anthora, tousled and fresh from her shower, considered this ensemble with head tipped to a side. He thought that she would make an argument, though the ether displayed no such brewing storm.

After a moment, she nodded.

"Surely, it is neither a shame nor a wonder, that one of Korval should arrive as a pilot," she said calmly. "Will you call for a car, love? I'll be another moment, only."

The car, having brought them from the port into the city, now drew to the curb. The back door slid open. Ren Zel touched the intercom, murmuring, "Wait," to the driver, before he swung onto the walk, and bent down to offer Anthora his hand.

She did not require his assistance, of course. But she put her hand in his as she rose lightly to his side.

Together, they turned—and it was then that his heart utterly failed him.

Confronting them—was nothing but a short walkway, and a fence, high and white, with a gate set center to the walk. Beyond, one saw the tops of small trees, such as trees grew on Casia, and beyond those a hint of the house, roof line taller than the trees, and the wink of a window, down below.

Obrelt's Clanhouse. He had grown up here—on this street, inside that fence, within the House, protected by clan and kin.

Until neither had protected him, at the last.

His chest constricted, the fence, the gate, the house blurred out of sense, and it was hard to breathe. He *remembered*—he remembered walking out of the gate, down the walk, to the empty street—incompletely healed, grieving, stunned—*alone.*

Cast out.

Nothing.

Dead.

It was true, he thought, breathless: The dead did not live again.

Despite everything Korval might do.

He could not—gods, he *could* not face this. Dead—twice dead—but for the kindness of Terrans, and the meddling of Dragons.

Three times dead, if he could not get air into his lungs, or calm the frenzied pounding of his heart. Perhaps someone spoke; he thought—but there was the roaring in his ears.

Quick or dead, he *was* a pilot—and in his need he reached for a pilot's calming exercise. The familiar discipline shattered on the rocks of his pain, leaving him lost in a disorienting blackness, chest laboring now, and it was desperation, or instinct, that threw his will into the ether, where there was silence, and the weaving of fine golden threads, calming, and . . . correct—correct beyond logic, or the designs of men, or the principles set out in the Code.

Ineluctable, the weaving stretched as far as he could compass—farther, in space, time, and beyond—with nary a thread out of place, nor any disruption of purpose.

Peace filled him; wit returned. He cast about, as one did in this place, and perceived nearby a complexity of silver and azure, lightly stitched with ebon and scarlet.

So did Anthora manifest in the ether. His lifemate, his soul, she for whom he would do anything—even live, if she required it of him. He felt a wave of tenderness, wrapped her in it, felt her love fill and strengthen him.

It required an active application of will; he opened his eyes once again.

The fence was in repair, he noted coolly, and had recently been painted. The trees and the roof were in good order. He sighed and felt a burden he had not known he had carried fall from his shoulders. Obrelt prospered. Jabun had honored, at least, *those* conditions of Balance. The clan had not foundered into poverty on his account.

He took another breath, felt Anthora's thought touch him, questioning, and nodded.

"Lead," he said softly, "and I will follow. My print no longer opens the gate, and the House may yet recall that I am forbidden."

• • • ✧ • • •

CHANE DEA'JUDAN sat in what had become her favorite chair in the solar at the back of the house, reading. She had since her retirement rediscovered the joys of fiction, surprising herself by finding that her taste ran to tales of high adventure and high *melant'i*, with improbable twists based on obscure points of the Code.

She had been for many years thodelm, Obrelt's *working hand*, as the vernacular had it, as if the delm had not, indeed, worked tirelessly for the clan and the well-being of all, until one evening he had simply sat down in his chair during the hour before Prime and declared that he was rather tired.

When she had come to wake him, just a half-dozen minutes before the hour, he had already left clan and kin far behind.

In the solar, Chane sighed over her book. Even in death, Arn Eld left Obrelt's affairs in good order—the nadelm had been working at his side for more than a year and knew the status of every bit of the clan's business. She had stayed with the new delm until it was plain that the child was steady, then stood aside for her own successor, likewise well-trained and able.

Not that her retirement afforded her endless days of reading. An elder of the house taught the youngers, listened to the halflings, counseled the working adults, and commiserated with her age-mates. All that, and there was still time to read in the sun, vicariously tasting adventure.

From behind, there came a small noise, as if someone scuffed uncertain boots on the warm stone floor.

"Yes?"

"Excuse me, Grand-aunt," Den Ton, who at eight years local was standing his first shift as doorkeeper, said breathlessly. "There's a lady—a pilot. She asks for your kind attention."

Her kind attention? Chane frowned slightly, then made her expression serene, lest the child think that he had erred.

"Come to me," she said calmly, and when he had done so, asked gently, "Has the pilot a name?"

"Indeed, she sends her card." He produced it, relatively unrumpled, from his pocket.

Chane glanced down—and blinked; in that first moment, the clan sign was everything that she saw. Tree and Dragon.

She took a breath. And what had Korval to do with Obrelt, save what they had already done? It had been a Korval Master Pilot who had so enraged Jabun that Obrelt must need forfeit not only their sole pilot, but a clan member of strong *melant'i*, a tolerant brother, an affectionate nephew, giving to the youngers, full of life, blameless—oh, without a doubt, blameless.

. . . Which Korval had known, and having done damage, repaired what they might, taking Obrelt's dead up into their lead trade ship—no less than *Dutiful Passage*—under the hand of that very same Master Pilot, so came the tale from out of the Port.

Alas, that had been the last tale touching them to come out of the Port, and the delm had forbidden her to seek further, for fear, at first, of what further ills Jabun might visit upon Obrelt. Later, when Jabun's fortunes had turned, and Arn Eld had gone beyond care, it was fear for the boy himself that had restrained her, for whatever—if anything—Korval had contrived, it surely would not suffer a stranger's hand upon it.

And it had been so . . . very . . . long. Surely, whatever further doom awaited the innocent dead had long since fallen.

"Grand-aunt?" Den Ton asked, his voice uncertain.

Chane swallowed old anger and sorrow, smoothed her face and looked again at the card, now quivering a little in small, uncertain fingers.

Anthora yos'Galan Clan Korval the legend ran. Not the Master Pilot, then. Or, at least, not the *same* Master Pilot.

"She asked first for Obrelt," Den Ton said. "But the delm is from House. Then it was you that she asked to see, Grand-aunt."

Chane sighed. "The lady perhaps works with an out-of-date book," she said. "In the delm's absence, you must offer the thodelm, child. Where have you placed the pilot?"

"I asked them of their kindness to wait in the visitor's parlor," he said, which was perfectly correct. "But, Grand-aunt, I *did* say that the thodelm was to House, if she pleased, and she said that she wished to speak a word to Chane dea'Judan, if the House permitted." He swallowed, his cheeks flushing.

"I ought to have gone to Wil Bar in any case, oughtn't I?" he asked, voice trembling.

"When a stranger comes unexpected to the door and asks for one of the clan by name, yes, my child, it is correct to bring the matter to delm or thodelm." She glanced again at the card, took her decision and slipped it from the child's fingers, closing her book as she rose.

Den Ton looked up at her, mouth sightly open. "Grand-aunt?"

"I will see the lady," she said quietly. Wil Bar would only have to call her, anyway. After all, the tragedy which bound Obrelt to Korval had happened on her watch.

• • • ✧ • • •

THE REPAIR JOB had gone well, the crew working in harmony and with goodwill. Not a little of that goodwill had to do with the bonus promised by the client, should the business take no more than forty-eight Standard Hours, which deadline they handily met. This was entirely due to Kei's Satchel, which he had insisted on bringing, despite the protests of both Jon and Marsel, both of whom swore that their kits were complete and they needed no such ragtag collection of odds and ends as resided in the Satchel.

Only, the ship under repair had not quite the standard locking mechanisms, and it had seemed that the bonus and the contract, too, would falter on the lack of a particular nut, absent by age from both Marsel's kit and Jon's, but present very near the bottom of Kei's.

That circumstance had seen the job complete an hour before the client's deadline, and the bonus had been transferred with the repair fee before they undocked and began the long spiral in to Casiaport.

She trusted that the lesson was learnt—and was certain of it when Marsel joined Kei in the galley, and asked how he chose the contents of the Satchel.

Later, when they were returned to Kunkle's small yard, and she had locked down the board, herded her crew to the office and signed the job complete with Nan, since Sal was not to hand—after all that was done, she walked cross-port to the Guildhall—the *Liaden* Guildhall—to show her card and file her hours.

"The record will relay from the Terran hall," said the clerk on duty—a man she did not know from previous visits.

"I prefer to come here," she answered, sharply. "Is there a problem?"

He stared at the screen for a long moment; the screen where he would see, in addition to her piloting record and Guild information, her name.

"No problem," he said softly, and pulled the card from the reader, offering it to her on the tips of his fingers. "Pilot Meriandra."

"Thank you," she said, snatching the precious thing. She turned, her temper unsettled, and looked up by habit, to the ship board.

Kunkle's vessel, being registered to the Terran side of the port of course did not display, but—

"*Korval*, here?" asked one of those nearby who was also perusing the board, perhaps of the room at large.

She frowned and stared up at the board on the tradeship side, thinking that it was come at last and again, as it had once before—*Dutiful Passage*, which had rewarded the enemy of her clan. Her heart began to beat faster, her hands curling into fists.

"Courier," someone else said, and her eyes jumped, found the name in the middle of the third column—*Dragon Song*—and the name of the pilot who sat as first.

Ren Zel dea'Judan.

• • •✧• • •

CHANE DISMISSED DEN TON to the doorkeeper's station and continued alone to the visitors' parlor. She paused a moment outside of the closed door to compose herself and to still a sudden qualm upon the realization that the costume she wore was more suited to the comfort of reading in the solar than greeting High House guests.

Well, she thought, smoothing her sleeves, if Korval *would* call unannounced, demanding speech with one of the clan, then Korval could take what was found—and well it was that she had not been working the garden this noon!

One more deep breath to center herself, then she slid the door aside and stepped through.

At first glance, the parlor was empty—second glance found two evenly matched silhouettes against the sun-filled window through which the pilots doubtless admired the small garden planted just outside for the pleasure of those who waited.

Pilots. Chane hesitated, then recalled that the boy had said he had put *them* in the visitor's parlor.

Even as she recalled it, one of the two turned, and came forward into the less dazzling center of the room, where she paused, and bowed.

Deeply.

Chane had been schooled in the forms; Casia might be an outworld, but that did not mean the Code or proper manners were lost. Having thus been properly and thoroughly schooled, Chane recognized that the bow was of one acknowledging a debt too great to Balance.

Precisely, in fact, the bow she had been about to offer the lady who was now straightening.

"Anthora yos'Galan Clan Korval," the lady stated, in a voice like rich, dark velvet. She gave Chane her whole face, a bit wide in the cheek, with a strong nose, and a chin that was frankly pointed. Not approaching a beauty, this Korval. Which fact one entirely forgot upon meeting her wide silver eyes. Eyes and face were solemn, for all the world as if the lady were an erring halfling awaiting her elder's judgment.

Her elder, in the meanwhile, recalled her own manners, and bowed, not as she had intended, but a civil welcome to the House, and said, gently, "Chane dea'Judan Clan Obrelt."

She straightened. "How may I serve you, Anthora yos'Galan Clan Korval?"

The eyes smiled.

"To serve *me,*" she said, "you need only greet my lifemate, and, of your very great kindness bestow upon him your kiss."

Her heart constricted painfully and for a moment she thought she might follow Arn Eld, on whom—save one—the burden of the death had lain heaviest. It had been his decision, that the clan could not sacrifice itself entire for the life of only one. His decision, too, to thwart Jabun as much as might be done, within the line and letter of the Code, though he would never after hear praise for that.

"Ren Zel?" she scarcely knew the voice for her own, rough as it was with tears and loss.

The silhouette that had remained at the window turned now, slowly, and walked deliberately forward, stopping at the lady's side, his face set and closed.

It was a man's face she saw, honed by the events of a dozen Standards. A man's eyes, wary, but steady on her own. His shoulders had broadened, filling the jacket he wore with a pilot's easy pride.

A death wounds all it touches, Anthora yos'Galan said—or did she? It seemed that the words had the quality of her own thought, and yet—

This can be Healed.

Of a certainty, Chane thought—can be and *should be* Healed. Arn Eld had taken the worst wound to himself, as a delm must, for the best good of the clan. But the clan—knowing that their safety was bought with life of one of their own? It had made them timid, that death; it had lessened them and made them aware of how fragile a thing was honor.

"Ren Zel," she said again, and reached to him, her hand shaking as her fingers brushed his cheek. "Child."

Her vision blurred; she felt her fingers caught in a strong grip, and the warm pressure of his lips.

"Aunt Chane," he whispered. "I've missed you so much."

• • • •✧• • •

IT WAS SOME FEW MOMENTS before she composed herself sufficiently to allow the child of her heart to seat her, and accepted a handkerchief from his lifemate's hand.

"Shall I call for tea, ma'am?" that lady asked gently, and Chane half-choked a laugh.

"You will terrify the kitchen, if you dare," she said. Ren Zel knelt beside her chair, her hand held between his palms. She blinked the last of the tears away and looked up at Anthora yos'Galan.

"In a moment, I will call for refreshments, and the thodelm, but first, if you will, what it is that *Korval* wants of us?"

"For of course Korval must want something," the lady said ruefully and sank to her knees at Chane's other side. She folded her hands on the arm of the chair and rested her pointed chin on them.

"And yet, as it happens, Korval *does* want something," Ren Zel murmured.

"True enough," the lady agreed, and slanted her eyes whimsically at Chane's face.

Ren Zel, thought his aunt, must find life interesting with such a charming scoundrel at his side. Anthora yos'Galan laughed, merrily, but with no cause that Chane detected. There were rumors, she thought, recalling them now, that the youngest yos'Galan was not quite right in her head . . .

"You must forgive my lady," Ren Zel murmured. "She is from time to time flutter-headed." He glanced at the lady in question. "Are you not, beloved?"

"Indeed I am," she answered. "I will also allow *quicker to school than to be schooled*." She smiled, sweetly.

"You were," Ren Zel prodded softly, "charged by the delm to speak."

"So I was." Anthora yos'Galan sat back on her heels, folded her hands onto her knees like a good, obedient child, and inclined her head gravely.

"I am to say, on behalf of Korval, that Obrelt's loss is three times Korval's gain. Korval therefore seeks Balance between our two clans. That custom does not allow us to sign contract and compensate Obrelt rightly for its treasure, we are aware. However, Balance may be achieved in other ways, if Obrelt is willing." The lady paused, her head tipped, as if she regarded a written page before her.

"There is," she said, looking to Ren Zel, "a list of arrangements and accomodations that might be made and met, but truly, beloved, I think those best left for Obrelt or for dea'Judan's thodelm."

"I think so, too," he said gently. "Aunt Chane? We had heard that the delm was away . . ."

"So she is." She felt him start, and extended her free hand to stroke his hair. "The years bring change," she said softly. "Farin is delm now; and Wil Bar stands thodelm."

"And Uncle Arn Eld?" he asked softly.

"Arn Eld embraced peace," she answered, and saw the sweet mouth tighten.

"I had wished," he said, glancing down, "many times I had wished to thank him, for having contrived so well on my behalf. To have managed it so that I kept my license . . . I would have died in truth, had he not been so bold."

"So I told him, again and again," she said. "Perhaps he would have believed *you*." She took a breath and looked back to Anthora yos'Galan.

"The delm will return by Prime. Will you wait?"

"Gladly," the lady said. "And Ren Zel may renew the acquaintance of his kin."

• • •✧• • •

SHE CHARTED a rambling course through the port until the horn sounded for Night Port. The racket of day-side security screens going down, while night-side screens rattled up had roused her from thoughts that had only gotten more tangled the longer she walked.

Night Port. She should go home. Sal would be worried. No, she reminded herself, Sal was not there. Likely, he was engaged more pleasantly, a thought that did nothing to lighten her mood or ease her thoughts. And who was *she*, she thought angrily, to begrudge Sal joy? If she truly valued him as a comrade, she would rejoice in his good fortune.

The crew-room was empty when she pushed the door open. Night Port though it was, it was not so late as that. Her crew had worked hard and on long-shift—they might well have gone upstairs to the dorm. Or they had gone out to celebrate the bonus by drinking it, though surely Dorlit would have—

"Stop that!"

She turned, seeing the door to the back office standing ajar, which it surely should not be, now that Day Port had turned.

There was a confused sound from the dimness beyond the door, as if of boots scuffed on the 'crete floor, a sharp cry and a low grunt.

"Stop it!" the voice came again—"I don't *want* to!"

She threw herself across the room, slamming the door open with one hand, and hitting the light switch with the other.

It was Rijmont she saw first; Rijmont with his back to the door, his weight pinning Lorin against the wall.

"Don't want to, is it?" he snarled. "You wanted hard enough just a minute gone!"

"Stop!" Lorin twisted. Rijmont grabbed her chin in his free hand and forcibly tilted her face up, bringing his lips down on hers.

Cyrbet moved, grabbed the man by his shoulder, spun him 'round and slapped his face so hard he staggered back, away from Lorin. She put herself in front of the girl, and stared at Rijmont, who stared back, the mark of her hand livid on his pale cheek.

"Lorin said no," she said, hearing her voice steady and hard. "Leave."

"She said yes, too," he spat, his hands curling into fists. "Which one should I believe?"

"You should believe *no*," Lorin shouted, and Cyrbet inclined her head.

"You should believe no," she repeated. "Leave, Rijmont," she said again, and added something she had heard Sal say, when tensions ran high, "Take a walk."

"Well, I don't wanna take a walk, *Bethy. I* wanna finish what I came in here for, and it ain't no bidness of yours. Who named you crew boss?"

"Sal did," Dorlit's shadow moved in the door. She stepped into the office, Jon, Marsel, and Kei filing in behind her.

"Bethy," she said, with a respectful nod. "Need us to do some clean-up?"

• • •✧• • •

THE THODELM, his cousin Wil Bar, had cannily handled the matter of introductions to the larger House by presenting Anthora yos'Galan Clan Korval and her lifemate. It was, strictly, proper, and gave those who could not meet his eyes leave to look elsewhere.

Of those who was his sister Eba, her distress overflowing into tears and a wordless, hasty retreat into the depths of the house.

His eldest sister, Farin, now Obrelt Herself, had no such difficulty. She embraced him, cheek to cheek, as she had sometimes done when he had been more regular, and gave Anthora full honor as Korval's representative. Nor was she behind in the news.

"One hears that the Council banishes Korval from the homeworld," she said, having heard Korval's greeting from Anthora's lips. "Forgive me if I seem pert, but this does seem an odd time to be pursuing new alliances. Surely Korval must look first to themselves."

"Korval has always counted allies above cantra," Anthora responded—an answer that had become rote for them both over the course of their journey. "And before you protest that we are not allies, ma'am, only consider that Korval and Obrelt are bound together by two events—a death, and a lifemating. We have the opportunity, now, to decide which of those events will inform the future."

He had scarcely to speak at all, it being very quickly settled in principle that Obrelt and Korval would turn their faces together toward the future.

Anthora then presented the delm's list, which Farin received, prudently requesting time to consider the various items in light of the best good of Obrelt. This, his lady readily agreed to, and so they went down to Prime,

Any awkwardness at table was handled simply enough by seating him, with Anthora, at the top, bracketed by delm, thodelm, and Aunt Chane. This left those lower down-table free to talk among themselves, which they did, so the ether told him, with considerable relief.

As Anthora was speaking with Farin and Wil Bar, he applied himself to Aunt Chane. She asked what his life had been like, after he had left Casia, and he truthfully told her that it had been well enough in terms of work and health and friendship.

"How strange, all that came of us wishing to see you properly wed, and the clan enriched by your child," she said pensively. "And how much better for all, had we never gone down that road."

"No," Ren Zel said softly, casting a glance into the ether and the orderly waltz of the threads. "No, that I cannot allow. Had you not done as you did, I might never have met, and been joined with, my lady." He smiled at her frown and dared to place his hand over hers, where it lay near her plate.

"Indeed, Aunt Chane, you have contrived to make me happy beyond anything I could have known to hope for. I thank you, with all my heart."

• • •✧• • •

MARSEL AND JON stayed with Lorin, while she, with Dorlit and Kei, took a rather bruised Rijmont to the port proctors. There he would be held until Sal came to arrange his release, or eighteen local hours had elapsed, whichever came first. She had Rijmont's Kunkle ID and pass-keys in her pocket; they would be turned over to Sal when she saw him.

But Sal was still absent when they returned. Nan said, worriedly, that she hadn't thought it would take so long . . .

"It?" she asked, but Nan only pressed her lips together and shook her head.

"Boss bidness," Dorlit said, around a sudden, wide yawn. "I'm beat."

There was a mutter of agreement from those present, and a

movement toward the stairs to the dorm. Dorlit stopped with her foot on the bottom step and turned.

"Coming, Bethy?"

She shook her head. "I'll wait for Sal."

"See you in the morning, then."

The footsteps faded. She heard the dorm's door cycle, and sighed. It was not conceivable that she would be able to sleep until she had told Sal what had transpired, given over the things from Rijmont's pockets, and heard what he thought of her actions.

That she had done well in the main—she did think so. Though taking one of the crew to the proctors, she thought, carrying a cup of strong tea to the table—bringing the port into a dispute between comrades—perhaps *that* had not been best done. Had there been any room, closet or cubby inside Kunkle's where they might have confined him without the possibility of mischief . . . but not even Kei could think of such a place.

The more she thought on it, the more it sat ill with her. Kunkle's crew held itself close, meted reward and punishment within the terms agreed upon by the crew. It was as if she had called the proctors into their rooms to restrain Grandfather during one of his tempers. Such a thing would have been improper. Disloyal.

Sighing, she nodded over her cup, half-dreaming and half-remembering . . .

She remembered Grandfather drilling her with the weapon, striking her when her aim was less than true. Once, the blow had landed more heavily than he had intended; she had fallen and struck her head—and awakened, moments or hours later, in Grandfather's arms, his tears falling hot on her face as he called her over, and over, "Elsu . . ."

She shook her head, rousing to drink some tea. Out on the port, a horn sounded the half-night.

Sal had still not returned.

It was familiar, this sitting in the dark alone. For a moment, she wondered why—and then she remembered. Before Grandfather had died, when all the rooms except the kitchen, the informal parlor, and the study had been sealed . . . she had often sat late alone, nodding over a cup of tea, listening to the night-sounds, thinking of death and duty.

That Ren Zel dea'Judan was the author of all the misfortune that had befallen Clan Jabun in the years following her mother's death . . . by then, she no longer believed. The clan had shrunk to herself and to Grandfather; her elder kin escaping as they could into apprenticeships, alliances, partnerships off-world, where *Jabun* was not a curse, nor *Meriandra* a threat.

After, when Grandfather, too, had gone, leaving his debt and his anger for her to resolve, she took her license, her ring, what coins were hers by right, and walked out of the great, empty house; down to the port, intending to buy passage or find work.

Her coins had not been enough to buy her way off-world in emulation of her cousins; and her second-class license did not trump the peril of her name. It was then that she sought the Terran side of the port, and put her name on every available employment list.

So at last she had come to Kunkle's, accepting the comradeship of Terrans; the doubtful camouflage of Bethy.

But she was *not* Bethy—a Terran with neither past nor *melant'i*. She was Cyrbet Meriandra Clan Jabun, the last of her clan, and by that fact, the delm. The last possession of the clan, saving herself, its instrument, was a debt. A debt she had never thought she might see Balanced. Until now.

Ren Zel dea'Judan had returned to Casia.

She could redeem everything. No more dishonor. No more nightmares.

She needed only to rise, and to act.

• • •✧• • •

IN THEIR CABIN aboard *Dragon Song*, Ren Zel waked of a sudden, certain that someone had called his name. Anthora lay with her head on his shoulder, her breath deep and regular. He looked into the ether, thinking that she might have inadvertently engaged him into one of her dreams, as had happened once or twice—but it seemed not. Her pattern on the ether was consistent with one who was profoundly asleep, glowing yet with the aftermath of energetically enjoyed lust.

And, yet, it had been so clear. A woman's voice; his name; a sense of—

He laughed, softly. Perhaps, he said to himself, it was you who dreamed yourself awake? Have you become so accustomed to the strange that you fail to consider the commonplace?

Amused, he closed his eyes, settling his cheek against Anthora's hair . . .

Ren Zel dea'Judan.

This time he opened his eyes to a cabin shimmering with gold.

He blinked, trying to return himself to everyday sight, for surely he needn't see this *now*—when the business with Obrelt was done in all but detail, and Korval, in their wisdom, had begun a healing long delayed.

His daily sight did not return, however, and the threads began to beguile his sense, so that he found himself following this one and that one—and *that* one, which was oddly kinked, hot—feverish.

Ren Zel frowned, reached—and snatched his awareness back to himself. It was not lightly done, to interfere with the threads. Indeed, it were best to have nothing to do with them at all, which he would not, excepting that it was his gift, to be Sighted in this way—and a blessing it was, for it allowed him to share fully with Anthora.

Again, he considered that odd thread, bringing his awareness close, subjecting it to minute study.

The thread pulsed, shedding flakes of gold, showing a core of molten red, like a raw wound.

Ren Zel bit his lip. That was . . .unnatural. That, he needed to deal with.

Tenderly, he slid Anthora's head from his shoulder to the pillow, and slipped out of bed, rapidly dressing in the glow of golden threads.

"Love?" Anthora muttered sleepily from the bed. "What—" Her voice sharpened, no longer sleep-drenched. "Ren Zel! Where are you going?"

"I am going out on the port for a moment," he said softly. "Sleep, beloved; I'll be back soon."

"Stay!" she cried—a Command, spoken with all the power of an extremely powerful dramliza. He felt the disruption it made in the ether, extended his will and batted it aside as he exited the cabin.

Behind him, Anthora scrambled out of bed and snatched up her clothes. It was a matter of moments only, but he had already descended the gantry by the time she reached the hatch.

Swearing, she ran after, following his signature in the ether.

• • •✧• • •

THE GUN WAS HEAVY—heavier even than it was in the dream—but she had no care for that. Was she not Cyrbet Meriandra Clan Jabun? She could bear any burden, save dishonor.

No, that was wrong—no, it *was* right! Grandfather had used to say so, and Grandfather was right. He had been delm, had he not? The delm was always right.

Now, she was delm. And she would also be right.

How noisy it was on the port this evening. She could scarcely hear herself think.

"Bethy!" The voice was familiar—beloved, she admitted it. On this night, she would finally and entirely be truthful with herself. She slowed briefly; he caught up and put his hand on her arm.

"Bethy, hey, I've got something to tell you. Said you'd be the first, didn't I? I'm sorry it took so long to get the papers signed, but—"

"Sal . . ."

"Are you OK?" He extended a blunt hand and brushed her hair from her brow—tenderly, as if she were a child. "Bethy, listen, I've got news. Good news."

"Good news?" She stared, seeing the smile, the *happiness* in him, then turned and resumed walking.

"Hey, aren't you interested?" Sal cried, running after her.

"I am interested—after," she said. "Sal, I have a duty. Please, when I return, you will tell me everything—this good news."

He cocked an eyebrow and kept pace with her, his eyes shrewd now.

"Something heavy in that pocket," he noted. "You ain't after beaning Rijmont with one of my good wrenches, are you?"

It was a joke. She was expected to laugh. She shook her head. "The proctors have Rijmont," she said.

"'Bout time. Bethy, you're scaring me," Sal said, and grabbed her arm. Her hand slid out of the pocket, showing the gun.

Sal's fingers tightened. He stopped and pulled her to a stop beside him in a pool of light.

"Sal, let me go."

"Hell I will! Bethy, where're you going? This like that dream you told me about? The one about your grandfather and that burden he put on you? Give me the gun."

"No." She tightened her grip and looked into his face. It would be easy, to give Sal the gun, to let him turn her from this. Bethy might do so. Delm Jabun . . . could not.

No. She straightened. Delm Jabun *would* not. She would have Balance. For the best good of the clan.

"Release me," she said, as gently as she might. "Sal, I have duty."

"Any duty involving a gun needs some close examination," Sal said grimly. "Bethy . . ."

"My name is not Bethy," she told him, sharply now. "It is—"

"Cyrbet Meriandra," a man's gentle voice said out of the shadows before them. "Clan Jabun."

Sal's grip loosened in surprise. She took advantage of his lapse to pull her arm free.

"Show yourself," she snapped, wrapping both hands around the gun's grip.

The shadows moved, reshaped themselves into a pilot in plain port leathers. His hair was brown, his face calm and comely.

"Ren Zel dea'Judan," he said, with a nod that was courteous, between pilots. "Clan Korval."

"If I was you, I'd run," Sal said frankly. "Bethy's a little off her head right now."

The pilot smiled, and shook his head; she could feel the weight of his attention on her and squared her shoulders, the better to bear it.

"You called me, perhaps, Pilot?" he asked.

"Perhaps I did," she replied. There was a small sound in the night, and she looked to Ren Zel dea'Judan's right, where another pilot stepped out of the shadows, dark hair stirring about her head, though there was no breeze on-port tonight.

"Ren Zel," she said, her voice soft and strong.

He raised a hand and she took a breath, folded her hands before her and said nothing more.

So, then. Cyrbet raised her chin and looked into his eyes.

"You killed my mother," she said. "My grandfather never forgave you."

"It is a terrible thing," Ren Zel dea'Judan said, "to lose a child."

Cyrbet licked her lips.

"You ruined Clan Jabun," she said, continuing the litany of those things this man had visited upon them. "My grandfather hated you for that."

The pilot bowed his head; said nothing.

She raised the gun, slowly, as Grandfather had taught her, until she still practiced what she must do, in her dreams.

"He taught me," she said. "He taught me to hate you. He taught me to use this, so that I would, one day, achieve Balance."

The other pilot, the woman, moved sharply, and subsided at once, a hand fisted at her breast; she saw it from the corner of her eye. Ren Zel dea'Judan never looked aside, his face calm, as if the gun had no meaning for him.

"I am here, now," Cyrbet said, going into the High Tongue for the correct phrase, "as Jabun's delm and the instrument of my grandfather's will. He last wish was for Balance with Ren Zel dea'Judan. I hereby fulfill his Balance, for the best good of the clan."

She reversed the gun and extended it to the brown-haired pilot, butt-first.

He stepped forward to receive it; held it with the muzzle pointed toward the ground.

Gently, he bowed.

"Lady, we are in Balance. Your grandfather's will is achieved; Jabun's honor is restored. Let there be peace, and let all wounds heal."

It was done.

Cyrbet felt her knees begin to tremble; felt Sal's hand come under her arm, supporting her.

"All done, now?" he asked, his voice careful.

"All done, now," she agreed, and nodded to Ren Zel dea'Judan and his second.

"Good e'en, Pilots."

"Good e'en," said the woman, coolly.

"Good e'en," said the man. "Sleep well."

"Let's go, Bethy," Sal said, turning her back toward Kunkle's. "You had a long day and a busy night, and you ain't told me yet if you're gonna marry me."

"Did you ask?" she inquired, and the two of them walked away without a backward look.

• • • ✧ • • •

ANTHORA STEPPED to his side.

"That," she said, "was extraordinarily dangerous. Please do not expose yourself so, beloved! What should I have done if you had been killed?"

"But how could I have been, when you extracted the pellets?" he murmured, slipping the gun into his pocket and turning to offer her his arm. "Where are they?"

She extended her fist, opening the fingers one by one to show six pellets lying in her palm—and suddenly laughed.

"All for naught. The young delm was wiser than I guessed."

Ren Zel sighed, looked into the ether and smiled.

✧ Eleutherios ✧

***THIS STORY WAS WRITTEN** for Baen.com, in advance of the release of* Necessity's Child, *in which the Bedel play an important role. The word "eleutherios" is an epithet of the Greek god Dionysus; it means, "the liberator."*

IT HAD BEEN MANY YEARS since the organ had last given voice. Friar Julian had been a younger man—though by no means a *young* man—then, and had wept to hear the majesty brought forth by his fingers.

Godsmere Abbey had been great, then, before the punishments visited by earth and air. Now it, like the city surrounding, was . . . not quite a ruin. Just . . . very much less than it once had been.

Though it no longer worked, Friar Julian cared for the organ, still, waxing the wood, polishing the bright-work, dusting the keys, the bench, the pedals. As the organist, it had been his duty to care for the organ. Duty did not stop simply because the organ was broken.

Indeed, it was all of his duty, now: The care and keeping of odd objects—some whole, some broken, others too strange to know—and odd people in similar states of being. The odd people brought the odd objects, for the glory of the gods and their consorts, and the Abbey sheltered both, as best it might.

It seemed fitting.

Before the earthquake, before the Great Storm, Godsmere Abbey had the patronage of the wealthy, and the high. Witness the walls: Titanium-laced granite that withstood the quake damage-free, saving some very small cracks and fissures; the roof-tiles which had denied wind and rain; the rows of carven couches in the nave—why, the organ itself!

They were gone now—the high, the wealthy, and the wise. Gone from the city of Collinswood, and from the planet of Fimbul, too; gone to some other, less contentious place, where they might be comfortably safe.

In the meantime, there was no lack of work for those few friars who remained of the once-populous spiritual community of Godsmere. With loss and want, their tasks had become simpler—care for the sick, feed the hungry, nurture the feeble; and curate the collection of artifacts that filled the North Transept, and spilled into the South.

From time to time, the Abbey accepted boarders, though a far different class than had previously leased the courtyard-facing rooms, seeking tranquility in the simplicity of their surroundings, and the sloughing off, for a time, at least, the cares that weighed their spirits.

A bell rang, reverberating along the stone walls: The call to the mid-morning petition.

Friar Julian passed the dust cloth over the organ's face one more time before tucking the cloth into the organist's bench.

"I will come again," he promised it, softly, as he always did.

Then, he turned and hurried down the steps, out of the organ niche, to join his brothers in faith in giving thanks to the gods and their consorts for the dual gifts of life and conscience.

• • • ✧ • • •

LATER IN THE DAY, another bell rang, signaling a petitioner at the narthex. Friar Anton stood ostiary this day, and it was he who came to Friar Julian in the kitchen, to say that two city constables awaited him in the nave.

Friar Julian took off his apron, and nodded to Layman Voon, who was peeling vegetables.

"Please," he said, "call another to finish here for me. I may be some time, and the meal should not be delayed."

"Yes, Friar," Layman Voon said, and reached for the counter-side mic, to call for Layman Met, which was scarcely a surprise. Voon and Met had vowed themselves to each other in the eyes, and with the blessings of, the gods and their consorts, and worked together whenever it was possible.

Friar Julian and Friar Anton walked together along the back hallway.

"How many?" asked Friar Julian.

"One only," replied Anton.

That was mixed news. They had been without for some number of months, and while one was certainly better than none, two—or even four—would have been very welcome, indeed.

On the other hand, it was true that supplies were low in these weeks between the last planting and the first harvests, and one would put less strain upon them than four. Unless . . .

"In what state?" Friar Julian asked.

"Whole." Anton was a man of few words.

Friar Julian nodded, relieved that there would be no call upon their dangerously depleted medical supplies.

They came to the nave door. Anton passed on to his post at the narthex, and the great, formal entrance, while Julian opened an inner, passed through it into the clergy room, and thence, by another door, into the nave itself.

Three men stood in the central aisle, among the rows of gilt and scarlet couches. Two wore the dirt-resistant duty suits of the city constabulary. Out of courtesy, they had raised their visors, allowing Father Julian sight of two hard, lean faces that might have belonged to brothers.

The third man was shorter, stocky; dressed in the post-disaster motley of a city-dweller. His hair was black and unruly, his face round and brown. Black eyes snapped beneath fierce black eyebrows. An equally fierce, and shaggy, black mustache adorned his upper lip.

He held his arms awkwardly before him, crossed at the wrist. Friar

Julian could see the sullen gleam of the binder beneath one frayed blue sleeve. He turned his head at Friar Julian's approach, and the cleric saw a line of dried blood on the man's neck.

"Just one today, Fadder," called the policeman on the prisoner's right. "He's a sly 'un, though."

Friar Julian stopped, and tucked his hands into the wide sleeves of his robe.

"Is he violent?" he asked, eying the man's sturdy build. "We are a house of peace."

"Violent? Not him! Caught 'im coming outta Trindle's Yard after hours, wida baga merch on his shoulder. Problem is, nuthin' caught 'im going in, and t'snoops was all up and workin'. 'Spector wants a vestigation, so you got a guest."

"There's something strange with his ID, too," said the other policeman, sternly. "Citizens Office is looking into that."

"But violent—nothin' like!" The first policeman took up the tale once more. "He ran, sure he did—who wouldn't? Nothin' to be ashamed of, us catching 'im. And he's smart, too—aincha?"

He dug an elbow into the prisoner's side. It might as well have been a breath of wind, for all the attention the man gave it. The policeman looked back to Friar Julian.

"We put the chip in, then stood back, like we do, so he could make a run fer it and get The Lesson. 'cept this guy, he don't run! Smart, see? We hadda walk away from 'im 'til he dropped off the meter and got the zap." He looked at the prisoner.

"Gotta have The Lesson, man. That's regs."

The prisoner stared at him, mouth hidden beneath his mustache.

"Not very talkative," the second policeman said, and opened one of his many belt pouches.

"The judge says board for two weeks," he said. "If the investigation goes longer, we'll re-up in two-week increments. If it goes shorter, the next boarder's fee will be pro-rated by the amount of overage."

Friar Julian slipped his hands out of his sleeves and stepped forward to pick the coins off of the gloved palm.

"Yes," he said calmly, fingers tight around the money, "that is the usual arrangement."

"Then we'll leave 'im to ya," the first policeman said. "Arms up, m'boy!"

That last was addressed to the prisoner, who raised his arms slightly, black eyes glittering.

The policeman unsnapped the binders while his partner walked across the nave to the safe. He used the special police-issue key to unlock it, and placed the small silver control box inside. Then he locked the safe, and sealed it.

He looked over his shoulder.

"Ponnor!" he called.

The prisoner pivoted smoothly to face him.

"You pay attention to this seal, now! It'll snap and blow if you try to get in here—that's the straight truth. The blast'll take your fingers, if it doesn't take your head. So, just sit tight, got it? The friar'll take good care of you."

"I have it," the man said, his voice low, and surprisingly lyrical.

"Right, then. We're gone. Good to see you again, Friar."

"May the gods and their consorts look with favor upon your efforts," Friar Julian said, seeing Friar Anton approaching from the direction of the North Transept. He had been listening, of course. The ostiary always listened, when there were policeman in the nave.

The policeman followed him out, leaving Friar Julian alone with the man named Ponnor.

• • •✧• • •

THE *GARDA* LEFT THEM, escorted by the *gadje* who had admitted them to this place. Niku rubbed his right wrist meditatively, and considered the one who would *take good care of him*, Fadder Friar.

This *gadje* holy man was old, with a mane of white hair swept back from a formidable forehead. He had a good, strong nose, and a firm, square chin. Between chin and nose, like a kitten protected by wolves, were the soft lips of a child. White stubble glittered icily down his pale cheeks. His eyes were blue, and sad; far back, Niku perceived a shadow, which might be the remnants of his holiness, as shabby as his brown robe.

It was, Niku reflected, surprising that even a *gadje* holy man should accept the coin of the *garda*. Niku had no opinion of *gadje* in general, but his opinion of holiness had been fixed by the *luthia* herself. And among the blessed Bedel there was no one more blessed than the *luthia*, who cared for the body and soul of the kompani.

Well. The *luthia* was not with him, and he had more pressing concerns than the state of any single *gadje*'s soul. It could be said that his present situation was dire—Niku himself would have said so, save for his faith in his brother Fada.

Still, a man needed to survive until Fada could come, so he looked to the holy *gadje*, produced a smile, and a little nod of the head.

"Sir," he said. *Gadje* liked to be called *sir*; it made them feel elevated above others. And the *garda* had shown scant reverence for this one's holiness.

The holy *gadje* returned both smile and nod.

"My name is Friar Julian," he said. "I am the oldest of the friars who remain at Godsmere, and it is my joyous burden to bring the prayers of the people to the attention of the gods and their consorts."

Niku, to whom this was so much nonsense, nonetheless smiled again, and nodded.

"Within these walls, my son, you are safe from error, for the gods do not allow a man to sin while he is in their keeping."

"It is well to be sinless," Niku said flippantly.

It seemed to Niku that the holiness far back in Friar Julian's eyes burned bright for an instant, and he regretted his impertinence. Truly, the gods of this place had failed him, for it *was* a sin to mock a holy man, even a *gadje* holy man. The *luthia* would say, *especially* a *gadje* holy man, for *gadje* are so little blessed.

"Let me show you where you will sleep," said Friar Julian, "and introduce you to the others."

Niku froze. Others? *Others* might pose a problem, when Fada came.

"Other prisoners?" he asked.

Friar Julian frowned.

"You are our only boarder at present," he said stiffly. "The others to whom I would make you known are friars, as I am, and lay brothers. This we will do over the meal." He raised a hand and beckoned. "Come with me."

• • • ✧ • • •

PONNOR WALKED the length of his room, placed a hand on the bed, opened the door to the 'fresher, closed it, opened and closed the closet door.

He turned, and asked, in his blunt way.

"What will be my occupation?"

Friar Julian was pleased. Despite his rough appearance, it would seem that this boarder had a sense of what was due a house of the gods. Most did not understand, and in fact, the agreement between Godsmere Abbey and the city constables stated that no boarder would be required to labor.

So it was that Friar Julian said, "You may do whatever you like."

Bright black eyes considered him from beneath lowering brows.

"If that is so, then I *would like* to return to my grandmother."

Friar Julian sighed, and held his hands out, palms up and empty, to signify his powerlessness.

"That," he admitted, "you may not do."

Ponnor shrugged, perhaps indifferently, or perhaps because he understood that there was no other answer possible.

"If I am to remain here, then, I would prefer to work, and not be locked all day in a room."

"We do not lock our boarders in their rooms," protested Friar Julian. "You may walk the halls, or the garden, meditate, read . . ."

"I prefer to work," Ponnor interrupted. "I am accustomed."

Were a boarder to volunteer to work, the agreement between Abbey and police continued, they might do so, without the expectation of compensation.

"If you would like, Friar Tanni will add you to the roster." Friar Julian hesitated, then added, in order that there was no misunderstanding. "Your work would be a gift to this house of the gods."

"I would like," said Ponnor firmly, and, "Yes."

"Then we will see it done," said Friar Julian. A bell sounded, bright and sharp, and he waved Ponnor forward.

"That is the dinner bell. Come along, my child."

• • • ✧ • • •

THE DINING HALL was full of people—*gadje*, all. The six friars sat together at one table near the hall door. To these, Niku was made known, and Friar Tanni that moment added him to the lists, and promised to have work for him by meal's end.

He was then released to stand in line, and receive a bowl of broth in which some sad vegetables floated, a piece of bread the size of his fist, rough, like stone, and as dense, and a cup of strong cold coffee.

This bounty he carried to a long table, and slid onto the end of the crowded bench, next to a yellow-haired *gadje* who looked little more than a boy, and across from a woman who might have been the boy's grandmother.

"You're new," the grandmother said, her eyes bright in their net of wrinkles.

"Today is the first time I eat here," he admitted, breaking the bread and dropping hard pebbles into the soup. "Is the food always so?"

"There's bean rolls, sometimes," the yellow-haired boy said with a sigh. "Bean rolls are good."

"Having food in the belly's good," his grandmother corrected him, forcibly putting him in mind of the *luthia*, the grandmother of all the *kompani*. She looked again to Niku.

"Don't know what we'd do without the friars. They feed who's hungry; patch up who gets sick or broke."

"They do this from their holiness?" Niku asked, spooning up bread-and-broth.

The *gadje* grandmother smiled.

"That's right."

"Some of us," the boy said, "bring finds—from where we're clearing out the buildings don't nobody live in now," he added in response to Niku's raised eyebrows.

"Isn't the same as before, when this was a place for the rich folk," the grandmother said. "When it was over, and those of us who were left—you're too young to remember—" So she dismissed both Niku and her grandson.

"Well, I don't mind telling you, I was one thought the friars would leave with the ones who could—and some did. But some stayed, all of them hurting just as much as we, and they opened up the door, and walked down the street, and said they'd be bringing food, soon, and was there anybody hurt, who they could help."

She glanced away, but not before Niku had seen tears in her bright eyes.

"Wasn't anything they could do for my old man, not with half a partment house on top him, but others, who they could."

Niku nodded, and spooned up what was left of his soup. After a moment, he picked up his cup and threw the coffee down his throat like brandy.

The grandmother laughed.

"Not from around here," she said. "Or you'd be going back for more of that." She looked to her grandson.

"You done?"

"Yes, ma'am."

"Then come on."

The boy rose nimbly and went to her side to help her rise. Then the two of them moved off, the boy supporting the grandmother, which was Bedel-like. Niku sat very still, caught with a sudden longing for the sight of his own grandmother.

When it had passed, he rose, and went to find Friar Tanni.

• • • ✧ • • •

HIS ASSIGNED WORK was to wash the floor in the big room—what the *gadje* called *the nave*. This suited him well, since the door to the street outside stood open during day-hours, and *gadje* of all description were free to come inside, to wander, to sit or lie down for an hour on one of the wide couches, to partake of the offered food.

It was this continual passage of feet that dirtied the nave floor, and Friar Tanni had told him that he might wash it every day, if he wished.

For the moment, he wished, for Fada, when he came, would surely enter by the day-door. It would be best were Niku near at hand to greet him. He had no clear idea what the friars would do, if they found a stranger wandering their halls in search of his brother, but there was, so Niku believed, no reason to discover the truth.

So, he washed the floor, simple work, and soothing, as simple work so often was. When he was done, he took his broom down the long hall to the left of the nave.

This was filled with cabinets, shelves, and tables, and those were filled with this and that and the other thing—an unrelated jumble of objects and intent that vividly brought to mind the work spaces of his brothers and sisters. The "finds" these must be, with which the *gadje* boy and others like him repaid the god-house for its holy care of them.

Dust was thick on surfaces and objects alike, but Niku had the means to deal with that.

He used the broom first, to clean the dusty floor. When that was done, he pulled the duster from the broom's handle, and addressed the collection.

Taking care to keep an eye on the nave, in hope of seeing Fada, Niku set himself to methodically dust the objects.

It was an interesting collection, to put it no higher that its due. One piece he picked up, his fingers curling covetously around it; another he could scarcely bring himself to touch. Valuable, dangerous, fascinating . . . all jumbled together without regard for utility or merit. It was as if the friars did not know what they had, nor how best to make use of it.

Niku had been born after the earthquake and the storm that had destroyed the city, but he had learned from the tales told by his elders. He learned how those who had means had fled, leaving behind those who suffered, and also much of their own property. The Bedel, scavengers and craftsmen, had recovered items similar to those here, in order to repair, destroy, or dream upon them, as each required.

A bell rang, startling Niku, as if from a dream. He walked out of the transept, into the nave, and looked about. There were a number of people about, as there had been, none of them was Fada, which saddened him. If the bell was a call of some kind, it had no power over those in the nave.

Well enough.

Niku returned to the transept.

• • •✧• • •

SOME TIME LATER, and Fada still not with him, he took the broom and duster, which would explain his presence, if he were found where he ought not to be, and explored further.

The South Transept was much like the North, save not yet so full of treasure. He did not pause there, but ascended a flight of stairs, to a loft which was very full of dust, and a standing desk facing a tiered platform. There was a low rail behind the desk and Niku stepped up to look below.

A wondrous sight met his eyes—a device he had only seen in dreams, brass glittering in the muted sunlight admitted by tall soot-stained windows. He stood for a long moment, wonder slowing his heart, then setting it to pounding.

Dazzled, he put one booted foot up on the rail, meaning to make the jump to the floor below.

He stopped himself as he leaned forward to grasp the rail, withdrew his foot, and rushed down the stairs.

A moment later, he crossed the threshold into the sunlit niche—and paused, gazing up at it, its perfect form haloed; light running liquid along the silver pipes.

Softly, Niku mounted the dais.

Gleaming dark wood was like satin beneath his fingers, the bone keys were faintly rough. There was no dust on wood or keys; the brass stops had recently been polished.

Niku sat on the bench and looked over the three tiered keyboards, matching the reality before him with his dreams. Reverently, he extended a hand and touched the brass knobs of the stops, pulling one for each keyboard, those being named the Choir, the Great, and the Swell. He placed his feet on the pedals; leaned in and placed his fingers *so* upon the Choir keyboard, pressed, and . . .

. . . nothing happened.

Fool, Niku told himself; there will be a switch, to wake the blower.

He found a small brass button set over the Choir, and slightly to the left of center, and pressed it. Then, as memory stirred a little more robustly, he located the *mute* stop, and engaged that, as well.

He pressed his fingers once more against the keys.

Nothing happened.

Frowning, Niku closed his eyes, striving to call up a more detailed recollection of the organ and its workings. It was several long minutes before he opened his eyes again, rose from the bench and descended to the floor.

The trap was behind the organ set flush to the boards.

Niku pulled it up, and sat on his heels, looking down into the dimness. Unlike the instrument, the rungs of the ladder were furry with dust, and likely treacherous footing. He had reached to his pocket before he recalled that the *garda* had taken his light-stick, along with the papers his clever sister Ezell had made for Ponnor Kleug, his *gadje* name.

For another moment he crouched there, debating with himself. Then, with regretful care, he closed the trap, stood—and froze.

He had heard a step, nearby.

Quickly, he ducked out from behind the organ, and went up the dais, pulling the duster from his pocket.

The steps came nearer, and in a moment Friar Julian came into the niche.

He paused for a moment, startled, as Niku read it, to see someone in this place, engaged in admiration of this instrument. Niku smiled.

"It is very beautiful," he said.

The *gadje*'s worn face lit with pleasure.

It is," he agreed, coming up the dais to stand at the organ's opposite side, "very beautiful, yes. Sadly, it is not functional."

"Has she ever shared her voice?"

The friar frowned, then smiled, as softly as a young man speaking of his lover.

"Yes. Oh, yes. Years ago now, she . . . shared her voice often. I was, myself, the organist, and—" He shook his head, bereft of words, the soft lips twisted, and the sad eyes wet. "She was damaged in the earthquake. I fear that I will never hear her voice again, on this side of the gods' long river."

"Perhaps," Niku suggested, softly, "a miracle will occur."

Friar Julian's eyes narrowed, and he glared at Niku, who kept his face innocent and his own eyes wide. After a moment, the old *gadje* sighed, and gave a nod, his anger fading.

"Perhaps it will. We must trust the gods. Still, even silent, she—she is a wonder. Would you care to see more?"

"Yes," said Niku.

• • •✧• • •

THEY TOURED THE PIPE ROOM, descending the stairs to the blower room, with no need of the trap and ladder. Niku inspected everything; he asked questions of Friar Julian, who was sadly ignorant of much of the organ's inner functions. For the old *gadje*, Niku realized, it was the voice, the opening of self into another self, that mattered. The mechanics, the why, and the what—they did not compel him as they did Niku.

Some while after, they came through the door, back to the organ niche. Niku smiled and bowed his head and thanked the friar for his time.

The sun was low by then, and Niku hurried out to the nave, to see if Fada had come.

• • •✧• • •

FADA HAD *NOT* COME before day had surrendered to night, and the day-door closed and locked. That was . . . worrisome. He depended upon Fada, to bring him, quickly, away.

Niku shared the evening meal of a protein bar and a cup of wine with the friars and the laymen. To take his mind from worry, he listened intently to all they said.

They forgot he was there, tucked into the corner of the table, and they spoke freely. The *garda*'s money was to go for medicines. Where they were to find money for food, that was a worry.

A very great worry.

The simple meal done, the *gadje* joined hands, and prayed together, as brothers might do.

After, Friar Julian stood, and the rest, also, and filed off to their rooms. Niku rose, too, and went to the room he had been shown.

There, he showered, his worries filling his belly like so many iron nails. The message that had come to the *kompani* had not been specific as to time, but it was certain that their ship was approaching. What, indeed, if it had already come, and he was left here, alone among *gadje*—

He raised his face into the stream of cleansing spray, and with difficulty mastered his panic.

The Bedel did not leave one of their own among *gadje*. Ezell, Fada—the *luthia*—they would not hear of such a thing. They *would not* leave him alone among *gadje*, not while Bedel knives were sharp. He knew that; and it comforted him.

But, still, a man would wish to continue his life, as long as it might joyfully be done.

His best hope yet rested upon Fada. But hope mended no engines.

It is said, among the Bedel, that gods help those who help themselves.

Accordingly, Niku stripped the blanket from the soft, *gadje* bed, wrapped himself in it, and lay down on the floor.

Arms beneath his head, he closed his eyes, and breathed in that certain way that the *luthia* had taught him. And so slid into the place of dreams.

• • •✧• • •

THE ACCOUNTS PAGE was bathed in red.

Friar Julian sighed, and shook his head, his heart leaden.

A shadow passed over his screen, and Friar Julian looked up, startled.

"Yes, Ponnor?"

The stocky man ducked his unkempt head.

"Friar, I come to offer a bargain, if you will hear it."

Friar Julian frowned.

"A bargain? What sort of a bargain?"

Ponnor stroked the air before him, as if it were a cat—perhaps the motion was meant to soothe him—and said, slowly, "I am an artificer, very fine, and I have studied many devices, including such a device as your lady organ in the niche." He leaned forward, his hands still, black eyes hypnotic.

"I can fix her."

Fix—? Friar Julian's heart leapt painfully in his breast. But surely, he thought, around the pain, surely that was impossible. The earthquake . . . they had done all they knew . . . and yet—

"An artificer?" he said, faintly.

Ponnor nodded. "My brothers—all of us—there is *nothing* that we cannot repair, sir," he said, with a matter-of-factness far more compelling than any more humble declaration.

"And you believe you can repair my—the Abbey's organ."

"Oh, yes, sir," Ponnor assured him. "But there is a price."

Of course there was a price. The gods themselves charged a price, for admission into the Life Everlasting. Friar Julian took a breath, careful of the pain in his breast. The price named by the gods was a soul. Perhaps Ponnor would ask less.

"What is this bargain?" he asked, speaking as calmly as he could.

"I fix your lady organ, and you release me, to return to my grandmother," Ponnor said, and rocked back on his heels, his hands folded before him.

The price was a soul, after all.

Friar Julian swallowed.

He could not, *could not* free Ponnor from his bonds. The chip implanted in his throat would activate and render him unconscious if he moved outside the field of the device locked into the safe in the nave. The police were not idiots, after all; they held the key to the safe; they held the code to the chip.

It was not in Friar Julian's power to release Ponnor to his grandmother, or to anyone else.

But . . . tears rose to his eyes. To hear his organ, once more? To play—did he *remember how* to play? Absurd doubt. He played every night, in his dreams.

He could not agree to this. He—

Stay. Ponnor offered his work to the house of the gods and their consorts. That had already been agreed upon. This other thing—what harm, if it gave him some ease while he worked? After all, the police would surely be back soon, to take him before the judge.

Friar Julian took a breath and met Ponnor's black, compelling eyes.

"After you repair the gods' organ, I will release you," he said steadily.

One side of Ponnor's mustache lifted, as if it hid a half-smile, and he continued to hold Friar Julian's gaze for a long, long moment . . .

. . . before he bowed his head, murmured, "I will begin now," and swept from the office.

Friar Julian, abruptly alone, covered his face with his hands.

• • • ✧ • • •

FADA ARRIVED as the sun was sinking. Niku had come out of the organ niche to clean the floor in the nave, seeking to ease muscles cramped by long hours of kneeling inside small places, and saw his brother enter, sidestepping those day-folk who were already leaving.

His brother saw him instantly, and raised a hand to adjust his hat, the smallest finger wiggling, which was a request to meet somewhere private.

Niku fussed with the duster, and the broom, in between which his fingers directed his brother to the inner garden, and warned him it would be some time before Niku could join him. He then turned his back and reactivated the broom, in order to clean up a spot of mud that had dried on the floor since his morning pass.

When he looked 'round again, Fada was gone.

• • •✧• • •

NIKU HAD TAKEN a battered lantern from among the clutter in the North Transept to light him on his way. He found Fada lying on a bench under a fragrant tree, hat over his face, snoring.

"Wake, foolish one!" Niku said, slapping his brother's knee. "How if I had been the *garda*?"

"For the *garda*, I am only a man who came to the house for the meal, and fell asleep in the garden," Fada said, swinging his legs around and sitting up.

"I cannot work here," he added, "even with the lantern."

"That is why we are not staying here. Come, Brother; let me show you some things that I found."

• • •✧• • •

"THIS," Fada said, some minutes later, placing his hand reverently on the organ's polished wood. "*This*, Brother, is something, indeed! Has it a voice?"

"Not presently," said Niku, from his seat on the dais.

"That's too bad." Fada stroked the wood once more, then turned and sat down next to Niku. He reached into his pocket and brought out a flat black rectangle, which he proceeded to unfold until it was a smaller, flatter black rectangle, with various protrusions, like the segmented legs of a river crab.

"First, I take readings," he said, straightening and rebending the legs. "After I have read, we will know how to proceed, which will we do. You will eat breakfast with your brothers, Niku!"

Hope made him giddy. Fada was the cleverest of his very clever brothers; surely no device of mere *gadje garda* could outwit him. Was it not said of the Bedel—admittedly, by the Bedel—that there was nothing they could not fix, nor any trap that could hold them long?

Fada placed one of the legs against Niku's neck, over the new, pink scar.

"Be still, now—no talking, no moving. Do not *breathe* until I say!"

Niku closed his eyes and held his breath. He heard a high, poignant hum, which might have been the device, or only his ears, ringing from tension.

"*And* breathe," Fada commanded.

This Niku did, reaching up to scratch at the scar.

"Now what do we do?" he asked, when Fada had been silent for what seemed too long.

There was no answer, his brother continuing to stare at the face of his device, his own showing lines of what might be worry.

"Fada?" Niku touched his shoulder.

His brother shook his head, and raised his eyes.

"Niku—Brother, I cannot . . ."

"Cannot?" he repeated. "But—"

"This—thing. It is . . . In a word, Brother, it is beyond me."

"You cannot remove it?"

"That—no. It appears to have established tentacles, and those have intertwined with nerves in your throat. It can never be removed."

Niku felt his stomach churn; the thought of this *gadje* device forever a part of him was enough to make him vomit. He swallowed, hard, and looked back to Fada.

"But you *can* disarm it," he said.

"That—yes. But at risk of your life. I may . . . I will need our brother Boiko for this . . ." His voice faded out, which meant he was thinking.

Niku sat, thinking his own thoughts. Boiko meant frequencies. Frequencies meant there was a way to turn the blessed thing *off*.

"We have heard again," Fada said, interrupting his thoughts, "from the ship. We have a day and a location."

Niku's mouth dried.

"What day?"

Fada looked at him bleakly. "Two days beyond a world-week."

"Surely Boiko can find the frequencies . . ."

"Surely he can, but if we must build a device, in among the packing of all the dreams and findings, for the ship . . ." His face firmed. "We will do it. Brother, you must trust us."

"You are my brothers," Niku said. "But, if Boiko can find the frequencies, we have here a device, Brother." He flung his hand out, showing Fada the organ.

His brother considered the organ over his shoulder, then turned back.

"You said it had no voice."

"And so it does not. But I will fix that."

Fada's face did not lose its expression of worry.

"I don't say that you cannot, Brother, but can it be done in time?"

"It must be done in time," Niku said firmly, "and so it will be."

Fada took a breath. "If you say it, then it is so."

Niku nodded. "And we have another path, Brother. I have a bargain with the *gadje* who loves this organ. When I fix it, he will free me."

"Has he this power?"

"It may be. The *garda* have sealed the control box into a safe. I think that Friar Julian is not a man who allows such things into the gods' house unless he has some measure of control over them."

Niku straightened, and looked at Fada with a surety he did not entirely feel.

"Boiko will find the frequencies. I will repair this organ for the *gadje*. You will bring the frequencies—in three days' time."

"Three days!"

"Three days," Niku said firmly. "By then, she will have her voice."

"And if it does not?"

"Then there are still seven days left for my brothers to build their device."

A bell rang somewhere in the Abbey, and they fell silent.

Niku then took Fada by the arm and brought him to his feet. "Come, there is something else you should see."

• • •✧• • •

"MORE TREASURE, Brother," said Fada, overlooking the tables in the North Transept. "Do they know what they hold, these *gadje*?"

"I think not," said Niku. He stepped over to a particular table and held his hand over that object that had so concerned him. "What do you think of this, Brother?"

Fada stepped up beside him and considered the thing with a critical eye.

"I think that it ought to be destroyed. Of course, they don't know how."

"That would be my guess. It ought not to be sitting here where it can work mischief. Will you take it, when you go?"

"It's best, I think," said Fada, and reached into his pocket, producing a muffling cloth, in which he wrapped the thing, before slipping it into a pouch and sealing the top. "That will keep it."

"There is also," Niku said, reaching carefully into a glass cabinet, "this."

Fada pursed his lips in a whistle, and held out his hand.

Niku shook his head.

"You must do another thing for me, Brother. You must sell this at good terms—bargain hard!—and bring me the money, when you return with the frequencies."

Fada frowned.

"Money?" he asked, doubtfully, as who would not? The Bedel did not have much to do with money.

"Money," Niku said firmly.

Fada shrugged and accepted the little figurine, wrapping it also with care and stowing it in an inside padded pocket. Then, he looked about.

"Brother, I will stay here until the door opens, and then I will be gone. What will you?"

Doubtless more of the collection would find its way into Fada's pockets, but that hardly gave Niku a qualm. What the Bedel found belonged to the Bedel. It had always been so.

"I will go back to the organ," said Niku.

"Should I come?"

"I think not."

Niku embraced his brother.

"Go safely," he said.

"We will not leave you alone," Fada said, and hugged him hard

• • •✧• • •

PONNOR WAS AT THE ORGAN every waking hour, and Friar Julian suspected, every hour that he ought to be sleeping, too.

The man's diligence shamed Friar Julian—and how much more shame would he feel, he wondered, if Ponnor did restore the organ?

When he had first come to Godsmere Abbey, as a boy, he had an elder brother—one Friar Fen. Among the many pieces of wisdom Friar Fen had given his young brother was this—that priests have no honor, for they must always, and first, do everything in their power to serve, without fault, the gods and their consorts. And then they must serve, without fault, those who needed their care the most.

It was not honor, then, that prompted Friar Julian's search of the file cabinets, table drawers, and bookshelves, looking for the key to the constable's safe in the nave.

Surely, he had once had it; therefore, he must have it still. He had given his word, that he would free Ponnor, should he succeed in repairing the organ. Given his word, in *this* house, where the gods allowed no man to sin.

Late in the night of the second day—or, more accurately, early in the morning of the third—he found it—stuck to the back of the top drawer of his desk. He gripped it in trembling fingers and went out to the nave to test it.

It was only after he stood in front of the safe that he recalled that the police had also applied a sealant, and had taken care to warn Ponnor of its danger.

And for that, he had no answer.

• • •✧• • •

"FRIAR JULIAN?"

He started from a doze behind his desk and looked up to find

Ponnor in the door. His heart took up a hard, sluggish beat that made him feel ill.

"Yes, my son?"

"It is done," Ponnor told him, black eyes fairly sparkling. "She sings again."

The words—it seemed as though he had heard the words, but lost their sense immediately. The organ—what?

"Friar? Will you come?" Ponnor held out his hand.

He sent a prayer to the gods and their consorts, and rose from his chair, willing shaking knees to support him.

"Of course I will come," he said.

• • •✧• • •

HE SAT ON THE BENCH, placed his feet on the pedals, and rubbed his cold hands against each other. Ponnor stood next to the organ, at his left, and he was pulling a much folded sheet of paper out of his pocket, which he unfolded onto the wood, and smoothed with his palm.

"Here," he said. "This is a song that I write in celebration of her voice. If you will play this, Friar? I will stand—" He looked over his shoulder and pointed, seemingly at random, "there."

"Even muted, that will be far too close for the safety of your ears, my child."

Ponnor gave him a wide grin, his eyes seeming, in Friar Julian's judgment, just a little *too* bright. But, still, the work he had put into this, the hours of labor and the several nights short of sleep—such things might push a man to frenzy, especially if he labored in a house of gods.

"Please, you will play this?" Ponnor asked again.

Father Julian had long planned what he would play, should the organ ever be repaired, and it grieved him, a little, to cede pride of place to an inept bit of music scribbled onto a grubby sheet by—

By the man he had lied to, and was about to betray.

Friar Julian picked up the paper, running his eye over the notes.

"Of course, I will play this first," he said.

NIKU HURRIED to the front of the organ, pushing the stops into his ears as he did. When he reached the place Fada and Boiko had determined to be the best, he turned into the sound, and deliberately relaxed.

It was, he thought, a very beautiful thing, this organ. It had been a good thing to do, to repair the blower that had been broken in the quake, and reseat the pipes that had been shaken loose. Very simple repairs. A child could have made them.

Well. Whatever happened in the next few heartbeats—and Boiko himself warned that the outcome might not be happy—he had done well here. This was a deed the memory of which he would wear like a star upon his brow, when he passed to the World Beyond.

Beneath the floor, he heard the blower start.

He heard Friar Julian shift on the bench.

Niku closed his eyes.

The first note sounded, flowed into the second, the third, ascended to the fourth—

Niku felt a jolt of pain, a burning along his throat, he gasped, his hand leaping to the spot . . .

The organ went on. The skin of his throat felt normal, save for the roughness of the scar under his fingers.

Friar Julian played on to the end of the little piece of music Ezell had composed from Boiko's frequencies.

There was a small pause, as perhaps Friar Julian adjusted the stops.

The organ burst into song; a wild, swinging music that had much in common with the music the Bedel made for themselves, when there were no *gadje* to hear.

His feet twitched into a half-step. He laughed at himself, realized that his ears were ringing, despite the stops, and stepped away from the organ.

• • • ✧ • • •

FRIAR JULIAN frowned at the scrap of music Ponnor had left, his eye moving over the lines. There was something—a progression, a linkage of line and tone . . .

It was, he understood suddenly, a test pattern; a technical exercise, and no music at all.

He smiled, pressed the blower key, and the mute, and placed his fingers on the keys.

The pattern completed, he paused only to set the stops, his hands moving on their own, surely, no shaking now, and he leaned into the keyboards with a will.

He had planned . . . For years, he had planned to play the stately and glittering Hymn of Completion, which celebrates unions of all kinds, but is most particularly played when one man and another have chosen to pledge themselves to each other for the rest of their mortal lives.

What flowed out of his fingers, however, was not the structured elegance of the Hymn, but the provocative and lusty Dance of the Consorts.

Friar Julian closed his eyes and allowed his fingers to have their way.

• • •✧• • •

HE CAME TO AN END, and lifted his fingers from the keys, listening to the final reverberations from the pipes. He sighed, his heart full, and his soul healed.

"Friar?" a voice said, very close to his left elbow.

Hearing it, his soul shattered again, and when he turned his head to meet Ponnor's eyes, his own were filled with tears.

The other man smiled.

"I am sorry that I will not be able to stay and hear the rest of the great music," he said. "My grandmother calls me."

Friar Julian shook his head.

"I bargained in bad faith. I cannot release you."

Incredibly, Ponnor's smile grew wider.

"I think you are too hard on yourself," he said, and extended a large, calloused hand. "Come, let us celebrate this lady and her return to song."

Friar Julian hesitated, staring from hand to face.

"Did you understand what I said?" he asked. "It's not in my power to release you."

"That!" Ponnor said gaily. "We will see about that, I think! Come, now, and walk with me. We will test this thing. Let us go together down the street to the tavern. We will drink, and bid each other farewell."

"I tell you, it is impossible!" cried Friar Julian.

His wrist was caught in one large hand, and he came to his feet, reluctantly, and Ponnor's hand still holding him, went out of the niche and into the nave, where the day visitors and the laymen, and all of the friars, stood, their faces bathed in wonder.

"Was that," asked a woman wearing a flowered apron, "the organ?"

"Julian?" said Friar Anton. "Is it—I thought I heard . . ."

"You did hear!" Ponnor answered, loudly. "Your organ sings again! Soon, Friar Julian will come back and play for you all, but first, he and me—we have business to conduct."

No one questioned him, least of all Friar Julian, the music still ringing in his head. The crowd parted before them, all the way down to the day-door.

Friar Julian came to his wits as the sun struck his face, and he pulled back.

"You will be struck!" he cried.

"Not I!" Ponnor declared. "What a beautiful day it is!"

That was so, Friar Julian saw, the sun smiling cheerfully upon the broken street, and the children playing Find Me! among the piles of salvage.

Halfway down the street, the bright red sign of the saloon mere steps ahead, Friar Julian exclaimed, "But you're out of range! The chip should have activated!"

"You see?" Ponnor grinned. "You have kept your word! The gods of the house would not let you sin."

A miracle, thought Friar Julian. I am witness to the movements of the gods.

Dazed, he followed Ponnor into the room, and allowed him to choose a table near the door.

"Sit, sit! I will fetch us each a glass of blusherrie! A special day begs for a special drink!"

The friar sat, and glanced about him. The hour was early and custom was light. Across from him a dark haired man wearing a hat sat alone at a table, nursing a beer. On the other side of the door, near to the bar, a young woman with red ribbons plaited into her black hair, black eyes sultry, sat by herself, an empty glass on the table beside her.

"Here we are!" Ponnor returned noisily, placing two tall glasses of blue liquid in the table's center, as he sat down in the chair opposite.

"We will drink to the lady's restored health!" Ponnor declared, and they did, Friar Julian choking a little as the liquid burned down his throat. It had been a long time since he had drunk such wine.

"We will drink to the wisdom and the mercy of the gods and their consorts!" he cried then, entering into the spirit of the moment.

They drank.

"We will drink to fond partings," Ponnor said, and they did that, too.

Father Julian sighed, surprised to see that his glass was nearly empty. He felt at peace, and more than a little drowsy.

Across the table, Ponnor set aside his glass and rose.

"I leave you now," he said. Father Julian felt his hand lifted, and blinked when Ponnor placed a reverent kiss upon his knuckles.

"Enjoy your sweet lady, sir," Ponnor said, and was gone, walking briskly out the door.

At once, the man and the woman at the single tables rose and followed him out.

That was odd, thought Friar Julian, and sleepily raised his glass for another sip of blusherrie.

"Hey," said a rough voice at his side. Friar Julian blinked awake and smiled sleepily up at a man wearing an apron. The barkeeper, perhaps.

"Yes?" he said.

"What I wanna know," the man said, looking down at him with a thunderous frown, "is who's gonna pay for them drinks."

Friar Julian sat up straight, suddenly and vividly awake.

Money! He had no money! Ponnor—

"The guy with the mustache said you'd pay for them, too," the barkeep said, using a blunt thumb to indicate the two single tables, now empty. "We ain't the church, here, see? You drink, you pay."

"Yes, I understand," said Friar Julian, his heart sinking, thinking of the few coins left in the cash box, after the medical supplies had been purchased.

Futilely, knowing they were empty, he patted the pockets of his robe. The right one was as flat as he expected, but the left one . . .

Crinkled.

Wondering, Friar Julian pulled out a bright blue envelope. He ran his finger under the flap, and drew out a sheaf of notes. Notes! Not coins.

He offered the topmost to the bartender, who eyed it consideringly.

"Hafta go in back to change that," he said.

Friar Julian nodded.

Alone, he fanned the money, seeing food, medicines, seeds for their kitchen garden . . .

Something fluttered out of the envelope. Friar Julian bent and picked it up off the floor.

It was a business card for one Amu Song, dealer in oddities, with an address at the spaceport. Father Julian flipped it over, frowning at the cramped writing there.

The gods help those who help themselves.

He stared at it, flipped the card again, and there was the word, *oddities*. He thought of the North Transept, the cluttered tables of worthless offerings there.

. . . and he began, very softly, to laugh.

✧ The Rifle's First Wife ✧

***COURTESY OF A YOUNG MAN** we didn't expect to survive his first meeting with Clan Korval, we get to look at the interplay of the suddenly mixed cultures of Surebleak. Needing to meet his new troop's expectations, Diglon Rifle, former enemy combatant, has been studying to become a more independent person. Noticed by Lady Anthora, he gets to work with plants, and to pursue his own individual interests—one of which happens to be card playing. What could go wrong? We had to ask this question because Diglon Rifle, much like the Taxi Driver and the Uncle, became far more of a character in the Liaden story than first expected. Enjoy—we did!*

THE SWEAT FELT GOOD to the Rifle; the effort did, the whippy wind gusts and sudden lulls providing an extra challenge to a course laid out in part by the blind necessity of defunct mining machines and part by the will of men long gone. Clan Korval and their minions had yet to exercise their will on most of the land, other than bringing the impossible tree and likewise impossible house to what had been a quarry, and starting an experimental joint farm with the bordering landholder.

In the distance, seen between the spiky pathside thistle-grass, were rows of extra-hardy vegetables—and many days he was among them, along with the small expert who was Alara chel'Voyon, Field Ecologist. Thus did Line yos'Phelium, Clan Korval, dispose of his time this work stretch, for which he was not at all unglad.

He held a look in that direction momentarily, sometimes she acknowledged his passing, as did all of the folk here, particularly those in charge. She'd been there today when he started his run, but Alara wasn't visible now, nor her field kit. He'd been concerned these last several days, that he'd not been performing his duties properly, or that the anomalous results they'd had were discovered to have been due to some error of his. The ecologist's usual low-key banter had been missing, and she both shorter of temper and of praise.

"Did you triple measure? Have we got the image?" Not only had she asked such self-evident questions, but at the end of the day yesterday she'd neither offered a Liaden bow or a Terran-style wave, merely pointing out that she'd see him on his next work shift in the fields.

In going over the social parts of his interactions with the biologist it seemed too that Alara—as she expected to be called for the everyday work transactions—had been less talkative for some few days, perhaps even from the last morning in the city. Something was perhaps not in order, then, at the center of her work . . . or in her need to come out to the fields, as much as she sometimes seemed to enjoy it. His duty, of course, was set by others.

He did not dispute Korval's right to place him in the fields with a sometimes sharp-tongued Scout who was bent on making each and every plant in the experimental rows grow larger and more edible than the one next to it. They owned his oath, did the yos'Pheliums, and if his fitness for work in the fields was determined by the one the Explorer called Scout, it was not his to deny it.

It had seemed odd at the first that he'd passed review with not only the elder Scout, who had taken their temp oath in order to see one of the troop reach medical care while there was still hope, and then the Scout and the Captain, to whom Nelirikk was expressly sworn, but also had been presented to the Scout's almost respectably sized cousin—called brother, a sub-commander and his wife—Shan yos'Galan and Priscilla Mendoza—and then, to the machine that wandered the house feeding cats, and to the woman Anthora, also a yos' Galan.

That one, oh, that one. She'd looked to him at first like a cuddle-girl, impossibly tiny and soft, vulnerable and needing protection . . . and then she'd really looked at him. Her eyes—he still blinked at the thought of her eyes, never doubting that she was one of the Liaden witches he'd been warned of in training, and never doubting, either, the warmth of her smile as the several kittens had wrestled at his feet.

It was the kittens he thought, and the hearty Terran-style nod Lady Anthora gave, that had brought him to the work in the field: she'd turned to the Captain and the Scout and said "This one will much prefer growing things to shooting things, once he is used to it." And then she'd laughed, turned back, and told him to always mind the cats, if they spoke to him, and wandered off.

His breath was comfortably labored, and he turned for the last of the run, preparing, and then busying himself as he usually did with a sprint to finish.

The tree shadowed him now and in that shadow he felt an extra warmth, as if the tree's very bulk forced the winds to flee before its willingness to stand firm, or else that it exuded a welcome to those who belonged.

Belonging to a world was an unusual thing—he'd grown up as a man of arms, expecting that all he belonged to was the Fourteenth Conquest Corps. That was when the Yxtrang High Command had been his decision maker, a time he was, in retrospect, glad was over. He had stood on seventeen worlds in his life, counting this one, and this was perhaps the third where he stood somewhat welcome. Large by most Terran standards, to Liadens he was out of reason large, overly muscled, and menacing. He'd discussed Liad's reaction to him with the Explorer, Nelirikk, who also owed allegiance to Korval's uncanny leaders and their line, and the Explorer had it that Surebleak welcomes them, and that Liad must be considered a toss-up.

While breath was being caught back to normal, he shook his hands, stretched his arms, allowed the thoughts he'd been thinking to creep back to the world, the people he knew here, and his duty to Line yos'Phelium. A spray of dust carried a flimsy light-green leaf, and he bowed to temptation, and swept it from the air, noting approximate time, and shoved it in his pocket. He'd recognize it, or the Field ecologist would . . .

As was, then, it was otherwise a wild and strange world, here, far from the spaceport he was posted to as a shift guard every other tenth day, and the weather, though seasonably warm by local standards, was uncertain as it always was, and then bordering frigid. He'd fought in more comfortable places.

And then he was back in a calm provided by the towering tree overhead and the outer walls of the tiny fortlike house that enclosed its base. He had not worn off the euphoria of the run, and that was good.

His run had been a moderate one, by choice, given his evening plans, and he'd received the news that he'd exceeded his average time for the relumma by a healthy four percent. The rest was due, he expected, to his concentration on thoughts other than running, and to the fact that one of his objects of consideration had been visible during his courses.

"Hello, I am present in the house," he said, having entered the small side-hall that he and other staffers used, "and on rest day. Is there need for me to alter my schedule?"

The "house" in term of personnel was not only the security 'bot, but also a butler, several house folk, a cook, a handyman, and himself and sometimes his several non-clan superiors. Elsewise, guesting in the house could be just about anyone, ranging from Boss Conrad, ruler of the world, to children of Korval clan members, to cats, to visiting scouts, pilots, musicians, and just strange odd folks. Since he was on garden security at this time rather than house security, his position didn't require him to report to the butler as long as the 'bot knew of him . . . not that reporting to the butler was onerous, though one did sometimes have to search the maze of rooms for some time to find him.

This was day six of this tour of what he called Tree Home; day six was a day largely of his own necessities, a luxury he appreciated very much. That his immediate superior was on duty elsewhere this day made it even less likely than normal that he would be interrupted at his private studies and work. That he was permitted private study and work—was far beyond luxury. That he, Diglon Rifle, the only certified Rifle on this world—even the only one in this system!—would have R&R leave this evening would have astonished someone more used to allowing such concepts their sway.

He had always been a simple man. Through creche and schooling and training, and through seven rotations of the vaunted Fourteenth Conquest Corps, he'd taken what life brought with little question, accepting the rights of others to order his presence and actions: it was a given that a soldier of the Yxtrang would revere honor and order, and even orders themselves, requesting little for himself. It was only lately that his life had taken an odd turn for an Yxtrang, for now he was oft expected to both know and to pursue his choices when they did not conflict with the needs of his superiors.

He had spoken on entry, knowing that the house, in the person of the security 'bot, Jeeves, was already well aware of his presence, if not by the touch of his hand to pressure plate, then by the weight of his step on the foot mat at the door, or the sound of his breathing. It was the way things were properly done, the announcement, and few on the planet Surebleak were as happy to do things the way they were done, as was he.

The house had delighted him by giving his run time and allowing him to know that no schedule change was required.

"Welcome, Diglon Rifle. The research information you requested is available; shall I save files to your data trees, deliver hard copy to your quarters, or deliver by voice as you work? Shall I mark this restricted personal, general research, or place it in the open query bin?"

It bothered him that he was addressed in Yxtrang troop mode, but it was part of his duty to the new Captain he was sworn to. Perhaps he should ask if he might be free of that on his day off . . .

The voice had been practicing with someone, or several someones; not only was the inflection closer than it originally had been to that of active troopers, now it began to come close to the proper accent and timing as well. True, the voice had also been practicing with *him*, but he felt that the inflections were likely due to study and dialogs with his elders-in-former-troop.

Diglon had long ago gotten over the odd fact of the robot's apparent self-animation and personality as well as his seamless integration into house systems; in fact he'd long ago gotten over many things about his new station in life. That was a troop's job after all: To put behind past actions and necessities in order to concentrate on the present order set, to follow orders, to . . .

Well, he thought, a rare Terran sound momentarily burying a phrase translated out of Liaden for a phrase out of Trade, and then the stutter as the Terran, direct from the Captain, returned to echo across his life, having lost the war to irony and become fact.

The Yxtrang concept, learned at first by a story told by an elder Troop, was rote as a child and reinforced at first once per ten day and then once per five day and then once per day until at last it was part of his very waking thought: Today I will joyfully do the work of the Troop, without delay, remorse, reserve, or restriction.

That the head of local security was both a bot and available to him as a unparalleled library of information resources . . . well then, he understood that the bot had once been a butler for Clan Korval and a war robot. The robot, then, was of the troop as much as he . . .

"Please, place it in my day file, under personal," he said, elated, moving through the halls leading to what once had been servants' quarters and now was Security's small corner of this house under tree. He could use a shower, and then study. On impulse, he added, "On my non-duty day I would prefer to speak in one of the locally used languages, if that is practical."

"As you say, Rifle." Those tones were in a strict Terran, without recourse to the Surebleak slang the troop was also absorbing.

The idea that he might have an access-restricted personal file that his troop mates and even his immediate superior might not enter at whim—an amazing thought that had frozen him for minutes the first time it was explained to him—continued to elevate him. That he could alter policy by expressing his wish! The Conquest Corps had been inadequate!

"This troop, this Line yos'Phelium, Clan Korval," Nelerikk Explorer had explained early in his relationship with the house, "is a troop of victors. It functions well by following orders and commands, as any well-organized troop may be expected to function, but it is victorious because it assumes and it demands that all troops are capable of making decisions. Personal initiative is not only expected, it is required. From the very oldest to the very youngest, all are expected to exceed norms, to excel at their own assigned duties as well as at duties or arts they choose themselves. Culture, arts, science, skills of joy or skills of survival, it is not expected that any one owing allegiance here should be backward in the pursuit of accomplishment. One must study what is at hand, and seek to improve the lives of all."

His independent accomplishments thus far included a modest facility with the Trade language and likewise a modest facility with Terran, many words of Liaden if not a casual speaking ability and a well-studied ongoing interest in the casual games of chance he was able to take part in when on Portside duty, where games of cards were a staple of the day's schedule. There his tendency to taciturn study of his hand did him well, and had led to his part in a public card tournament, and then to tonight's plans, for having won . . .

If the card games were not the kind of study that was expected of him, no one complained, and indeed, he had discovered that several of the ex-mercenaries in employ of Port Security would hold the start of the evening hands if he was expected. It was a comradeship not quite the equivalent of troop, but then it had become clear to him over time that he could not expect to find that exact feeling again in his life.

The feelings he did have in his life now were . . . different. He'd noticed almost at once, starting with looking into a mirror to assure his readiness for duty after the Captain's order was followed and he'd had his *vingtai* removed as neatly as mud and blood might be swabbed off after an engagement. He'd been both surprised and pleased at his face, finding his aspect not uncomely and his wrinkles not oversetting; he looked younger than Nelirikk Explorer and felt that was, somehow, an advantage.

More, it seemed to him that it mattered more to him what his face looked like, and as cut-short as it still was, the arrangement of his hair made more of a difference to him now. Now, why? Because now there was not a troop regulation style required of him, nor as far as he could determine a troop regulation length. It felt odd, but he was comparing the styles of those around him.

Hazenthull Explorer . . . now that was another thing. If he'd found his own face acceptable, he'd found hers worrisome, for the animation was largely gone from it, as nicely shaped as it was. He'd seen her in the throes of duty, where there was strength and courage and . . .

But there, he was noticing more about the Explorer than her face, and it had come to him in the night why that might be so, given the general exuberance he'd enjoyed since his face-cleaning.

The med-tech had apologized for "taking the pair of you into overtime" and that pair, Hazenthull and himself, had been in a unit where rations where short and command stingy in the best of times, and certainly more so after the landing. The only thing they'd not been short of were their inoculations. And in a combat unit those inoculations would have included medical restraints on the distractions of boredom, hunger, and more hormonal issues like anger and sex.

Having divested himself of the outdoors comm unit and running shoes in favor of house boots, he was about to start on his way to his upstairs staff quarters when the security 'bot rumbled into view.

"Ah, Rifle," the AI said familiarly, in Terran, "I have a message from Nelirikk Explorer that will interest you. He apprises the house that he will be somewhat detained this evening . . ."

Diglon paused, his feet suddenly leaden with concern. It had been a very long time . . .

Turning to face the 'bot, sorting choices, in his mind, sorting sudden back-up plans. His made plans included a time scheduled ahead with those at Ms. Audrey's, for never before had he had a visit to that place. As he was going as winner of a Poker Night Special at the new Space Port Lounge, there was to be a ceremony as well, as he understood it, a—

"Oh, forgive me, Rifle," said the AI, "please! I had not meant to alarm you! The Explorer informs the House that he has made arrangements for a ride: If you'll be ready at the front door they'll take you directly and on time to Ms. Audrey's where he'll meet you. He reminds that, in his absence, you should confer with a member of the house about proper dress."

"Can you not suggest proper dress, House?"

There was a pause, which was unusual, and then a nearly diffident reply.

"I have not been long enough in this house, in this place, to feel confident of such suggestions, Rifle, given that they affect many protocols and expectations I do not have direct experience with. I suggest that though I, the cats, and the Tree may wish you well, all of us together would not be able to establish the proper dress mode for a celebratory visit to Ms. Audrey's. Perhaps an adult male member of the household would be best."

Brought to a standstill momentarily, the Rifle stood rooted, gathering to his mind's eye interleaving chains of command, recalling that most things in the house could be sorted out immediately by one resolute person.

"Yes," he said with determination, "an adult male!" Holding his wind jacket close to him, he went in search of the butler in the more formal front of the house, the AI's rumble behind him.

• • •✧• • •

ALARA CHEL'VOYON CLAN SILARI, Field Ecologist, Scout, Daughter . . .

Today, she was working in a field far from the Port of Surebleak, and far from her recent haunts of rugged rooftops and near-secret garden rooms filled with old dirt and tired strains of tubers, greens, and vitaplants. She knew her thoughts ought to belong to the leaves she measured and photographed, but Ecologist was not the top role in her thoughts today, *melant'i* be damned.

Her recent arrangements with Conrad, Boss of Surebleak, were as temporary and as non-standard as any she'd had since she'd been a working Scout: Local expenses, food, and housing covered here on this end-of-spiral-arm planet in exchange for agronomy expertise and insight. The duties-as-assigned part was not unexpected in a situation where her home-base had been destroyed, the scout home office couldn't tell her when, if ever, the exploration team she'd been destined for might ever be reconstituted, and the field situation was elsewise fluid, if not chaotic. Staying *here*, on Surebleak, meant at least some stability in a life and career that was otherwise in extreme disarray. Staying here with the tacit connivance of her superiors was useful. Staying here when it was the destination of her soon to be displaced clan . . . was only common sense.

The manual leaf-sorting she was doing was on automatic, which it most assuredly should not be.

Alara, Delm Silari . . . and no, that did not bear thinking on with everything else going on—her delm lived, the clan—if inconvenienced—was still intact, and it fell to her to recall her role as Daughter.

All thoughts *must* come back to *daughter*. Her own daughter had gone to Line chel'Mara in a contract marriage before she took on her Scout training, and had been an appropriately squalling and healthy bundle when released into the care of the chel'Mara nurse. It wasn't that child that brought the daughter to mind, but the note that had gone through a tortured line of hold-boxes and Scout-tracking to get to her, a note headed URGENT, addressed to Alara chel'Voyon, Daughter of Clan Silari.

In truth, she wasn't much used to thinking of herself in the daughter role, and particularly not in the favored daughter role. It had come to that, though, with Delm Silari, long thought to be bordering his dotage, not unexpectedly favoring the Korval side of the business of the great hole put in Liad by Korval's forces.

Here she sighed, and put the leaves down a moment to wipe unexpected sweat from her brow; sometimes the thinking was an effort, especially the thoughts of these recent events. Korval's retreat into Plan B, the Scout's suffering a rebellion in their midst, and the attack on Liad itself by the very clan thought by most as the great protector of the planet.

Yes, the attack had been a threat to the home world, but Silari himself had long muttered about the Council of Clans eating up progress for comfort. His having been a deciding vote in allowing the quite young Pat Rin yos'Phelium into Teydor's at Daav yos'Phelium's suggestion also figured into the question, but then he'd been a contemporary of that delm's mother.

It should not have mattered, given his age, but he'd promised her he'd not make her delm while she was happy as a scout, and now things had to change because Silari had been the subordinate business partner in an arrangement generations old . . . and so Clan Forban taking both the other two daughters of Silari—and the daughters of those daughters had not seemed so out of place until the weak-brained council had thrown Korval off world. Forban supporting the Council, Silari—in the person of Delm Valad chel'Voyon—had opted out of the partnership. Someone needed to be in charge.

Valad was not such a one to be stupid after having made such a momentous decision, and having unretired from the world at large and begun the slow dissolution of business and homestead to vacate Liad along with a hundred other clans, he'd issued orders to the one remaining member of his clan who had not yet fulfilled the second part of her duty to the clan and demanded her duty of her: A replacement heir for herself.

That had been the first shock, but they kept coming, for his orders had included the necessity that she do this soon, without coming home to Liad, in place on Surebleak for the love of space!—because the clan would likely relocate itself there!—and . . . with a husband buy-in price of a pair of cantra now, and the rest to be determined as the clan settled.

Then the surest shock: "The delm wishes this at the earliest moment; my physicians complain of my recent exertions and while I mean to leave them and their strictures both on Liad in the near future it is certain in my mind that we must move forward—that *you* must move forward so that when the clan lifts from Liad your tenure as nadelm may begin in earnest, and with an uncomplicated heir in hand. Changes are happening and it would be good to know Silari will one day be led by a Scout."

Nadelm. Heir to the delm! He was too young to be thinking thus—she was too young . . .

Knowing she was both resourceful and a biologist, he'd leave the choice of an acceptable marriage to her, other than requesting that the genes be of a long lineage, the husband respectful of her and the rules of marriage they'd long followed. And he'd invoked old names and relationships and short lists of rules . . . including the hint that if all else failed, she could go to the Delm of Korval, and a reminder that yes, a husband closer to Korval's interests would be closer to Silari's.

So she vaguely sorted leaves, here where plants did better than they ought, as long as . . . as long as . . . as long as something she wasn't sure of happened, and pondered the necessity brought down upon her.

That the Delm of Korval was uniquely available to her, she knew. The delm—at least one of them—was in the house right there, under the tree. As for the other, she knew the Scouts on port included any number willing to bed her. Her doubt was that there were many, given ties of clan and the uncertainties attendant to the evolving role of the Scouts, able to fall in with the kind of wedding-contract her own delm desired, one at least shadowing the proprieties.

Alara found her ankle cramped, and stood, suddenly, letting the leaf stay where it was. She found the work a little more awkward without the Rifle, who often carried, dug, and searched with her. Paradoxically, his height allowed him to work closer to the ground it seemed, and he could hold position immaculately in pulling and replacing probes.

He was an odd man, was Diglon, though perhaps not as odd as some of the scouts she knew, large even by Terran standards and thus huge to her. He'd first been an extra guard to her as she studied the plantings at the spaceport, where he apparently envisioned his role of bodyguard to mean he literally stood between her and threats, daring any such to come through his bulk.

And there was one of the mysteries she'd someday tell her grandchildren about—that she was relying heavily, in the city, on the ability of a genuine Yxtrang to guard her. Liadens were taught to fear and despise the soldier hordes, to consider them forever a threat to the universe, a menace to civilization. And here was Diglon, who a city contact not knowing his background had declared to be a *pussycat* of a guard: Polite, efficient, watchful, helpful, aware, respectful, honest.

His eye being good and his ability to hand-carry phenomenal, he'd become both guard and assistant during her tour of the in-city grow-rooms and private gardens. He'd been excellent with the grandmothers, especially, who shared as much with him as with her the secrets of their medicinal plots, the special timing of the tuber plantings, the necessity of planting in rotation of these groups, this way.

Thus, she, Liaden and daughter of a Liaden, had swept aside her cultural schooling in favor of her Scout-training, and requested him as her daily guard and then asked he be allowed, later, to accompany her to the fields at Yulie Shaper's place when the farmer himself was unavailable—and then, as the project grew, the assignment became a matter of requesting attendance when his schedule matched hers, and finally, that he be assigned as assistant in title. If he no longer thought himself Yxtrang, then neither would she.

She'd seen him earlier, on his off-day run, but had been unable to acknowledge him, her body shielding an in situ absorption study from the breeze then, and she wondered if she'd missed seeing his return. It was perhaps best, since his concept of duty made it far too easy to hold him over hours, and more than once he'd joined the field work in his own time. It had slipped, at one point, from an exchange she'd overheard between Hazenthull Explorer and the delm's aide Nelirikk, that Diglon's need was occupation.

Standing, the wind buffeted Alara's face, and the smell of soil carried with it grit and a hint of moisture. Her day . . .

Her day, checking the chronometer, had been over sometime before. She laughed, knowing that her thinking had put off thought and action. Her stretch told her the cramp of legs could use true relief, and she began gathering together her supplies. She'd be staying here *under tree* this night, as those of Korval sometimes called it. Maybe tomorrow, before she packed for a five day at the cramped laboratory in Boss Conrad's block, perhaps tomorrow she could approach one of the house to see if the Korval might spare a moment.

A half-dozen days now, and she'd yet to reply to her own delm. He was not only dear to her, and her father in fact, he was the delm.

Pulling her jacket a little against the wind, she poked a marker into the ground, firmly, so she'd know tomorrow where she had stopped. Picking up her supplies after a final friendly brush at the leaf she'd been studying, she emulated Diglon's march, and headed off. Today, today—right now—she would ask staff to inquire of a moment with the delm.

The protocols of a proper Liaden house in the country might see a member of the clan on door duty assuming a secure situation, else as security an inconspicuously armed doorman or woman, front and back . . . but then Jelaza Kazone, the house, had hardly been a proper Liaden house for these last seven or eight hundred Standards and was not likely to start now, nor was a house staffed with a robot . . .

She regretted the robot, at times, as polite as it was. Korval, though, must be seen . . .

Ah, and *why*, Alara asked herself as she approached the door, was she trying to do this by the book now? By the Code itself? With Liad's influence clearly fragmenting, with—

She caught her breath, feeling the urge to back away from her mission strengthening the more she questioned, and knowing that, indeed, she was at risk at disobeying her delm, her father, her . . .

She *was* a Scout, and knew better.

The rainbow of serenity flashed through her consciousness, and the resolve to do this rebuilt itself before her eyes, as well as the recollection that she gave importance to her universe and not the other way around.

Her delm's decision would not be wasted by her: Liad itself might falter but her clan would hold the loyalty that had supported Korval and the pilots of Korval. This arrangement had kept her clan and her line steady these centuries, and if Liad varied there was no cause for *Silari* to vary.

And so, though she was by rights guesting in the house and able to enter a side door, she still went to the front entrance, and rang.

• • •✧• • •

MR. PEL'KANA'S demeanor so far had been fair, but stern. They stood in the hall; the conversation not loud, nor was it precisely heated. It was pointed, however, and Diglon Rifle, permitted presence, was quick to note that the butler and the former butler had resisted going up the ladder of command all the way to The Captain herself, but they had both, without hesitation, referred concisely to the strange bit of Liaden troop lore called the Code as if, in fact, dealing with standing orders.

With Jeeves calling on the necessities of security and the fact that the matter had been referred to him by the Captain's aide, Nelirikk Explorer, Mr. pel'Kana's side of the discussion drew heavily on his own role as butler and head of internal operations for the house, explicitly drawing on the notes of his predecessors as well as the Code.

"I've never had the dressing of a soldier for a visit to a whorehouse, Jeeves. The house is unused to maintaining quite so wide a measure of clothing as you assume; certainly you have access to the records and can understand that the house has not generally outfitted our security—and particularly one of such proportions—for their own private amusements."

They'd both argued around the conflicting bunker of truth that Nelirikk, as the Captain's aide de camp, was able to give instruction to both of them on some topics, as if the order came from the Captain. The difficulty was the bunker pel'Kana had built around his own lack of experience at dressing for such an outing and the necessity—agreed by both parties—that an inappropriate suiting decision would be worse than none at all.

"You have a visitor at the door, sir," said Jeeves in a formal Liaden, which Diglon took to mean both that there was someone coming to the door and that security was building status points against the butler's arguments.

For his part, Mr. pel'Kana stood straighter, showing form altogether as nice as that you'd show at a Commander's parade, and waited until the bell actually rang though the hall before moving toward it, and then, pausing to bow and mutter, "by your leave, Mr. Rifle, I must attend the door," he opened it inward with a flourish.

Diglon, for his part, was surprised—surely the ecologist retained the same privileges he had to enter by the common door near the back staircase rather than the formal door at the front of the house.

Not only did she come by that way, she also performed an extremely elaborate bow, executed to all of them and including the building itself, as she spoke in a Liaden so complex Diglon could only gather the sense of the words rather than know them.

"The house of Korval is of the oldest and most honorable and it is with all humility that I enter. A clan's hope is that Delm Korval will see and advise this one, far from home, with an urgent delmic order upon me and necessity crowding possibility until confusion reigns. As Clan Silari has always acknowledged a debt to the clan of the Pilot, and as Clan Silari follows Korval's lead even now, this traveler seeks a word with the Delm of Korval, that I may be enlightened and empowered to act with propriety in an uncertain moment, on a mission most urgent to my clan. A word, a moment, an audience, I beg of the house, in the name of Silari, with utmost humility."

The butler made a hand gesture that became a lean, that became a bow, his voice firm.

"I hear for the house, oh traveler, and for the house I offer welcome to one on a mission. If you will but accept the hospitality of the house I will ascertain as soon as I may the delm's availability."

The butler bowed her toward a sitting room, but Diglon saw the concern in her eyes and leaned toward her for a moment, catching her eye, opening his hands in question . . . "Please," she told the butler, suddenly bereft of flowery language, "I'll wait here if it isn't long . . ."

Pel'Kana bowed to Alara, half-nodded to Diglon before saying, "Your situation is not forgotten," and strode away at a respectful pace, and then around the corner, where his rapid footsteps faded as he mounted the stairs.

"What do you do, my comrade?" Diglon asked her in Terran. "Are you in danger? May I aid you?" he bent toward her, voice soft and even concerned.

Alara struggled for a moment with the question, the irony of being named comrade at this moment hard on her sensibility. Her role was stretched across so many *melant'i* points that she could see herself in a play . . .

"Thank you, Diglon," she managed. "Not in danger, but in flux. I'm not sure anyone can help me, which is why I am here. . . ."

"If this flux regards the fields, can you share with me . . ."

She waved him off with a Scout sign, *allow space, please,* and he saw it, hands testing . . .

"Another room?" she heard him venture, and then he admitted, "I have not all of the languages yet, Ecologist, and not all of the forms. There is very much in flux also for me, I fear!"

She sighed up at him, nodding.

"Yes," she agreed, "the whole of the world is in flux, and us within it. But how came you here to be delayed by my needs . . . ?"

He moved his hands now, willing to express hand signs if they might work, and she picked up and offered, "A trench across the road?"

He nodded a Surebleak nod of yes, a quick three bounces of the chin.

He raised his eyes to the silent AI, their heights being nearly equal, and spoke distractedly away from her, so she barely heard the edge in his voice.

"I too have requested help of the house." His hands repeated the hole-in-the-road sign, and he continued . . . "It is not a secret, I believe, that my over-senior, Nelirikk, was to assist me here today, and deliver me to Ms. Audrey's, there to accept my winnings of the card game."

Alara nodded, smiling—"Yes, I'd heard of that, and it was in the papers that you'd won something . . . congratulations!"

His chin moved again, nodded thanks. "Yes, a win. A double-dip, they call it, and I was much looking forward . . ."

Alara started, suppressing the chuckle while managing to get out . . . "At Ms. Audrey's, this double dip?"

"Indeed, at Ms. Audrey's. I've not been there, and have very little liberty, and now the senior cannot direct my clothing, for I'm told that my work clothes are not appropriate to such celebrations."

Alara nodded in gentle agreement, aware though that Ms. Audrey's front door opened to a wide spectrum of folks. Surely he'd not be turned away if he appeared thus attired.

"I sought assistance," Diglon accused, "of Jeeves, who declares ignorance of the topic. And thus, we have arrived at Mr. pel'Kana's office."

"Mr. pel'Kana," came a sharp voice, "has no experience of dressing for pleasure houses on Surebleak, or anywhere else!"

That gentleman was rushing forward, and gave her a rapid multifaceted bow, which read out in short as, "By the delm's order, a respectful reply to a supplicant welcome to the house and its comforts."

"I am to inform you, Daughter of Silari, that Lady yos'Phelium is napping with the heir, and that she has left orders to be awakened in time to see you before dinner, which she will do in the . . ." here he struggled for a moment, his mouth pursing slightly, obviously quoting verbatim, the Terran falling oddly off his tongue, "in the rumpus room, if you don't mind, so the child may wear herself out enough to sleep tonight. If the delm is required for a solving, the delm will be available there."

Alara struggled to regain proper composure, bowing grateful acceptance of the delm's word, daring to breathe. This was a good sign, a delm able to show moderation, a delm . . .

"I shall await Lady yos'Phelium's pleasure, thank you, Mr. pel'Kana."

He bowed in reply to hers, and Alara thought to go to her room . . .

She found Diglon's concerned eyes on her, and she gave a wan smile.

"A solving," he asked, "is this good?"

Her breath came easier now, and she gave the half-and-half hand sign, which he knew from their work together. "We only know that when we hear it, my friend."

His turn to nod, and waggle the same sign.

"I wish you success in your endeavors," he said, "and after, if you need assistance, please allow me . . ."

Flattered, she bowed a wordless formal thanks to him while pel'Kana was saying to Jeeves behind him—"You, you have the records of available house clothing—do we even have anything in stores that this man can wear? And how should I know what is proper. . . ."

Alara saw Diglon go wooden-faced with worry as Jeeves was answering.

"We have many items that will fit Diglon Rifle. I cannot tell you we may outfit him appropriately as a member of Jelaza Kazone's household! . . ."

"Mr. pel'Kana?" she offered.

He didn't hear immediately, having ratcheted up his volume to say, "There are no fashion sources on this planet that I know of, and if you know of them you haven't explained to me how we might . . ."

"Mr. pel'Kana," she insisted, this time moving within reach of his eyes and bowing an eloquent "offer of information."

"Yes, Daughter of Silari?"

She dismissed that title with the appropriate bow and laughed.

"Oh, no, in this I am a Scout! Scouts are very experienced people, Mr. pel'Kana. I believe, if I may be permitted to assist, that I might be able to discover among your clothes items that, if not appropriate to everyday dress, will be all that is acceptable at a house of pleasure on Surebleak. Scouts, you see, dote on such places; I have seen several sides of such establishments over the course of my studies and I'd be honored if I might be able to assist."

Diglon was nearly radiant, but it was Jeeves who spurred them to action.

"The cab reports itself on the way, Diglon Rifle. You have approximately an hour to prepare."

• • •✧• • •

"WE MUST USE OUR IMAGINATION," she said quietly in his ear, her gentle hands still brushing his hair with the softest brush he'd ever experienced, perhaps lingering on the back of his neck where his hair exceeded troop norm in a style Surebleak recognized as comfortable. She applied a light dressing of some ethereal scent familiar at the edge of consciousness. Alternating with the brush, her hands touched his back, his shoulders, the admonition, "Patience, troop, patience. If the fit is not exact, we must make it work, and it must last the evening. Let us be artists. . ."

Surely such attention was that reserved for commanders and generals?

Now her hands spanned his back and shoulders, touching skin with knowing hands, for she'd long since explained that the soldier's preferred light-sensitive camouflage shirt was inappropriate to such a night . . . though she allowed his chameleonic shorts to be just the thing . . .

"We must be prepared to let inner energy flow, to take full advantage of what comes . . ."

He sighed. His shower over, Diglon stood entranced at parade rest in front of the large mirror as Alara worked, standing on a stool behind him. Mr. pel' Kana, having delivered the last of the "waist clothes" laid across the bed for display, was off now looking for better boots, for neither of the Rifle's two pairs were capable of being "date-night fresh," as the ecologist had put it with a wrinkled-nose shrug at them.

"We have no dresser or valets here, Lady," pel'Kana had explained to her, "for the staff situation is not yet stable following our move, and other than Lady Kareen, we have no one at house who might consider such a necessity. And Lady yos'Phelium was quite clear in the matter—'our Rifle,' she told me, 'is going to a public place, where he is a winner, celebrating an earned victory. It was reported in the news. He represents the house. Surebleak runs on blocks and territories and talk on the street, and he best look *fine* because every local in Audrey's place is going to notice him to start with, and they'll be weighing the house on his turnout and turn-up. He best look *fine*.'"

Jeeves appeared after a perfunctory knock on the door, carrying other items, some hung, some not, which he began to display.

On the bed, Diglon knew, there was a kilt-wrap that looked over large, even for him, and of a color that displeased him greatly, as it echoed the colors of the Fourteenth Conquest Corps. Jeeves had admired it, since there was some military history to it which they had not time to explore. He'd held it before him for size and suspected it would be somewhat scratchy if he were careless.

There was a pair of sturdy pants with many pockets—he'd ask after it, later, perhaps, but since he was going visiting he doubted he needed those pockets and suspected he harbored a troop's tendency to regard empty pockets as things to fidget with, or fill. The cloth was sturdy.

The other item he'd not yet touched, and he hoped that when he did that it would fit; it was a pair of slacks, an admirable red-wine color which he'd have never been permitted as infantry. That looked soft and comfortable. It was belted already with a leather belt, it called out luxury to him, and if the Captain wished him to march bravely he'd be pleased to march through Ms. Audrey's doors in them.

"Tops," said Alara, "are important for first impressions. This one, try it on."

She held out a fabric bit that shimmered, white and smooth one moment and then smoother and silvery the next.

As he donned it, she asked Jeeves, "Are there other singlets like this, in colors that perhaps match the slacks there?"

There were not though, and it didn't matter. He hesitated, feeling that the sleeveless shirt did not really cover—so much hesitation in fact that Alara smiled at him.

"You have a party, my friend. There's no reason why you should not be as enticing as may be, yourself."

She made a motion he took to mean he should handle the fabric and indeed, it felt good, and too, it did show him to be fit in muscle and tone.

Alara climbed down from the stool and pointed to the antique-styled button-shirt to go over the singlet; it too had shimmer and felt good. So dazzling was it, with a touch of ruff at the collar, that he was again afraid that it was no shirt for a simple trooper—but then, he was representing the house, and if the house felt him up to it, so be it, so long as it fit. There was question to that, for surely the sleeves ought to be longer—but Alara soothed.

"Jeeves, surely there is a bracelet or cuff in the house. Matching. Then, the sleeves may be rolled on each arm just so"—here she clinically adjusted them to the length she meant—"and as this is Surebleak, none will doubt that in fact you wish to display your very handsome arms for the delight and edification of others."

Then she patted his arm and smiled up into his face, saying: "You look very well, my friend, and will do the house honor, besides making observers wonder who it is that has won a prize!"

The call came then: The taxi was approaching the drive circle!

Alara stroked three coats that Jeeves held, one in each arm, and Diglon watched her, trusting her judgment in these things now, seeing results already in the mirror—

Her mouth made a silent "Oh" . . . and then she said it, out loud, "Oh, Diglon, I think this will set you off to look very fine indeed."

He backed away, though, as she held it up to him—a jacket, a leather jacket!

"I must not, comrade, for I surely am not a pilot and none will mistake . . ."

She gave then a peremptory hand motion, identical to the ones she used in field when, from a distance, she meant him to stop a measurement or motion in progress.

"Hush, Diglon," she said to him softly, "we do not ask you to sully honor. Feel this coat—and see the lining? Pilot's jackets are not so lined with simple wool. As pretty as it is, would a pilot trust it to fend off a bad landing? Hardly, but still . . ."

He had touched it, led by her words and her hands, stroking the silky leather . . .

"This is a jacket from the house of Korval, my friend. If it is offered, I would say wear it in health. . . ."

She surprised him then by swinging the coat around her own shoulders, where it looked more like an officer's greatcoat than an item of evening wear . . . and she spun, before handing the jacket over, her grin infectious.

"Try it, it must fit because there's no time for another choice! I envy your evening, Diglon!"

It came to him then that perhaps he owed Alara for all this assistance—

"But you can come as well, if I've won a double!"

Mr. pel'Kana's intake of breath was palpable, and Jeeves maintained silence.

Her smile deepened and seemed to take in her whole body, and then her face went blank, and he wondered if he'd overstepped. Surely offering a comrade a visit to a house of pleasure could not be so . . .

She made a hand motion then, of clearing away.

"Dismiss the thought," she managed, almost a sputter, "as much as I appreciate it. Your taxi awaits, there's no time for me to dress properly and indeed, I myself have a pressing engagement on the night. Go, please, cover yourself and the house in glory!"

Rushing his boots, Diglon did as he was told.

• • •✧• • •

"THIS WAY PLEASE, SCOUT," was what Jeeves said, and she followed, wondering if the use of the security 'bot to call her to her meeting was a subtle warning, a hint, or . . . mere convenience. Her delm had met the 'bot himself at Trealla Fantrol and spoken of it more than once, the usual result being a discussion of the proper upbringing of a clan's children and the subtlety with which Korval balanced debts . . .

The room was small and warm, and—soft.

That was Alara's reaction to the rumpus room: Soft. Not only were there rugs in multiple depths strewn about, but there were pillows and sit-cushions scattered about on floors and chairs and against shelves, and there were wondrous quilts of multiple sizes draped from chair-backs. There were walkways, cleared here and there, with various plush items that were cats or norbears or dragons or spaceships, and, higher, there were shelves with adult-stuff on them and—Oh!

Barely noticeable on the corner, was a woman altogether Liaden-sized, long red hair wrapped in a spiraling braided coif, who was kneeling, warily watching a child with wide eyes and a wider grin standing, bouncing experimentally on bowed legs, intent and wonder warring on her face as excited but nearly inaudible *whuffs* escaped her smile.

"Lady yos'Phelium," announced Jeeves, "Alara chel'Voyon, Clan Silari."

The gray eyes fixed her instantly, smile still strong.

"Please come on in, Scout, over this way," she said. "Pull up a chair, a cushion, a rug—I'm on baby-watch tonight."

The eyes had surveyed her, seen that she was dressed respectfully but was ringless, and then gone back to the child, still standing.

Alara was torn by the comfortable informality of the greeting, knowing her mission deserved some seriousness of attention . . . and yet knowing all too well the stricture that one went to Delm Korval only in peril.

And there, she was in peril, for the her own delm felt the clan at risk, and what could she do but . . .

The room was as quiet as it was soft; Jeeves said nothing and the child, after an extra-exuberant bounce, settled in front of her mother.

"Good!"

That was Lady yos'Phelium, deftly changing her kneel to a cross-legged seat on the rug next to the youngster, and a hand casually sweeping the closest chair, cushion, and floor in a reaffirmation that they were all the same as far as she was concerned.

Soldier, married to a Scout. Yes, that's what she recalled, daring to go cross-legged herself on the rug, a few hands-breadths away from the child, facing the mother. Soldier-woman, being comfortable in her own house, of a quiet evening, in house boots so light they were almost leather socks . . . not expecting, and perhaps not *wanting*, to deal with bows and layers of protocol.

Already she could imagine herself reporting such a meeting to her father, who'd never think to meet someone in such an informality, but who would no doubt accept that his daughter stood on such footing. . . .

"Jeeves, please bring us some morning wine if you please, and some of that spring-cheese we just got from Yulie."

Jeeves assented and started out immediately.

"Lady, I must . . ." Alara started, but found herself waved aside nonchalantly.

"How about Miri, while it's just us and Lizzie relaxing, right? As long as I can call you Alara? I grew up hereabouts and some days doing the pretty gets a girl tired . . ."

"Yes, Miri, thank you . . . I am sorry to intrude on your day . . ."

"Not an intrusion; you didn't even have to come through the front door to talk to me, though I have to tell you it did get Mr. pel'Kana's attention. He likes the formal sometimes, and I guess we gotta keep the home folks happy if we can. . . ."

Miri laughed, and untangled the baby's foot from the edge of one of the soft rag rugs that populated the corner.

"But anyhow, I need to thank *you* for helping out with our Diglon. You 'betcha Nelirikk's going to shine your boots for you one day over this—leaving the poor troop to the last minute over something as important as his first leave on world and then hanging him out for a quick-dress and a cab-ride on his own? And really, not sure I could have done it any better myself, dressing a guy to run to Ms. Audrey's—"

Alara tried to school her face to the idea of a delm dressing a security guard for an evening's romp, but there, Miri had been a soldier, after all, and not just a soldier, but a Captain . . .

Here there was a short break as Jeeves returned with bottle and glasses, and small plates, and a z-gee bulb of something for the baby as well. A tray on short legs went between them and some home-made crackers and a dish of soft-brown cheese. . . .

"That's fine, Jeeves; we'll call if we need you."

Lizzie's eyes followed Jeeves' departure with interest; and Miri smiled and shook her head over something before returning to her topic, a wry grin on her face.

"As I was saying, I appreciate you picking up the slack there. A good thing, I guess it was, to have a Scout in that mix, else they have sent him off in something as ordinary as they could, and that just wouldn'a done. Saw the vidfeed on his way out to the taxi—you got him right up handsome, you did. I seen troops his size couldn't put on comfortable unless it was sloppy. He'll have the city-girls all pleased, I expect . . ."

"Really, it wasn't a difficult thing," Alara said. "He has a sound body to start with, and the choices—well, it works that way, doesn't it, that if you have only a few choices one of them usually looks much better! I merely imagined that I was assisting a cousin with a festival preparation, and the choices became clear!"

Miri nodded, gave the grasping child her z-gee bulb to chase a bit of cracker, and they settled for a moment to sip wine and have cheese themselves. Miri finally deposited an empty glass, and said to her guest in local Terran.

"I was talking about choices afore, and I guess we got some to make here. You already made one, coming to me with a problem, and you say it's a delm thing you got, so you brought it to Korval. How about you explain gentle . . . ," and here Miri made scout-like hand signs, *simple good quick easy gentle*, "and remember I wasn't born to Liaden, myself, but I can pretty well get by however you want to talk it."

Alara bowed lightly, *Simple simple* repeating mildly in her pilot's hands, and laid the basic situation out succinctly, avoiding the formal as much as she could, and also at the end of her explanation, not quite avoiding the spray of water from a thrown water-bulb, the bulb itself snatched out of the air by pilot-quick hands.

"Ring the bell and she'll be playing bowli ball if we're not careful!"

Miri handed a small hand-towel to her guest, nodding, and then adjusting the child's position to sit easier against the pillow-back, she sat straighter herself before turning back to Alara.

"Listening for Korval," she said, "I hear that your clan's going through some changes and your delm's dropped you into a hard spot. And I can see what's some behind it, 'cause I hope you don't mind, but I did some research, and pretty much Silari's been one to lean toward Korval almost since that tree out there took root on Liad."

Abruptly Lizzie rolled from her sitting position and worked her way to standing against the pillow, sharing a self-pleased smile with her onlookers despite a not-quite firm stance.

Miri watched, absorbed for several seconds in the gentle swaying, and then, assured there was some stability there, looked at Alara seriously.

"Don't know we need me to come delm for this, but I can tell you there's a case here, over time, that Silari ought to have a connection with Korval, money in the budget or not. We got council votes, we got old farming agreements, we got help with—heck, Silari himself knows it . . ."

Alara, startled—it might have been what her delm had thought but the idea hadn't crossed her own mind—raised her hand as if to protest, but Korval was shaking her head gently, hands saying, *wait wait.*

Miri paused, pursed her lips, and looked straight at Alara again.

"Just like Silari, though, Koval's a bit thin right now. We got Syl Vor or Quin a few years down the line, but parents are already thinking there, and I'd hate to have to make call for six or eight years out, if you hear me."

Mother instinct, she reached over just in time to steady Lizzie against a sudden rocky step, and turned back, still serious and thoughtful, as much talking to herself as Alara.

"There's Gordon Arbuthnot, but again, he's more out of the yos'Galan side of counting, and not necessarily going to get into the contract stuff. No one's talked about that with me, busy as we all been. Details, all these details."

Now she was touching fingers, and then almost snickered, "I dunno, I think we can't figure Pat Rin's gonna have much free time any year soon . . ." which made them both laugh, even as aghast as Alara was at Korval assuming . . .

"And I think we might need to figure that altogether, we're in a spot with you. I'm doing my part here, but lifemates being lifemates, Val Con's in the same spot as Pat Rin, and if we was to go to bel'Tarda I'm thinking that's another thing would have to be worked out—

Bel'Tarda? The rug merchant? Alara ran the connections in her mind, and saw the odd subordinate line—yes, he stood as foster father to Pat Rin in the lists, and as old as . . .

"Korval," she said, though in reality Korval had yet to be invoked directly in this catalog of potentially available gene donors, "it is my understanding that Silari is not as bold, nor as demanding, nor as acquisitive, as these choices you mention, and which honor me even if not possible. I suspect that my delm, at least, will be pleased to see a contract produce a child of a connection favorable to ourselves *and* to Korval. That our long-connection is fractured I have mentioned, and it is clear that Korval has many more connections within reach than Silari . . ."

Scout-talk in the hands, from Korval: *shredded more nets than we've mended, orbits on remainders still computing . . .*

Alara signified, *read that message and match it.*

The child made a noise that made Alara cringe and Miri laugh. The redhead shook her head, muttering something about being glad when Val Con was back for kid-duty, and then smiled brightly up at her guest.

"So, Alara, I think what we both need to do is to think; and for our side, we'll read the records deep and see if we spot anything to bring to you. Look at the details. If you are thinking of someone else on port, not directly of Korval, it might be good if you could have names and information to hand so that our connections might be considered, and their own needs. Take the day tomorrow to think of it. Certainly I can understand that Silari, moving in support of beliefs, is as worthy as any, and more so than many, when it comes to our consideration. Let us agree that the conversation is not over, and we'll talk in the afternoon, tomorrow. Let us say an hour after the midday meal is cleared here."

Taking child to her then, Korval rose, and the interview ended, Alara still in amaze.

• • •✧• • •

DIGLON'S NIGHT had ended with a quiet cup of whipped-top cocoa, an unexpected gift of the house on his return from Ms. Audrey's in the early hours, brought by Jeeves in his role as night sentry and door master. He doubted that there'd been a sleep agent in that draught, yet he'd slept exceptionally well, and was wide awake and well-satisfied with himself some moments before the call-tone on the chronometer chirped.

Surebleak, he'd heard from his poker combatants, was a place where the good things were hard to come by, an inhospitable place on the fringe of civilization, a hardship post, a place to escape from if at all possible . . .

But, in the afterglow of his night, he considered that perhaps not all eyes saw the same world. Here, there was relative quiet, and though the security work he'd been doing was serious enough, there'd not been open fighting for some time, and Boss Conrad's dominion was secure, particularly with the backing of the rest of Line yos'Phelium, who could command battleships to stand off-planet if need be.

Surebleak—he'd done his research and knew the name of the planet itself to be a sign of the original colonists' disapproval—but there, after their hard work Surebleak had breathable air, drinkable water, and land that could support farms and a spaceport, and—and he'd discovered last night that Ms. Audrey's was but one of a dozen or more pleasure houses! How could port security think it such a burden, when the duty helped make it all safer?

He dressed quietly, taking time to glance out his window into the inner garden where grew the tree and its surround of flowers. In the morning light the usual heavy dawn mist was giving way to dew-topped fronds and flowers, and to the flowers came birds, some few, the winter having been gone some weeks now, and parading about were several cats. Cats amused him, and apparently he, the cats; he was not yet entirely used to them and still, on Hazenthull's standing order, he found he needed lock them out of his quarters else he'd wake to purrs and clothes covered in cat hair.

A motion among the bushes, and from a spot that seemed far too small for him, Jeeves emerged, several more cats in his train. Jeeves offered names to the cats, fed them, communed with them. Truly, Surebleak was a world of marvels, and he pleased to be part of it!

He wondered who else might be seeing the mist drift away. Was the Captain up? That was likely, he supposed, for the baby kept her own hours and he often found the Captain at common table when he arrived, if the one she called Tough Guy were away, as was often the case.

Was Alara the biologist up? No way of knowing that certainty unless he met her: her room was on the opposite side of the tree's incredible trunk. He'd walked the gardens until he was sure of that, supposing it was his security consciousness at work. It comforted him to know where the folk who were important were . . .

There was a sigh then, recalling that she was Liaden and her ways were not the ways of the troop, nor of Surebleak, nor of Liad, either, since she was a Scout. She was, however, comfortable to work with and he wondered how he might Balance her assistance for what had truly been a memorable experience. He doubted he should share that he'd thought of her there at Audrey's, for as surely as he would have enjoyed sharing his bounty with her, she'd have cited something from the Code, or from a rulebook, explaining why it couldn't have been so.

A bird, launched by a stalking cat, fluttered very nearly into his window and he knew that the day was upon him, and opened his door, to find two dark cats sitting primly in front of it, as if waiting for him. Indeed, they became his escort, and walked him knowingly to breakfast, their feet avoiding his on the back stairs.

The common table was set; nearby on the old wooden side tables sat the breakfast teas, coffee maker, juices, nut-milks, water, and even the carafe of Yittle, a yeast and caffeine drink he'd asked after one morning and which had been added to the menu. He often started with a few sips of that, and when Haznethull was on-station she, too, would have some. He'd been startled to see several other guests partake as he assumed it was a vestige of his trooply upbringing . . . but several claimed to appreciate the robust flavor, and considered it food rather than beverage.

And so, Yittle first, with a side of coffee, and a flash toast of hearty bread brought up from the city. No one else present, he still sat at the end chair, which for the youngsters like Syl Vor or even for the absent Quin and Padi, might be a two-person bench, leaving the places he'd decided were preferred in case others joined. There being rank within rank even here, where so often the unannounced guests might be pilots having left their jackets in the room, or commanders, on holiday, his current spot was the most practical.

A sound behind him as he slathered nut spread on his first flash-toast, and he smiled wide for Alara, who was dressed for—not for field work, but not yet for visiting the city. Perhaps it was her day off . . .

She'd come in with a commpad and missed his first look; when she did see him she'd already been aiming for one of the seats at the other end of the table, which surely was her right . . .

Then, seeing no others in the room, the scout caught his glance and gave a wan nod, changing course to place her keypad across the square angle of the table, to his left side, before angling back to the beverages.

"Diglon, I hope the morning finds you well and in spirits?"

This was said over her shoulder, in Trade.

The words were there, he heard, but her concentration was elsewhere, he thought, and not simply on the morning duty of her tea.

The languages of this house were slippery; unlike the small spaceport guard garrison in the city, where the common language was Terran with as much Surebleak dialect as possible, and fell back first to basic Terran, and then to Trade, moving on to Liaden rarely and against custom, to the tongue of the troop not at all, here, sentences might vary from one to the next, and at times, even with the sentence words, tense, and dialects might be sprinkled about with impunity, and with great accuracy. Even in the presence of the youngsters, who were all now away from house, it was the expectation that communication would take place. He himself was picking up some of this side-language spoken with fingers. Rarely would a sentence be spoken in troop—if the others of his background were there, principally, but then from time from some hidden necessity might come a phrase, a word, even a paragraph or two—not necessarily well-formed—from those two who were Korval, and as well from the elder Scout when he was present.

Yet the Trade Alara offered was a distancing effort, more formal rather than the everyday. He had recourse to his Yittle, and then nodded, though she might not have seen, agreeing.

"The morning fog found me happily awake; my spirits are high and I am well, and I am rested. And yourself, if I may inquire?"

This, of course, could be shunted aside; their relative ranks being such that permitted casual discussion but did not encourage it.

The musical sound of spoons and ceramics and such came to him, and then she returned, steaming beverage in one hand and a simple buttered cheese roll wrapped in one of the impeccable cloth napkins in the other.

She sighed as she sat, raised her cup toward him as if a salute, and sipped carefully before answering.

"I am well, that I am."

She stopped there, took a bite of her roll, and leaned back into the seat, sipping again soon, and then stared into her cup reflectively, then tapped on the commpad idly to bring forth a screen already waiting. What she might see there he couldn't tell, yet such total distraction was unlike her, and he leaned forward to offer a gentle observation.

"I see you are not dressed for field duty this morning. Have you information or orders for me?"

Her cup to lips, her free hand danced over the keys, and she stared at the screen, sighing, before looking up and bowing a bow of contrition.

"Diglon, you are correct. I have . . . other necessities today, and a meeting this afternoon as well—in fact, thinking of it now, I should have left a message for you that you might also have the day free for yourself. I am behind hand on this."

Now his concern rose, and he weighed his thoughts before making them into words.

"Is it possible that my performance has not been up to standard and that you must make amends with the Captain? I have seen, without understanding, that there has been an issue. I am proud of my posting with you, and your regard, and will do what whatever I may improve. If I may assist your work today, whatever it may be, that we may continue with our studies and bring the fields to full and timely production—"

She startled him, clinking the cup on the table and rising.

She gave him a bow, full of import that he could not read, and then shook her head Terran style, admitting in a quiet voice:

"I have been unkind to you, have I not, these recent days? And you, you with an event of importance I have not honored. We do, very much, need to work as a team and I am foolish to forget. Teammates should help each other."

She paused, spoke a brief line of Liaden:

"Let us do this: Give me a moment or two and I shall return and we will begin the morning again, in better Balance. I will put aside this cloud . . ."

She gathered up her commpad, slapping it into clear screen and tucking it into her belt loop, and then quick marched out of the room, placing the used cup on the side table and leaving him briefly to wonder if she had a pressing physical need. A time passed, of perhaps ten breaths, and she returned.

What exactly she had done in that interim he was unsure; it was said that Scouts had attention exercises, and perhaps it was that. Yet she arrived with a hint of energy and awareness that she had lacked on her first entry; and it was if she spotted him for the first time of the day.

"There you are, Diglon," she said now, and a smile touched at the corners of her mouth. "I hope your day is well-started?"

This was an oddity, but indeed, he had trained well enough to understand when a situation was reviewed and begun again.

"Yes," he managed, and added, "the Yittle is an excellent start and soon I shall move on to meat!"

"And good!"

Now she scooped up a new cup and new tea, and along with that, some fruit and another roll. She selected the same seat, and began, as if newly arrived indeed.

"Ah, my friend, I have been remiss; duty calls me to other necessities for much of the day and I'm inclined to permit us both a day away from the field. Indeed, I should have told the house so last night, that you might have slept in after your date in town, for surely a lazy morning would have treated you well!"

She spoke in Terran, with more ease about her.

"I woke easily as I always do," he told her, "and ready to work."

"We shall amend your day in any case, I fear, for the field can use a day or two of growth before we recheck. I'll let Jeeves know you are available, if the house needs you, else, perhaps it would be wise of you to study on what clothes you may need for future civilian use so that we may not have Jeeves and Mr. pel'Kana in such a sweat as last night again."

He laughed despite himself, allowing the image of their rush of the evening before to be the stuff of stories, had he but a troop to share it with.

"Nelirikk Explorer has suggested as much for the future, though I doubt that I shall often win such a prize. . . ."

He went silent with consideration of his prize—and after a respectful moment she asked him:

"And were you dressed sufficiently finely?"

He nodded, and allowed, "The staff of Ms. Audrey's told me so, and, and in particular, Tova was appreciative. The shirts were very fine, she told me, and she took special care to . . ." here he fumbled, having run out of the correct words in any of the languages he had quick to tongue, "that is, she helped to get me out of them, gently and with much touching, and admired how well they fit, and how well-formed they were for me."

He paused. "I was struck there, with Tova and Diam, that it would have been a good moment for, for . . ." he struggled, started again. "I lack a full troop here, of course, and some events are as good to share as they are to experience. You had paid such attention to finding these correct choices, these choices that helped—and your own adjusting of the clothes had begun to give me the feeling that this was special. I thought that it would have been good if a comrade, a team member, that is . . . had someone like you been there to share in this triumph!"

"Teams," she said, "can do some things together better than others. And some teams can do everything together. Triumphs . . . some share better than others, I think."

"It would have been good," he said, but honesty took over and he said, "It was good, it just could have been better! And they told me to come back as soon as I might, because I was not so foolish as to be stupid drunk, nor drugged to numb, and I paid attention, which is good and would I please come back . . . they were afraid I was one of the new spacers and would be gone after last night. And for me to dress in fine clothes they thought a present to them!"

Alara laughed, which made him smile, and she said, "Yes, but see, perhaps you can have such a time again and you'll wish to have the dressing of yourself. There's no reason why, in this house, you may not order the clothes you wish!"

"But I am not sure of which clothes there are. I have never seen the like of Tova's . . . undersuit. And then she first and then the pair—they know such techniques as are amazing! I must practice! Did you know that. . . ."

Alara was now eating her fruit, with tea to hand; she was laughing, and in some haste she managed to say, "Perhaps those techniques are discussions for another time and place! Please, do not fail to eat!"

Diglon's stomach agreed with that suggestion, and he rose now to gather his meat and tubers, more Yittle, and some juice. Having thought about the techniques Tova and Diam shared with him, he sighed. He recalled from training that Scouts frequently worked in teams, and wondered how much those teams might share . . .

Alara sat, brighter than she had the first time into the room, but as she glanced toward the window it was as if a shadow had fallen on her again, or duty pressed, and the edges of her smile filed off to seriousness.

"Do you know," Diglon said around his food, "that Tova and Diam think that those clothes as you fit me with are such fine things that they are too expensive to have and wear. And Tova wished to know if I was married, on account of she said she could marry someone in three years, when she retires . . . especially someone who wears such nice clothes! And I—I am not a commander, I doubt that I can afford really fine clothes . . ."

Absently, considering the dressing of him, she said, "You deserve nice clothes, Diglon, and *here* there is opportunity, because several of the plants we are looking at make very fine fibers and very fine cloth as well as food. We can have samples made—you could even perhaps model them for Tova and Diam as a test!"

Diglon was much taken with that thought, and several others, and it was only after he realized that Alara had fallen quiet and withdrawn again that he returned to an earlier topic, and as he spoke he saw her turn to him, studying his face.

"If it is not my performance that is a difficulty, can you tell me what I may do to help with this difficulty? It affects how our little team works. I have been researching the flowers and the food, and there is so much that we can do—we can grow storage foods that will have the house eating well all year . . . but the work is important."

He gathered his strength, dropped his voice to nearly a trench-whisper to insist.

"You must tell me how I can help—I will do extra work, I will do whatever I may, within the service I am sworn to yos'Phelium. If you can tell me how to help, you must!"

He realized he'd been leaning toward her, and that she'd been leaning toward him as well, her brown eyes riveted.

She was silent, and he was, which was awkward, and more so when they found themselves unalone, the silent Captain standing as she was a few scant paces away.

"Service to yos'Phelium, is it? Well," she said in Terran, "yos'Phelium's got lots of needs, and me and my other half, we're pretty flexible. That's why we have folks like dea'Gauss work with us, people who can spin a contract like one never been written and make it look all everyday and acceptable. Heck, that's why we signed a contract to be Road Boss on an outworld."

The Captain's eyes were on him, firm, appraising. Diglon didn't flinch, unsure what the contract talk was about, but sure it was important. She nodded, and said, "You're a good man, Diglon Rifle."

"Thank you, Captain," he said from his seat.

She smiled and added, "You stand with us, right?"

"I do stand with you, of course!"

The Captain turned to Alara.

"He stands with Korval, Daughter of Silari. Just so you know."

"I am informed," Alara said, with a bow, and turned to him—

"Let us walk beneath the tree, Diglon," she said to him, "and you and I will discuss this idea you have, of doing what you may to help. I believe we have many details to discuss!"

✧ The Space at Tinsori Light ✧

__THE FIRST MENTION__ of Tinsori Light is in the heading preceding chapter twenty-nine of Scout's Progress. The heading purports to be part of a beam-letter sent from Jen Sin yos'Phelium to his delm, complaining of the cost of repairs at, and impugning the reputation of the keeper of, the Light. It was meant to illustrate the use, and worth, of a Jump Pilot's Ring, which figures in the storyline of the novel. We never intended to write a story about the Light, or the Keeper.

Well.

It turns out that Tinsori Light has a mind of its own.

SPACE IS HAUNTED.

Pilots know this; station masters and light keepers, too; though they seldom speak of it, even to each other. Why would they? Ghost or imagination; wyrd space or black hole, life—and space—is dangerous.

The usual rules apply.

SUBSTANCE FORMED from the void. Walls rose, air flowed, floors heated.

A relay clicked.

In the control room, a screen glowed to life. The operator yawned, and reached to the instruments, long fingers illuminated by the wash of light.

On the screen—space, turbulent and strange.

The operator's touch on the board wakes more screens, subtle instruments. A tap brings a chronometer live in the bottom right of the primary screen. Beams are assigned to sweep near-space; energy levels are sampled, measured, compared.

The clock displays elapsed time: *293 units*.

The operator frowns, uncertain of what units the clock measures. She might have known, once. Two hundred ninety-three—that was a long phase. At the last alarm, it had shown 127 elapsed units; on the occasion before that, 63.

The operator turns back to her scans, hoping.

Hoping that it would prove to be *something* this time—something worthy of her. Of them.

The last alarm had been triggered by a pod of rock and ice traveling through the entanglement of forces that supported and enclosed them.

A rock pod . . . nothing for them.

She hadn't even had time for a cup of tea.

The alarm before the rock pod—had been nothing for them, either. Though they hadn't known that, at first.

They pulled it in, followed repair protocols, therapies, and subroutines . . .

She'd had more than a cup of tea, at least—whole meals, she'd eaten. She'd listened to music, read a book . . . but in the end there was nothing they could do, except take the salvage and ride the strange tide away again into that place where time, all unknown, elapsed.

The scans—*these* scans, *now*—they gave her rock, and mad fluctuations of energy. They gave her ice, and emptiness.

There ought to be something more. *Some*thing more, worthy or unworthy. The geometry of the space about them was delicate. The alarm would not sound for nothing.

The scans fluttered and flashed, elucidating a disturbance in the forces of this place. Breath-caught, the operator leans forward.

The scans detected, measured; verified mass, direction, symmetry . . .

The scans announced . . .

. . . a ship.

Any ship arriving here was a ship in need.

The operator extended her hand and touched a plate set away from all the toggles, buttons, and tags that attended to her part of their function.

She touched the plate. And woke the Light.

• • •✧• • •

THIS, thought Jen Sin yos'Phelium Clan Korval, *is going to be . . . tricky.*

Oh, the orders from his delm were plain enough: Raise Delium, discreetly. Deliver the packet—there *was* a packet, and didn't he just not know what was in it. Discreet, the delivery, too. Of course. Delivery accomplished, he was to—discreetly—raise ship and get himself out of Sinan space, not to say range of their weapons.

Alive, preferably.

That last, that was his orders to himself, he being somewhat more interested in his continued good health and long-term survival than his delm. *Package delivered* was Korval's bottom line; the expense of delivery beyond her concern.

In any wise, the whole matter would have been much easier to accomplish, from discreet to alive, if Delium wasn't under active dispute.

Not that this was the riskiest mission he had undertaken at the delm's word during this late and ongoing season of foolishness with Clan Sinan and their allies. He was, Jen Sin knew, as one knows a fact, and without undue pride, Korval's best pilot. Jump pilot, of course, with the ring and the leather to prove it.

Of late, he would have rather been Korval's third or fourth best pilot, though that wouldn't have prevented him being plucked out from the Scouts, which had been clan and kin to him for more than half his life. No, it would have only meant that he would have served as decoy, to call attention away from Korval's Best, when there was a packet for delivery.

Well, the usual rules applied here, as elsewhere. If working without back-up, always know the way out, always carry an extra weapon, always know the state of your ship—and know that your ship is able and accessible, always be prepared to survive, and always remember that the delm was Captain to the passengers. Being Korval's best pilot, his job was to fly where the passengers needed him to fly, at the direction of the delm.

Jen Sin sighed. Gods knew he was no delm, and thankful for it, too. Delms did math in lives, set in courses that would be flown by pilots not yet born. The delm decided who to spend, and when, for what profit to the clan. And just as well, Jen Sin acknowledged, that he wasn't clever enough to do those sorts of sums.

His attention was occupied for a bit, then, dodging various busy eyes in orbit, and when he had time to think again, at his ease between two security rings, he found he was thinking of his team.

When he'd first come out from the Scouts, he'd thought of them often—the comrades closer than kin; the six of them together stronger, smarter, faster than any one of them alone.

Well.

There was a time when he could have gone back, delm willing, which she hadn't been. *Could* have gone back, no questions asked, no accommodation required. *Could have*, then.

Now, what he had was *couldn't*, though *would* still burned in his belly, even now that it was too late. His team had long ago moved past their grief, taken on someone else, shifted tasks and priorities until they were, again, a team—different from the team it had been.

And no room for Jen Sin yos'Phelium, at all.

• • •✧• • •

"I WOULD PREFER the Starlight Room, if it is available," he said, and passed over the identification for one Pan Rip sig'Alta, and a sixth-*cantra*, too.

The desk-man took both, bland-faced, scanned the card and returned it, the coin having been made to disappear.

"Sir, I regret. The Starlight Room is unavailable. May I suggest the Solar Wind?"

"The Solar Wind, excellent," he murmured, and received the key-card the man passed to him.

"The hallway to the right; the second door on your left hand. Please be at peace in our house."

That was scarcely likely, a certain tendency to unpeacefulness in perilous places being one of his numerous faults. Thus far, however, all was according to script. That, he told himself, firmly, was good.

Jen Sin entered the hallway, found the door, and used the key, stepping across the threshold immediately the door slid away, a man with no enemies, in need of an hour of solitude.

Two steps inside, the door already closed behind him, he checked—a man startled to find his solitary retreat already occupied.

This was also according to script—that there should be someone before him. Who, he had not been privileged to know. No matter, though—there were yet another few lines of code to exchange, which would in theory assure the orderly transfer of the packet tucked snug in an inner pocket of his jacket. And the safe departure of the courier.

Jen Sin allowed himself to display surprise before he bowed.

"Forgive me," he said to the severe young woman seated by the pleasant fire, a bottle of wine and two glasses on the table before her. "I had thought the room would be empty."

"Surely," said she, "the fault lies with the desk. However, it seems to me fortuitous, for it seems I am in need of a companion other than my thoughts."

All and everything by the script. He ought to have been reassured. He told himself that.

Meanwhile, acting his assigned part, he inclined his head formally.

"I am pleased to accept the gift of comradeship," he murmured, and stepped toward the table with a Scout's silent footsteps.

He paused by the doubtless comfortable chair, the back of his neck feeling vulnerable. There remained one more matched exchange, to prove the case. Would the child never speak?

She looked up at him, and smiled, wistfully, so it seemed to him.

"Please," she said, "sit and share wine with me."

That . . .

. . . was *not* according to script, and now he saw it—the anomaly that his subconscious, ever-so-much cleverer than he, had noticed the moment he had cleared the threshold.

The wine bottle, there on the table between the two glasses . . .

Was uncorked.

Jen Sin kicked; the table, the glasses, the wine becoming airborne. He slapped the door open, heard glass shatter behind him, and a high scream of agony.

He did not look back as he stepped into the hall, turning left, away from the foyer where the doorman presided. Deliberately bringing to mind the floor plan he had memorized to while away the hours alone in transit to Delium, he ran.

Less than a half-minute later, he let himself out a service door, wincing as the alarm gave tongue. Then, he was again running at the top of his speed, down the delivery corridor to the street beyond.

• • • ✧ • • •

HE HAD NOT SURRENDERED the packet, his ship, or his life, though he had pretended to give up the two latter.

The man hidden on the gantry, justifiably proud of the shot that had dropped him at the ship's very hatch, had taken the key from Jen Sin's broken fingers, turned, and slapped it home.

Obediently, the hatch rose. Jen Sin, slightly less dead than he had appeared, lurched to his feet, and broke the man's neck. The long rifle clattered to the landing pad, where he doubted it disturbed the gunman's three associates. The body he left where it fell, as he staggered into the lock, and brought the hatch down.

He crawled down the short hallway; dragged himself painfully into the pilot's chair. Gripped the edge of the board until his vision cleared. It hurt to breathe. Cunning thrust of the knife, there—he ought to remember it.

Time to go. He extended a hand, brought the board clumsily to life, his hands afire, no spare breath to curse, or to cry. The 'doc, that was his urgent need. He did know that.

Not yet, though. Not *just* yet.

He sounded a thirty-second warning, all that he dared, then gave *Lantis* her office, sagging in the chair, and not webbed in, and in just a while, a little while, only a while, a while . . . He shook his head, saw stars and lightning.

As soon as they gained Jump, it would be safe enough then, to tend his hurts.

An alarm screamed. He roused, saw the missile pursuing, initiated evasive action and clung to the board, to consciousness, in case his ship should need him.

So much for discretion, that was his thought, as *Lantis* bounced through lanes of orderly traffic, Control cursing him for a clanless outlaw, and not one word of sorrow for those firing surface-to-air into those same working lanes of traffic.

Korval either would or would not be pleased, though he had the packet. He kept reminding himself of that fact—he had the packet. The woman at the meeting room spoke the lines out of order, no sense to it. If she were false, why not just finish the script and take what was not hers? If she were an ally, and captured—then, ah, yes, *then* one might well vary, as a warn-away—

She had not survived, he was certain of that, and to his list of error was added that he had cost Korval an ally . . . and added another death to his account. He might almost say, "innocent," save there were no innocents in this. He might, surely, say "dutiful," and even "courageous" might find a place in his report—and Korval—*he*—was in her debt.

His ship spoke to him. Orbit achieved. At least, he could still fly. He set himself to do so, heading for the up and out, the nearest Jump point, or failing that, the nearest likely bit of empty space from which he might initiate a Short Jump.

His side, where the knife had gotten past the leather, that was bad; his fingers left red smears on the board. The doc . . . but *Lantis* needed him.

They had almost reached the Jump point, when a ship flashed into being so close the proximity alarms went off. Jen Sin swore weakly at pinheaded piloting, and a moment later discovered that not to be the case at all.

The new ship fired; the beam struck directly over the engines.

The shields deflected it, and there came evasive action from the automatics, but the other ship was a gunboat, no slim and under-armed courier.

The Jump point was that close. Once in Jump space, he would have some relief. Enough relief that he might live through this adventure.

There really was no other choice; he had no more time on account.

Blood dripped from fingers remarkably steady as they moved across the board, diverting everything but the minimum amount necessary to function—from life support, from auxiliary power.

From the shields.

He fed everything to the engines, and *ran* for the Jump point, as if there were no gunboats within the sector, much less the ship that even now was launching enough missiles to cripple a warship.

They hit the point with too much velocity, too much spin; in the midst of an evade that had no chance of succeeding. He greatly feared that they brought missiles into the Jump field with them.

Jen Sin groped for and hit the emergency auto-coords, felt the ship shiver, saw the screens go gray—

And fainted where he sat.

THE LIGHT PULLED and riffled the files from the ship. The operator kept one eye on its screen while she pursued her own sort of data.

Engine power was minimal, and life support also; the shields were in tatters. The dorsal side showed a long, deep score, like that delivered from an energy cannon. That the hull had not taken worse damage—that was something to wonder at. Still, her readings indicated life support and other services low past the point of danger.

It was, the operator acknowledged, a ship in dire trouble, yet it held air, it held together, and it had come under its own power into the space at Tinsori Light. All those things recommended it, and the operator felt a cautious thrill of anticipation.

If the ship were fit to be repaired—but that was for the Light to decide.

If the pilot lived—her duty fell there.

The operator shivered, in mingled anticipation and fear.

• • • ✧ • • •

THEY'D TAKEN BAD HITS, him and his ship, and unless they raised a repair yard or a friendly station soon, there was no saying that they'd either one survive.

He'd come to in Jump with emergency bells going off and a blood-smeared board lit yellow and red. It took determination, and a couple of rest periods with his forehead pressed against the board while pain shuddered through him, and his sluggish heartbeat filled his ears—but he pulled the damage reports.

Whatever had hit them as they entered Jump had been—*should have been*—enough to finish them. The main engine was out; the hull was scored, and there was a slow leak somewhere; life support was ranging critical and running off impulse power, along with the lights and screens.

In short, he was a pilot in distress and with a limited number of choices available to him.

One—he could manually end Jump and hope *Lantis* held together, that they would manifest in a friendlier portion of space than the port they had just quit, and within hailing distance of, if not an ally, at least a neutral party.

Two—he could ride Jump out to its natural conclusion. Normal re-entry would be kinder to his ship's injuries. His own injuries . . .

He looked down at his sticky hands, the Jump pilot's ring covered with gore, and allowed himself to form the thought . . .

I am not going to survive this.

Oh, he could—probably—crawl across the cabin and get himself into the autodoc. But under emergency power, the 'doc would only stabilize him, and place him into a kindly sleep until such time as ship conditions improved.

He may have blacked out again, just there. Certainly it was possible. What roused him was . . . was.

Ah.

Lantis had exited Jump. They were . . . someplace.

Gasping, he leaned toward the board, squinting at screens grown nearly too dark to see.

The coords meant nothing to him. He remembered—he remembered hitting the auto-coords. But the auto-coords were for Korval safe spots—the ship yard, the Rock; quiet places located in odd corners of space, such as might be discovered by Scouts and pilots mad for knowing *what was there*? Auto-coords had taken stock of *Lantis* as injured and hurt as she was, and, measured through some prior delm-and-pilot's priorities, cast them together through limitless space to one particularly appropriate destination, to one last hope.

He looked again at screens and arrival data. The coords still meant nothing to him, though their absolute anonymity to a pilot of his experience and understanding gave him to believe that pursuit was now the least of his problems.

The space outside his screens was a place of pink and blue dusts pirouetting against a void in which stars were a distant promise.

If there was a friend of Korval in this place, it would, he thought, be good if they arrived . . . soon.

As if his thought had called the action, an interior screen came to life. Someone was accessing the ship's public files.

Hope bloomed, so painful and sudden that he realized he had, indeed, given up himself and his ship. There was someone out there—perhaps a friend. Someone who cared enough that it did them the honor of wanting to know who they were.

Jen Sin reached to the board, teeth gritted against the pain, and did pilot's duty, waking the scans and the screens, directing the comp to pull what files might be on offer at the address helpfully provided by their interrogator.

He found the visual as the files scrolled onto the screen—stared at both in disbelief, wondering if everything, from his waking at Jump-end to this moment, were nothing other than the final mad dreams of a dying mind.

A station rose out of the dust, like no station he had ever seen, all crags, sharp edges, and cliffs. There were no visible docking bays, nor any outrigger yards. From the center of the uncompromising angularity of it, rose a tower; white light pulsed from its apex in a rhythm of six-three-two.

On the screen, the information: *Welcome to Tinsori Light, Repairs and Lodging.*

He touched the query button, but no further information was forthcoming.

An alert trilled, and Jen Sin blinked at the stats screen even as he felt the beam lock around *Lantis.*

For good or for ill, friend or foe, Tinsori Light was towing them in.

• • • ✧ • • •

THE PILOT had queried the Light.

The pilot was *alive.*

The operator rose, hands automatically smoothing her robe. Once, she thought, she must have had a robe that wrinkled, showed wear, became stained. This garment she wore now, here, in this role—this robe was never mussed or rumpled. Always, it was fresh, no matter how long she wore it, or how much time had elapsed.

But the pilot—alive. She stared at the screen, as if she could see through the damaged hull, into the piloting tower, to the one sitting conn. Was the pilot wounded? she wondered. It seemed likely, with the ship bearing such injuries.

Wounded or whole, there were protocols to be followed, to ensure the pilot's safety, and her own. The Light would have its sample—that she could not prevent. Though, if the pilot were wounded, she thought suddenly, that might go easier; there would be no resistance to entering the unit.

The Light was not always careful of life. That the pilot might be frail would not weigh with it. It was hers to shield the pilot, to follow the protocols, and to insert herself between the Light and the pilot, should it come to be necessary.

She looked again to her screens, at the progress of the ship toward the service bay.

Should she, she wondered suddenly, *contact* this pilot? If she *was* injured, she might want reassurance, and to know that assistance was to hand.

The operator studied the screens; the lines of the ship being towed into the repair bay.

She sighed.

It was *like* a design she knew. The Light obviously considered it *like enough* that repairs could be made. But languages were not so easy as ships.

In the end, the operator tucked her hands into the sleeves of her robe, watching until the ship entered the repair bay.

• • •✧• • •

BLACKNESS EBBED.

He observed its fading from a point somewhat distant, his interest at once engaged and detached. First the edges thinned, black fogging into gray, the fog continuing to boil away until quite suddenly it froze into a crystalline mosaic, the whole glowing with a light so chill he shivered at his distant point of observation.

In that moment, he became aware of himself once more; aware that he was alive, healed, perhaps returned to perfect health.

The chill light sharpened, and from it came . . . nothing so gross as a whisper. A *suggestion*.

A choice.

He *had* been returned to optimal functioning; to perfect health. But there existed opportunity. He might become *more* perfect. His abilities might be enhanced beyond the arbitrary limits set upon him by mortal flesh. He might be made stronger, faster; he might sculpt the minds of others, turn enemies to allies with a thought; bend events to favor him—all this, and more.

If he wished.

The decision-point was here and now: Remain mortally perfect, and perfectly limited. Or embrace greatness, and be more than ever he had—

A sharp snap, and the complaint of pneumatic hinges shattered the crystal clarity of the voice. Warm air scented with ginger wafted over naked skin.

Jen Sin yos'Phelium opened his eyes. Above him, a smooth hood, very like to an autodoc's hood. To his left, a wall, supporting those hinges. To his right, the edge of the pad he lay upon, and a space—dull metal walls, dull metal floor, and, nearby, a metal chair, with what was perhaps a robe draped across its back and seat.

He took a deep and careful breath, tears rising to his eyes at the sweet, painless function of his lungs. He tasted ginger on the back of his tongue—knowing it for a stimulant. She'd gotten him to the 'doc after all.

That thought gave pause. He closed his eyes again, taxing his memory.

There had been a woman—had he dreamed this? A woman with a pale pointed face, her black eyes large and up-slanted, and a hood pulled up to hide her hair. She had picked him up—surely, *that* was a true memory! Picked him up, murmuring in some soft, guttural tongue that was almost—almost—one that he knew . . .

And there, a key phrase or sound, a match in a part of his memory he was sure was as new as his health.

"Do you wish to sleep, a better bed awaits you," a voice commented. The voice of his rescuer. Now that his brain was clear, he understood her perfectly well, though she spoke neither Liaden nor Trade, nor the Yxtrang language, either, though closer to that tongue than the other two. Sleep-learned or not, it was a language his Scout-learning marveled at even as he heard it.

He opened his eyes and beheld her, standing quite in plain sight next to the chair. Wordlessly, she lifted the robe, shook it, and held it wide between two long, elegant hands.

"My thanks." He rolled off of the mat, expecting the shock of cold metal against his soles; pleased to find that the floor was warmed. The robe, he took from her hands and slipped on, sealing the front, and leaving the hood to hang behind.

That done, he bowed, deeply, giving all honor to one who had saved his life.

"I am Jen Sin yos'Phelium Clan Korval," he said. "My name is yours, to use at need."

"There is scarcely any need of names here," his companion said, coolly amused. "Keep yours; it will profit you more."

"Will it?" He straightened and looked at her.

She was taller than he, the starry robe hiding the shape of her. Her face was as he remembered, pointed, pale, and solemn; the hood was cast back, revealing tumbled curls of some color between yellow and white. Relieved of the burden of his garment, she had tucked her hands into the sleeves of her robe.

"I wonder if I may know your name," he said.

"It is possible that you may know it," she answered. "If you do, you might tell it me. It would be pleasant to hear, and to remember from time to time, though as I said, there is little use for such things as names, here."

He cast her a sharp glance, but she seemed serious, and there was the language interface; this near-Yxtrang tongue had an ambiguous question protocol.

That being so, he moved a shoulder in regret.

"I have said the thing badly," he admitted. "What I had wished was to learn your name, or what you are called by your comrades, or yourself."

"Oh." It seemed that she was disappointed, and he was, foolishly, regretful, that he had no name to bestow upon her. "I am the Keeper of the Light at Tinsori. Others before you have chosen to address me as Keeper. It is enough of a name, I suppose."

He bowed gently. "Light Keeper, I am in your debt."

"I do my duty. There is no occasion for debt."

"And yet, I place a value upon my life. That you return it to me—that is not without value. My ship—"

She raised a hand. "Your ship is under repair. Our facilities here are . . . old, and perhaps non-standard. However, with some small modification, your ship can be brought back to functionality. The Light proceeds with that work."

"Is there an estimate for completion?" he asked.

She frowned. "No."

That made him uneasy, but he merely inclined his head. "It is true that such damage as *Lantis* sustained might require some time to repair. I regret that I must ask—"

"Ask what you might," she interrupted, brusquely. "I am not so accustomed to company that I will naturally realize what you wish to know."

"To give a Scout permission to ask questions is generous beyond sense," he said, attempting lightness. "Immediately, I take advantage, and ask if there is a pinbeam unit on-station."

She tipped her head, and he saw the glint of what might have been drops of crystal in the tumble of her curls.

"There is not," she said.

That was disappointing, but not necessarily fatal.

"I then ask—may I gain access to my ship, which has such a unit? If I may draw power from the station, the message might be sent." He added, as gently as he might, "I mean only to let my delm know that I am well. This is no ploy to call enemies down upon you."

She laughed at that, which was as startling as it was engaging. No sooner had the sound faded then he wanted her to laugh again.

"To call enemies down on Tinsori Light! That has been done. It did not go well for them." She slipped her hands out of her sleeves and smoothed the front of her robe.

"Look you, Jen Sin yos'Phelium Clan Korval—messages do not travel outward from Tinsori Light; and in all the time that has elapsed since our founding, no message has ever reached us from elsewhere. The space . . . does not behave as normal space must do. Worse, even the attempted transmission of such a message might disturb the balances that keep us here and now. I cannot allow it. The Light, I fear, will also not allow it."

He took that as his answer, for now, and assayed another question.

"May I know where my clothes are? There was something . . . dear in my jacket, and I would not see it lost."

"I have placed your possessions in your quarters," she said. "Do you want to go there now?"

His quarters, was it? And no time estimated for the completion of repairs, nor access to a pinbeam. It began to seem as if he were a prisoner, more than a customer, but until he knew more of this place, he dare not do anything but bow his head and murmur.

"I would very much like to see my quarters, thank you."

• • • ✧ • • •

HE HAD EXPECTED standard station accommodations—which was to say, slightly smaller than his quarters aboard *Lantis*. Instead, he was shown to a room very nearly the size of the apartment he so seldom rested in, at Jelaza Kazone. The metal walls had been softened with hangings, and the floor had been spread with rugs. Pillows and coverlets in bright colors covered the bed. There was a screen mounted in such a way that it could be easily seen from the bed, and a small carved chest on which the contents of his pockets had been scrupulously placed.

Leaving his host by the door, Jen Sin approached the chest—*cantra* pieces and lesser coins; a flip-knife of Scout issue; his snub-nosed hideaway; a leather-rolled tool kit; and the green-wrapped packet, its ribbons and seals undisturbed, though displaying a few distressing stains upon its surface.

"The leathers are being repaired," she said in her abrupt way. "There are robes a-plenty."

"I thank you," he murmured and turned, holding up his hand. "I had been wearing a ring . . ."

"Yes." She tucked her hands into her sleeves and came like a wraith across the rug-strewn floor. She was well within kin-space when she finally stopped her advance, and he using all a Scout's discipline to stay easy where he stood.

She slipped her right hand out of her sleeve and extended it, fingers curled. He held out his hand, and felt the cold heaviness of it strike his palm. A downward glance told him it was his own ring, sparkling as if it were new-made.

"I cleaned it," she said.

"And I thank you for that kindness as well," he said sincerely, remembering the gore-encrusted stones. "A third time, I am in your debt."

"No," she said.

"But I stand at a disadvantage," he protested. "Is there nothing that I might do for you, to balance us?"

The black eyes lifted to his face.

"I wonder," she said slowly, "if you play cards."

• • • ✧ • • •

THE DECK HAD BEEN STRANGE to him; the game stranger, though he had the rules to a hundred card games committed to memory.

The Light Keeper played with an intensity that was somewhat alarming, and when they paused the play for a meal—the most basic of yeast-based rations—she ate with that same intensity, as one starved for sensation.

After the meal, he pronounced himself weary—which fell short of being a complete falsehood—and she obligingly led him back to his room, standing aside while he entered, the door closing behind him.

Panic took him in the instant he heard the door seal, and he spun, threw himself at the blank wall—and all but stumbled out into the hallway and the Keeper's arms.

She frowned.

"Are you not tired, after all?"

"I had wanted to see if it opened for me," he said. "The door."

"That's wise," she answered gravely, and left him there, vanishing 'round the corner of the hall.

He stood for perhaps two dozen heartbeats after she was gone, feeling foolish. Then he turned and re-entered his room.

• • •✧• • •

THEY FELL INTO A SCHEDULE of sorts. The Light Keeper had duties that held her at odd hours, during which time Jen Sin partook of the station's library. When the Light Keeper's duty permitted, they walked together, she showing him somewhat of the station.

It was a strange place, the station, and it seemed that he and the Light Keeper were the only persons who walked its halls. He inquired after other travelers, traders, or those in need, but his guide only said that there was very little traffic in the space about Tinsori.

Moreover, the station contained such amusements as were strange to him. One room she led him to simulated planetary weather, so that they were rained upon, dried by a warm wind and then snowed on. The Light Keeper laughed, and spun, shaking her crystal-beaded curls, her robe flaring out to show naked long toes and trim pale ankles.

Jen Sin caught her arm and pulled her out into the warmer hall.

"Is it not delightful?" she asked.

"Truth said, it casts me off-balance," he answered, trying

unsuccessfully to dry his face with a snow-spangled sleeve. "Weather changes on-planet come with warnings, to simply have random weather flung at one—it distresses me."

He was likewise distressed by the room that produced odors in an indiscriminate olfactory medley, though the green room found his favor—flowers and vegetables alike.

"Here, this one is ripe," he said, touching the round red cheek of a tomato. "Shall we take it back with us for the evening meal?" This was his third day on the station, and he was growing tired of yeast.

The Light Keeper frowned at him. "Eat a plant?"

"A vegetable, but yes. Why not?"

"I never thought of it," she said.

"Someone must have done," he said lightly, plucking the fruit. "Most stations have hydroponic sections, so residents may reap the benefit of fresh food. Yeast alone does not satisfy all one's appetite." He smiled at her. "I would have thought that one as open to sensation as yourself would have sampled every leaf here."

"Truly, it did not occur," she said, and he could see that she was troubled. "How . . . odd. I must have forgotten."

They exited the garden and continued their walk.

"What duty are you called to," he asked her, "in the control room?"

He thought for a moment she would not answer him, and indeed, it was impertinence to ask. But his browsing of the library, of those volumes written in a language he could read, had begun to fill him with unease.

The Light Keeper shrugged. "I prevent the Light from doing mischief," she said. "And keep it to its location."

It was his moment to frown.

"The station drifts?"

"No," she said. "The station moves of its own volition, within the constraints of coords that balance with the expanding edge of things. Part of my function is to keep us at that expanding edge, to maintain the energy levels that keep the coords constant. The Light would be better pleased, if we were closer in, where it could wield its influence."

"Influence," he repeated, as they came to a place where the

corridor split. Unthinking, he turned right—and stopped immediately when she caught his sleeve.

"Not that way."

"Why not?"

A hesitation. "Old damage. The hall is not safe."

"May I assist? I am a Scout, and have strange abilities of my own."

She looked doubtful. "If you like, I will open the schematics to you."

Oh, would she, indeed? Jen Sin bowed softly.

"I would like that very much, indeed."

• • •✧• • •

THE LIGHT KEEPER ate her half of the fruit greedily, then grilled him on what else out of the garden section might be edible. He laughed and threw his hands up, palms out, to fend her eagerness.

"Come, if you will open the schematics, then open the garden records, as well, and I will apply myself to research."

"Done!"

He laughed again, lowering his hands.

"I see I have my work in line."

"You asked for work," she pointed out in her practical way.

"So I did."

She tipped her head. "Jen Sin, I wonder if you might do something . . . else for me."

He looked into her tip-tilted black eyes, and thought he knew what she might ask. Indeed, he was surprised that she had not asked before, as sense-starved and solitary as she was.

"I will do anything that is in my power," he told her gently.

• • •✧• • •

"WHAT ARE THESE?" he asked, later, fingering the crystal drops in her hair.

"My memories," she said drowsily, her head on his shoulder.

He was drowsy himself, but a Scout fails of asking questions when he is dead.

"If you brush them out, will you forget yourself?"

"No. But if something happens and I am not wearing them, I will have no prompts and the Light will be unwatched."

Perhaps that made sense in some way, but he lacked context. He would have pressed her, but her breathing told him that she had slipped into sleep.

He sighed, nestled his chin against her curls, and followed.

• • • ✧ • • •

"WHAT PROGRESS," she asked the Light, "on the repairs?"

Progress, came the reply.

The Keeper bit her lip.

"When will repairs be complete?" she asked.

Unknown.

This mode was unfortunate. It was behavior from a distant time, when the Light had first come into the care of the Sanderat. The Keeper closed her eyes, called up her will, thrust it at the Light.

"You will tell me when repairs will be complete and when Jen Sin yos'Phelium Clan Korval may depart, to continue his lawful business."

Are you ready to be alone again? The pilot amuses you, does he not? What harm to keep him?

Yes, this was very bad, indeed. The Light was at its most dangerous when it offered your heart's desire. She breathed deeply, and made her will adamantine.

"I will have a time when the ship in your care will be repaired and able. The pilot is his own person; he has duty. It is our duty to assist him, not disrupt him."

It is your *duty to assist.*

"It is, and as you serve me, it is your duty, also."

There was a silence. Rather a lengthy silence.

The ship will be able to depart in six station days.

So soon? She bowed her head.

"That is well, then. Keep me informed."

THE SCHEMATICS were fascinating—and horrifying.

Jen Sin had been a member of a Scout Exploratory Team. He, as all explorer Scouts, had been well-drilled on the seeming and the dangers of what was called Old Tech. His team had discovered a small cache of what might have been toys—small, crude ceramic shapes that might infiltrate a man's mind, make him receptive to thoughts that he would not recognize as belonging to an Other.

The cache of toys they had found had been depleted, being able to effect nothing more than a sense of melancholy and foreboding in those unheedful enough to pick them up. His team—well. Krechin had wrapped them in muffle, and sealed them into a stasis box until they could be properly handed over to the Office of Old Technology, at Headquarters.

The toys had been frightening enough, but he had an extra burden of knowledge, for he had read the logs and diaries of Clan Korval, as far back as Cantra yos'Phelium, who had brought the understanding that the old universe and the old technologies had together been the downfall of vast civilizations. And that had been old technology in small gulps, as might be found in a toy, or a personalized hand-weapon, or a geegaw worn for nefarious purpose.

To find a working, *aware* structure entirely built from forbidden tech—that was enough to give a Scout nightmares. Even Korval might quail before such a thing.

And the Light Keeper's purpose was to keep it from *doing mischief*?

Mischief, by the gods. And his ship was in its keeping. Worse. His ship was in *its power*, being modified, never doubt it, as he stood by—and did nothing.

Jen Sin closed the schematics and rose from the desk. He quit the library, and walked toward the hub, where there was a gym.

Exercise would calm him.

And then he would need to speak with the Light Keeper.

• • •✧• • •

"TELL ME," he said to the Light Keeper, as she settled her cheek on his shoulder, "about this place."

She stirred, eyelashes fluttering against his skin.

"This space?"

"No, the station," he murmured. "The schematics woke questions."

She laughed softly. "What sorts of questions, now?"

"Well. How did the station come to be? Who built it? How did you come to keep it? Where are the others? . . . Those sorts of questions. I don't doubt I can find more, if you wish."

"No, those will do, I think."

She sighed, relaxing against him so completely that he thought for a moment that he had been cheated, and she had slipped over into sleep.

"How the station came to be. My sisters of the Sandaret believed that the Great Enemy built it. We found it abandoned, and riding in space where a waystation had been sore needed. The Soldiers were in favor of destroying it, but it was in Sandaret space, and we undertook to Keep it.

"Three of our order were dispatched . . . Faren, Jeneet, and . . . Lorith."

She tensed. He held his breath.

"Lorith," she breathed. "That is *my* name."

"May I address you thus?" he asked, when several minutes had passed and she had said nothing more, nor relaxed.

"Yes." She sighed again, and became . . . somewhat . . . less tense.

"What happened," he murmured, "to Faren and Jeneet?"

"Faren died in the storm," she whispered. "We were without power, adrift, for many elapsed units. When we came to rest, and repairs were made—it was no longer possible to reclaim her. The Light took new samples, from Jeneet, from me."

Samples. He repressed the shiver, sternly, and asked his next question softly, "What storm was that, Lorith?"

"Why, the big storm, that shifted everything away from where it had been. When it was done, the Light was . . . where you found it, and not in orbit about Tinsori, as it had been. Tinsori, we were not able to locate. The coordinates of our present location . . . were not possible. Jeneet took our boat and went out to find where we were. That was . . . Much time has elapsed, since then. I fear that she has been lost, or died, or taken up in battle."

Korval had an odd history; it was odder still to hear that history from other lips, from another perspective, and yet, *that* war, that had displaced a universe or more . . .

from one space-time to another.

That war had ended hundreds of years ago.

He stroked her hair, feeling the crystal beads slide through his fingers.

"Lorith," he said, gently, oh, so very gently. "I cannot allow my ship to rest any longer in care of the Light."

She raised her head and looked down at him, eyes wide and very black.

"It said . . . six days, as we measure them here, when time is aware. Six days, and your ship will be ready." She frowned. "I have exerted my will. You will come to no harm, though I will . . . miss you."

"You need not. Come with me."

"No, who would Keep the Light? It might do anything, left to itself."

So it might.

He sat up, and she did, drawing a crimson cover over her naked shoulders.

"I must go," he said, and slid out of bed, reaching for his leathers.

• • • ✧ • • •

HE WAS DETERMINED and she could not—*would not*—influence him to wait. She showed him the way to the repair bay, hearing the voice of the Light.

Little man, you will have your ship when it is properly prepared.

Jen Sin checked, then continued toward the place where the tunnel intersected the hall.

"The pilot decides when his ship is ready," he said aloud. "I go now, and I thank you, and the Light Keeper, for your care."

She hardened her will, and pushed at the Light.

"Let him go to his duty," she said, and added, terrified for his safety, "unless the ship is not functional."

She was an idiot; her fear for him softened her will. And in that moment, the Light struck.

The walls crackled; she felt the charge build, and simultaneously threw her will and herself between Jen Sin and the bolt.

She heard him scream, her name it was—and then heard nothing more.

• • • ✧ • • •

HE CAME TO HIMSELF in the library, with no memory of having arrived there. He supposed that he had run—run like a hare from Lorith's murder, to save his own precious self, to *survive* against every odd—*that* was Korval's talent.

Craven, he told himself, running his hands into his hair and bending his head. He was weeping, at least he had that much heart.

But the Scout mind would not be stilled, and too soon it came to him that—he dared not leave the Light unwatched. For who knew what it might do, left alone?

He had the schematics, and his Scout-trained talents. Did he dare move against it and risk his life? Or ought he to stand guard and prevent it doing harm?

"Jen Sin?" He would swear that he felt her hand on his hair, her voice edged with concern. "Were you hurt?"

Slowly, he lifted his face, staring into hers, the pointed chin, the space-black eyes, and the crystal beads glittering in pale, curly hair.

"You were killed," he said, toneless.

She stepped away. "No."

"Yes!" He snapped to his feet, the chair clattering backward, snatched her shoulders and shook her.

A thought tantalized, then crystallized.

"*How many times* has it killed you?"

"I don't know," she said, shockingly calm. "Perhaps I die every time we drift back to quiet after an alert, and the Light remakes me at need. Does it matter? I am always myself, and I have my memories. The sample, you know."

He stared, speechless, feeling her fragile and real under his fingers.

"The sample, of course," he agreed when he could speak again. "What came of Jeneet's sample, Lorith?"

"She did not use the beads, and when I called her back, she remembered nothing."

He closed his eyes briefly, recalling the unit he had risen from, and the crystal-cold voice, offering him a choice.

"Jen Sin?"

He raised his hand and ran his fingers through her hair, feeling the cool beads slip past his skin.

"I wonder," he said, softly. "Is there a . . . sample of me?"

Her eyes flickered.

"Yes."

"And have you more beads?"

"Yes."

"Then this is what I think we should do, while I wait for my ship to be . . . properly prepared."

• • •✧• • •

THE OPERATOR SAT at her board, and watched the ship tumble out of the repair bay. The scans elucidated a vessel in good repair, the hull intact, all systems green and vigorous.

She took a breath, and watched her screens, dry-eyed, until the Jump-glare faded, and the space at Tinsori Light was empty, for as far as her instruments could scan.

• • •✧• • •

HE BROUGHT THE PINBEAM ONLINE, entered the message, in Korval House code. The message that would warn the clan away, and see Tinsori Light scrubbed from the list of auto-coords in Korval courier ships. The message that would tell the delm the Jump Pilot's ring was lost, along with the good ship and pilot. The message that would tell the delm that when she needed another packet delivered, it could never again be Jen Sin who would do it.

Emergency repairs at Tinsori Light. Left my ring in earnest. The keeper's a cantra-grubbing pirate, but the ship should hold air to Lytaxin. Send one of ours and eight cantra to redeem my pledge. Send them armed. In fact send two . . .

The 'beam went. He waited, patiently, for the ack, looking down at his hands, folded on the board, ringless and calm.

He reviewed his plan, and found it, if not good, certainly necessary.

A ship *properly prepared* by an agent of the Great Enemy? How could he bring such a ship into the galaxy proper, save for one thing only?

Comm chimed; the 'beam had been acknowledged by the first relay.

Jen Sin yos'Phelium Clan Korval pressed the sequence of buttons he had preset, and released the engine's energy at once, and catastrophically.

• • •✧• • •

SHE FELT A HAND settle on her shoulder, and looked up, finding his reflection in a darkened screen.

"He's gone?"

"Yes."

She spun the chair and came to her feet; he dropped back to give her room, the beads glittering like rain in his dark hair.

"Now, it is for us," she said. "Will we survive it?"

He smiled and held out his hand, the big ring sparkling on his finger.

"Many times, perhaps," he said.

• • •✧• • •

SPACE IS HAUNTED.

Pilots know this; station masters and light keepers, too; though they seldom speak of it, even to each other. Why would they? Ghost or imagination; wyrd space or black hole, life—and space—are dangerous.

The usual rules apply.

✧ Landed Alien ✧

"LANDED ALIEN" happened in part because Theo Waitely had gotten herself thrown off a world—and we needed to get her belongings back to her. That meant that her friend Kara had to get into the act, and that meant—well, we knew what it meant, but we hadn't told the story to you, and not exactly to us, it being in notes and partials for several years until the opportunity to mark it into a full story came along. Opportunity? Indeed, because we'd been so busy during the start of the Fledgling *and* Saltation *stories all we had time to do was to write novels. There are still spin-offs that need to be written . . . but you've got "Landed Alien" here, now, thanks in part to the folks at Baen.com putting it on a front burner for us.*

POOL PILOT and Tech Kara ven'Arith sat in the Station Master's office, on an uncomfortable, and cold, steel chair.

She sat alone, hands folded tightly in her lap, face under rigid control. Waiting . . .

A man was dead. A *pilot* was dead.

By her hand.

She turned her head to the left, and stared for a long moment at the door to the outer hallway and the rest of Codrescu Station. She turned her head to the right, and gave the door to the Station Master's inner office similar close study. Neither door was locked. Why would they be?

There was no place to go, and nothing, really, for her to do.

Save wait.

Wait on the verdict of those now discussing her and her actions, there in the inner office. Would she live? Would she die? Would she be banished to the planet's surface, to take her chances there?

They would decide: the Station Master, the Guild Master, her immediate supervisor, the head Tugwhomper, and the associate supervisor of the pilot pool.

Kara took a deep breath, and wished they would decide *soon*.

• • •✧• • •

IT WAS SILENT in the common room as the graduation list scrolled across the community screen. They were all seniors in this dorm; and each a deal more solemn than even the suspense of the scrolling list might account for.

At the back of the room, Kara ven'Arith stood alone, and hopefully out of the eye of the dorm's loyalty monitor. *That* one had been dogging her steps for the last semester, trying to catch her in a "subversive" act. The monitor had been at great pains to explain Kara's precarious situation to her—the lack of three black marks was all that stood between Kara and the fate of her *very good friend*, Expelled Student Waitley.

The monitor had stared at her in what Kara supposed was intended to be a sad-but-stern manner, and which had been so ludicrous that she had been hard-put not to giggle. Worse, the thought of what Theo might say upon hearing her new title of honor was almost enough to send her into whoops.

It being fairly certain that she would earn one, if not two, of those missing black marks immediately for a failure to show proper respect, Kara had bitten the inside of her cheek and bowed her head, striving to give the impression of one too cowed by authority to speak.

The monitor *hrummphed*.

"You'd do better to sit up and meet my eye," she had snapped. "Sneaking alien ways won't improve your record."

Well, and that *had* almost brought her to join Theo. Kara had taken a deep breath, and lifted her head deliberately to meet the other woman's eyes.

"I am not an alien," she said calmly, in the Eylot dialect of Terran. "My family has held land on this planet for ninety-eight Standards."

The monitor, whose name was Peline Graf, frowned.

"And you think that makes you Eylotian?" she asked.

It was on the edge of Kara's tongue to say that she had been born on Eylot—but, after all, that did *not* make her Eylotian—even her delm taught so. They of Clan Menlark were *Liaden*, though based upon Eylot.

"You're nothing but a landed alien," Monitor Graf added, in a tone that made plain that she found this Eylotian legal reality not in the least amusing.

Kara folded her lips together and held the monitor's gaze until the other woman waved her hand in abrupt dismissal.

"I'm required to warn students who are in danger of expulsion. This has been your warning, ven'Arith. Watch yourself."

It had been, Kara had admitted to herself, after a long walk, a long shower, and a long, sleepless night, a fair warning, of its kind, and worth taking to heart. She had so much hanging, as the Terran phrase went, in Balance. Very nearly a Liaden meaning to Balance, there.

Well. She had seen what had happened to Theo, who had committed the dual crimes of not being Eylotian, and excelling beyond those who were. For those crimes, she had been targeted, trapped, and expelled. She, Kara ven'Arith, was the designated instrument of Theo's will in *that* matter. As such, she was honor-bound to keep all and any doors open through which Balance might enter.

That—and there was her family to consider. To be expelled so near to the completion of her course and flight-work, even if she could show political malice as the cause? That would scarcely please her mother or her delm. Indeed, it was very likely that she would be roundly scolded for having been so maladroit as to allow her enemies to prevail against her. Clan Menlark had not prospered as pilots and as mechanics on a culturally diverse world known for its effervescent politics because its children were either maladroit or stupid.

All that being so, she had watched herself, and also, with a sort of black humor, watched those who watched her. She held herself aloof from any ties of friendship, that she might not be tainted by another's error; she studied; she flew; she tutored; she slept; and ate; and attended all and every politically significant rally and workshop offered on campus.

By doing these things, she insured her graduation, pilot's license in hand, as her mother and her delm expected.

Her mother next expected her to offer herself for hire as a pilot, that being the clan's main livelihood. There, duty . . . diverged. Kara's heart had long been with the clan's secondary business. Even as a child, she had dogged Uncle Bon Sel's every step in the repair shop, until in self-defense he gave her a wrench and taught her how to use it. Her determination was to continue in that line, now that she had done as her delm and her mother had commanded.

That being so, she filed her app with Howsenda Hugglelans, where she had a good multi-season record as a temp worker, and excellent relations with her supervisors, and with Aito, the Hugglelans' Third Son. It was not at all unreasonable to think that she might be hired there as a mechanic or a tech, and best to have all her cards in hand before she brought the matter to her mother.

The application had not yet gained a reply, but here—here came the approach to her name on the screen. She straightened, waiting, hardly daring to breathe. What if something had happened? What if someone in Admin had decided to withhold her last grade points? What if she *had* been given a black mark, despite all her care? What if there was some new reg, put into place secretly, that had to do only with those who weren't "truly Eylotian"? It had happened before . . .

Her chest was tight. Surely the feed had slowed? But no, that was foolish, and there! Her name!

And next to her name, her standing in the class—low, but she had expected that—and at the end of the line, her license certification . . .

Candidate Second . . .

"Candidate Second?" she gasped, stunned. She had *earned* a firm second-class license. She had the hours, she had passed the tests, she—

"Something wrong, ven'Arith?" asked Droy Petris, with false concern. Droy Petris watched her, also, though less diligently than the monitor.

She had spoken out loud, Kara thought. *Stupid*, to let caution go *now*. Still, there was a recover to hand.

"I was astonished," she said, truthfully. "I had no idea I'd graduate at such a level."

He looked at her suspiciously, and Loyalty Monitor Graf was seen to frown, but there wasn't a regulation forbidding a pilot to express surprise.

She hoped.

• • •✧• • •

THE FIVEDAY between the end of class and the senior graduation ceremony was traditionally a festive time, featuring parties, and picnics, dances, and epic games of bowli ball. It was a time when friendships were reaffirmed; when new addresses and mail drop codes were exchanged.

Kara, who deliberately had no friends, dutifully attended the meetings mandated by Admin. As she was a past-champion, she also took part in the bowli ball tournament where she reveled in the play until, in the quarter finals, her lack of current connections made it easy for her to be ganged up on and evicted early from the game.

Not wishing to risk any unpleasantness in the stands, she avoided spectating. Instead, she volunteered to polish one of the long-wing training sailplanes, that it would be a welcome meeting for its next pilot, and thus received the benefit of exercise.

She also took long, solitary walks around campus, carefully avoiding such places as might call unwanted attention to her, such as Belgraid dorm, which had once housed the Culture Club, since "discovered" to be a hotbed of subversive activity, designed to indoctrinate the unwary into the customs and lifestyles of planets that were not Eylot.

She returned to the dorm from one particularly long walk to find herself the sole occupant. That would have been more pleasing if she didn't suspect that Monitor Graf had planted spy-eyes about, to watch when she could not.

Still, the absence of her dorm-mates did give pleasure. Kara stopped to withdraw a fruit drink from the cold-box, and went to her room, shaking the bulb absently.

She closed the door—senior privilege—and sat down at her desk, bringing the computer live with a light touch, snapping the bulb open while she waited for her mail to download.

Three letters came in-queue. Kara ran her eye down the list as she sipped her drink.

The first letter was from Hugglelans. She opened it, bottom lip caught in her teeth. If she had an offer, or perhaps an invitation to interview . . .

But no.

> *Dear Applicant.*
>
> *This letter is to inform you that your application for employment has been received. We regret to inform you that Howsenda Hugglelans is not hiring at this time.*
>
> *Thank you for your interest, and the best of luck in your search for employment.*
>
> *Human Resources Form Number 3*

Kara stared at this missive for much longer than required to master its contents. *Not hiring?* she thought. *Or not hiring Liadens?*

The thought made her angry—and then frightened. If *Hugglelans* had bowed to the rising tide of politics . . .

She took a breath, filed the form, and looked to the next item in-queue.

It was from the Dean of Students office. Her stomach clenched, and her mouth felt dry, despite the juice. She put the pod down on the edge of her desk, and opened the letter.

> *TO: Kara ven'Arith, Candidate Pilot Second Class*
> *FROM: Anlingdin Pilot Certification Office*
>
> *Candidate pilots are required to attend a re-orientation session immediately following graduation. At the conclusion of this session, those qualifying will see the candidate status*

removed and their license properly registered by the Eylot Pilots Guild.

Please report to Gunter Recreation Area on . . .

Kara squeezed her eyes shut, and mentally reviewed an exercise designed to restore clarity to a pilot's tired mind. That done, she took six deep, calming breaths before opening her eyes again and re-addressing the letter.

Her hands were cold and she was shaking, just a little, though that was anger, because they had found a way to hold her license hostage still longer! She had *earned* her second-class license! Earned it! And now, she was being required to complete some other requirement—a requirement, she was certain was in place only for those who were not *truly Eylotian*! And what chance had she to qualify, to see her license properly recorded at the end of it all?

"Wait," she told herself, closing her eyes again. "Wait. Think."

She accessed another mental exercise, this to impose calm; then she did, indeed, think.

She had come this far. She had completed her coursework, gained her second-class license, despite the oppressive oversight that had caused others of her classmates—friends from the Culture Club, and various others who had come from outworlds—to drop out and return home. Kara ven'Arith hadn't quit. She had been clever, she had kept her head down, she had kept herself informed of the changing requirements, and she had graduated.

She had done what was needed, and she could—she *would*—do whatever was necessary to clear this new barrier to claiming that which she had earned.

When she opened her eyes this time, her feelings were firmer, though they suffered a ripple when she saw that the re-orientation "session" was indeed a planetary month long.

And Gunter Recreation Area . . . was a wilderness campground, without even an air-breather landing field.

Her stomach clenched again, and she hurriedly closed the letter, marking it for later review, and opened the last file in the queue.

It was a personal note from Flight Instructor Orn Ald

yos'Senchul, her academic adviser, inviting her to take tea with him—in an hour.

Kara smiled with real pleasure. Pilot yos'Senchul had been a support and a comfort, subtle as he was. He remained at Anlingdon, so he had told her, in honor of his contract, which the new administration was unexpectedly too canny to cancel out of hand, having perhaps learned a lesson from the Slipper instructor's dismissal.

But—good gods, the time! Kara leapt to her feet and ran for the shower.

• • •✧• • •

"A TENDAY TOUR?" Kara took the paper Pilot yos'Senchul held out to her across the tea-table, and sat somewhat ill-at-ease, cup in one hand, folded printout in the other.

"Please," her host murmured, "take a moment to familiarize yourself. I thought first of you when I read it, and I am curious to know if you feel the same."

Immediate need. Codrescu Station, Eylot Nearspace. Student mechanic to tour, inspect, and repair station systems under supervision of Master Mechanic. Long hours. Union rates. Teacher recommendation or references required. First qualified hired.

Kara felt her pulse quicken. It wasn't a full-time job at Hugglelans, but it was far better than a walk in vacuum without a spacesuit.

She frowned, calculating. The graduation ceremony was in three days—an empty formality since her mother had let her know that *circumstances* would unfortunately keep her kin from making the trip to Anlingdin.

"I have my ratings and references from my break-work at Hugglelans," she said, speaking aloud, but more to herself than to Pilot yos'Senchul. "A tenday tour . . ." She frowned at the print-out again. "*Immediate need*," she mused, and looked up to find his gaze very attentive on her face.

"If *immediate* means that I may start within the next two local days," she said slowly, "I can do the tour and return in good time to attend the re-orientation class."

"Do you mean to do so?" Pilot yos'Senchul asked.

She looked at him in surprise.

"Well, I *must*, if ever I want to free my license of that wretched notation of *candidate*!"

"Yes, of course," he said, and used his chin to point at the paper she still held. "Do I hear that you are interested in filling that position, assuming that *immediately* is found to be accommodating?"

"I am, yes."

"Very good." He put his cup down and stood, slipping the paper away from her with his natural hand while the fingers of his prosthetic spelled out, *rise! quick lift!*

Startled, she came to her feet. "Sir?"

"Go quickly and pack. If I may—pack heavy, lest there is a dorm cleaning while you are away. I will meet you at the shuttle in an hour."

"Sir, but—"

"I had said that I thought first of you. Having done so, I sent the master mechanic my recommendation, forwarding your references from Hugglelans, which were available to me, as your adviser. He replied that he would have you, if you were interested. We have established that you are interested. And I should tell you that *immediately* in this instance means, according to Master Thelly, *three days or a week ago*."

"But, I—"

"You may send an introduction from the shuttle," he interrupted. "Or perhaps you've changed your mind, and that is why you stand here when your ship needs you?"

"*No*, sir!" She cried, and bowed—respect to an instructor.

Then, she ran.

• • •✧• • •

KARA'S PERSONAL EFFECTS, with those things that Theo had entrusted to her, were in the shuttle's modest holding area. She was in the pilot's chair, Pilot yos'Senchul sitting second. Once they had broken orbit, she had 'beamed a message to Master Mechanic Thelly, introducing herself and informing him that she was on her way to take up duty.

She was doing the set-up for Codrescu approach when the master's reply arrived, telling her to find him in Sub-sector Blue Eleven's machine room after she'd been cleared through.

"I'm going to have to hit the deck running," she commented, not unpleased by the prospect of getting right to work.

"Union rates," her copilot murmured. "Be certain to keep track of your hours; Master Thelly is quite capable of working three shifts in four, and he expects his assistants to do as much."

She shot a glance at him, but only saw the side of his face, calm as it usually was, his eyes on his screens.

"That sounds like the voice of experience," she said. "Did you 'prentice with Master Thelly, Pilot?"

"In fact, I did, some few years ago. He was at first . . . doubtful . . . regarding the utility to himself of a one-armed assistant. I was able to put those doubts to rest, and learned a good deal in Balance." He glanced at her.

"You will find the master a thorough teacher."

"Good," said Kara.

The board pinged for her attention, then, and she gave it.

• • •✧• • •

"THIS WAY, PILOT," yos'Senchul said, waving her into a dim side passage that was definitely not the route to the Station Master's office.

"Master Thelly . . ." she began.

"Master Thelly will still have work for you in half an hour," he said.

Kara sighed and followed him, the peculiar taste of station air on her tongue. She had been to Codrescu Station a dozen times or more, and thought she knew its maze of corridors pretty well. This hall, so thin that she and Pilot yos'Senchul—both comfortably Liaden-sized—needed to proceed in single-file, wasn't at all familiar. It was a utility hall, she thought, noting the access panels set high and low. Well, perhaps it would soon become familiar.

Ahead, their hall ended in another—and this one Kara did recall.

"The Guild Office?" she asked.

"Indeed," he answered. Before them was the door, and a guard beside it, sidearm holstered.

"Yos'Senchul and ven'Arith, to see the Guild Master," her companion said. "We are, I think, expected."

"You're on the list, Pilots," the guard confirmed, opening the door for them. "Straight ahead."

• • •✧• • •

GUILD MASTER PELTZER ran her card, made a noise strongly reminiscent of a snort, and nodded in her direction.

"Be a couple minutes to review your files, Pilot. You wanna make yourself comfortable here? I got a feeling Pilot yos'Senchul wants to have a private word with me. Is that right, Orn Ald?"

Pilot yos'Senchul inclined his head gravely. "You know me too well."

"Just about well enough, I'm thinking. Step into my office. Pilot, please, take some rest."

The two men stepped in to the Guild Master's inner office and the door closed. Kara, too energized to sit, *or* to be comfortable, walked quietly to the small green garden across from the intake desk, its tall fronds waving in the breeze from an air duct. An agreeable gurgle of running water came from somewhere in the depths of the tiny jungle.

Kara knelt down and considered the greenery. There were, as she knew from previous visits, norbears living among the fronds—one quite old, and the other quite young. She would, she thought, like to have the attention of a norbear at the moment, though it would be rude to wake them, or to disturb their pretty habitat.

She was about to rise again, when the fronds dipped more deeply than could be accounted for by the small breeze, and here came the elder norbear—rust colored and thin of fur—marching deliberately forward, through the fronds and out of the garden entirely, climbing familiarly onto Kara's knee.

"Hevelin, good-day to you," she said, stroking his head gently. He burbled and pushed into her fingers, demanding a more vigorous scrubbling.

Kara smiled and settled cross-legged to the floor, careful of the old norbear's balance, and rubbed his head with vigor. His pleased burbling seem to leach her restlessness, and she sighed, half-closing her eyes.

An image came into her head, lazily, like a dream—an image she recognized as Pilot yos'Senchul. She recalled him entering the Guild Master's office, and the image faded, to be replaced by the impression of a pointed, pale face dominated by fierce dark eyes, framed by blow-away pale hair that Kara knew to be as soft and warm as feathers.

"No," she murmured. "Theo's not with me, though I have her things. I'm here for a tenday tour, to assist Master Thelly."

A man's round, red-cheeked face faded through Theo's, his eyes blue and sharp, the lines around them made by worry, laughter—or by both. Master Thelly, perhaps.

She felt herself sinking into a languor; almost, she felt she could have a nap.

Happily for her dignity, the door behind her opened at that moment. The languor fled, leaving behind a feeling of tingling alertness. She opened her eyes to look up, at Orn Ald yos'Senchul, and, further up, at Guild Master Peltzer.

"Hevelin took the edge off, did he?" he said with a nod. "Worth a full night's sleep, one of Hevelin's purr-breaks. If you'll stand up, Pilot, we can get your little matter finished up and send you to the Station Master for registration."

"Thank you," Kara said to Hevelin. "Would you like to go back to the garden?"

It appeared that Hevelin did not. He clambered up her arm to her shoulder and grabbed onto her collar to steady himself.

"I'd say that's plain," said Guild Master Peltzer, moving over to the intake desk. Kara came to her feet, careful of her passenger, and stepped up.

"All right now, Pilot. This'll take a bit to propagate across the databases, so I'll just drop a note to the Station Master and to Master Thelly, letting them know the news." He tapped keys, and Kara, Hevelin humming in her ear, waited with what patience she could muster for someone to tell *her* the news.

"Right, then. Here you are, Pilot." He held her license out in her general direction, while his other hand and his eyes were still on the computer.

Kara took the card, Hevelin all but deafening her with his purr, and slipped it away into an inner pocket.

"Sir?" she said. "May I—"

He looked up, catching her gaze with his, and inclined his head formally.

"Congratulations, Second Class Pilot Kara ven'Arith."

She stiffened. "Your pardon, Guild Master. I am, I believe, *Candidate* Second Class Pilot ven'Arith."

He shook his head, his smile tight.

"That's according to the so-called Pilots Guild of Eylot, which has no standing with the Interstellar Starship Pilots Guild. Eylot Guild can deny our licenses and our regs 'til they're short of air, but at the end of the shift, they're a local independent piloting group. Anybody lifting with an Eylot Guild ticket is just another indie flyer, far as *this* Guild is concerned."

Hevelin's purring hit an ecstatic crescendo.

Kara looked closely at the Guild Master's grim face. She transferred her gaze to Pilot yos'Senchul, who inclined his head gravely, and murmured, "A signal achievement, Pilot. Well done."

"You brought me here for this, didn't you?" she demanded.

"In part," he allowed, with a slight smile. "I did also think of you first when the tenday tour came into my queue."

Kara took a breath. "Pilot yos'Senchul," she began—and stopped as he held up his hand.

"Please, honor me with the use of my given name, now that we are colleagues—and comrades."

She frowned at him. Colleagues, yes, because they were now both certified by the same guild, though he was Master to her Second Class. Comrade, though . . .

"Do you have work on-station? But your contract at the Academy—"

"The present administration has placed conditions upon my continued employment which I cannot in conscience accept. Therefore, I have offered myself to Guild Master Peltzer, who believes he may be able to find a use for me."

The Guild Master laughed.

"More like sixteen uses for you!" he said. "I figure to whittle it down to three, after I talk with people."

"The Academy's shuttle . . ." Kara protested, thinking of *Cherpa* in Berth Fourteen.

"I will send the key down on the station shuttle. Whomever the Academy chooses to take it down may ride the jump seat on the supply wagon."

"Details," pronounced the Guild Master, waving a bluff hand. "What the two of you need to do is get registered with the Station Master's office. Soon's that's done, we can start getting some work out of you!"

"Indeed," said Pilot yos'Senchul, with a slight, comradely bow. "After you, Kara."

"Yes," she said, and turned to put Hevelin back among the greenery.

• • • ✧ • • •

THE PILOT handling her forms for the Station Master was called Fortch; his work blouse was that of a commercial transfer company. He looked her up and down before she announced herself, and then with a spark of interest when she did.

"Ven'Arith, eh? I gather you've been expected for a day or so. Forms have been waiting—fill and sign and . . ."

Seeing her glance at his name and the Certified Pilot logo on his breast pocket, he nodded and tapped it with one finger.

"Company gave me my uniform the day the newest rules came down," he told her as he checked her work. "All I needed was the paper. But you know what's happening, and I do; they say I'm no pilot until I get *their* paper. Can't get *their* paper 'cause my father's brother was suspected of being on the wrong side twenty years ago. I get to do some tugwork here, they put me in the pool. I help out here on the slow days." He sighed, glancing at the form screen. "At least you'll get a chance to pick yours up."

Kara nodded. Tugwork meant he was likely a third-class, maybe an air pilot too—and that was hard. If his family went back for generations and was thought unreliable, he might never get work on-world.

There was a small chirp and he started nervously; and out of the air the order, "Send in the new one, Fortch! Master Thelly's in a snit to get her on the job!"

The aide jerked his head at the inner door, and handed the forms back to her.

"Luck. Hope to catch you around."

• • • ✧ • • •

SHE'D WORKED OVERSHIFT—not unusual, and becoming more usual as she double-timed herself—working two full shifts, then cramming a class into her so-called rec shift. The class she was currently embroiled in, remote repair, required not only coursework, but board time, not with a sim, but with an actual remote, out on Codrescu's skin. Time and necessity being what they were, she had to grab her practice sessions betwixt and between. The work shifts today had gone long, whereby she had been late to log into class, and so last to take the remote.

The work had not been mere practice, but real work, resetting a trio of lock-anchors on Ten Rod Two, the arm that the Guild supply ship *Zircon Sea* was due to use. With the strangenesses attendant to Eylot's politics, the *Sea*'s technical and parts refills were much needed to make up for several quarters worth of back-orders, missing items, and out-and-out damaged-on-receipt goods. Given the state of supplies, she'd triple checked her work, and delayed herself more . . .

And now, she was *starving*.

At least there was an easy answer to that; very possibly the first easy answer she had been confronted with today.

She turned down the hall to the Hub Caf, ran her station card under the reader and picked up a tray.

Quickly, she onloaded soy soup, fresh salad, and a more-or-less fresh-baked roll, and a cup of lemon-water. She turned from the serving bar, expecting at this shift and hour to have her choice of tables—which wasn't . . . quite true.

There was only one other diner in the Caf—a man in coveralls much like those she wore. Uncharacteristically, his shoulders were hunched, his arms crossed on the table before him, his attention wholly on the screen before him.

Kara hesitated, took a breath and went forward. Comrades held duty to the well-being of each other; and even if they had not been comrades, she owed him the same sort of care he had shown for her.

"Orn Ald? May I join you?"

He looked up, and even in the dim lighting, she could see that his cheeks were wet.

For a Liaden to so far forget *melant'i* as to weep in public—that was appalling. That *Orn Ald yos'Senchul* should do so could signal nothing less than a cataclysm.

Kara clattered her tray to the table, staring at him.

"*What has happened*?"

For answer, he spun the screen.

She recognized the *Eylot Gazette*, the Liaden community's social newspaper, open to the death notices.

There was only one.

Lef Nal vin'Eved Clan Selbry, of injuries sustained during Anlingdin Academy Graduate Re-orientation camp. Selbry Herself stands as the instrument of his will. Clan and kin grieve.

Kara remembered him only vaguely—they had been in few classes together and he hadn't been a bowli ball player. He had, in fact, been rather frail, all the more so for a certain single-mindedness that allowed him to discount every obstacle between himself and a goal. Lef Nal was, thought Kara, easily the sort of person who might fall off a cliff by reason of having momentarily forgotten about the effects of gravity.

She raised her eyes to Orn Ald's ravaged face.

He had, she saw in relief, used a napkin to dry his cheeks, but not even Liaden social training could hide the desolation in his eyes.

"I have also had a private letter on the topic," he said quietly. "It would appear that Pilot vin'Eved has been reft from clan and kin as a result of what is termed a *hazing*. He and several others had been identified as lacking a proper reverence for the new political scenery, and so were placed in . . . special circumstances, in order to cow them. The others are injured, but will survive." He sighed, and spun the screen to face him again.

"One save a year," he murmured, and she looked at him sharply.

"What is that?"

"Ah." He raised his eyes to hers, his mouth twisting. "When I was newcome to Anlingdin Academy, the elder instructor who was assigned as my mentor taught that we who teach must sometimes rescue our students—from themselves, from bad advice, from the expectations of kin, or of the world. She had it, as a point of philosophy—or perhaps of honor—that *one save a year made all the rest worthwhile*."

Kara slid onto the stool across from him, pushing her tray with the cooling soup and wilting salad to one side.

"You saved me," she said, very softly; and then, whispering, because even the thought was too terrible to bear.

"Was it only *us*—the landed aliens—who were given conditional licenses, Orn Ald?"

He shook his head. "A few less than half, by my count, were in your case, and in . . . Pilot vin'Eved's case. A handful of outworld students received conditional licenses, also, but they were merely required to certify that they would be leaving the planet after graduation."

It was easier to breathe. She sighed, slipped off of the stool and bowed as one who was cognizant of debt.

"Do not think of it," he murmured. "Our relative *melant'i* at the time placed one in the position of protector. Honor is fulfilled, on all sides, and Balance maintains." He shook his head, and said, in subdued Terran, "I advised him to go home and place it in the hands of his delm."

And Lef Nal had decided that school matters were the student's to solve, and matters of one's license best resolved by the pilot.

It was, Kara thought, precisely what she would have done.

Indeed, it was precisely what she *had* decided to do, until Orn Ald yos'Senchul had whisked her off for a tenday tour, and showed her a way to gain her license without condition.

When the fill-in assignment had come open, near the end of her tenday, she had contacted her mother and her delm, who had advised her, in their separate faces, to pursue opportunity at the station. Her mother had said that their own small yard was for the moment empty and thus closed, for want of business. Her delm had noted that all Menlark pilots were for the present pursuing hire contracts out-world, and that none were expected to return to Eylot in the foreseeable future.

Failing an outworld piloting contract, Codrescu Station was, said her mother, the best place for her.

She looked again to Orn Ald. As the one owed, it was his to assert what might be the cost, or if they resided in Balance. A comfort, certainly, but rather chilly. A comrade might offer more warmth.

Kara inclined her head.

"Forgive that I notice your distress. I merely do so that I may offer relief, if it is desired."

His eyebrows rose, and she braced herself for a light comment regarding their relative ages. But, when it came, his response was only a mannerly, "The offer is gently made. However, I fear I would bring little to the cause of comfort—and you are wanted in not too many hours at your duty."

He slid off his stool and bowed to her as between comrades, indeed.

"I will leave you to your meal. Speaking with you has been a balm. Good shift, Kara."

"Good shift, Orn Ald," she answered, and turned to watch him walk away before once again taking a stool and pulling her meal toward her.

After a moment, she stood again, picked up the tray and carried it over to the disposal.

• • •✧• • •

THE BOWLI BALL ZAGGED, then zagged again, avoiding Bilton's grasp as adroitly as if it had eyes and reason. Kara, next nearest, jumped, spinning lightly, and capturing the ball against her chest. It kicked, not hard, and the moment her feet hit decking, she threw it well to the left of Yangi.

The rangy red-haired pilot showed her teeth in what might equally have been a savage smile or a grimace of pain, and launched into a long vertical lunge. She snatched the ball, holding it in the crook of her elbow as she tucked to roll mid-air, coming down flatfooted, knees bent. Her smile grew positively feral as she threw ball with considerable strength, straight down at the decking.

Predictably—at least to those wise in the ways of the device and the game—the ball shot upward. Unpredictably, it skated to the right, into the space occupied by the hapless Fortch, the least apt of their players, nearly as new on station as she, and yet unaccustomed to his local mass.

He jumped for the ball, twisting in an effort to eat his unwanted momentum, actually got a hand on—

"Kara ven'Arith!" The all-call rattled the walls of the so-called Arena.

Bilton leapt, and came spinning to the deck, the bowli ball dancing along his fingers, shedding energy as it did.

Yangi grabbed Fortch by the belt just in time to keep him from ramming his nose against the wall.

Kara, flatfoot and hands at her side, stood waiting.

"Kara ven'Arith to Central Repair," Master Thelly's voice blared. "Kara ven'Arith to Central Repair, *now*!"

• • • ✧ • • •

"SORRY 'BOUT IT, Kara—know it's your rec shift. Vechi had an accident in Green-Mid-Six. Got 'er out to the clinic, but the work'd just got started, and needs to be finished. You got least hours on the card."

"So I win," she said, showing cheerful in the face of his worry, though she was worried, too. This accident was the fifth among the tech-crew in the last eighteen Station-days; more than the total accidents for the last six Standard months. Not only newbies, either—two old hands had spent a couple work shifts each in the station's autodoc, getting patched up from injuries from "freak accidents."

Kara finished belting on her kit, and looked 'round.

"Vechi's wagon's still down in Mid-Six," Master Thelly said. "Had to carry her out."

Kara stared at him.

"What happened this time?"

"Wild charge," Master Thelly said, looking even more worried. "You be careful, hear me?"

"I'm always careful," Kara told him, picking up her tea bottle.

He grunted. "So's Vechi."

• • • ✧ • • •

GREEN-MID-SIX was a well-lit and roomy utility hall in a low-grav segment of the station. Kara had helped with the complete maintenance overhaul of the systems housed in this hall during her tenday tour. Vechi's orders, still up on the work wagon's screen, were to check an anomaly in Bay Four. The hatch was off, and leaning neatly against the wall. The test leads were still tidily wrapped on the wagon, so the wild charge must have struck Vechi either as she removed the hatch, or when she did her first eye-scan. That was standard procedure for a tech with an anomaly report to retire: A visual scan to make sure there wasn't any obvious damage—melted leads, snapped fuses, anything broken or compromised.

If the tech's eyeballs or nose didn't locate a problem, then the leads from the wagon were attached, and a series of diagnostics were run.

A wild charge build-up, thought Kara, pulling on her gloves, while contemplating the open access from the side of the wagon—that would create an anomaly, all right.

It would also create damage with a very particular signature. Once identified, all that remained was for the tech to pinpoint the cause, for the reports, and file a work order for rebuild.

Gloves on and light in hand, Kara advanced on the open access port.

Even though she knew what she'd see, Kara still blinked as her light illuminated the interior of the hatch.

Carnage was the word that came to her mind; and also the thought that there would be no identifying the failed source. There simply wasn't enough left to support a forensic diagnostic. The smell of ozone was not completely gone, nor that of the antiseptic sprays they'd used on Vechi.

She returned to the wagon, tapped up the main schematic screen and traced the power flow.

The station operated with tertiary back-ups, only sensible in so vulnerable a habitat as a space station. She was pleased to see that the back-up had come online without a glitch and there had been no discernible disruption of service.

So much was to the good. She opened another screen, logged the damage and created the work order for the rebuild. In plain truth, she was likely to draw that one, but right now she was Vechi, with Vechi's orders to clear.

She tapped the screen, bringing up the list of work orders. Anomaly resolution went to the top of a given roster-list, so this had been Vechi's first stop on her shift. It glowed yellow on the screen—begun, but not logged as complete.

Below was a long list of work orders, all patiently showing green—waiting for tech.

Kara sipped from her tea-bottle as she created a ref-file, attached the open, incomplete, order to the rebuild order, raised her finger to tap the next task in line—and stopped, frowning.

Vechi was the fifth tech injured in the line of duty. Had the others all been checking anomalies, too?

In less than thirty seconds, she had the anomalies report open on one side of the wagon's screen; on the other, the tech department's injury report.

The injured techs: Vechi, Mardin, Whistler, Harfer, and Gen Arb—and yes, each had been checking an anomaly report when they had been injured.

Kara's fingers were quicker than her thoughts. She called up the real-time functions, using her key for the big ops board, that she sat on rotation every eight Station-days.

The wagon's screen was too small to accommodate the whole function screen, but all Kara wanted to do was to set an alarm. That done, she opened up the next work order in-queue.

• • •✧• • •

ABOUT HALFWAY THROUGH Vechi's shift, Kara paused between jobs to file a manual schedule adjustment. There was, she reasoned, no sense going off-duty for one shift, only to have to report back for her regular work-shift. Best to just keep on, with the loan of Vechi's wagon, and swap out her second shift for rest. That would get her two rest shifts in a row, and put her back onto her regular schedule.

The system OK'd the change, which meant that Master Thelly was on maintenance himself, and would scold her the next time they met, per standard procedure.

Content with her changes, Kara finished out Vechi's shift, closed the list of completed work orders, signed in as herself and downloaded her own run of work.

She was in Green-Mid-Forty-Five; her work started in Blue-Mid-Twelve, conveniently near. Kara regarded the change of venue as a break.

She sipped tea as she walked, the wagon following. The best route to Blue-Mid-Twelve involved a shortcut through Orange, where the root of Ten Rod Two joined the station structure proper.

And there she quite unexpectedly found Fortch, the pool pilot who had not yet mastered the station's gravity, in front of the utility-core for the arm, an access hatch wide open, and several tools haphazardly sticking from his pockets and belt.

"What are you doing in the tech-tunnels, Pilot?" she asked, using her tea-bottle as a pointer, her voice sharper than it ought to be, for truly, he could be temp-help, or—

But if he was temp-help, where was his repair wagon? Where was his kit?

Fortch seemed to feel himself at a disadvantage. He licked his lips.

"Kara! I didn't know you were working down here!"

"And I didn't you were working down here."

"Oh, well I am—working. Filling in. Just checking something out for Master Thelly, that's all. There was a glitch on the screen and he asked me to—but wait, I need to talk to you about your license problem . . ."

He was moving, as if trying to stay between her and the open hatch. Lights were on, and covers hinged back from equipment.

Behind her, the anomaly alarm went off on the work wagon, and three things happened in a quick succession.

Fortch jumped toward her, a spanner suddenly in his hand.

Kara spun as if she were playing bowli ball, ducked under his outstretched arms, using the open tea-bottle to fend off the tool he swung down. There was a clang, the bottle was torn from her hand and spun away, splashing tea everywhere. Her spin continued as his lunge faltered; she came up behind—and pushed him away from her, hard as she could, toward the open utility room.

He, inept in the station environment, skidded on the tea-splashed deck, arms pinwheeling now, half-fell and half-slid, snatched for his balance, cursing—and lost his balance altogether, striking his shoulder on the access door and crashing heavily into the room, arm up in a desperate and failing bid not to fall into the panels and wiring.

There was a sharp snap and a dazzling flash, and he collapsed to the decking, unmoving.

• • •✧• • •

THE DOOR TO the Station Master's private office opened, and Kara stood up, preferring to meet her fate thus.

"Tech ven'Arith, thank you for your patience," the Station Master said gently, giving her a bow as well-meaning as it was meaningless. "You're free to go."

She blinked at him.

"To go?" she repeated. "Go—where?"

"To your conapt, I'd say," Master Thelly stuck in. "You got the next three shifts off—use 'em to sleep!"

"But—" She looked among them until she found Orn Ald yos'Senchul's face. "Fortch is dead."

"So he is, and that is unfortunate, since there were questions that various of us would have liked to ask him. Clearly, however, he was undertaking sabotage against the station and his efforts might have killed hundreds. Stopping him was of utmost importance—and stop him you did." He inclined his head.

Kara noticed that her hands were clenched. She opened them, and shook her fingers out.

"But—why?" she asked. "Why was he trying to . . . harm the station?"

Bringo, the Chief Tugwhomper, looked grave.

"Had a drink wit' the boy not so long ago," he said slowly. "Shortenin' it considerable, he told me he figured out how to get his paper, Eylot-side."

Kara shivered, suddenly cold.

"By killing the station?"

"Now, missy. Coulda just drunk too much coil fluid and talkin' big. Cheer 'imself up, like."

"There will be an investigation," said the Station Master. "Might be something in his quarters will be helpful. In the meanwhile, Pilot ven'Arith, the lesson you're to take away from you is that you acted in self-defense—properly acted in self-defense. If Fortch hadn't had the main power bus to the arm open he'd be alive. I'd say the fatal mistake was his, not yours."

Orn Ald's voice then, quick, comforting Liaden preceding a gentle bow between comrades.

"The station is in your debt, Kara."

"That's right, and we don't aim to stay that way," said Guild Master Peltzer. "There's a reward for preserving environmental integrity. Understand, it's not what any of us can call exact Balance—more like a symbolic Balance. Be as may, I reckon that reward's gonna show up in your account." He gave the Station Master a hard look, and that individual smiled.

"Without a doubt, Guild Master. Without a doubt."

"That's all set now," said Master Thelly, firmly. "Kara—go get some rest."

"Yes," she said, numb, but with a dawning sense of relief. She bowed a simple bow of respect to the group of them, and turned toward the door.

As she stepped into the hall, she found Orn Ald yos'Senchul next to her.

"Will you share a meal with me, Comrade, and allow me escort you to your conapt?"

"Yes," she said again, and considered him. "And you will tell me everything that the others didn't want to tell me, won't you Orn Ald?"

"Oh, yes," he said serenely. "I'll do that."

✧ Moon's Honor ✧

***IN ADDITION** to their involvement in the events culminating in* Crystal Dragon, *we've written several stories about Lady Moonhawk, priestess of the Goddess, and Lute, an itinerant sleight-of-hand magician. "Moon's Honor" was intended as the beginning of the Lute-and-Moonhawk novel we* really wanted *to write; it was the "chapters" part of a proposal package. Sadly, no publisher could be persuaded to take the novel on, and the partial languished on Sharon's hard-drive from 1996 until early 2013, when we published it to Splinter Universe.*

THE MOON

Caution, danger, error, disillusionment

OUT OF THE HIGH COUNTRY it drove him, lashing him through and around places where normally he would have tarried, displayed his skill, collected a coin, an egg, a cheese.

At first he fought it, this vast and reasonless compulsion, though his master had always urged him to heed the lesser sendings he had experienced in the past.

Those had never frightened him.

This—this chilled his soul. So he fought, striving to bring his own will to the fore—and lost, as the compulsion moved him, puppet-like, down from the mountains where breath still showed frost at dawn and at sunset, into the high valleys and further, to the river plain itself, where spring was already blooming.

He must reach Dyan City by full Moon. So little to know, when one was accustomed to being one's own master. Certainly too little to keep him on his feet and traveling well into the night, with only the racing Hounds to light him. Far too little to raise him from his fireless camp at dawn's first blush, walking again as he broke his fast from the dwindling supply of journeybread.

The bread was gone by the time his feet touched the road to Dyan City, and he walked the last miles hungry, passing through the gates as they were closing for the night.

It was Beltane Eve.

The compulsion shoved him through the gate-market, past the rim of cheap inns and beer-rooms, through a ragged ring of houses, toward the city's center.

He hurried across the warehouse district, and a zone of painfully tidy houses, each with its own tiny garden spot; through the midpoint market and the streets of upscale inns; past shops and through wide cobbled streets faced by spacious houses where music and laughter spilled from walled and secret gardens. On and on his demon rode him, through odorous crowds, past perfumed pavilions, until he reached Goddess Square.

There, facing the glory of Dyan Temple, at the very foot of Maidenstairs, with the Elder Hound just rounding the Eastern Tower—there, the compulsion left him.

"Crone's teeth!" An oath, though he was not in general a man who cursed.

He swayed, so suddenly was he free, and his knees began to go. Teeth grit, he caught himself, determined that none of the Temple should see him kneeling and mistakenly bear him inside as a supplicant.

His master had maintained that these incidents of compulsion were Goddess-sent, thus holy, and had adjured his apprentice to heed the sendings and obey them with grace.

Sadly, the 'prentice had never been so sweetly devout as the master, and endured these moments of the Goddess' favor with wariness, not to say dislike. Endured he had, however, and learned that a foretelling of gold eventually turned golden, and a whiff of disaster held real danger. Thus, he added another weapon—chancy as it was—to his arsenal of survival.

But such a compulsion as this? Never before had he experienced the like: To be herded like a cow, five days down from the mountains, neglecting both work and food—neglecting even the all-important practice!—to be dumped at the foot of Maidenstairs like a sack of wheat, without the first notion of why he should be there? His life disrupted and his stomach growling, all for the Goddess' mere whim?

He was inclined to be annoyed.

However, it was not politic to be annoyed at the foot of Maidenstairs within the heart of one of the Three Cities, and he was a man possessed of shrewdness.

Deliberately, playing for those who might be watching from tower-top or window-slit, he made obeisance, cloak swirling gracefully as he sank to one knee in the Houndlight. He held the genuflection for a long beat of three, head bowed in reverence, then came straight in one fluid movement. Carefully, he backed nine steps from the foot of Maidenstairs, his eyes on the pinnacle of the Eastern Tower.

Then, ritual flawlessly performed, he turned gently on his heel and walked back into the city.

There was a guildhall in Dyan City, but he was not wishful of meeting his fellows thus new from the kiss of the Goddess. The few coins hoarded in the lining of his cloak were enough, he reckoned, for a meal at one of the outer inns. He trusted to his skills—rusty as they must be from so long without practice—to earn him a place near the hearth for sleeping, and a bit of sausage wrapped in fresh bread to see him along the road, tomorrow sunrise.

Mind made up and course once more his own to chose, he sauntered through the streets of Dyan City, taking leisure to look about him, now that the lash was off his back. He marked the silks, furs and fine woolens; the gilded doors and the locked gardens, gates lit by the steady glow of electric lanterns, gift of Dyan Temple's generator.

He sighed and went away from the avenues of nobles, crossed the empty evening market and passed into a gaggle of thinner streets, most lit with candle-lanterns. More folk were about here, there being no pleasure-gardens to lock themselves into, and he went freely among them.

Those who saw him at all merely marked a thin man, a bit taller than some, with a face that might have seen twenty years or forty, in the way of faces sun-browned and scoured by the winds of turning seasons. His neatly braided hair was black, showing no lighter strands; under the road dust his cloak was likewise black. He carried a bag beneath it, slung over his shoulder by a leather strap. But none passing him on the street would note that.

The inn he chose, by and by, had a remarkably lifelike carving of a snowy owl aside the door, talons gripping the wooden peg it stood upon. On the wall above someone had shakily hand-painted the legend: Hunter's Moon.

He had not expected such erudition in this ring of the city and turned eagerly toward the merry red door and the wooden owl's baleful stare. He moved his hand as he did so, conjuring a bright green counter from the air. He walked it across the back of his hand, vanished it, reached out and drew it from the carven feathers on the owl's snowy cheek, grinning in unselfconscious pleasure. His fingers were not so stiff, after all.

It was then he saw the parchment.

Real parchment, such as Temple Proclamations were written upon, inked in green and signed in silver, with official ribbons dangling from the pentagram that sealed it. Heart unaccountably stilled—for what did Temple Proclamations have to do with him?—he leaned forward to read it.

Let it hereby be known that all and any practitioners of the so-called "Craft Magic", which is that fraud and sleight-of-hand designed only to trick the naive eye and beguile the foolish from the True Wonder of the Goddess, shall fail to display these supposed arts within the sight and hearing of the Circle.

Let it also be known that any who in defiance of this order of the Temple persevere in displaying the "Craft Magic" shall be considered to have performed blasphemy and shall be schooled accordingly.

This by the order of the Inner Circle, Dyan Temple, whose will is set forth by the hand of Greenlady upon the thirty-second night of the waxing moon looking toward Beltane.

"Blasphemy." His fingers flicked, vanishing the damning counters even as he tried to breathe normally, to hide all outward signs of fear. The "schooling" that drew one away from blasphemy had to do with incarceration in some deep room within the Temple, and the constant company of those of the Circle, whose purpose it was to bring the sinner to honest abhorrence of his sin and repudiation thereof.

Some even survived the experience.

Was this why he had been driven to Dyan City? he wondered, and then shook his head. The Goddess knew each of Her children by name and every soul was as a crystal for Her scrying, so the teaching went. Armed with such knowledge, She could not for a moment have supposed that Her son Lute would gladly walk up Maidenstairs, declare himself magician and practitioner of the so-called "Craft Magic" and joyously embrace *schooling*.

"We are all as the Goddess made us," he whispered, and smiled thinly. It was a thing his master had been prone to say; the comfortable mantra of a man comfortable in his faith. Goddess thanked, he had not lived to see this.

He looked again at the proclamation, at the unweathered parchment, the crisp ribbons, and the bright nail holding it to the wall over the owl's left wing. Posted new this morn, or so he judged it.

There was a guildhall in the city. A very full guildhall, no doubt, this being Beltane and practitioners of the "Craft Magic" standing at least as devout as the rest of the populace. On average.

Behind him, he heard steps—voices bearing down toward the merry red door. In that instant, he made his decision, flicked a hand out, then melted into the shadows aside the doorway. The two customers—younger sons of outer-ring market families, by their dress and accent—passed within a finger's breadth and never saw him.

The door swung closed and Lute stepped into the street, moving with long, unhurried strides—back toward the deep of the city.

Behind him, the carven owl stood vigil over sign, door and a bright, new nail.

THE HIGH PRIESTESS

Wisdom, serenity, judgment, learning, sagacity, common sense

"Lady Moonhawk! Lady Moonhawk, come quickly!" The novice who demanded it hurtled pell-mell into the library, sandals grating on the polished wooden floor. She hit one of the red and yellow rugs with no diminishment of speed, skidded—and would have fallen except that the woman curled in the window glanced up from her book and prevented it with a flicker of long fingers and the breath of a Word.

"Thank you, Lady!" the novice gasped, belatedly recalling her bow. She performed this ritual hurriedly, straightened without having received the Lady's aye and blurted again: "You must come quickly!"

Lady Moonhawk lifted an eyebrow, dark blue eyes sharpening on the novice's face. "Oh," she said, in dangerously sweet accents, "must I?"

The novice gulped, nervously tangling her fingers together before her. "Please, Lady, it's—"

"Keela's baby." Moonhawk was up in the same instant, moving with long strides across the slippery floor. "Fetch Mother Portal," she snapped over her shoulder as she vanished into the hallway.

"Yes, Lady Moonhawk," the novice said, and quit the room herself, forbearing to run until she hit the stone-floored hallway.

• • •✧• • •

IT HAD BEEN A HARD BIRTH and the baby had not been hale, so both mother and child had been brought to the Temple Infirmary, to be cared for by the Circle until both were strong.

Keela did well, gaining weight and strength with joyous ease. The babe had not done as well, though neither Moonhawk nor any of the other Healing Sisters could determine what it was that ailed him.

"He has no will to live," Greenlady had said, though not in the mother's hearing. "Poor babe, he hangs by a thread, as if life were a fault in the weaving, rather than the purpose of the loom."

There was wisdom in that, Moonhawk thought, for the boy certainly showed no spark of the all-consuming interest characteristic of other children his age. She probed him, seeking his soul, seeking the nature of his mind—and found only weariness, as one might find when aiding those full old to prepare for their reunion with the Goddess.

Just as well, she thought, that he return to the Mother now . . .

Aye, the next thought intruded, and what of Keela?

Keela, who had lost her man this winter past, when the river ice cracked wide and the frigid waters dragged him down; who had rejoiced in a son to bear his likeness—and his name. Keela, who nursed the sickly boy with fierce patience, holding him in her arms, willing him to life with a potency that bordered upon a Sister's skill.

What of Keela, should the child die, too?

Moonhawk began to run.

• • • ✧ • • •

THE INFIRMARY WAS QUIET as she dashed into the common room, so that she dared hope—and then she saw Keela, bent over the cradle, her arms moving in the way Moonhawk had taught her. She was pressing on the child's chest, helping him breathe.

Moonhawk stopped at the cradle's side, watching Keela work, caught a whiff of the other woman's desperate terror, saw the thin chest rise and fall under his mother's hands.

"He breathes," she said. "Keela, let him take it up."

"He breathes," Keela said grimly. "Three times before I thought so, and when I stopped, he did as well!" She glanced aside, face grim and wet with sweat. "Lady Moonhawk, my child is dying!"

It seared of Truth. Moonhawk opened herself to the trance, stepping into it even as she moved forward and put her hand beside the other woman's hand, upon the baby's breast.

"Let me See," she said, and then she said no more, nor saw more, either, except what lay before the Inner Eyes.

A wasteland lay stretched before her, parched, misbegotten and doomed. There was no air, nor sun, no water, no joy.

In the world she had left, Moonhawk's other hand moved to rest atop Keela's own.

A second landscape overlay the first, this one lush with life and love and joy, save that where it crossed the wasteland, patches of lush greenery became tainted; here and there strands of grass were seen to die.

And as the two landscapes stretched further together, each bound into the other, the first began to leach more life from the second, killing wholesale, until, on the edge of the horizon, Moonhawk could see no difference between them—only deserted waste, stretching onward forever.

Chilled, she closed the Inner Eyes, took one glimpse at the mother's grim desperation, moved both her hands and lifted Keela away from the child.

"No!" One cry, anguished, and Keela slumped against her, face hidden against Moonhawk's shoulder. Moonhawk held her close, stroking the disordered hair, opened the Inner Eyes—and Watched the baby die.

It came quickly—only a fading, a shuddering sigh of ultimate easement, with no need of her to smooth the path, without a note of the singing joy so commonly heard at the last instant. Joyless alive, joyless he died, giving up the life that had been only burden.

"Gone," she said, and felt Keela shudder, then move away. The Inner Vision spun for a heartbeat, then steadied again on the exuberant land that was Keela, a small near patch of blight showing, then a lush regrowth. The sun was warm, and Moonhawk thought she heard birdsong.

She opened her eyes.

Keela was holding her son in her arms, tears running her face, breast heaving. "The Goddess gives," she gasped, half-raising her face.

"And the Goddess receives us back," murmured a soft voice from beside Moonhawk.

"Lady Portal."

The Mother of Dyan Circle bowed slightly. "I see I am too late."

She lay a tiny hand upon Moonhawk's sleeve. "Come to me after Tenth Chant."

"Yes, Mother." Dismissed, Moonhawk bowed deeply and turned away. Mother Portal's soft voice followed her out of the room, accompanied by the first subtle flavors of a Heart Heal: "There, there, my child. Come, lay the lad down in his crib. No, there's no shame in crying. Such a bonny boy he was and so strongly did you fight for him . . ."

Except, Moonhawk thought, she'd lost, despite the love and the fight, and the combined efforts of three Witches skilled in healing. In the end, the babe *would* die, and perhaps better he had never lived at all. She caught her lower lip in her teeth at such a thought and turned her mind forcibly to the prayers to establish serenity.

• • •✧• • •

SHE RETURNED to her own rooms, bathed and dressed in a fresh gown of the shade known outside Temple as "Circle blue," and cut to fully reveal the breasts.

Any other of the Sisters would then have repaired to the Lady's Chapel in Temple's center or to the private altar each kept within her room, to meditate on events just past, to seek portents and signs of things left undone for the soul returned, to achieve communion with the Power that moved the universe.

Moonhawk went to the East Tower.

There, she stared up into the late day sky, and when the hawk spiraled into sight, she brought her arm up, crooked so, as if this were a tame beast and not wild the length and breadth of its days.

She held her arm up and, obedient, the hawk stooped, cruel talons digging tight into the invisible shield she conjured to protect her fragile flesh.

The invisible shield was a small magic, in Moonhawk's estimation. The miracle was having one of the Goddess' wildest children with her of its free feral will, looking without fear into her eyes.

They stayed so, Witch and hawk, for a timeless time, staring deeply into each other's eyes, drinking each of the soul of the other. Then the woman moved, slowly bringing up her other hand, and trailed her fingers through the chest feathers in caress.

The bird allowed it: One stroke, from beak to belly, then it flicked its wings, and broke the gaze that had bound both.

Obedient in her turn, Moonhawk brought her arm sharply up and the bird was gone in a blast of wings, soaring upward into the purpling twilight, until it was lost to the Witch's straining eyes.

Regretfully, she brought her eyes down, bent and picked up the barred brown feather from between her bare feet. "Thank you," she murmured, and moved to the parapet.

One hip braced against the low wall, she gazed down into Goddess Square as her fingers separated a lock of hair and began to make a braid into which the hawk's feather would be woven.

Pilgrims had been flowing in for the past half-moon, two, three, a dozen every day, and now, on the evening before Beltane, it would seem that all had gained the security of the Supplicant's Courtyard. The plaza she gazed down on was empty, except for those townfolk who crossed it in the course of normal business. At the foot of Maidenstairs there was no one, travel-stained and weary, come down from the mountains to partake of Beltane at the Temple, to offer themselves up to the Spring Goddess and beg for good growth, good fortune, good health.

But no, what was this? From the ring streets came a man, dark-cloaked and dark-haired, barely more than a blot against the shadowing air, striding purposefully toward Maidenstairs.

Straight across the plaza he came, looking neither right nor left, eyes seemingly fixed on Maidenstairs. He moved with long graceful strides, but Moonhawk caught a sense of weariness rise up from him, as if he had kept the pace for longer than was wise.

At the foot of Maidenstairs, he stopped, cloak swinging into stillness, embracing him with shadow.

The First Hound was barely around the edge of the tower where she leaned, braiding the feather into her hair; the supplicant had time, just, to climb the stairs and beg Sister Doorkeeper the boon of shelter and food for the night.

He remained quite, quite still, as if having come this far his resolve now failed him. Moonhawk leaned more nearly over the parapet, heedless of the dangers of overbalance, and sought him with the Inner

Eyes. If she could but discover the fading ember of courage, entice it to flame once more . . .

Weariness she read in him, as clearly as if he were a Sister in Circle; hunger, and a spark of honest anger, overridden at once by wariness. Moonhawk blinked, very nearly overbalanced at Center by the clarity with which he could be read. Yet, she Saw no trace of that which must have carried him many days and miles.

Biting her lip, she embraced the prayer for serenity and prepared herself to attempt a deeper Reading.

The man in the plaza below moved.

Gracefully, he sank to one knee, sleek head bent in respect.

Three heartbeats later, he came as gracefully to his feet, and backed nine smoothly precise steps away from Maidenstairs, his shadowed face lifted to the East Tower. If it had been day, Moonhawk thought, he might have seen her; she might have been able somehow to influence him to mount the stairs, and enter the comfort and safety—

The man turned away, walking back across Goddess Square, his stride still smooth, though less long, less—driven.

Moonhawk watched until he vanished into the shadows of the ring-street, unaccountably troubled by his failure. So small a thing, to climb Maidenstairs, to ask the ritual question and be welcomed within. So small a price to pay for relief of whatever had driven him to such weariness. To lose a soul from one instant of human fraility—

She shook her head, smiling wryly. Peace, Lady Moonhawk, she told herself. Well you know that no soul is ever lost. The Goddess speaks to us all in the tongue we know best. Yon seeker this time heard imperfectly. Next time he'll doubtless hear fully.

Doubtless. She raised her face to the Hound and stretched both hands high, palms open, naked feet braced against the tower stones, welcoming the weak power of the lesser moon into her, letting it wash away her grief for the dead child, the lost seeker, allowing her soul to take wing and soar as the hawk had soared, spriraling gloriously upward.

The bell-notes preceding Ninth Chant brought her to herself with a gasp and she lowered stiffened arms. The Hound was behind her, half-done its first circuit of the night. The Moon itself would rise at Twelfth Chant, at which time the Founding Ritual that prepared all for Beltane itself, would take over the attention of the Circle. Goddess Plaza, deserted now below her, would be crowded with townspeople eager to lend their energy and good heart to the ritual.

Her talk with Mother Portal would be over by then, and she would be with the others in the center courtyard, raising her voice with them in the opening songs, merging her being with the beings of her Sisters, raising and sustaining power—the first complex level of power needed for the coming joyous ritual . . .

She should, she thought abruptly, eat something. In general she was careless of meals, but the hunger she had tasted of the seeker nagged at the pit of her own stomach. Food, she thought, firmly, and so thinking climbed down from the tower and went down the long hallways to the kitchen.

When she arrived there, she made a good meal of roast lamb and spiced vegetables and fresh bread with sweet butter. She ate methodically, and more than she would have eaten for herself, as if she might feed the unknown seeker, too.

• • •✧• • •

"AND SO YOU FELT it time to allow Keela's baby his death?" The question was mild, as all of Mother Portal's questions were mild, but Moonhawk felt a chill pebble her skin.

"With the Inner Eyes I Saw how it was with the babe, how he would take all of Keela's joy and remain joyless. How, if he were to return to the Goddess, she would heal, and he would have the Summerland, and rest before his next incarnation. It was True Seeing." She heard the defensive note in her own voice, bit her lip and moved her eyes to contemplate the green-and-silver candle burning upon Lady Portal's private altar.

"True Seeing." The tone was bland, empty of any compulsion or command. "But not Goddess-moved."

Moonhawk turned her head to stare at her interrogator. "Goddess-moved?" she echoed. "No, Mother. It was myself who Saw, who knew right action and acted."

"So," Mother Portal said. "Lady Moonhawk takes it upon herself to judge who should live and whose life is a burden no longer to be borne."

"It is what the Sight is for!" Moonhawk cried. "It is what I was trained for, why I was shown to the Goddess and taught the Inner Magics—"

"And you believe that attaining the Inner Circle makes you like unto the Goddess, able to give life and take it?" Sharp as ice now, Lady Portal's voice, and each small cold cut hurt and bewildered, so that Moonhawk sat back upon her heels and merely stared.

"Answer," Lady Portal directed and Moonhawk licked her lips.

"Mother, I have told you what I Saw. I believe that I acted rightly, in accordance with the Way I was shown and with the Will of the Goddess as I have been taught to understand it. It is my private belief that the child wished to die and that as he grew older his wish would grow greater until it would have taken all the Circle, concentrating all their energy upon him and him alone to keep him from the Summerland."

"And so you acted and took away the hands that might have saved him one more time and allowed him to slip away now." There was a pause during which Moonhawk ran through an exercise to embrace Serenity and abandoned herself to the will of the Goddess.

"How do you know," demanded Lady Portal, "that it was *time* for that child to die, Lady Moonhawk? Did your True Seeing show you that?"

Within the warming cloak of Serenity, Moonhawk felt a spear-thrust of ice pierce straight to her heart.

"No," she murmured. "I did not know that."

"So." Lady Portal stared at her, eyes showing sadness. "I have had reports from others of our Sisters," she said slowly. "They tell me that Lady Moonhawk is full with herself, that, though her talents are great, so is her pride. That Lady Moonhawk alone is the best judge of ritual rightly done, of results correctly obtained." She glanced down at her hands, folded upon her lap; looked up again into Moonhawk's face.

"How long have you been in Circle, Sister?"

"How long—" Moonhawk caught herself staring again; blinked.

"All my life, Mother," she said carefully. "I was brought here as an infant, to fulfill my birth-mother's vow to the Lady."

"And, showing talent as soon as you could walk, you were trained, knowledge poured into you until you were full to bursting. With a flick of your fingers you can conjure a spell that another of our Sisters, less talented, yet industrious and good-hearted, may spend days of careful ritual to achieve." She closed her eyes.

Moonhawk sought again the green-and-silver candle, and abandoned both thought and unease. It would transpire as the Goddess willed it, she thought firmly, pulling the rags of Serenity about her. Whatever punishment might be hers, for failing to read fully, that she would do. Neither Mother Portal nor her Sisters in Circle nor the Goddess would put upon her more than she might bear.

Mother Portal opened her eyes. "You are arrogant," she said slowly, each word a pebble, dropped into the still pool of Moonhawk's mind. "Further, you are ignorant. It is our duty, who have trained you, to see that these faults in you are amended, so that you may serve the Goddess to the full extent of your powers. I shall meditate upon it, as shall the Circle." She moved, rising to her full, diminutive height, and smoothed her hands down the front of her rumpled robe. Moonhawk rose as well and stood looking down at her, Serenity yet cloaking thoughts and emotions.

"You will go to your rooms," Mother Portal said. "You will cleanse yourself and you will do a Crossing Over ritual for Keela's child. You will then fast and meditate and await my call."

Within Serenity, a spark of panic. "But—Beltane . . ."

Lady Portal looked severe. "Beltane was before there was Moonhawk," she said sternly. "And Beltane there will be long after Moonhawk is returned to the Goddess. Do not add disobedience to your transgressions."

Moonhawk stood, and stared.

Lady Portal sighed. "You have your instructions, I believe?" she said, voice unremittingly even.

The panic had gone from spark to conflagration, through which that dangerously mild tone cut like a honed blade. Moonhawk bowed low—"Yes, Mother. Blessed be."—and left the room.

Numb, she walked down halls glowing with the lambent energy of nearly a hundred excited Witches and novices. She was bumped once or twice by those hurrying toward Moon Court for the midnight ritual, but most of the tide she moved against avoided her scrupulously. No one called her name in friendship. No one caught her sleeve and laughingly scolded her for walking the wrong way. She moved alone, as she ever did, through halls crowded with the Sisters of her Circle.

It wasn't until she reached her own room, the door closed and sealed behind her, that she released Serenity and began to cry.

THE ACE OF PENTACLES

The beginning and the end

THE MOON HAD RISEN since he had quit Goddess Square, and the access streets were crowded with those who wished to partake of the foundation rituals performed on Beltane eve.

The devout made a river of humanity, carrying Lute toward Dyan Temple and the living heart of the city.

A human river, however, could be fought as a Goddess-sent compulsion could not. Lute used shoulders and elbows to steer himself through and across the current, to land at last, ill-tempered and sweaty, at the door of the Magician's Guildhall.

It was locked.

Lute stared for a long moment, bag heavy across his shoulder, then grabbed the bell-rope and pulled. The door remained shut.

"Damn you," he gritted and renewed his grip on the rope. Over and over, he hauled down, waking such a peal that his head fair rang with it—and at long last the door came open a cautious inch.

"Go away," snarled someone from within. "It's Beltane eve."

Lute glared into the dark as if he could see the speaker well. "Tell the Guildmaster that Master Magician Lute is here to speak to him upon a matter of utmost urgency."

"Be silent, or are you Moonkissed?" The keeper would have shut the door then, except that Lute's foot prevented it. "Maiden's tits, man, will you have us all called to Circle? It's Beltane. Go away."

"It is most certainly Beltane eve, and I will just as certainly not go away." Lute snapped. "I will see the Master of this Hall if I have to ring the bell until the roof falls in! Let me in—my right as Guildsman!—and fetch the Master." He paused for the beat of two, called up the voice-power as his master had taught him and released it in one word: "*Now.*"

It worked. It nearly always did work, even against those who knew the trick of it. The doorkeeper sagged back a step, the door widened an inch more, Lute got his shoulder into the gap and shoved.

A half-beat later he was standing in the dim entrance way, closing the door behind him over the keeper's sputtering, and scrupulously lowering the bar. He fixed the older man with a stern eye.

"Fetch the Guildmaster."

"He's not here," said the keeper, sullenly. "Nor should you be, if you have a taste for health."

Lute lifted a brow, magnificently ignoring the man's surliness. "If the Guildmaster is not here," he said, keeping his voice sweet, "then send for him."

"But—"

"And after you've done that," he continued, brooking no debate, "you will show me to a parlor and bring me the latest log books, and a sup of ale. And some cheese. That is all."

The doorkeeper gaped at him, so Lute was forced to clap his hands sharply and flick the voice-lash: "*Go!*"

"Yes, Master," muttered the servant, startled into a bow. He scuttled off down the hallway, leaving Lute in dimness. Sighing, he walked to the wall, noting the position of the three ready sconces—set well above his overlong reach, a silly place, really, for torches, unless one wished to make a point.

He backed away from the wall, counting his steps, then, exactly centered upon one of the fine-cut granite blocks flooring the hallway, he stamped his heel three times, cried, "Ho!" and flung his arms high, fingers stretched wide, miming the flames that leapt instantly in all three sconces at once.

Slowly, he lowered his arms, keeping his face as solemn as if there were a crowd to impress, and as if satisfaction did not soar in him, that he had not lost the trick of it.

"Master's work," commented a voice to his right, abruptly enough to intend to startle. Lute finished the gesture properly, allowed his cloak to wrap him in mysterious stillness and held it for one long beat before he turned to face his audience.

"How pleasant to hear you say so," he purred and had the satisfaction of seeing the man's jowly face take on a pinkish tinge. He bowed, sweeping the cloak out and making it seem of velvet and ermine, to thus place it on a level with his host's 'broidered scarlet sash and silken shirt.

He of the scarlet sash bowed also, with grace, but without wit. "I am Feldris, newly Master of Dyan City Magician's Hall."

"And I am Lute, Master Magician, who had been apprenticed to Master Magician Cereus."

"Registered of what Hall?" The question was an insult; the names of all Master Magicians were inscribed in the *Book of Masters* kept in each Guildhall and it was the duty of each Hallkeeper to have that Book by heart. Lute lifted an eyebrow.

"Hagsmere, and it please you, great lord."

Feldris colored again, mouth tightening ominously. "I regret," he said stiffly, "that I am new to the house and have not committed the names of all the Masters to memory."

"A failing deserving of regret," Lute acknowledged, around a sudden sense of foreboding. "Let us step over to the Common Room and pull down the register, that you may satisfy yourself of my—authenticity."

The other man fluttered his hands—a formless thing, and thoroughly unlike the measured gesture one expected from a brother magician. Lute felt his foreboding grow, the parchment in his sleeve as heavy as stone.

"I am certain you are who—and what—you say you are," Feldris Hallkeeper said soothingly. "Did I not with my own eyes see you light the torches? But the doorkeeper spoke of an urgent matter you must discuss, and I have kept you waiting long enough. In what way can Dyan Guildhall aid you?"

Foreboding flared into active dismay. Here? Lute wondered,

keeping his face bland. In the very entrance hall? With neither table nor greet-wine nor the witness of others of the Guild?

"It is a matter of sufficient import," he murmured, "to interest all currently resident within the hall."

"Ah." Feldris folded his unschooled hands before his sash. "That would be myself," he said. "And the doorkeeper, of course."

"Is everyone at the Foundation Rituals, then?"

"They are no longer in the city," the Guildmaster said softly.

Lute took a breath, and then another. "Well," he said lightly, "I can see that I've wasted my time and yours, sir! Good Beltane to you—" He turned smoothly and went, smoothly, toward the door, ignoring his stammering heart and the lungs that wished to labor.

"Hold!" The Guildmaster's tread was heavy behind him and Lute was too far from the door—fool that he had been to bar it!

"Hold!" Feldris cried again as Lute laid his hands upon the bar and—

"Hold!"

"Hold!"

"*Hold!*"

Cried three separate voices from three corners of the entrance way, so that Feldris spun on his heel, surprised by words in the hall he knew to be empty. Lute flung the bar aside with a clatter, jerked the door wide—

And ran.

• • • ✧ • • •

TO BECOME INVISIBLE it is merely necessary to become one of many.

Thus had his master taught him, and good lore it was, as far as it walked. It was certainly no failing on the part of Master Cereus that his apprentice wished most ardently to avoid the place where the shielding crowd was thickest.

"If I wanted congress with Circle, I could as easily have clung to Master Feldris' side."

So saying, Lute left the crowd two streets short of Goddess Square and ducked into the shadow of an ornate garden gate, there to complete his preparations in private.

Master Cereus had been a gentle man, but no one's fool. He had walked a rough road for upwards of forty years and took no lasting harm from it. It had been his ardent wish that his 'prentice did as well.

"Of course," Lute muttered to himself in the privacy of the gate-shadow, "he never meant you to fight Circle, either. Each as the Goddess made us, master. Excepting only that the Goddess has lately reached forth her hand and made some of us more perfect than others."

He freed his bag from its carrying strap and knelt by it on the paving stones, hands hasty on the secret clasps. In the very act of unsealing it, he stopped, hands gripping the worn black leather.

The Guildhall where he—three times a fool!—ignored the gatekeeper's most obvious warning. And Feldris—no magician he, nor even one who had much experience of the breed, to be so startled by a minor bit of ventriloquism. Newly come to the post, was he, by the Moon? And by whose aye, with the Guildhall empty and Dyan City's magicians "gone"? Lute sat back on his heels and shivered as might-have-been ran down his back on many cold feet.

Feldris might well follow him: For his own safety, Lute must suppose that the hunt was already on. However, the pretty sash and soft hands spoke of one not so familiar with the rough, twisty streets along the city's outer ring. It was in those streets that Lute intended to pass the night, and be out the Western Gate the moment it opened, tomorrow.

"Fortunate, indeed, if dawn sees you out of the city," he told himself grimly. "Remember this and never again go within gates."

He took a deep breath then, and performed the linked series of mental images that had been the first magic his master had taught him. Calmed by the exercise, hands steady and mind cool, he finished the necessary adjustments to the bag.

A moment later he was out on the street, joining the crowd running there, and let it bear him, resistless, toward Goddess Square and the choice of multiple routes to the outer city.

• • •✧• • •

SOME TIME LATER he was moving toward a spur street tending westward and out and feeling a bit more sanguine regarding his chances of winning clear. So he ambled along, angling through the crowd, the picture of a man vaguely questing—for a lover, perhaps, or an aged parent—nothing frantic, to draw the eye, nor even particularly purposeful.

Inside the cloak, he rounded his shoulders to disguise his height and took care to walk heavy on the paving stones, to foster the illusion of bulk.

It took time to do the thing thus, but he judged it to his advantage to allow time for his scent to grow cold to the nose of whatever hounds the false Guildmaster might call out to the chase.

So he thought and so he believed. And so did this endeavor appear to have the Mother's smile, for he had the proper street in his eye; and was beginning to count the steps until he began once more to be safe—when he of the 'broidered sash, Master Feldris himself, stepped out of the street that Lute had thought his salvation, stopped and looked directly into the magician's eyes.

His jowly face lit as if he'd been chosen for Temple consort, flushing pink as he pointed at the place where Lute had been and looked over his shoulder to call out, "Here he is, Lady! Come quickly!"

But whether the lady obeyed such ungenteel summons or not, Lute could not have said. He was running, pushing and shoving and not caring whose feet he trod on—running, back into the thickest of the crowd.

THE FOOL

Simplicity, Faith

UPON HER BALCONY overlooking the innermost garden, Moonhawk sat in meditation. Outer eyes closed, she yet saw the greening bushes, the budding trees and the soft new grass with exquisite clarity. The garden was a haven of tranquility, after all, and many potent spells had been woven to insure that tranquility. It was a fitting model for the meditations of one judged by her sisters to be hasty and arrogant.

It had taken work to shed her bitterness at being excluded from Beltane eve circle; work that, in her current meek state, only illustrated more painfully that she was not fit for Inner Circle; and much less than fit for her duty as a vessel of the Goddess.

With these realizations newly in hand, she had eschewed the more sophisticated trance-patterns and opted for one that needed no drawn-out ritual to birth it, but merely required her own unimpaired Sight, and a relaxing of her arrogant will.

Upon the balcony, deep in meditation, Moonhawk *was* the garden and the peace therein.

Until, in the garden, there was—discord.

It was a slight thing, quickly gone, but it was enough to pain her, linked as she was—more than enough to break the web of trance.

Eyes still closed, but alert now, and seeking, Moonhawk cast her net out to capture the cause of discord.

She found it nearly at once: A pattern startling in its clarity, tinged with elusive familiarity. From the surface thoughts she caught frustration and anger, desperation, yet not despair. She received the impression that the intruder was being hunted, without expectation of either mercy or succor.

Hunted, on Beltane! Moonhawk stood, and opened her outer eyes, coordinating what she saw with what her other senses brought her. She established the intruder's location and nodded.

Hunted, in the very garden of the Inmost Circle!

Moonhawk went to the edge of the balcony, stepped off and walked the air down to the ground.

Feet upon the path, she paused once more to be certain of her direction, then set off at a rapid walk.

• • • ✧ • • •

HE HAD BEEN A FOOL to think that the hounds Feldris would bring to the hunt could be any less than Witches.

Not one Witch, as he had first thought, but *three*. Almost, he laughed. Three Witches and a false Guildmaster to run one ragged conjurer to ground? Soberness claimed him in a chill rush. Was *this* the reason the Goddess had herded him to Dyan City? That he might be held as an example to others of his profession?

Yet, for whatever reasons, three Witches. More than enough to push him in the direction they chose, and to deny him any hope of the streets beyond the square.

What they had aimed for, he thought, was to pin him against the base of East Tower, there to gather him up at their leisure. But he had moved a little too quickly; played the crowd-currents a little too adeptly. He came to the wall near the tower, certainly, but to the north, hard by the wicket he had noted earlier in the evening. It was the work of a moment to pick the lock and slip through, and hardly more than that to make sure the gate was locked again behind him.

He doubted his ploy would hold his pursuers long, but he hoped it would hold them long enough for him to hide himself. For in all the great pile of Dyan Temple, he thought, treading the conch-lined path with care, there must be one small hole into which he might crawl, there to sleep through Beltane. He would let himself out the way he had come in tomorrow.

The path made a sharp turn and twisted through a taelberry arbor, turned again . . .

And ended at a blank wall.

The wall must protect a private garden, Lute thought, refusing to accede to despair. The private garden, perhaps, of some Witch, who, if she held rank high enough to possess such a quiet spot, might well be a part of the Beltane eve rituals taking place in the Moon Court even now.

Beltane itself did not come to fruition until Moonrise tomorrow and there were certain other rituals after, so he had heard, that might keep a ranking lady well away from her garden.

It was the best gamble he had, who should have quit the table long ago. He brought gloves from beneath his cloak and pulled them on before he set his hands carefully among the wallstones and began to climb.

The wall was admirably supplied with hand- and footholds. Moments later Lute dropped lightly into the garden beyond, stripped off his gloves and headed for the shalmon bush at the base of the cort tree. He slipped in tight against the trunk, cloak melding with the black bark. The bush clothed him with leaf to the knee.

He leaned his forehead against the tree and deliberately emptied his mind of everything that was Lute or of Lute's concerns. He was a part of the garden, just quickening with spring. He was the cort tree, warm, smooth bark, widespread branches, soft, feathery leaves.

And then he was nothing, merely a blot of shadow among the other shadows beneath the tree. Invisible, not there, never there, safe and calm and—

"It is you!"

The voice shattered his self-hypnosis and he jumped; stumbled within the embrace of the shalmon bush, and would have fallen except that strong hands caught his shoulders and held him gently upright.

"It *is* you," the voice reiterated. "But however did you come here?"

The speaker was nearly his own height; yellow-haired and angular, dressed in the blue, breast-baring robe of an Initiate. Lute felt his heart go to ice.

As if she felt his dread, the woman held out a slim hand and stepped away from his hiding place. Rings of power glittered in the moonlight—enough silver to feed him for a goodly number of years, baring an unnaturally short life.

"Come," the woman said gently. "You don't need to be afraid. No harm will come to you here, I swear it!" She moved her fingers, beckoning, as if he were a bashful child.

"Come," she said again, and he stepped out of the bush and went two steps toward her across the grass. He could think of no place, now, to run.

"Good," said the woman—the *Witch*. "I saw you earlier, at the base of Maidenstairs and was sorry you had not come in. But you are here now and may find peace, for the Goddess is Mother of us all and Her Temples are safe havens for all Her children." She tipped her head.

"You are still afraid, but you needn't be. No one will hurt you here. Haven't I said so?"

"There he is!" He heard the words and felt the blow at the same time: A blow as from a giant's fist, slamming into his skull, driving him to one knee as the world shimmered and started to go gray . . .

"No! I have said he is safe here!" The world steadied and took back its colors; the pain in his head receded to a dull ache. Lute looked up, saw Feldris and another woman in Circle blue coming toward himself and his champion. This woman was smaller, rounder, darker, and frowning like a thunderhead.

"*You* have said he's safe here," she snapped. "And what have *you* to do with it?"

The yellow-haired Witch pulled herself up. "He failed at the door at First Hound—I saw it! Now, he comes to us, but afraid. Afraid of being hunted, Sister! Remind me, is it not Beltane eve?"

The dark one lifted a brow. "You know very well the name of the ceremony from which you are excluded."

"Yes?" the taller woman said with a false sweetness that set Lute's teeth on edge. "And yourself?"

"You—*dare*! On what hour was Moonhawk named Circle's Center? *I* draw my duties from the Circle, and to the Circle alone do I explain my reasons!"

"Strange," murmured Lute, climbing to his feet and wincing at the persisting headache, "I'd have thought you might reserve time for that which the Goddess sends you."

"Be silent!" snapped the dark woman, tracing a sharp sign before her. Lute saw the image shine against the air for an instant, then vanish.

"Certainly," he said and bowed, slightly and with irony. "Since you ask it so nicely."

The dark woman fairly gaped, but her escort was at no loss of words.

"Respect for Lady Rowan!" he cried and came two strides forward, fist rising. Lute watched his approach calmly; saw him stop as if suddenly rooted as the tall Witch wove her hand through glittering air.

"Shame, Feldris Circleman! To move for violence within these walls!"

Feldris Circleman. Lute stared at the other, searching the soft face and haughty eyes. A servant of the Temple, perhaps even the angry lady's consort. Thus might Lute have been . . .

"This man," Lady Rowan was telling—Moonhawk?—pointing at

Lute's very self, "is a breaker of the peace and one who actively works to rend Circle and lead the ignorant into error. He must be brought before Truth-seers at once."

Lute stirred. "I am of course honored that word of my skill has come to the ears of the ladies of Dyan Circle," he said smoothly. "However, I have traveled hard the last few days and doubt not my work is grown ragged." He smiled, noting how Lady Rowan's eyes sparked with fury even as her cheeks seemed to pale.

"I would bring nothing less than my best performance," he said gently, "before your sisters."

Lady Rowan walked forward, heavy, deliberate steps that crushed the new grass beneath her bare feet. Straight past Feldris Circleman she went until she stood less than an arm's length from Lute and there stopped, looking up at him with her hands on her hips.

"I bade you be silent. *Magician*."

Lute felt a spark of anger, though he kept his face pleasant. Make a curse-word of his profession, would she? He bowed once again, slight and mocking.

"Why, so you did," he said, smiling down at her. "Forgive me a faulty memory."

Her lips tightened, and she brought her hands sharply up, tracing a design that shone like living bars of fire in the air between them. He heard the other woman make a small sound even as his tongue began to burn.

Never anger a Witch, he thought as the pain grew and he felt the roof of his mouth scalding. The inside of his cheeks began to fry and he wanted, desperately, to scream—

"Avert!" One word, that seemed to lance through his tortured mouth like a spear of ice. The pain died on the instant and Lute closed his eyes in blessed relief. He opened them again to see Lady Rowan turning toward Moonhawk.

"You will cease to meddle! You will free my servant and return to your meditations. When Mother Portal hears of this—"

"Which she will better hear from my lips than yours, I think, Sister," said Moonhawk coolly. "Let us go together, why not?"

"Together?" Lady Rowan had gone very still.

"Together," Moonhawk replied, looking down upon her. "Where should this man better go than to Mother Portal, who knows Truth as plain as any other Seer?" She smiled, but not warmly. "And how better to bring word of my trespass most quickly to her ear?"

There was a hard silence, then a nod. "Very well," said Lady Rowan stiffly. "Join with me in subduing the magician—"

"Subduing?" Lute felt Moonhawk's glance like a physical thing. "He hardly seems frantic, though he has every right to be. Few folk, you know, Sister, would stand calm while their tongue was set afire."

"Oh," said Lady Rowan, ignoring the rebuke. "So you think he'll come quiet, do you?"

"Why should he not?" returned Moonhawk, then lifted her shoulders in a shrug. "But, there, you're distraught yourself and hardly in condition to lend support. I'll lead him and there will be no trouble." Another thoughtful blue glance at his face. "Will there, Master Lute?"

His name, which he had not told her. He stared, speechless now that he was required to speak, then drew himself up, conjuring a grin.

"No trouble at all, Lady. My word upon it."

• • •✧• • •

MOTHER PORTAL'S ROOMS were hung with silvery tapestries, upholstered in velvets and furs. Green and silver candles burned at the four prime points—green for the Spring Goddess, silver for the Moon. A fat white cat with a green riband about his neck sprawled across a low round table inlaid with gemstones. Incense hung in a pall, overburdening the air with the scent of false roses, and the windows were shut tight against the fine spring night.

"Take off your cloak," Lady Rowan snapped and Lute froze, eyes going to his patroness.

Moonhawk returned his glance gravely. "You've no need of your cloak here, Master Lute. The room is warm. And it is discourteous to come covered before Mother Portal."

"Ah," he said, around the dread in his heart. "Moon knows I would not be churlish."

He raised his hand and twisted the copper brooch at his shoulder, let the cloak slip free and caught it up in a practiced motion that never brought the lining to sight. Feldris Circleman had it off of his arm the next instant, and Lute bit back a protest.

"He's only gone to hang it up," said Moonhawk. "You shall have it again when you go."

"Yes," said Lute gently, for she seemed out of reason young and touchingly certain of his eventual freedom. "Of course I shall."

Lady Rowan was a different matter. "That!" she snapped, pointing at the bag, suspended from its leather strap and hanging at his hip. "Give that to me!"

It was the command voice again. Lute stilled the involuntary move of his muscles to obey, took three deep breaths and looked into Lady Rowan's eyes.

"No."

Her breath hissed. "You—*charlatan*! Have a care what enemies you make, lest you buy above your means." She snapped her fingers. "Give me the bag."

"No."

"And why should he?" Moonhawk demanded, cutting through whatever new pain Lady Rowan was doubtless contemplating inflicting upon him. "It is his, after all."

"It is proof of his villainy and it shall be set out now, ready for Lady Portal's hand."

"It is my life and my livelihood," Lute cried, anger breaking its barriers for an instant. "Nor is it safe for Lady Portal or any other except myself to touch it!"

"That is True," said Moonhawk into the small silence that followed this outburst. "He believes what he has said, completely."

There was more silence, then a flicker of Lady Rowan's fingers. "Show him the logic of putting it aside, Sister, do," she said, but to Lute's ear it sounded more an order than a request. "If the thing is as dangerous as that and he the only one who may control it, we can hardly take the chance of him unchaining it and making good his escape."

"Escape." Once more those blue eyes rested fully on him. "Do you wish to escape us, Master Lute?"

"Yes," he told her with utter truth.

She frowned. "I am sorry to hear it," she said gravely, "but I can scarcely blame you. Rough treatment has been your share here thus far. Still, Lady Rowan speaks sensibly, you know. If your bag is as dangerous as you believe, with yourself distressed and likely to err, perhaps it would be best for all, if you simply put the strap off and set the bag here." She pointed to a place upon the costly carpet exactly halfway between them. "Is that an acceptable compromise?"

He stared at the spot where her finger pointed, felt the weight of the bag across his shoulder, and thought, briefly and wildly, of the mountain village he had quit nine days ago, when the compulsion had come upon him—

"Lady," he said, seeking Moonhawk's glance, willing her to see the Truth in him. "I have no more will to break Circle than that cat!"

She held his eyes for a long moment, until Lute felt himself sliding into lightheadedness, then glanced aside, a tiny line between her brows.

"But you know," she said in her grave deep voice, "that is not *quite* true, Master Lute." She moved her hand, showing him the spot on the carpet once more. "The bag here, if you please."

There was no help for it. With a flourish he slid the strap free, leaned forward and placed his bag precisely upon the designated place, face betraying none of the profound dismay in his heart.

"Thank you," said Moonhawk. "I will see that none harm it, Master Lute. I say so before the Goddess."

"Fine promises," mocked Lady Rowan, and Moonhawk spun quick, eyes flashing and lips parting for a scorching reply, so Lute was certain. But—

"Enough!" cried a new voice, accompanied by the sharp sound of a clap. "Can I not be out of my rooms for an hour without returning to find two Sisters squabbling like brats?"

The lady who demanded it wore a shawl across her bony shoulders, and her fine Circle robe was rumpled as if she had passed many nights in it. Her hair was gray, with a bluish cast to it, snarled as if she had been out in the wind. Overall, she was tiny—small on height and short on meat, as the country folk told it—and her face was rodent-sharp, dominated by a pair of enormous brown eyes. Her hands glittered with the inevitable Moon rings, but she held them poised, ready for any movement, as if she were a magician trained.

Lute bowed. "Mother Portal."

The bright brown eyes locked on him with a force that nearly took him to his knees. She returned his bow with a nod of her head. "Child. Be welcome." Her voice was unexpectedly soft.

Lady Rowan thrust herself forward. "Mother Portal, this—"

But the older lady's eyes had moved, to rest upon Moonhawk.

"I had thought you were to meditate until I called you here."

"Yes, Mother," said Moonhawk, with poise.

"'Yes, Mother,'" repeated the sharp lady. "And have I called you here? Refresh my memory."

"No, Mother," Moonhawk returned, never moving her eyes from those of her interrogator.

There was a small pause before Mother Portal moved her eyes and walked across the room to the cat. "How extraordinary. No doubt you have your reasons." She extended a wire-thin hand and stroked the cat from head-top to rump. Satisfied rumbling rose in the scented air.

"So," said Mother Portal, looking down at her hand stroking the cat. "But Rowan had something of urgency to impart. What was that, Rowan?"

"Mother, this man is a Circle-breaker and an intruder. He was found within the walls of the Inner Garden." Malice glinted in Lady Rowan's dark eyes. "With Sister Moonhawk."

"Circle-breaker. That is serious," Mother Portal told the cat. She glanced up, capturing Lute's gaze. "Are you a Circle-breaker, my son?"

Lute met her eyes straightly, and held himself utterly calm. "No, Mother."

"Said plainly enough. Were you in the Inner Garden with Lady Moonhawk?"

"Yes," said Lute, and folded his lips tightly over. *But*.

Mother Portal's eyes sharpened. "There were circumstances, were there? But you don't care to name yourself a fool. Pride belongs to the foolish, you know, but no matter. Lady Moonhawk."

"Mother?"

"How came this man to be in the Garden with you?"

"I was meditating upon the Garden, that its peace would fill me, when there was—discord. Only an instant—only a flicker. If I had not been one with the Garden, I would never have noticed. As it was, trance was broken . . ." She tipped her head, a trick of the pathetically young, thought Lute, watching her.

"I sought the source and touched a thought—a thought of being hunted, Mother, and a taste of desperation. So I descended into the Garden, to see if I might aid one who was being hunted upon Beltane."

"And you found this man?"

"Yes, Mother."

"What was he doing?"

Moonhawk's lips curved upward, very slightly. "He was being invisible."

"Invisible!" That was Lady Rowan. Mother Portal spared her a glance and she subsided.

"Invisible," Moonhawk reiterated. "He did well with it, too. If I had not been looking for him, I would have passed within a yard and never known he was there."

"Unconvincing," snapped Lady Rowan, "when it most likely yourself who let him in—just as you let him in the Plaza Gate!"

"Alas," Lute said gently, "I fear you are out there, Lady. I let myself in through the gate."

"Certainly you did," she said with cordial sarcasm. "And with merely a wave of your hand."

"No," said Lute, "with a picklock." He gestured and the instrument in question appeared between his fingers, vanished. "I've studied the old locks. The type you have on the gate is very simple. No trouble at all to pick."

"No trouble to pick." That was Lady Portal, who had turned away from the cat. She pulled a tarot deck from a fold of her robe and began to shuffle, the cards nearly as large as her small hands. She looked up, deep into Lute's eyes.

"But who showed you where to look for the Gate, I wonder?"

He moved his shoulders in an irritable shrug. "No one needs to teach me to see what is in plain sight. I had noted the gate earlier this evening. When three of your Temple were striving to herd me against the wall, I recalled its location, and made use of it."

The cards made a slight sandpapery sound in the silence.

"Lady Rowan," Mother Portal said dreamily, "you were once a novice. How many levels of spell are woven about that Gate?"

"Twenty-six, Mother."

"Twenty-six. And also the several layers of spell we have woven about the Temple entire." She shuffled in silence, her eyes on the cards, then glanced up, sharp, into Lute's face. "You interest me, child. Have you perhaps had Circle training, as I hear is sometimes offered boys in the out-country, in years when girls are few?"

He laughed; he could not stop himself.

"Respect for Mother Portal!" cried Rowan, and Lute raised his hand in protest.

"Every respect for Mother Portal," he replied, bringing himself under control. He bowed to the tiny woman. "Forgive me, Mother, but Circle would not have me. My mother brought us to the Temple, she having fallen into hard times, and offered us both for service. They wanted only her daughter and turned her and me out with a loaf of bread in trade." He deliberately relaxed his shoulders, which were tense with the old bitterness.

"What came forth then?" asked Mother Portal.

He smiled at her. "Why, then, my mother sold me, Lady, to a man with clever hands who said he had need of an apprentice, and who promised to feed me and give me a trade and who paid her in good minted silver."

"He did those things?"

"Lady, he did. Only imagine my dismay to find that the trade I learned so well now makes me outlaw." He gestured and the parchment came to hand, unrolling with the weight of the ribbons and pentagram. He held it steady for her to read.

"*By the hand of Greenlady . . .*" she said softly, and her eyes when she looked into Lute's face were knife-sharp. "Lady Moonhawk, what do you make of this?"

The tall woman came a few steps forward, frowned at the proclamation. "To name an entire guild outlaw?" she said in wondering accents. "For what wrong?"

"An excellent question. Perhaps Lady Rowan may instruct us."

"Certainly," said that Lady, nervously folding her hands before her. "It was decided among Thirteen that the kitchen and hearth magicians confuse the simple, who are not trained to mark the difference between mere trickery and the true magic of those who are Circle. The Way is difficult enough, to the simple, and we owe them the care of removing falsehood from their path, that they not stumble because of our inattention."

"And so this—document—was drafted and posted in the city?"

"Yes, Mother."

"And it was considered too small a thing, I gather," pursued Portal, unrelentingly gentle, "with which to trouble the High Priestess of Dyan Temple?"

There was silence; a beginning of speech, cut off as Mother Portal turned back to Lute.

"Where were you bound with this thing, child?"

"To the Magician's Guildhall, Mother, to show it to the Master." He looked down at her bleakly, the hairs standing tall on his nape. If the Mother of Dyan Temple were not impervious to political maneuverings within her own Circle . . . He broke her gaze, looked up, located and pointed at Feldris.

"This man was there. He told me he was newly named Guildmaster. He said that the magicians of Dyan City are no longer within walls. I ran, thinking to lose myself in the outer rim and win free of the city tomorrow. He and three Witches pursued me across Goddess Square. I saw the gate, picked the lock . . ."

"And thus came to the Inner Garden. I see. Lady Moonhawk, take that document, if you will, and put it on my desk. Master Lute."

He started, looked down to find the tarot deck fanned face down, in a half-circle that all but hid her hand. "Draw a card."

He did so, holding it between the tips of his fingers, face still toward the floor.

"Show me," Mother Portal said, and he turned the card up, swallowing his shock, staring at the horrific black figure that leered from the creamy background.

"Do you know what card that is, Master Lute?"

He swallowed. "Death."

"Hah. And it frightens you, does it? Lady Moonhawk—what card is this?"

A quick blue glance. "The change card, Mother."

"So." She folded the deck, shot a glance at Rowan. "Bring me my pen. Master Lute, your card."

She took it from him, and the pen from Rowan, and scrawled some lines across the creamy stock before offering it back.

Lute stood still. "Mother . . ."

"Take the card, child. I've no doubt you'll find it as dangerous as you find it useful. Balance in all things is the way of the world." She thrust the card at him and perforce he took it, glancing down at the words: "The man who carries this is my emissary. Portal, Dyan Circle."

He looked at her. "I am free to go?"

"Presently," she said, frowning up at him. "You have brought me good coin, Master Lute. You must not think me ungrateful, though I give you dubious fortune in return. Why did your master wish an apprentice?"

He lifted an eyebrow. "All masters wish an apprentice, Mother. It is one's duty, to pass on knowledge. And it is a way to keep one's own skills sharp, for there is nothing so challenging as to teach." He smiled. "So my master taught me."

"A wise man, your master. His name?"

"Cereus, who made his return to the Goddess six years ago."

"Blessed his memory. Have you an apprentice, Master Lute?"

"No one likely has come my way. Doubtless, when I have need, the Goddess will provide."

"Doubtless." She shuffled the cards again, fanned them. "Lady Moonhawk, draw a card."

The blue eyes flashed, startled. Then she extended a slender hand, pulled a card free and turned it up.

"The High Priestess." Mother Portal sighed, folded the deck and pulled from her robe a silver string with which she bound the incomplete tarot.

"Lady Rowan, there are several decks being made for me. Inform the cardmaker I will chose from those completed at full Moon. These shall stay always with me.

"Lady Moonhawk, the time has come for you to leave Circle. Master Lute, the Goddess, as you had predicted, has provided you with an apprentice. I hope you will not find her hopelessly stupid, though I must tell you that she has spent all her days within these walls."

Lute stared at her, the card held loose between his fingers. "Mother, I do not understand."

"You relieve me. Suffice that you are my emissary and this is your apprentice. Return here in a year, I think, and do then as you think best."

"Mother, you cannot send one of the Inner Circle to travel the world with a—magician! It—"

"Oh," said Mother Portal, turning quick on her heel, "can I not? And what else, Lady Rowan, may I not do within the Temple where I am High Priestess?"

Lady Rowan's face had gone white and Portal nodded, sparing one last glance at Lute. "Take your apprentice and go, child. Now!"

The command voice, yet again. But this time he had no mind to resist it. He vanished the card, bent and caught up his bag, pushed past a gaping Feldris and swept his cloak from the hook by the door.

He was five strides down the hallway when he realized that Moonhawk was right beside him.

✧ Quick Working Glossary ✧

cantra—A Liaden coin. By Terran standards, a cantra piece represents quite a lot of money. Other coins are tenth-cantra pieces and (at least according to King of the Cats) twelve-cantra pieces, which, given the worth of an ordinary cantra, ought to buy quite a bit more real estate than a mere hyatt. Say, a star system. Cantra pieces, by the way, are named after Cantra yos'Phelium, who . . . "lives inside," as the authors say, *Crystal Soldier* and *Crystal Dragon*.

delm—The head of a clan. In theory, the delm is the embodiment of the clan, and as such deals for the clan entire, and also for the individual clan members. The Delm's Word is law to members of their clan; there is no higher authority to whom one can appeal.

melant'i—Terrans frequently misunderstand this to mean "honor." While honor is certainly part of the equation, as Liadens believe that everyone should behave "honorably," *melant'i* is much more. A person may, for instance, be variously a pilot, a mother, a lover, and a delm. Each role carries its own responsibilities and abilities. It is therefore crucially important to know from which *melant'i* a Liaden is acting at any given time. A delm acting for the clan is a much more fearsome thing than a pilot acting for her ship. The Terrans who *get* this sometimes refer back to the old Terran concept of "hats," used to describe the busy person who performs many tasks. To make matters even more complex, *melant'i* also equates with "face" or "reputation." It is said among Liadens that a rich man who has squandered his *melant'i* is a beggar, indeed. It's also worth noting that mainstream Liadens (by which we mean, those who are neither Scouts nor of Korval) consider that Terrans in general "have no *melant'i*." This is not a compliment.

nadelm—The delm-in-waiting.

qe'andra—Another tricky concept. Terrans consider the *qe'andra* to be accountants, and it's true that a good many of their duties have to do with finances, investments, and just plain money. However, Liaden culture has elevated contracts to an art form, and the *qe'andra* are also those professionals who write, vet, and, when needed, interpret contracts.

relumma—A quarter of a Liaden year. Clan shares are typically paid on the first of each relumma, thus "quartershare."

vingtai—This is an Yxtrang word; it means "tattoos." Specifically the tattoos on the face, which designate such things as rank, troop, and honors.

For a more complete dictionary, list of character names, and all sorts of other interesting stuff, see the, Liaden Universe® wiki at: http://liaden.wikia.com/wiki/Liaden_Wiki.